I0654639

HOW GREAT IS THE
DARKNESS

A Pastor Butch Gregory Novel

by

Jamie D. Greening

ATHANATOS
PUBLISHING GROUP

HOW GREAT IS THE
DARKNESS

A Pastor Butch Gregory Novel

by

Jamie D. Greening

ATHANATOS
PUBLISHING GROUP

How Great Is The Darkness
     by Jamie Greening

Official website:
     www.butchgregory.com

Published by Athanatos Publishing Group
     www.athanatosministries.org

ISBN: 978-1-936830-83-1

The cover art for this novel is a 1599 painting titled *Judith Beheading Holofernes*. It was painted by the Italian artist Michelangelo Merisi da Caravaggio and is currently located at Galleria Nazionale d'Arte Antica at Palazzo Barberini in Rome. This is the painting Monica Bennett studied in college that would inspire her later in life.

How Great Is The Darkness is a work of fiction. All characters appearing in this work are fictitious—especially the evil ones—I just made them up and have never encountered people quite so horrible. Any resemblance to real persons, living or dead, is purely coincidental, although, I certainly hope you are blessed with a pastor like Terence or Butch, and a friend as interesting as Wyoming.

Jamie Greening's Pastor Butch Gregory Books:

> *The Haunting of Pastor Butch Gregory*
> *and Other Short Stories* (Athanatos)
> *The Land Begins to Heal* (A Bard And Book short story)
> *The Little Girl Waits*, a Butch Gregory Novel (Athanatos)
> Jamie Greening's *Deep Cove* series (all from Bard And Book)

> *Deep Cove*
> *Deep Cove: The Party Crasher*
> *The Deep Cove Lineage*
> *The Deep Cove Investigation*
> *The Deep Cove Confrontation*

> Other Short Stories from Jamie Greening (Bard And Book):

> *Jolly Rogers: A Story About Boyhood*
> *Speculation*
> *The Last Message*
> *Morbid* only available in the book *Terror On The Toilet*
> *The Big Wheel Blessing*

Jamie Greening blogs regularly on a wide variety of topics as Pastor Greenbean at jamiegreening.com and Pastor Butch can be found at www.butchgregory.com.

ACKNOWLEDGEMENTS

Church is a big word for me, and as such it comprises all people who follow Christ, regardless of labels or geography. The first Butch Gregory novel, The Little Girl Waits sought to show how dangers in the world are threats to the church as well, and those who are in the church have a responsibility to act. In many ways TLGW was a metaphor about the shepherd protecting and saving sheep. Some threats, though, come from within the church itself, and that is the key thought behind How Great Is The Darkness.

I owe a huge debt of gratitude to Elisha Pile, Jaclyn Dye, Dottie Gauvin, David Caddell, Patrick Shaub, Carolyn Fowler, Ken Campbell, The Freedom Writers of Burnet, Texas, and Iris Macek. The folks at ACM, as always, are a blessing beyond words, especially Maryann Spikes, Gerson Lacdao, Julius Broqueza, and the indomitable Anthony Horvath. The philosophy at ACM allows for the publication of books which reflect a Christian worldview but do not necessarily follow the formula of traditional Christian publishing houses.

My family is a never-ending source of strength and encouragement in all of my endeavors, and most especially writing. It started with my mom. When I was still very young she nurtured within me a desire for reading and stories. My wife tirelessly proofs over and over again my hacked ideas and run-on sentences. Thanks Kim! My two daughters have taught me more about love than I could ever teach them. Thanks Belle and Phoebe!

I also am thankful for you—a brave soul who picked up (or downloaded) this book. A writer is nothing without a reader, a storyteller is only a dreamer without an audience, and I am only wasting my time if it weren't for you. So thank you, and I pray the Lord's peace upon you.

Jamie Greening
Epiphany, 2016

—For Kim—

PROLOGUE

People receive inspiration for their behavior, whether good or bad, from all kinds of places. Take, for example, the story out of the Apocrypha about the brave woman named Judith.

The Assyrians had come to conquer Israel, just as they had conquered every other nation in the region. The Assyrian general Holofernes brought his troops against the Israelite town of Bethulia. The Israelites were feckless in their defense, and all seemed lost. A beautiful young Jewish widow named Judith understood what was wrong. The Israelites inability to stop the Assyrians was a result of their unfaithfulness in following God's laws as given to Moses. In her frustration, the heroine takes matters into her own hands with subterfuge that would make a Cold War spy envious.

She and her unnamed servant girl pretended to be willing to betray the Israelites, feigning the Assyrians and Holofernes with promises of secrets and strategic information. She ingratiated herself to the general, and so he lowered his suspicions of her. Holofernes got drunk and passed out under her seductive wiles. In this defenseless state, Judith and her servant beheaded him, sneaked out of the camp, and then carried the bloody trophy back home to the Israelites. The Jews received inspiration from Judith's bravery, thus they defeated the Assyrians.

The story is a morally ambiguous Hebrew novel designed to teach the importance of purity, law, faithfulness, and bravery in the midst of a polluted culture that stands in opposition to faith.

Monica Bennett first heard the story of Judith in an art history class lecture during her first year of college. It soon became her favorite story, as well as the inspiration for her terrible deeds.

Chapter One
A Phone Call

Frosty air shot out of Michael Westgrave's mouth. He glanced behind him to see if someone followed. He didn't see anyone, but he couldn't tell because of the darkness.

His breath quickened. The nighttime fog was heavy. November raindrops formed and fell to the earth. Michael ran off the trail. He sprinted across the shadowy baseball field in the middle of the park, then toward the lot lights. There was a tiny break in the hedgerow in front of him, and he slid through it, emerging into the parking lot where his Lexus sat. He pushed through the gap in the hedge and transitioned from mud puddles and wet grass to slippery pavement. When he did, his footing gave way. He fell to the ground.

Michael popped back up, wiped off his pants. There was a slight tingle in the right foot, like it might be sprained. He realized his left hand was throbbing. The humming overhead lights revealed blood gathering in the palm of the hand. Loose gravel had dug into him like burrowing worms. It burned. The crystal on his Omega Seamaster wristwatch was smashed, a victim of gravity and other forces of physics like momentum, velocity, and the crushing power of mass.

There was no time to worry about a little blood or broken glass now. Michael limped as fast as he could to the opposite side of the lot where his car waited for him.

Inside his car, he felt safe—safe from the darkness, safe from the people chasing him, safe from his own bad decisions. Michael Westgrave was smart enough to know the feeling of safety was an illusion. The interior of his luxury sedan was only a temporary sanctuary, a momentary elixir for the panic ripping his insides apart. Eventually he would be found, or found out, and then nowhere would be safe. Not even his car.

He needed to do something to fix this problem, and fast.

But what? They had trapped him like a wild beast, like a circus animal whipped into submission, forced to perform tricks at the sting of a lash. He had lost his freedom. Michael Westgrave was no longer the master of his

1

own fate. He was a slave, and the realization made him sick.

Michael didn't drive home. Instead, he drove from the park to his office on the other side of town, the money side, of Sydney, Washington. He found a large dishrag in the office kitchen. The gravel clanked against the porcelain sink when he pushed it out of his flesh. He wrapped the rag around his oozing hand. He hobbled back to his desk. Once inside, he took off his shoe to check his ankle. It had swollen but didn't appear to be broken or too badly damaged. It felt so good to take the wet shoe off that he took off the other one, along with his socks. Michael Westgrave let his feet relax in the luxurious carpet so richly provided for his study.

His watch, however, didn't make out as well. He took it off his wrist. He stared at it, snarled, and laid it on his mahogany desk. The destroyed timepiece looked out of place on the immaculate desktop, where everything was tidy and perfect—an opened organizer that only had his secretary's handwriting in it, a fancy desktop pendulum he bought years ago at Sharper Image, leather-bound books he'd never read, and an oversized lambskin Bible, positioned perfectly in the middle of the desk, opened, as it had been for almost five years, to the same page of Scripture.

The picture perfect desk told an idealized story about Michael's life. It was the life he wanted others to believe he lived, a life of order and stability, grounded in wisdom with an appreciation for the sophisticated blessings of life. Michael worked hard to cultivate the image of success.

The smashed watch told an altogether different story of Michael's existence. This was the life he worked so hard to keep hidden, a life of broken beauty, destroyed by carelessness and arrogance, clutched to a past that, if known, would ruin him.

Neither story was authentic. He'd lived both lives, but neither one was who he really was. He was somewhere in the middle; he lived between two worlds, at home in neither.

Michael opened the bottom drawer of his large desk. He pulled out a glass tumbler along with a half empty bottle of Macallan twenty-one-year-old scotch. He poured out two fingers, then savored its complex flavor and texture. He took another sip, then read the Scripture that was literally opened to him almost every day, but which he'd not read in years. It was the Twenty-Third Psalm, written in Petersen's popular modern translation.

> God, my shepherd! I don't need a thing. You have bedded me
> down in lush meadows, you find me quiet pools to drink from. True

to your word, you let me catch my breath and send me in the right direction.

Even when the way goes through Death Valley, I'm not afraid when you walk at my side. Your trusty shepherd's crook makes me feel secure.

You serve me a six-course dinner right in front of my enemies. You revive my drooping head; my cup brims with blessing. Your beauty and love chase after me every day of my life. I'm back home in the house of God for the rest of my life.

The irony of the passage cut his soul, dividing it as a sharp knife divides a slaughtered animal. He felt anything but security. He had caught his breath, though, and he did have a good drink. However, Death Valley felt close and he didn't think it was God's beauty or love that were chasing him. It was demons that chased him, vile demons that used his past to threaten his present and future. The Bible talked about heaven. The succubus promised him hell.

There was no escape. He was trapped.

Reaching down again to the same drawer that held the booze, he pulled out a SIG Sauer 9mm pistol. Maybe he could just go ahead and live in the House of God now. He'd really rather not give his enemies a chance to ruin him or hurt his family. His career and life would never be revived in this lifetime. He had managed to turn the cup of blessing into a bottomless brew of curses. It would be quick to end it all right here, right now.

Michael Westgrave grasped the custom rosewood grip, squeezed the cold steel, racked the slide to chamber a round, then put the barrel of the pistol in his mouth. His finger was on the trigger.

The thought that he should at least finish his drink before he pulled the trigger sparkled inside his mind. It felt like a good thought to him, so he put the pistol down beside the broken watch. Swirling the drink around in his mouth, he looked at the photographs on the wall. A sad smile swept across his face as he beheld the various photographs of him, his fashion-model-looks wife, and their three blonde children. There were other pictures as well. One of him with the governor at an awards ceremony for community service. There was a picture of him on K2, water skiing in Hawaii, and the obligatory photo from his African safari.

Taking his drink with him, he walked to the gallery wall. One particular picture captured his imagination. It was taken two years earlier at the dedication of the new children's hospital on the south side of town. Some of his colleagues were there: Stuart, John, Allison, Terence, Fred, Calvin, R. T., and several others he'd never gotten to know. There at the end, though, was Butch.

Michael took a drink.

Could Butch help him? Of all the people in the world, Butch Gregory was one of the few he trusted. Butch had been refined by fire. Maybe he could help Michael get out of the fire?

Sitting back down behind his desk, he set his drink down, pulled out his phone from his leather jacket.

"Michael, how are you old friend?" said the voice on the other end.

"Hi Butch. I'm okay—I guess?" Michael took the last drink from his glass tumbler.

"Then what's up?"

"Well, I guess maybe I'm not okay. Do you think we could talk tomorrow, I mean, do you have time in your schedule? I know that tomorrow is Wednesday and all, but if you're able, I'd like to talk to you about some things."

"Yeah, Michael, absolutely. I've got an 8:00 AM breakfast appointment, but other than that my day is open. When do you want to get together?"

"Is the morning too soon, say around 10:00 AM?"

"Sure," Butch said. "You want to meet at Starbucks for coffee? You can buy me a cinnamon dolce latte and a blueberry scone."

"Butch, I'll bring you a latte and a scone, but I'd like," he paused as he put down his empty glass, "no, I need to talk somewhere more private than a coffee shop. Is it asking too much for you to meet me here at my office? I don't want to be around a lot of people right now. It's inconvenient, I know, but is that okay, to meet me here?"

"Yeah Michael, that's fine, but are you sure you don't need to talk tonight?" Butch paused and then exhaled, "It seems to me like there is a bit of edge to your voice, not that I'm trying to overanalyze you. It's just that it seems like something is wrong. It wouldn't take but a few minutes for me to come meet you now."

"Butch, something is wrong, but now is no good. I'll tell you everything tomorrow. For now, I'm going to go home and go to bed. I want to be with Celeste and my kids. I suddenly miss my family very much."

"If that's what you want, okay, but . . ."

Before Butch could finish the sentence Michael ended the call. It was

4

enough for Michael that he would see Butch tomorrow. He could feel the strange and encouraging feeling of hope on the horizon, or at least on his calendar. He had hope, a hope that his friend might somehow show him the way out of this mess. Butch Gregory would rescue him. Everything was going to be okay.

Michael put his shoes back on, but he threw the wet socks into the garbage can. He hid the bottle of scotch and shot glass safely in its usual bottom drawer, away from any janitorial or administrative prying eyes. He left the broken wristwatch on the desk, but put the pistol in the inside pocket of his jacket.

No sense taking any chances.

He turned the light out in his office. His wet shoes squeaked all the way across the hall tile to the front door of the building. It could have simply been the alcohol, or it might have been the decreasing levels of adrenaline dissipating from his bloodstream, but Michael felt optimistic as he opened the door to the administrative complex and stepped outside. It was probably because he trusted Butch, and even though Michael didn't have any idea of what he could do to escape the situation, he believed Butch Gregory would. God was with Pastor Butch Gregory, recent history showed that, and everyone in Sydney knew it.

He punched the code to lock the door, then he walked down the sidewalk to the small parking lot behind the building. Just as he turned the corner, he heard the rush of footsteps. His movements were a bit slowed, so he didn't completely get turned around before the metal rod smashed down on his head.

Chapter Two
First Breakfast

Pastor Butch Gregory barely touched his eggs or gravy-covered potato hash. There hadn't been enough time in the pause of conversation to nibble on the sausage or sip his never-ending cup of coffee. It was always that way between Butch and Terence, and this morning in the Sydney Diner was no different. Butch and Terence became friends back in seminary, but after graduation they each landed in different parts of the country. Butch remained on the west coast to stay near his native Oregon, taking a call in the small Seattle suburb of Sydney. Terence, however, accepted an associate pastorate at a large church in Alabama. It was not a good fit for him, and eventually he moved to a smaller church in New Jersey where he was the lead pastor. The church hadn't remained small for long. Under Pastor Terence's leadership it grew to over five hundred people. Two years ago, though, he began to feel a desire to do something new, a yearning for a new challenge. He and his wife Muriel also wanted to be on the west coast again, so he accepted a call to Ebenezer Missionary Baptist Church in Sydney. Being close to his old friend Butch Gregory was an added bonus.

Terence Simon Harrison was average height, and he'd managed to stay lean even in the midst of middle age. His skin was a marvelous color of mocha. He shaved his head several years ago as a first strike against baldness, but it was the dignified Vandyke beard that was his most dominant physical attribute. He wore dark framed glasses, but they could not diminish the natural curiosity fueling the intellect that blazed inside his vivid eyes. There was a quality, a timbre, to his voice that demanded the hearer pay attention. He tended to pucker his lips when he was deep in thought, and would make an inverted whistle sound as he sucked in air through his lips just before he began to speak, like he was kissing his words goodbye before he released them into the open air.

Terence's arrival in Sydney, and in Pastor Butch's life, came just after the trauma Butch faced in the Tamara Rey incident. During those two years, Terence not only rekindled a long friendship with Butch, but he had served, in a way, as Butch's pastor. Pastors need a pastor, too, and God sent Terence at exactly the right time. Now their relationship had evened out. Terence's dad died in January, and Butch walked with Terence through that ancient, shadowy valley. Iron sharpens iron.

Of late though, their conversations had become typically mundane—church boards, eccentric church members, the mean church boss wannabes, and more than one story of sermons gone awry. Somehow, the theme for breakfast on this particular Wednesday morning was weddings. Terence had a wedding the previous Saturday that didn't go well. In the middle of the communion element of the service, the groom vomited into the wine goblet. Not to be outdone, the bride upchucked as well. Except she was somewhat conscious of the communion cup so she turned her head. Terence simulated the gag reflex as he told Butch, "She spewed bile all over the altar area. Most of it landed on the legendary one hundred and twenty year old altar Bible that had been prized by the church."

"Legendary?" Butch wondered. "What do you mean legendary?"

Terence jumped on the question. "Supposedly, that Bible was brought from an Underground Railroad home, via New Orleans."

"That's pretty significant," Butch was impressed.

"How it got to New Orleans no one knows, but it originated in Ohio. The church legend says Harriet Tubman herself read out of it. From New Orleans it came with a pastor who moved here in the 1950s."

"Is that true?" Butch said.

"It doesn't have to be true. It is a church legend. Every church has them."

"Heaven knows our does," Butch said. "Our legend is that an angel, disguised as a vagabond, painted the picture in the baptistery. I know it is not true because an angel would paint better, but that is the legend."

Terence nodded his head then continued his story. "It gets better with our Harriet Tubman Freedom Bible. They say infertile women can hold it during prayer in the worship service and they will be pregnant before their next birthday. I heard the story of a Vietnam War veteran who was deaf but was healed because he put that Bible under his pillow when he slept. That is just a sampling of the legends."

"And now it is covered in vomit," Butch said. "The legendary Bible is interesting enough, but a legendary fertility Bible covered in throw-up, now I can't really top that one," Butch sipped his coffee. "Usually, when I have puke at church, it is a baby dedication. Babies always find a way to barf or pee on me." Pastor Butch tilted his head and continued, "As far as weddings go, I consider a wedding successful if everyone is sober at the wedding rehearsal the night before. Other than that, most of the problems at my weddings involve mothers. The mother-of-the-bride is always unbearable. Always."

"You got that right," Terence swirled a piece of his blueberry pancake in the maple syrup puddled on his plate then popped it in his mouth. "One time I had this angry mother—I mean she was angry. Fire exploded out of her eyes. Smoke billowed out of her ears. Her fangs were sharp as daggers. I think she'd been sharpening them every night since a date had been set for the wedding. She dipped her long elegant fingernails in poison, ready to scratch the eyeballs out of anyone who dared to oppose her will. She was so angry even her hair looked mad." The whole time that Terence spoke his hands were waving wildly and his eyes were dancing, the way all good storytellers do when they exaggerate their subject matter.

"Who was she mad at?"

"Who wasn't she mad at? She was mad at her daughter for marrying that man. She was mad at that man for thinking he was good enough to marry her sweet darling. She was mad at her husband for not being as upset about it all as much as she was. She was mad at me because I agreed to do the service and thought it was a good match. But most of all, she was mad at God, because so far he had refused her request to strike the groom-to-be dead before he had a chance to lay a hand on her sweet, innocent baby."

"That's a lot of mad going on there," Butch said.

"She had plenty of mad to go around." Terence pursed his lips, kissed the air, and said, "Most of all I think she was mad at life, because her baby getting married meant she was getting old, and she was not the kind of woman who took well to the idea of growing old gracefully."

"Are you sure," Butch said, "that it was you who did that wedding? Because I'm pretty sure I married that woman's daughter off last summer. Sounds like you're describing the same person to me that I had to deal with. Was she a chubby, wrinkly, white woman from Bainbridge Island?"

"Nope. She was a skinny, fit, black woman from Sequim. But regardless of what they look like, Butch, they are all identical—every last mother-of-the-bride—they are all alike."

"True, except of course, when our own kids get married." Butch raised his eyebrows and opened his eyes wide.

"I don't even want to think about that," Terence shook his head, then fidgeted with the unused spoon beside his plate. "To be honest with you, I'm already practicing being mean to whatever young boys come around one of my daughters." He swallowed, "In fact, I think my goal is to make sure they never get married. That way, I'll always be the one they call when they are in trouble. I like being their hero. I don't want anyone edging me out of my spot."

"You don't really mean that, Terence. You know you want all three of your girls to have the same joy you and Muriel have. I know you do."

"You're right, of course. But I think I'll still be mean for a little while, just so I can feel good about myself."

"Do you plan on doing the weddings for your own children?"

"I've never thought about it Butch. What about you?"

"I don't think I could do Paul or Sarah's wedding. Lucy tells me I would cry through the whole thing and it would be a blubbering mess. She's right, of course. What Lucy talks about, and what she wants, is for the both of us to just be the parents, and not try to be spiritual leaders when our kids get married. I can't be the pastor and the father-of-the-bride or groom at the same time. I've always thought I'd get a trusted friend to do premarital counseling with them and to do the wedding ceremony. I just want to be daddy when that all comes down."

Butch nibbled again at his biscuit before he continued. "We're hopefully many years away from that, but if you're still around and Muriel hasn't yet buried you in the backyard, Terence, I think it'd be great if you did the wedding for my children when the time comes. There is no one Lucy and I trust more than you."

A broad smile jumped onto Terence's face. "I'm honored Butch, and it would be my pleasure. However, we'll have the wedding ceremony at your church so when they throw up it will be on your platform and not mine."

"Agreed. Keep in mind, though, we're talking about things that are a long, long way off."

"Not as long as you think, my friend. I got started on the baby-making business sooner than you did, so take it from a man who has two in college and one in high school, let me tell you that these years go very fast." Terence pointed to his Seiko and said, "Tempus fugit."

"Tempus fugit indeed. It doesn't seem like all that long ago I was in high school, and that was before I ever met you. The world has changed a lot since then. Our kids face so many dangers and challenges we never even dreamed of."

"For sure, for sure," Terence shook his head. "We were blessed, weren't we? We didn't have to worry about how many people followed us on social media or who downloaded our video on YouTube. All we had to worry about was being home before the street lights came on and making sure our fathers didn't see the bad grade we made on the spelling test."

Butch smiled, but then grimaced. "Yeah, Terence, that is true, but I remember how crazy the world was when LSD was making the rounds, strange cults erupted into existence, and don't forget we all lived with the Doomsday Clock ticking the slow and sure countdown toward nuclear annihilation. Every age has its unique challenges, but those challenges are also great opportunities."

"Point taken," Terence nodded in agreement. "Being a black man, I guess of all people, I should remember that the past wasn't always as Pollyanna as old timers like us sometimes want to make it out to be. As a species, humans have a tendency to block negative stuff out with selective memory."

Terence stared in the distance. He didn't tell Butch what he was thinking, but Butch knew behind those bright eyes his friend's mind was churning. Eventually Terence looked back at Butch, smiled, and asked, "Enough about the past. What have you planned for Christmas this year over at Sydney Community Church?"

Butch talked about the choir's attempt at doing some pieces from Handle's *Messiah*. It wasn't going well. He wondered if he should pull the plug on it.

Terence advised him to let it ride. "People will appreciate the effort, even if it is not a technical success," he said. "Remember, this whole thing about church is not about the music, it is about the community. You are like their parent. You need to let the children try, then celebrate their effort even if it's insufferably pathetic. You wouldn't pull the plug on your child's solo in the school play just because it wasn't technically perfect, would you?"

The two friends talked on for another half hour. They talked about what books they were reading. Both lamented the recent scandal with the big time pastor in Seattle. Then they talked about the increasingly sorrowful state of churches. Then politics. It wasn't long before the struggle with ISIS came up.

"I refuse to call it ISIS," Terence said. "I like the term that our missionaries in the Middle East use. They call it Daesh. They tell me the so called Islamic State doesn't like it when you call them Daesh. In some way beyond my meager mind, they take it as a pejorative."

"Meager mind? Your false humility is duly noted, and rebuked." Butch fidgeted with the bill that the server had put on the edge of the table. "I hadn't heard of that Daesh thing before. I think I might start using it, too." Butch frowned, "Do you think President Obama will send troops in?"

"Some, maybe." Terence shook his head. "But not enough. Our president is not particularly hawkish on sending troops anywhere, you know that. He only likes to use drones."

Over the next several minutes the conversation turned from politics to sports, then to the weather and eventually back to politics.

Terence wiped his mouth with a napkin. "I know I shouldn't be, brother, but I am worried about the world. I don't think it is headed in a good direction. It is only a matter of time before we end up with some kind of global struggle between those who value liberty and freedom, and those who want to suppress anything they disagree with. I worry about people who use violence to enforce their sense of holiness."

"Surely it will not come to that." Butch looked at his old Timex and said, "I wish we had time to solve all the world's problems, but I've gotta run. I'm supposed to meet Michael over at TLC. There is something he wants to ask me. He called me last night, which was weird. He and I only make small talk at the ministerial alliance meetings. We've never really talked before."

"Who knows? Maybe he has a new church growth gimmick to sell you." Terence's eyes lit up with an idea, "I got it, maybe he wants to finally become a Christian?"

"That wasn't very nice. You should be ashamed of yourself."

"I repent. You're right, that wasn't nice. True, but not nice." Terence shook his head, still laughing at his own joke. "Anyway, you tell that fat cat I said hi, and that I haven't forgotten he owes me a round of golf over at the fancy country club he belongs to."

Butch took one more sip of his coffee then stood up. "I will, as long as you remember that today's breakfast is on you, because I paid last time."

"Touché."

Chapter Three
Caravaggio

Pastor Butch hadn't really eaten much of his first breakfast at The Sydney Diner because he knew he was getting a second breakfast of scones later. He was thinking about those scones when his phone rang. He slowed his blue sedan down a bit as he pulled the phone from his coat pocket. He glanced down at the screen to see who was calling. Butch felt a twinge of guilt as he pushed the button to talk because he knew he shouldn't be driving while talking on the phone. It was another example of driving under grace, not law.

"Good morning Robert," Butch said. "What's up?"

"Erin is mad at me again."

"What did you do?"

"Nothing. Well, nothing that should make her mad."

"What did you do?"

"I might have bought a new riding lawn mower."

"Might have? Either you did or you didn't." Butch shook his head. "Robert, you are going to have to stop making impulsive decisions without talking to Erin first. Last week it was a car, three weeks before that it was getting another dog, two months ago it was a change in jobs. Now this?"

"I know I was bad, but it was an end-of-summer closeout sale, oh, and when spring comes we will need it."

"No, you wanted it. Don't confuse want with a need, but a want is not necessarily a bad thing. What's bad is that you didn't discuss it with Erin first. Marriage is a partnership, and you're not a very good partner if you act alone all the time." Butch stopped at a red light and swiveled his head around to see if there were any police patrol cars around. "How mad was Erin when you told her?"

"That's sorta of the thing. I haven't told her yet."

"Don't you think you should? And soon." Butch turned left up the long wooded road that led to True Life Center where the scones and Starbucks awaited him.

"I'm afraid to tell her."

"You should be." Butch thought of the time he bought a non-refundable February vacation to Chicago without checking with his wife first, and how Lucy chased him with a wooden spoon across the house when he told her.

Butch slowed down to merge left. "Look, you have to tell her, and the sooner the better. Is she at work right now?"

"No. Today is her day off, and mine, too."

"Where is she?"

"She is downstairs, I think reading or something."

He realized why Robert was so panicked. "You're just now getting worried because they are delivering the lawn mower this morning, right?"

"The delivery guy just called. It will be here in about twenty minutes."

"You better tell her, and fast."

"Can you come over and be here when I tell her?"

"No. I have a meeting in," he checked his watch, "in seven minutes. You need to hang up with me and go tell her right now." Butch could hear Robert's breathing change and he could tell that Robert was walking. Then he heard Robert say, "Hey honey, Pastor Butch has something he wants to tell you," and then Erin said, "Hello, Pastor Butch."

The first thing out of Butch's mouth was, "That's not what I told him."

"Told him what?" Erin said.

"I'm sorry, Erin. What I told your husband was that he needed to tell you, not for me to do it for him. Do me a favor, put down the phone for a moment and look at Robert and tell him that Pastor Butch wants you to tell me. Does that make sense?"

"Perfect sense," Erin said. There was a playful lilt to her voice.

Butch sat in the car listening to the brief conversation that ensued.

Erin relayed to Robert what Butch had said, Robert erupted with guilt and shame, and confessed, in about four seconds flat, that he'd bought a brand new lawn mower that cost over two thousand dollars and it was on its way.

Then Butch heard Erin say, "I know," as she explained how she set the bank account to notify her on her mobile whenever purchases over three hundred dollars were made. Then there was silence. For a split second he thought the situation had gone south. That was when he heard Erin's voice on the line again.

"Pastor Butch, are you still there?"

"Yes, Erin, I'm right here. Is, is uh, is everything okay? I couldn't help

13

but overhear some of the conversation."

"Oh, everything is fine."

"So you knew about the lawn mower, but you intentionally let him suffer all that anxiety?"

"Absolutely. But I love him too much to be mad for long," she chuckled. "I didn't know he would call you, though. I guess he was more stressed about it than I thought."

Butch said, "I guess so. It is probably true, though, that the two of you need to talk about this kind of thing, I think. Don't you think?"

"I guess so," Erin hesitated, "but, spontaneity and gusto for living is one of the things I love about that man. If Robert wasn't that kind of guy, he wouldn't be the man I fell in love with. He saw that mower in the store and all he could see was making a perfect yard, for our perfect house for us to live in together. How can a girl get mad about that?"

"I couldn't have said it better, Erin."

"Thanks for being there for us, for me and Robert. You have no idea how much you mean to us. But right now I'm gonna go take some pictures of my husband on his fancy new lawn rig so I can post them on Facebook. And I'll make him wear his muscle shirt, even if it is rainy and forty-two degrees outside."

"Before I go," Butch said, "I'd like to pray for you two."

"Okay, thanks Pastor Butch."

Butch began his prayer as he yielded to a dump truck.

> Dear Jesus, thank you for these two wonderful young people. My prayer is they will experience all the joys of marriage with wide hearts and gentle minds. Thank you for the way Robert loves Erin, and for the way Erin loves Robert. I ask, Lord, for them to grow spiritually together as they grow closer to one another becoming one flesh, one body, with one heart, mind, and soul united together in their love for you. In Jesus' name, Amen.

"See ya Sunday," Erin said.

"Yes, Sunday." Butch drove around behind the sanctuary to where the administrative building was. He got out of his car and walked into the office building of True Life Center, or TLC as it was known around town.

By any definition, TLC was the largest church on the western shore of Puget Sound. It dominated the church culture in Sydney. In the spring, TLC completed a ten million dollar building campaign, ran close to fifteen hundred people every weekend, and boasted of a large television and media presence. All of this had taken off after Michael Westgrave took the pastorate seven years earlier. Pastor Michael transformed the traditional congregation into an attraction model church and built the programs around what people wanted. Although Pastor Butch did not approve of such techniques in general, he still thought Michael had done a good job at evangelism and outreach. The world was changing, particularly the church world, and Michael had embraced that change and rode it as hard as he could. Butch felt that no one should blame or accuse TLC or Pastor Michael Westgrave for doing the best they could to grow the Kingdom of God.

"Good morning, welcome to TLC, my name is Pamela. How may I help you?" The young woman behind a large reception desk in the administrative building greeted Pastor Butch with the enthusiasm of a toddler for ice cream.

"Good morning Pamela, I have an appointment with Pastor Michael. My name is Butch Gregory from Sydney Community Church. Michael and I are friends."

"Oh, everyone knows who you are, don't you know. Let me see," she turned her attention to a computer screen, clicked a mouse two or three times, then looked up at Butch, "there is nothing in his appointment book about a meeting with you. Are you sure you have the right day?"

"Yes, he called me last night and we arranged for 10:00 AM. He even promised me scones."

"Yum, lucky man. I love scones." Pamela licked her lips in a way that made Pastor Butch very uncomfortable. "The problem is, Pastor Michael is not in his office. I checked when I came in at 9:00, but his car was here when I arrived. So he is here somewhere. I just don't know where." Pamela twirled her blonde hair with her left hand. "I bet he is over in the sanctuary. Sometimes he does that—he just walks around and will come back with a list of property issues that need to be taken care of before Sunday. He says things look different in the early morning light when no one else is around, that you can spot things that are out of place quicker. You know what Pastor Michael always says about growing a church, 'People want a clean, modern, well-kept facility that sparkles with excellence.' He really does practice what he preaches." She took a breath. "Do you want me to call him on his cell phone? I'm sure he'd come right over."

Butch thought a second, remembering the rather cryptic conversation from last night. Maybe Michael was in deep prayer. "No, Pamela, I think I'll just walk over, if that is okay with you, and find him. Is the building unlocked? Are there any security codes over there?"

"No problem, Pastor Butch, I can unlock everything from right here."

Pamela turned around, grabbed a computer notepad, punched in a code, and then turned to Butch and said, "All good. The tablet indicates that the alarm system has already been deactivated, which means Pastor Michael is over there. I also went ahead and unlocked all the doors. You can walk freely into any of the buildings, except the TLC Christian Academy across the street. They have their own system."

"Thanks." Butch was impressed. It would have taken his secretary fifteen minutes to rifle through all the keys and codes needed to get someone through Sydney Community's facility, and she would have been grumpy the whole time. He might have to look into an automated system operated by a digital device.

Who was he kidding? It would never work at his church. People valued their church keys like a dog does a bone.

Butch walked through the perfectly manicured garden that separated the different buildings on the sprawling campus. Rhododendrons and azaleas were the dominant flower, but there were also apple, plum, and pear trees galore. He'd been here several times for various conferences, a couple of funerals, and Pastor Michael had given him the grand tour three times, apparently forgetting each of the previous times. However, it had been a long time since he'd been inside TLC.

He finally came to the main building, where he assumed Michael would be waiting for him with the scones. There was a light on in the hallway. Butch hoped he'd brought both blueberry and cinnamon. The door, just like Pamela had said, was unlocked. He walked across the marble hallway toward the sanctuary. Somehow Butch just knew that was where Michael was, but he couldn't yet smell the scones.

The hallway was filled with large poster-sized photographs of people of all ages and ethnicities. An Asian woman. Children playing. A Latino man sitting at an engineer's desk, smiling. A black man and an Asian woman at a restaurant. An entire Nordic-looking family at the park. There was even a Native American, in traditional ceremonial attire, standing proudly with arms crossed. They were all too beautiful and perfect-looking to actually be people who go to TLC or who live in Sydney. There was a different kind of beauty that the authentic folks in the blue collar community have, it is different from staged fashion, faux diversity, and expensive haircuts.

Written in dramatic script on the bottom of each of the posters was "True Life."

The closer he got to the narthex, the pictures changed in subject and style. They were now black and white, Annie Leibovitz-esque still-lifes of Pastor Michael. One of him sitting behind his desk, dressed to the nines. Another of him preaching in the sanctuary wearing a Polo shirt and tweed blazer, then yet another of him and his family. Michael again, in some kind of meeting, where the image is crystal clear on his strong face but begins to blur as the clarity disintegrates toward the other people, the other faces around the table. The only face that matters is Pastor Michael's. One more picture of Michael kneeling in prayer with an opened Bible before him.

Michael was as handsome as the models in the earlier pictures, cast as an action hero and visionary leader. The cult of personality—hero worship—made Butch nervous. What's next, coloring pages of Pastor Michael in the preschool curriculum, staged pictures of him saving people from burning homes or using the Jaws of Life to rescue a crash victim just before the car explodes? A meeting of him and the Dalai Lama?

It was all a bit silly. He felt a little guilty for judging his colleague, but he couldn't agree with the whole package over here at TLC. It was one of the reasons why he loved his own church so much. They saw through the flash and glitz and were unmoved by sophisticated, manipulative marketing.

Butch saw no crosses. No Bible verses on the wall. No mention of Jesus.

The physical space was beautiful to behold. Any observer could tell the appearance of the building and the dazzling of the eye meant a great deal to the people at TLC. The floor transitioned from marble to carpet at the main entrance to the sanctuary. Butch pulled the handle, hoping it would open. It did.

The door was massive, but it opened far easier than one would have thought from its appearance. It was oaken with engravings of large trees on it. The doors rose to twelve feet, meeting the doorjamb frame about halfway up the wall to the drop ceiling.

The platform lights were on inside the sanctuary. Butch saw Pastor Michael sitting in a chair in the middle of the chancel area. The room was large and the ceilings so high that it took a minute for his eyes to adjust because the sanctuary was completely dark except for the spotlights facing forward.

It was indeed an impressive sanctuary.

Maybe Michael wants to show off some fancy new equipment they have installed? It was not beyond him to brag a bit when it came to his church's use or early adoption of the latest technology.

"Michael," Butch said. He thought his friend might be in prayer and that it would be best if he didn't sneak up on him.

There was no reply.

"Michael?"

Still no reply.

Pastor Butch Gregory increased his speed toward the front of the sanctuary. About halfway down the middle aisle he saw that Pastor Michael was not moving, and that was when he smelled the tang. What Butch saw next, as he walked up the stairs of the altar area toward the middle of the platform was something he would never forget for the rest of his life, although he would often try.

Pastor Michael Westgrave was bound with gray duct tape in one of the crimson sanctuary chairs. His hands were pulled behind his back and taped again. His feet were taped together too, and shoved underneath the seat. A small trickle of blood showed on his forehead, but Butch could see no other cuts or bruises on him. Michael's face was expressionless, drained of color. The life was gone, and seemed to have been gone for a while. The two dull eyes were open, with the head tilted back, staring upward as if in a pleading prayer.

His mouth was open, and something was stuck inside it.

Platform lights, chair, and head positioning made the scene look like a Caravaggio painting.

When Butch got close to the corpse of Michael Westgrave, he wanted to cut the tape and remove whatever was in Michael's mouth and lay him out on the floor. He didn't, though. His friend was dead, and this was now a crime scene. He shouldn't touch or do anything because it might disturb evidence that would be helpful to finding whoever did this. It felt so undignified to leave him like that, but he wanted to make sure that the murderer would be caught, so he resisted his instincts. Forensics does not care about dignity, and science is not sentimental.

Butch pulled out his phone and called 911.

"911, what is the emergency?"

"Something," Butch's voice squeaked. It was hard for him to talk. He started over. "Something terrible has happened. My friend is dead."

"What is your location, sir?"

"I'm in the sanctuary of True Life Church, over on Baron Forest Drive near the country club."

"Did you say True Life Church?"

"Yes."

"What is your name, sir?"

"I'm Butch Gregory."

"Who is deceased, sir?"

"My friend, Pastor Michael Westgrave."

"Are you in any danger?"

Pastor Butch did not know how to answer that question. It hadn't occurred to him before then. Might the killer still be here? Was he in danger? He looked around the sanctuary and didn't see anybody else, and he had not seen anyone other than Pamela since he arrived. Of course, a killer would not want to be seen, so that didn't necessarily mean anything. Butch looked down at his friend and realized that this was personal, and somehow what he was looking at was connected to whatever it was Michael didn't want to talk about last night on the phone.

"Sir, are you in danger?" the 911 woman again repeated on the phone, this time a little louder.

"No, I don't think so. I think someone killed him. And I think it was someone who knew him."

"Did you say that you think someone killed him?"

"Yes, most certainly someone killed him. I have no doubt about it."

"Why do you say that, sir?"

"Because," Butch looked around, "this couldn't be an accident."

As soon as the call ended, Pastor Butch sat down on the chancel stairs with his back to Michael's body. Several moments passed as Butch tried to gather himself. He'd seen death before, up close and personal, and he hated it. It made him feel sick all over, and a spiritual dread overcame him. It wasn't fear, but instead a knowing. He knew that this had somehow become a part of his life and that God wanted him involved. The tingling erupted in his gut.

Butch bowed his head and prayed.

Dear Lord, this is beyond terrible. Don't make me do this again. Please no. Haven't I done enough already? Haven't I suffered enough? Haven't I hurt enough? Haven't I cried enough? What more do you want from me?

Why this? I thought my life was now getting back to normal. How could you rope me back into another one?

He paused a moment in his prayer.

Okay, fine. I know not to argue with you. Please guide me and teach me, and help me. Send me help. We both know that I don't have any skills for this sort of thing.

Poor Michael, please bless his memory. I pray for Michael's family, for Celeste, Bobby, John Mark, and Paula. I don't know how a family could cope through such as this, but I do know that you are good and that somehow you will help them.

And what of this church—oh sweet Lord. There is obviously something nefarious here, some evil lurking in the shadows that has manifested itself in such a traumatizing act. Please spare this church from the certain scandal that will come. I pray you help their staff and lay leadership to know what to do and how to do it.

In the middle of his prayer he began to weep as the sorrow overtook his emotions. With sobbing, he finished his prayer by reciting the 23rd Psalm.

The Lord is my shepherd; I shall not want. He maketh me to lie down in green pastures: He leadeth me beside the still waters. He restoreth my soul: he leadeth me in the paths of righteousness for his name's sake. Yeah, though I walk through the valley of the shadow of death, I will fear no evil: for thou art with me; thy rod and thy staff they comfort me. Thou preparest a table before me in the presence of mine enemies: thou anointest my head with oil; my cup runneth over. Surely goodness and mercy shall follow me all the days of my life: and I will dwell in the house of the Lord for ever.

He walked back over to Michael's body, lifted his hands over the head, just above the vacant eyes. He was careful not to touch anything, although he desperately wanted to put his hand on Michael's head. He cleared his throat, then pronounced:

Give rest, O Christ, to your servant Michael Westgrave with your saints;

where sorrow and pain are no more, neither sighing, but life everlasting.

When he finished the benediction he pulled his phone out again and called Terence Harrison.

"Terence, drop what you're doing and get over to TLC right now."

"Why? I'm in the middle of a staff meeting. Can it wait?"

"No. Michael's dead."

"I'm on my way."

Just as he ended the call and put the phone back inside his coat pocket, two Blackjack County sheriff's deputies burst into the sanctuary, guns drawn and pointed at Pastor Butch.

Chapter Four
Detective Wright

One of the officers shouted, "Don't move!"

The other one yelled, "Lay down on the floor, right now."

Butch Gregory raised his arms and asked, "Which is it? Do you want me to not move or do you want me to lay down? I'm willing to do either, but can't do both at the same time."

"Shut up and lay down."

Butch did as he was told. Something about the moment, and the exchange with the police, reminded Butch of a slapstick movie.

Butch couldn't see what the officers were doing, but he could hear them walk up the platform. One of them said, "Sweet mercy" when he saw Michael in the chair. The other officer said something much stronger.

Suddenly he felt the steel of the pistol's barrel in the back of his head.

"Did you do this? Did you kill this man?"

"No. I am the one who made the 911 call. I found Michael like this when I showed up for our 10:00 meeting."

"Is that the truth?"

"Of course it's the truth. It shouldn't be too hard for even you to look at your records. If you do, you'll see that it was Butch Gregory who made the call. I am Butch Gregory. My wallet is in my back pocket. Take it out. Look at my driver's license. See that I am who I say I am. Then you can take your gun from the back of my head, and treat me like a human being who just discovered his friend has been killed."

"Watch your mouth!" The pistol pushed a little more into the back of Butch's head.

"Was it something I said?" He was pressing his luck, but he didn't care. The sorrow he'd felt moments earlier was unstable, and in the instability it transmuted into anger. Butch could feel this happening to him. He knew the psychology of what was going on inside of him, yet he felt helpless in controlling it. "Look, this is ridiculous. Let me up. You have no right to treat me like this. I didn't do anything."

"I said don't move." The officer's voice was elevated.

"I'm not moving. But at least go over to the office and talk to Pamela. She should know what has happened, and she can tell you who I am."

"That will not be necessary, Pastor Butch," another voice interrupted. "Deputies, put your firearms away and let that man up. Go out and keep the paramedics outside this room until we get a chance to go over the sanctuary and the evidence. One of you go over and talk to the office staff and tell them that they need to cancel all their activities on site until Sunday. Also, find out who their security company is and see if they have video camera surveillance. Tell them I'll be over to talk to them later. When you're finished with that, put up roadblocks on the driveway to the church. Then cordon off the area extending out to the tree line on all four sides. Until further notice this entire area is off limits and under investigation."

The two men scuttled away. Pastor Butch stood up.

"Sorry about that Rev. Gregory, but they get a little excited sometimes. Things like this don't happen very often around here, and when they do, well, sometimes the deputies lose themselves in the moment. I'm afraid they've all seen one too many crime dramas on television."

"I'm glad you came along when you did," said Butch. "I think he might have really shot me."

"That is unlikely. My name is Richard Wright. I am the lead detective for Blackjack County. The dispatcher told me to expect you at the scene. I need you to have a seat right over there on the front row of chairs and wait until I get a chance to question you. Do you understand?"

"Yes. I do. Thank you. Can I call my wife and tell her what is going on?"

"Yes, you can call her. Tell her that you've been detained, but don't give her any other details. As you can imagine, this story is going to hit the media pretty fast. We'd like to try and delay that as long as possible. Okay?"

"Okay," Butch replied.

Detective Wright looked at the corpse, then turned back to Butch, "On second thought, you might want to wait in the anteroom. What we're about to do in here might be difficult to watch."

"No, I'm fine," Butch said. He thought that might be a lie, because he didn't feel fine. Nevertheless, his curiosity overpowered his repulsion.

Butch had been so caught up in the moment that he didn't notice that while he was talking to Detective Wright, the sanctuary had begun to fill up with technicians and investigators. Some were brushing the area for fingerprints, others were taking photographs from various angles, and still others were sweeping the platform and surrounding areas with what looked to Butch to be an ultraviolet light. The scene was surreal, yet, at the same time, like a familiar nightmare that had returned yet again.

He felt a comforting arm on his shoulder.

Terence sat down beside his friend.

"How did you get through the police line, Terence?"

"One of the officers sings in the choir at Ebenezer."

"What did he tell you?"

"Nothing, except that you were in here, and the last time he saw you, they had you laying on the ground with a pistol barrel in the back of your head. Is that right?"

"Yeah, apparently they didn't get the message that I was the one who made the phone call to 911. I guess the officers sometimes get a little over-zealous in their application of justice."

"Welcome to the club, brother. That is what every black man in America already knows. But that is beside the point. What happened to Michael?" Terence pointed at the platform chair. Pastor Michael's pale corpse was still taped to it.

Butch told him about how Michael was not in his office and Pamela in the administrative building had told him to come on over. He described the lights on in the hallway and that the platform light was on in the sanctuary. He told him that he found Michael all bound up and dead and that he called 911, and then him.

They were both watching the macabre scene unfold. The two pastors saw investigators with feet covered in black plastic shoe covers walked around the platform, waving their special lights, and like magicians of old, plying other mysterious tools of their trade. Butch could tell from their reactions that blood was found on the carpet and that more blood was on Michael's shirt. Apparently he'd bled worse than readily apparent. He pointed this out to Terence.

"Hmm," Terence said. "That makes me wonder."

"Wonder what?"

The two men whispered, but in a sanctuary everything echoes.

"If someone hadn't cleaned him up a bit after they killed him, or maybe he had time to clean himself up before he was taped up like that."

"That is curious."

"Detective," one of the light operators said. "Looks like there are, in all, seven different footprints. One of those belongs to the victim. The other is the man who found the victim, then there are the two deputies who responded to the scene. So that is four. Three other footprints have definitely been here in the past twelve hours."

"Good work. Can you get some pictures of those footprints and begin trying to determine shoe size and what kind of shoe."

"That shouldn't be too difficult."

When all of that work was done, Detective Wright walked over to the body and did what Butch had been wanting to do since he first made the discovery. Except, Detective Wright was much more careful. He pulled out a plastic bag from his coat pocket, then he put a latex glove on his left hand. Then he slowly placed his hand into the mouth of Michael Westgrave. Butch and Terence both noticed that the jaw was set tight from rigor mortis.

Detective Wright noticed it too and said to one of his people, "Rigor has set in good, which means he's been dead at least six hours. I would put it at between six and eleven hours since the victim was killed." He paused and thought for a moment, "And it looks like he was killed right here."

"You sure about that, sir?" One of the women working the equipment said. "From what I can see, there isn't enough blood in this location to account for bleeding to death, and I see no signs of strangulation on the neck."

"True," said the detective, "But Christine, there are more ways to kill someone than bleeding them to death or strangling with the hands."

He put on another plastic glove so that he could use both hands to pry open the locked jaw. Then he pulled out paper. It was thin, crispy paper with words on it.

"This is a book." He kept digging more and more paper out, then what looked like a cardboard cover of some sort. It had all been shoved down Michael's mouth, and pushed down into his throat.

Detective Wright said to Christine, "I would say it looks like the good reverend here was strangled to death from the inside. They—the three other footprints—shoved a book down his throat; he choked. The book clogged his airways, and he either suffocated to death or he drowned in his own fluids, one of the two."

"What book is it?" asked Terence.

"It looks like the Holy Bible," Detective Wright said, not realizing who had asked the question. "Specifically it looks like a Gideon Bible," he turned aside and asked, "But who are you? Is the press here already?"

"No, I'm not the press. My name is Terence Harrison. I am," he stammered, "I guess I was a colleague of Michael's. I pastor the Ebenezer Baptist Church."

"Oh good. More preachers. Just what we need." He shook his head in mock disgust, but then added. "Maybe you two can actually help. What sections of scripture is this? Is it random or intended to pass along some meaning of some sort? Come on over here."

The two rose from the first row and approached Detective Wright and their dead friend with cautious reverence. The pages had been ripped from the binding, wadded up and shoved down Michael's throat. The detective had flattened several of them out, although they were all wet. Terence took a peek and said, "These appear to be random pages from the Bible, detective. I don't see any pattern."

Butch agreed.

"You can go sit back down now."

The pages that were easy to get at were pulled out and put in plastic evidence bags.

The police continued their work. Soon Michael's phone, his wallet, his keys, and a Cross pin were all inside of evidence bags.

"What do we have here?" asked Detective Wright, to no one in particular. He let out a long whistle. "I think I feel something very interesting." He reached inside of Michael's jacket, to the inside pocket, and then pulled his hand out revealing a handgun.

"Looks like the good reverend was afraid of something besides the Lord. Let's see, this is a SIG Sauer. 9mm. Nice choice on the grip." He slid it into another evidence bag.

"Great," Butch mumbled. "Guns. Why is it always guns?"

Detective Wright continued his preliminary investigation. "Looks like the magazine is gone." He held it up to his eye, peering through the plastic, "There is not a round in the chamber, either. That tells me something. I don't know exactly what, but it tells me something.

"Either of you two men," Detective Wright said as he looked down from the platform to Butch and Terence, "ever know of the deceased to carry a pistol?"

Butch and Terence glanced at one another and then turned back toward

Detective Wright. They said, almost simultaneously, "No."

"Are you sure?"

"No," Butch said.

Terrence added, "I'm beginning to think there was much about Michael Westgrave we didn't know about."

"That," Detective Wright nodded, "is likely very, very true." He shook his head again, then added, "It is true of most of the people we think we know. Everybody has secrets." He pointed at them as if it were a warning and repeated, "everybody."

They carried his body out on a stretcher. As he passed by, Terence noticed that Michael was not wearing socks. He pointed that out to Butch.

"A sharp dresser like Michael," Terence whispered, "would have never worn those shoes without socks. Maybe a pair of summer loafers or sandals, but not those shoes."

"It doesn't make sense."

"What about any of this makes any sense, Butch?"

Detective Wright came down from the platform to Butch and Terence. "Pastor Butch, I need to ask you a few questions about how you found the deceased. Relax and be calm, you are not under suspicion for the murder, but as the person who found him you might be able to give us some valuable information about what went on here. As you can probably tell, it is a bit gruesome, and more than a little strange."

"Sure," Butch said. He then went on to explain how he'd come to the church that morning and how Pamela let him in. "Hey," a thought occurred to him. "Pamela could tell from her tablet that the security system was already disarmed and that the doors were unlocked. She probably . . ."

"Can tell me when it was disarmed," Detective Wright finished his sentence. "Yes, we already thought of that and while we were in here, one of my people checked, and there is no help in that particular line of thought. Apparently the system's alarm was never turned back on yesterday evening after some musicians were here to practice. Pamela tells us that is not too uncommon as they often forget to arm the system. Good thinking there Butch, but no dice this time. But, we are hoping that the video cameras were working properly."

"Oh," was all Butch could manage.

He continued on with his narrative of how he found Pastor Michael right up to the moment when he was humiliated by the officer. As he finished with his account, Butch added, "Detective Wright, you should also know that Michael called me last night. It must have been around 9:00 or 9:30. He said he needed to talk to me, but wouldn't tell me about what. I tried to get him to meet at Starbucks, but he wanted to be somewhere more private. He wanted to meet here at his office. I don't know if that has anything to do with what has happened, but you should know anyway."

"Do you know where he called you from?" Wright said.

"No," Butch tried to remember the conversation, "but he wasn't at home. He told me he wanted to go home to see his family. So wherever he was, it wasn't home."

Terence said, "That makes me wonder, Detective Wright, why his wife didn't phone the police when he didn't come home last night. Seems odd that no one missed him until this morning."

"That is a good question, and it is one I'll have to find out the answer to as the investigation progresses. The short answer, and the one I find most common, is that he might be the kind of man who doesn't always come home. If you take my meaning." Detective Wright reached into his pocket, "Thanks for the information, gentlemen. Here is my card if you remember anything later on. We may need to talk to you later as we piece this thing together."

"Detective, do you think you'll find the killer?"

"I hope so. It's my job to find the killer. This looks definitely like something unusual is afoot. We're not dealing with anything normal here. It wasn't a robbery because his wallet had over $1,200 cash in it. Maybe it was a jealous lover or an angry parishioner, but I doubt that is all there is to this. There is more going on here. Angry people use guns or knives. The victim had a gun on him, which tells me he was probably afraid, but he was disarmed before he had a chance to use it, and whoever killed him was intentional enough to not use the gun. It seems to me that this was far too exacting, too planned to have been something like a crime of passion or a crime of opportunity."

Wright seemed to be calculating in his head, thinking about the implications of what he'd just said out loud. He pointed his finger at Butch and Terence and said, "I've got to go outside and talk to the news people now. They tell me two Seattle TV stations are already broadcasting from the parking lot. But before I do, I want to warn the both of you to be very careful. I smell a rat in Sydney."

Chapter Five
Snooping

"Come on," Butch said.

"Where to?"

"Just follow me, Terence." Butch Gregory backtracked his path toward the main administrative building. "I think Michael called me from his office, from this church last night."

"What makes you think that?"

"When we were talking, he said something like, 'come over here' or maybe it was 'meet me here' or something like that. It was the kind of phrase that someone would use to indicate they were already where they wanted you to be. If he'd been home or in his car or at a restaurant or something he would have maybe said something like, 'meet me down at my office' or 'over at my office' but he didn't. He said here—and by here he had to mean his office."

"Are you sure he said that?"

"Mostly."

"Do you think you should tell the Shakespeare quoting detective about that?" Terence's head jerked around from side to side to see if anyone was listening to them. There were two police officers standing beside the door to the main sanctuary. Terence added in a whisper, "Because I think you probably should tell him. He smells a rat in Sydney, and I don't want him to think I'm the cat that drug it here, if you get my drift."

"Maybe I'll tell him, eventually, I don't know. But not right now."

"What do you have in mind?"

"Well," Butch stopped walking for a moment and turned to face Terence. "I hope the police haven't sealed Michael's office or anything. I'd like to take a peek inside there and see if there are any clues. I'd also like to look inside his car."

"Are you crazy?" Terence almost shouted it. "Who do you think you are, Magnum P.I. or something? You need to let the professionals handle this one. That detective whatever-his-name back there is smart. And trained. He knows what he is doing. You don't, so don't tempt fate."

29

"Magnum P.I.? Really. You know that is a thirty year old reference, right?" Butch shook his head in mock disgust. "Besides, I only want to look around if the office hasn't been sealed off yet and if Pamela will let me in. Something inside me tells me that I have to do something about this," and then he grinned at his friend and said, "and you too."

"Me?"

"You."

"Hey, I'm a pastor, not a detective."

"I tried that line once, too, but it didn't work for me. I don't think it will work for you, either. Whether you like it or not, you're up to your neck in this already. We might as well see what we can find out while we're here. We might regret not taking advantage of the opportunity. Most of the police are all out front dealing with the media," Butch pointed in the general direction of the front of the property. "It is the perfect distraction. I'm parked in the back here by the office anyway, so it is natural for me to walk this path. We'll just take advantage of the situation God has given us, that's all."

Butch didn't give Terence a chance to respond, he just started walking again toward the administrative buildings. Terence remained still, doing a little thinking of his own. As he ran to catch up he shouted, "Maybe, but that is your fault. You called me."

A minute later they were through the pristine garden and at the small parking lot for visitors and staff.

Terence pointed at an emerald green Lexus. "That is Michael's car."

Butch agreed. "Yeah, check out the vanity plates—GODLUVS-ME— definitely Michael's."

Butch looked around as he took from his trouser pocket a dirty napkin he'd stuck in there from breakfast at the Sydney Diner. He used it to pull the handle on the driver's side door. It was locked. He grimaced.

He heard a click and turned to his left. Terence had pulled out his phone and took a picture of the windshield.

"What's that for?"

"That, my nosey friend, is for that piece of paper in the windshield, down low. Do you see it?"

"Yeah, I do."

It was a small slip of paper, roughly the size of a credit card receipt from a restaurant but stiffer. Butch leaned over to look at it. "Parks-A-lot" was written in bold red letters at the top and underneath it was the smaller, computerized print "Sealth Park." Still further down the sheet of paper, just barely visible over the bottom line of the windshield, where the crevice of the dashboard slips beyond view, was the military time 20:14:29 and the date 11/3/14.

"Looks like our friend was out and about last night. What do you think, Terence?"

"What the devil is he doing out at Sealth Park on a rainy and dark evening?"

"That is a good question," Butch said. "The devil indeed might have something to do with it."

Terence looked around the car and found nothing else.

As the two men entered the office door, one of the officers who had treated Butch so roughly was coming out.

"Sorry about that earlier business in the auditorium, Reverend," he said. "I guess I just got too excited back there."

"That's okay," Butch said. "It was a difficult moment."

The officer nodded his head, and continued on his way back to the sanctuary.

Pamela was still at the same reception station Butch had seen her about an hour earlier, but she was no longer happy and perky as before. Her eyes were puffy red, hair disheveled, face swollen. She was obviously in great despair. To Butch's relief there were no other sheriff's deputies inside.

"Oh, Pastor Butch," Pamela said as she jumped up from behind her desk and ran around to him and threw her arms around him. "I can't believe it. I can't believe it." The tears now flowed like the waters of Multnomah Falls. "They killed our pastor. Who would do this? Why? It doesn't make any sense. He was such a wonderful person." Pamela was beginning to hyperventilate. Butch patted her back the way a father would pat the back of a daughter, and let her cry.

He eventually pulled back and told her, "I don't know. Hopefully we'll find out answers to all those questions. The police are already working very hard on it." Butch needed to move quickly, but he didn't want to rush this moment of hurt and pain. He was, after all, a pastor, and when others hurt he felt a deep desire to bring as much comfort as possible. He decided he needed to press the issue.

"Pamela, can you let my friend, Terence and me into Michael's office? We'd like to just sit somewhere private and decompress a bit. Can you do that?"

"For you, Pastor Butch, anything." Thirty seconds later she deactivated the office door lock with her tablet, and let the two men in. Something like professional protocol, or perhaps Emily Dickinson's famous formal feeling that comes after great loss, must have kicked in because Pamela, in the midst of her personal tragedy, asked the two men if they needed any coffee or anything else, just as if they'd been there visiting on a normal day. They declined, and she pulled the door shut behind them.

"We may not have long, Terence, and we certainly can't snoop too much or we will leave a trail behind."

"Yeah, don't touch anything." Terence's eyes darted around the room.

"I don't have to. Do you see that watch on the desk?" Butch pointed.

"What happened to that?"

"I don't know, but whatever it was, it wasn't good." Butch glanced at his own watch as a comparison.

"Yeah," Terence shook his head. "Poor watch. I remember the last time I had lunch with him, all I could think about every time he brought his arm up with a fork to stick food in his mouth was how much I loved that watch of his. That night I had to spend some time with Jesus confessing the sin of envy; I loved that watch, and Michael wore it so well. Now look at it, all busted up."

Butch pulled out his dirty napkin again. He used it to pick the watch up by its polished metal band. He and Terence stared through the broken crystal to the cracked, but still stunning blue watch face. They both noticed the same thing. The date was off, stuck on the day before, matching the receipt for the parking stall. The time had also stopped because the smashed crystal had pushed against the hands, causing them to cease their winding. It was stopped at 8:46.

Terence took a picture of the watch, then he pivoted to his right and took another picture. "Yeah, well, look over here." Terence pointed at the trash can.

"Socks." Butch walked over to the can. He leaned in toward the trash. Both socks had caught the lip of the opening and hung on the edge. Butch leaned over, sniffed the air, then pushed his finger against one of them. "Wet socks."

"I can't believe you just did that? Why did you touch it? We agreed not to touch anything, didn't we? Now they have your fingerprints on his socks.

That was dumb." Terence's hands waved wildly, and he bounced on the balls of his feet.

"They looked wet. I don't think they can get fingerprints off a wet piece of clothing."

"What if they'd not been wet, what then? And do you know what they can and can't get fingerprints from? Did you take some kind of CSI learning annex or something?"

"Congratulations, you've gone from Magnum P.I. to CSI. Now look Terence, who are we kidding? They will ask Pamela if anyone has been in here, and she will tell them that she let us in. They will know we were here, one way or another. The key is just to not look like we're snooping. I suspect Detective Wright will not take very kindly to that."

"I guess you're right about that. I was only hoping to not cause any trouble for ourselves. However, I have a feeling we're swimming in a barrel of trouble."

"That's probably true." Butch was still holding the busted watch with the napkin. He put it back down on the desktop exactly as he had seen it.

"By the way," Terence said, "I couldn't help but notice the way you lied to the receptionist—what was her name?"

"Pamela."

"Yeah, you lied to Pamela back there about us needing to decompress or whatnot. Don't you think that was flirting a little bit with the dark side? I mean, last time I checked lying was one of the big ones."

"Yes, Master Yoda." Butch sat down in one of the oversized and overstuffed chairs. "But sometimes a higher truth must be served. At least, that is what I tell myself. Besides, it wasn't a complete falsehood. We do need to decompress and talk. Our friend was killed last night, and I think God wants us to find who did it."

"I was afraid you were going to say that." Terence sat down opposite Butch. "And you are definitely not Luke Skywalker."

"You're right on that count, I'm no Luke Skywalker. However, you know that I'm right about getting in here, and that God wants us to be involved in this. I feel it in my bones, in my gut. I know you do, too."

"I don't have to like it," Terence said, then he puckered his lips, kissed the air, and said, "I suppose the Lord thought my life was going along a little too smoothly, that I needed some shaking up. But I don't feel anything particular in my bones or anywhere else." Terence held his hands out and shook them as if he were shaking an imaginary person in front of him. Then he looked around the room. "Man, this is a nice office."

"I was thinking the same thing," Butch said. "I love my office over at Sydney Community, but it is nothing compared to this. This is the Taj Mahal of offices. All those pictures look like they were done for heads of state. These chairs probably cost more than I made all last year."

"What did you think about the desk? Looks like something from the Oval Office."

"I think it's big. But this office is big. I'd been here a couple of times, but just long enough to pop my head in. Usually Michael would take me out and walk me over to some new gadget or gizmo they'd just installed or purchased for ministry. We never sat and talked in his office."

"You know what is missing?" Terence said.

"What?" Butch frowned, "What on earth is possibly missing in a perfectly appointed study like this?"

"Books. There are no books. The one book shelf has trophies, plaques and pictures on it, but no books."

"You're right. Maybe, though, he kept a few books in those massive desk drawers over there."

"You think? Well, let's have a look."

"Now you're getting a little braver. All it takes is books to move you close to the dark side. Now, where is my dirty napkin?" Butch and Terence stood up and walked over to the stately desk. Butch used his napkin to pull open the top drawer. It was mostly empty, containing only a small package of tissue paper. Butch opened two other drawers and found only golf tees, golf balls, and golf gloves in one and toiletries in the other. Switching to the other side of the desk there was nothing in the top drawer but protein bars.

In the bottom drawer they found the glass tumbler and the half empty bottle of Scotch.

"That is some expensive stuff," Terence said as he grabbed Butch's dirty napkin. He picked up the bottle by the neck. "Aged twenty-one years. I tell you Butch, if it wasn't still in the morning I might have to have a sip of this."

"Heathen," Butch said. "Put that back."

"Yes, mommy, or should I say, Obi-Wan?"

Butch ignored Terence's word play. "There seems to be nothing else here of interest. Should we go before the detective finds us?"

"Probably."

The two left the room. Butch gave Pamela another hug on the way out. The poor woman was inconsolable.

As they stepped around the corner of the building toward the parking lot, Butch caught the sparkle of something in a rare autumnal ray of sunlight.

"What is that?"

He and Terence walked and stood over the golden gleaming object.

"You and I both know what that is. We found Detective Wright's missing 9mm shell from the chamber."

Terence took a picture.

"What do you think it means?" Butch said.

"I think," Terence puckered his lips, "it means that somewhere around here Michael had his gun taken away from him, and whoever did it popped the magazine out and emptied the chamber. That is what I think it means."

"Why? Why not just take the gun? Why empty it and then put it back in his pocket?" Butch shook his head.

"Yeah, well, I've got more questions than answers myself. None of this is making a lot of sense to me. I think we should show this to the detective." Terence got into Butch's car.

"I don't trust the police," was Butch's only reply.

Butch drove Terence around to the front of the church building complex where the barricade had been erected. Terence had been forced to park his white Ford pickup on the side street of the road leading to the facility. Butch pulled his tiny blue Honda up alongside the truck.

"I'll call you later this afternoon," Terence said as he got out. "We need to talk about all of this some more."

"I agree. But for the rest of the day, we need to play it cool."

Chapter Six
The Judys

"I see from the news reports that the deed is done," Monica Bennett folded her hands in her lap. "Did he repent?"

"Not at first," Stephanie tilted her head sideways as she elaborated. "Eventually, though, he repented with much sorrow and many tears. He confessed to sins of the flesh, lust of the eyes, and his greatest weakness, of the pride of life."

A tremor of satisfaction moved from Monica's brow down to the base of her spine. She knew it was wrong to derive pleasure from the necessary purging. It was hard not to, though. Knowing part of the disease had been eradicated made her feel something close to joy. She had been called by God to rid the world of false prophets and false teachers, and whenever she was able to fulfill this calling, it caused her delight. It would be a sin to enjoy her work too much, but she counseled herself that it would likewise be a sin to not enjoy it at all. A woodcarver may mourn the loss of a noble tree, but the artist would still celebrate the work of art that came from it. She had molded the Servants of Judith from the raw material of disaffected and disillusioned women. When they performed their God-given function it was like beholding a masterpiece.

Monica Bennett was a brunette with a serious face. In her late-thirties, her complexion was light. Small brown eyes sat narrow on her face, framing her sharp nose. She wore dark clothes. Her posture was perfect, and it was evident she was in absolute control of herself, her people, and the world around her. She believed this control came from her spiritual focus: Purity, cleansing, wholeness, integrity, and decency were noble. The pursuit of those qualities kept her from the pollution of sin.

"Because he repented," Monica said, "we should have every confidence that he has entered into eternity clean and forgiven. We have done him a favor. It is far better to enter eternity maimed than to enter hell completely whole. May the Lord have mercy on his soul." She crossed herself.

"As for you, well done, good and faithful Servant of Judith. How did your team perform? Were there any problems?"

"Michelle was perfect. When the false teacher ran from us in the park, she was able to follow him back to his office without him or anyone else noticing. Then she easily disarmed him as he left his office. Likewise, Jeannie was on point. She overrode the security system of the facility just like we talked about in our planning meeting. She turned off all the security cameras which fooled the system into thinking that it hadn't been turned on again after the musicians left. That gave us complete access to the entire facility."

"What about Nicole?" Monica did not veil her curiosity about Nicole's performance.

"Nicole was another issue. She was fine until we got to the church, but when she saw the false teacher in the flesh, her resolve became shaky. She decided she couldn't go through with it, so she agreed to wait outside the building and stand guard while we worked inside. This she did, without incident, but I don't think we can trust her on future operations. I recommend we move her back to the Discovery Team and take her off the Remove Team. She's not disloyal; I simply think she just would do better as a researcher. It is hard in the heat of the moment to concentrate on the mission."

"I agree," Monica said. "Not everyone can be as purposeful as the prophet Samuel when he hacked King Agag to pieces. Some of us have a bit of King Saul in us, and we want to show compassion to the sinners."

"It is hard to do, Monica," Stephanie said, sitting upright in her chair. "I've been doing this since we started, but I don't think I'm completely at ease with it. It doesn't come natural."

"Dearly beloved Servant of Judith, I understand," Monica reached out and put her hand on top of Stephanie's. "Doing what comes natural leads to sin. We must put to death the natural man so that the spiritual man may thrive. I know it is hard to do this, but we have a job to do, a calling from God himself. Because our work is so vital, Nicole must be punished for not following through on her commitment. She made a promise to the team before it launched. Our word is our bond; it is our integrity. Everything we've built with The Judys depends on integrity and our verbal oaths. If she had backed out before the team started its mission, before you were in place, it would be different. But once she made the promise, she had to follow through. She put the entire operation, and the identity and purpose of The Judys in jeopardy. Therefore, we will have to act accordingly."

"What punishment," Stephanie's voice faltered as she looked down at her feet, "do you order for her?"

"Don't worry about Nicole. I'll take care of her. You are a strong leader, and I trust your judgment. But I don't think you have the gift for punishment or discipline. I, however, have a certain flare for knowing exactly how best to motivate a woman without breaking her."

"I understand, Monica. All I ask is that you not hurt her permanently. She is not a bad person, she just couldn't go through with it."

"Let your heart not be troubled. I will be tender. I am gracious and long-suffering, much like our Lord. However, unlike our Lord, I will be speedy in the distribution of justice. It will be done before our next mission. For some reason, which I cannot always fathom, the Lord seems to delight in delaying punishment."

"When is the next mission?"

"Colleen on the Discovery Team identified a false teacher through her associations on Facebook several months back. I moved his case over to the Investigation Team. They will do their diligence, as they always do, but this seems a clear-and-cut case, so I expect to finalize the mission before the first of December. Does that sound good to you?"

"It sounds like we'll be giving Sydney a great Christmas present—the end, one way or another, of a false teacher."

"Excellent. I thought you'd like that." This time a smile came over Monica's face that she didn't even try to suppress. "Send me your field notes when you get home this afternoon. For now, though, we should probably get back to work. I know I have clients waiting and," she looked through the glass window of her office, "things are filling up out there."

"True," Stephanie glanced backwards, "I'm sure Edward is bogged down at the counter. My work shift is over at 3:00 PM. I'll get the notes to you by 4:00 PM because Nathan wants to take me out for fish-n-chips tonight before I go to church." Stephanie stood up, "so, unless you need anything else, I'll await your further instructions on these issues."

Stephanie strode out of the cozy cubicle office, across the lobby, and took her spot behind the teller's desk. She keyed her code into the computer, flashed a big, appreciative smile, and told Edward, "Thanks for covering for me. I had an issue."

"No problem. It will not take us long to clear the line out."

She broadened her grin, looked out at the line and said, "May I help the next customer, please?"

She spent the next three minutes collecting a mortgage payment for a middle-aged man named Trevor Morris. Mr. Morris also wanted a checking account balance statement. When he finished his business, he said, "Thank you, Stephanie, you're always a big help!" and then walked back across the lobby toward the large glass double doors. Over the doors was a large placard which read, "SeaTown National Bank, Branch #32" and it had an oversized photograph of Monica Bennett brimming with confidence, her dark hair coifed perfectly in a business style, her no-nonsense face wearing a professional smile, dressed in an expertly tailored, conservative navy blue suit. Under her image were the words, "Branch Manager."

***

Later that same night, Bennett sat in the bedroom recliner and looked over the notes Stephanie sent. Monica's husband was on a six month deployment with the Navy. Their fifteen year old daughter, Abigail, was upstairs taking a shower and getting ready for bed. She enjoyed a cup of chamomile with just a hint of half and half together with a packet of artificial sweetener.

Stephanie's notes were delicious and precise.

> I telephoned the false teacher named Michael Westgrave with the pre-paid phone you gave me at 1:05 in the afternoon on November 3. I told him that I knew about his embezzlement of crime money in 1997, and that Michael Westgrave was not his real name because he changed it in order to hide. I explained to him that if he didn't meet me that evening we would go public with the story, as well as the detail about his real name. I reminded him that drug lords have long memories.
>
> He agreed to meet.
>
> I told him to be at Sealth Park at 8:30 in the wooded area where the walking trail splits. I told him I knew that he knew where that was because I saw him there last week with one of his girlfriends. I also explained that he should come alone, or else the media and his church board would be contacted the next day.
>
> He arrived five minutes early.
>
> I concealed my face behind a brimmed felt hat, large sunglasses, and a black scarf wrapped around my neck, chin, cheeks and nose.
>
> I told him not to try to harm me, because there were many of us and that if he hurt me it wouldn't stop anything.
>
> He told me he had no plans to hurt anyone.
>
> After these preliminaries were made, I got down to business. I told him that not only did I, we, know about his financial swindling from

1997 but also that he and the financial secretary of TLC were siphoning off church receipts into separate accounts. I also showed him different photographs of him with his mistress. I told him we suspected there were probably more in other cities for when he traveled to conferences. Then I pointed out to him the extravagance of his automobile, his home, his clothes, travel, and entertainment.

He seemed shocked, but he was listening.

Then, following our protocol, I quoted to him the two sacred passages. First from Jeremiah about lying prophets, "For both prophet and priest are profane; yeah, in my house have I found their wickedness, saith the Lord." And then also from 1 John 1:8-9 "If we say that we have no sin, we deceive ourselves, and the truth is not in us. If we confess our sins, he is faithful and just to forgive us our sins, and to cleanse us from all unrighteousness."

I told the false teacher that we knew of his sacrilege and moral blasphemy. I told him we knew that he had bended the knee to the Baal of this age. He had only one choice. He had to agree, right there, to repent of his sin, resign his church, and never again engage in pastoral ministry.

He waivered. He agreed that what he'd done was wrong, but he was not broken. I could see the pride behind his eyes. The false teacher said that he needed time to think about it before making the decision to leave the ministry.

I told him there was no time for him to think about it. He had to choose right then whether he would change his ways and follow the path of righteousness or continue in his deceit and sin along the path of wickedness. I told him that one way led to life, but the other way led to death. I reminded him that obedience was instant or it wasn't obedience.

He ran away, like a frightened deer in the forest. He ran back to his car, falling along the way.

Bennett's engagement with Stephanie's notes was interrupted by the ringing of her phone. She snapped the cover over her tablet and picked the phone up from the table beside her chair.

"This is Monica."

"Hi, Monica. It's me, Carlotta. Hey listen, Samantha wants me to ask if Abigail can spend the night this Friday. I think they have already talked about it. We are going to the Seattle Aquarium on Saturday and probably do some shopping at Pike Place, and Sam wanted a friend to come along. Is that okay? We should have her back by around 10:00 Saturday night."

"Sure, Carlotta. Let me talk to Abigail about it later and confirm, but I don't see any problems. I will drop her off at your house after school on

Friday. However, as I think about it, that night is a football game. Do you want me to take Abigail and Samantha to and from the stadium?"

"Don't worry about that, Monica. We're going to the game anyway because we haven't heard the band this whole year. I think Sam told me you were there last week to hear Abigail. How did they do?"

"Well, I'm a little partial to the flutes, as you might have guessed, but I think they all were great. Samantha and all the other drummers did an outstanding job. I will say, though, I don't really like the choice of music this year. I preferred last year's swing music better."

"You don't like their 80s Madonna medley? Really, 'cause I love it," Carlotta nearly squealed. Monica held the phone out from her ear as Carlotta continued, "It brings so many memories when I hear Samantha practicing her music in her room. Sometimes, I can't help myself and I sing really loud along with her. It drives her crazy, which makes me do it even more. A couple of weeks ago I pulled out my old cassette tapes and blasted them while I cooked dinner. I mean, what good is life if we can't embarrass our kids with our wayward youth? Right?"

"Well," Monica said, "I have no such nostalgia for heathen art."

Carlotta stammered, paused to collect her thoughts, then added, "Anyway, don't worry about them getting to the game. I will take care of that."

"How much money will Abigail need for the trip to Seattle?"

"None, really. Only if she wants to do some extra shopping or something."

"Okay. I'll have her at your house right after school on Friday."

Monica ended the call without saying goodbye. She returned to her notes.

> Michelle followed him through the woods and then to his office. She waited outside until the rest of us arrived. We waited in the tree line that surrounded the church complex. When the false teacher came out of his den of iniquity, Michelle approached him from behind and hit him over the head with a tire iron. The three of us then taped him. We found a pistol in his pocket. I took the clip out of it and removed the round from the chamber. Then I put the pistol back into his pocket, thinking it might throw the police off a little.
>
> It was at this point that Nicole became noncompliant. It was clear to me that her resolution had faded and she would be a liability. I told her to stand guard, which she did.
>
> Jeannie was superb in her expertise handling of the electronics. I don't know how she did it, but somehow she was able to seize con-

trol, digitally, of the alarm from outside the building. She unlocked all the doors and turned off the security cameras. This allowed us to move onto the second part of our plan.

We dragged the false teacher into the sanctuary and taped him in a chair in the middle of his own platform. When he came to, he was afraid. I told him he had nothing to fear as long as he told the truth. After a few minutes of panic and crying, I again confronted him with his sins. Initially he protested, arguing that he was essentially a good person, but then he broke down when I told him he was a liar and that we knew about all of his evil deeds. Eventually he admitted to stealing the money we knew about, as well as two other incidents we didn't know about—one from a friend and the other from the denomination. When I asked him if there were any other sins, he admitted to fornication, lust, and greed. I gave him plenty of time to confess because he had a lot to work through. At 10:30 PM I decided we needed to move forward. His wife might miss him and come looking. So Jeannie and Michelle held his mouth open while I forced the word of God down his throat as the three of us prayed the prayers of forgiveness and the Our Father.

He choked to death and died before we ever got out of the Prophets. I went ahead and sealed the rest of the Word in his throat and then left the cover folded up in his mouth.

Follow Up Items: (1) I took a picture of the false teacher after he died. It is in an attachment. (2) I threw all of the bullets from his pistol into the Puget Sound. (3) All four of us left our cell phones, per your instructions, at our homes with the location devices on during the entire event. (4) We all wore latex gloves underneath leather gloves. There should be no fingerprints. (5) I checked his phone record on his cell to see if he'd called anyone between the park and the church office. The only phone call he made was to Pastor Butch Gregory. I know him, and know him to be innocent. I don't know why he called Pastor Butch. Maybe he was looking for help.

The attached photograph was gruesome even to Monica. The false teacher's eyes were bulging and his face, though relaxed, was still freshly coated with the patina of terror. There was one unavoidable injury on his body, and that was superficial.

Monica marveled at what she had wrought: Her people had done this as professionally and skillfully as anyone could. It proved Jehovah was with them, and that Jesus was on their side. The Holy Spirit had paved the way for her team's success. How else could one attribute such efficient justice to her rag tag group of housewives?

Monica picked up her cup of tea, but didn't drink. She enjoyed the warmth from the cup.

What was his last thought? Did he think of his family, did he think of how he had failed to be a spiritual leader for them? Did he think about his church? Perhaps his last few moments of life were spent dwelling on his many sins? Maybe he thought about heaven? Or hell? Perhaps there were no reflective thoughts, and all he was thinking about was trying to get one more breath, one more gasp, one more second of life? He may have been thinking it was all a scare tactic. He may have wrongly assumed that nice, pretty, young women like Stephanie and Michelle would never hurt anyone. Maybe his last thought was something along the lines of, 'who are these people?' or 'how did they find out?' kind of thing?

She looked at the image again.

He was frightened, that much was evident.

A longing to have been there when he received his punishment—to see him, hear him, watch him squirm, plead and beg. She felt cheated that she missed out on that moment, and that she'd missed all those moments.

She wondered what she might feel for the false teacher as he perished.

She didn't know how she might feel, but she knew that she wouldn't have felt sorry for him. Monica refused to go down that path. He did not warrant pity. Michael Westgrave's fate was that of all those who resist the Lord and his ways. His was the fate of those shepherds who hurt and deceive the sheep. He got what he deserved, and more will get what they have coming to them as well, and soon. She was the selected executrix of God's hand of vengeance upon those wolves who dress themselves in shepherd's clothing. No more will they get away with it. The Judys will make certain that every last one of the false teachers will either walk away from their role of leadership with repentance or they will most certainly die. It was that simple. There can be no gray in the Kingdom of God. It was black or white, yes or no, truth or lie, obedience or rebellion, life or death.

They were getting better at this, graduating from their clumsy beginnings. Now they had one more false teacher in their sights, but she had two more in hers. Monica knew in her heart why the false teacher would have called Butch Gregory. They must be confederates, in league together in licentiousness.

God, grant me strength and life enough to purge Sydney of all those who blaspheme your name by smearing filth all over the church. She crossed herself.

Just as Monica filed the note away into its proper folder on her tablet, her daughter Abigail came into the bedroom. She was wearing a fluffy, pink housecoat, and combing her wet hair.

"Hey mom, I heard you talking on the phone. Was it Sam's mom?"

"Yes, it was Samantha's mom. She told me that you and Sam had worked out a sleepover this weekend. Is that true?"

"Yes ma'am," Abigail said. Her posture went limp.

"Well, I will allow this trip. I'll even give you some spending money. You can buy your father a gift and we'll try to get it to him by Christmas. I think they will be in Hawaii then. However, I want you to be careful with Samantha's family. They are eaten up with this world. They do not share our values or our morals. They are not good people, honey, and if we're not careful they will corrupt us, they can influence us. That is what worldly people do, sweetheart, they delight in corrupting the good. You are good, but you can easily become bad if you let them influence your thoughts and behaviors.

"I don't want to keep you from being a kid and having a meaningful childhood, so I will not forbid you from having her as a friend, or spending time at her house. Besides, you and I have talked at length about choices. You are almost grown, almost sixteen years old. In Bible times, you'd likely already be married or near to it. So you've got choices to make on whether you will be a good person or a bad person. No one else can choose for you. One way leads to life, and one way leads to destruction. You have to learn to know the difference. Your father and I have taught you right from wrong, we've taught you Jesus' way from the world's way. You are coming of age where you must choose."

"Yes ma'am."

"Good. Now go get our Bibles for our nightly prayers."

When prayers were over, and Abigail was in her room working on going to sleep, Monica picked up her phone and called Theresa.

"Another target has been identified. Split the Investigation Team into two different workgroups. I want half to keep working on the false teacher from the Methodist church, but start the other two Judys on a new file. I want you to investigate Butch Gregory at Sydney Community Church." There was a pause as Monica listened. "You heard me right. It seems that the hero of Sydney might not be all he is cracked up to be. God has chosen us to discover who he really is, and to expose the truth."

Chapter Seven
Wednesday Night

Pastor Butch Gregory made his way home around 4:30 that Wednesday afternoon. The house smelled fantastic.

"Is that ham?" he said as he threw his satchel in the chair beside the door.

"Does it smell like ham?" Lucy said.

"Yes," he walked into the kitchen and lifted the lid on the crock pot. "I see that it looks like ham, too. Now, if I can just determine if it walks like a ham and talks like a ham, then I'll know if it is a ham because it's clear you're not gonna tell me."

"You're silly. Of course it is ham. I bet you're hungry after the kind of day you've had. Did you ever get a chance to have lunch?"

"Sure. I had a chocolate cupcake with a little map of Africa on it that was leftover in the church freezer from the Sunday missions festival, along with a lot of coffee."

Lucy frowned at him. "That is not exactly lunch."

"No, but it is typical pastor food. Don't worry, I also had two pieces of butterscotch left over from my Fall Festival stockpile." He reached inside the pot and pulled a piece of the tender ham off the shank and popped it into his mouth. "Yikes, that's hot."

"You stupid man!" Lucy said, slapping his shoulder, "it is cooking in the very hot pot, so, yeah, it is hot. You're supposed to be smarter than that, Dr. Gregory. Or should I call you Dr. Obvious?" Lucy gave him a kiss on the cheek as he chewed the meat. Then she took him by the hand and led him to the dining room table. He knew what was coming next; her mood had shifted.

They sat down at the table, opposite one another. Lucy said, "How are you? It couldn't have been easy."

"Are Paul and Sarah home?" Butch asked the question, hoping to avoid the conversation he knew Lucy was forcing him to have.

"Sarah is at practice. I called Jeremy's mom and made plans for Paul to stay with them until church tonight, so we're all alone."

"I guess that is good."

"Are you okay?" She tilted her head as she said it.

"Yeah, I really am. I mean, you're absolutely right, it wasn't easy seeing Michael like that and knowing that violence had been done to him. God knows I've seen enough violence. To see any human being treated like that is hard. I can only fathom the fear and the pain he would have felt, knowing they were going to kill him, and the way they killed him."

"I don't want to sound morbid, but I don't know how they killed him. Did they shoot him? Torture him?"

"Sorry, honey. I guess I forgot to tell you all the details. No, they didn't shoot him, and I don't know if torture is the right word either. What they did was, well, they strangled him with a Bible. It looks like they shoved it down his throat, and kept shoving more and more pages, until he choked and suffocated. I guess strangle is the right word. It was a kind of asphyxia."

Lucy tensed up her body. "That sounds terrifying."

"It must have been terrifying. He was duct taped to the chair. He was trapped on his own platform, at his own church, and he was being killed. And he knew it."

"How are you feeling?"

"Well, I'm okay, if that is what you're asking. Michael was a colleague, but he wasn't exactly a bosom buddy or a pal. We knew each other, sure, but we didn't really share life together. Michael turned in far different circles than we do. We're the ham-in-a-crockpot kind of people, while he was more of a filet-mignon-with-cocktails kind of person. I hang out with engineers and sailors, he hangs out, or I guess hung out, with executives and politicians. We wear Levi's and off the rack, he wears Armani and tailored. We didn't have a lot in common, and there was no gut-level connection."

"Are you jealous of him?" Lucy said. It was a risky question, because she knew her husband could become defensive, especially when his motives were in question.

"No, not at all," Butch said. "It doesn't bother me," he swallowed the last bit of his bit of ham, "we just had different kinds of ministries and we had different philosophies of ministry."

Lucy sat back in her chair. "Are you sure it doesn't bother you? I think I might hear a bit of envy in your voice."

"Do you? You must be hearing things then, because I am not jealous. Why would I be jealous of a dead man?"

"That's a little crass and insensitive, don't you think, Pastor Butch?" She exaggerated her pronunciation of pastor.

"Maybe. But, like I said earlier, Michael was a colleague, but he wasn't a buddy of mine. Seeing him murdered like that was hard, but hard in the way that if I saw anyone like that, it would be hard. I guess to put it succinctly, though I am startled and shaken that something like this happened, in a church, and in Sydney, I do not feel loss. Does that make any sense?"

"Yes, it makes perfect sense. What doesn't make sense is why down deep inside I feel like there is something else you've not told me yet."

"I hate when you do that. It's like you can see right through me. Every. Single. Time. In all these years of marriage, you never fail to pick me apart, like vultures on a carcass. You just swoop in and begin to work through me. How do you do it?"

"I'm a woman. God made us that way. You'll never understand so stop trying, because men are not as smart as women." She wagged her finger at him. "Now, tell me what else is going on."

"Well, you're not going to like this, but as I was in the sanctuary at TLC waiting for the police to show up, which, by the way, remind me to write a strongly worded letter to the sheriff; those deputies treated me like a criminal—gun in the back of my head and everything. It made a frightening situation that much more frightening. I really can't believe they treated me like that. They were really outrag—"

"I will remind you to write that letter," Lucy said, raising her hand like a stop sign, "but get back on subject and quit stalling. What else is going on?"

"Sorry, I guess I am easily sidetracked today. Anyway, while I was waiting for the police to show up, I got the definite impression from the Lord that I was supposed to find Michael's killer."

"Crap."

"Yeah, I thought the same thing. I think, though, it is what he wants."

"Wait a minute," Lucy cocked her eyes at her husband. "Are you sure it is God? It could just be you. Perhaps there is a part of you that wants to be involved, and you've interpreted the coincidence of being the one to find Michael as some kind of divine call."

"Maybe." Butch bit his lip. "I certainly don't rule that out. It wouldn't be the first time I misinterpreted something. However, Terence and I have already started."

"You've dragged Terence in on this? I bet he wasn't happy about that.

You know that if anything happens to Terence, Muriel will come looking for you. She's not as forgiving as I am."

Butch laughed because he knew it was true. "No, he wasn't happy, and I will try to not get Terence or myself hurt. However, I didn't drag him into it. I think the Lord did that, too. It just doesn't seem like an accident that we seemed to fall into this together."

"Back up a moment," Lucy said. "What do you mean you started the investigation? Do you think you know who the killer is?"

"Killers, actually. While we were waiting to be questioned by the detective we were able to watch some of the preliminary forensics. We overheard them say there were three different people on the platform. I am certain there is more information in their report that we didn't hear, so one of my first goals will be to find out if I can get a copy of the police report."

"How are you going to do that?"

"I have no idea. I'm sure something will come up. If experience has taught me anything, it is that the Lord tends to send information my way when I need it."

"When are you going to call Wyoming?"

"Why would I call Wyoming Wallace?"

"Please, put away your pride. You would never have found Tamara without Wyoming Wallace. And if you had found her, you'd never have rescued her from those evil people without Wyoming and Amber. Remember? Because I remember it every single day. I shudder at how close I came to losing you."

Lucy got up from the dinner table. She walked to the open window and stared out into the dark. I think if you're intending to do any snooping around you'd be safer with Wyoming Wallace around. Besides, I like him. He's got that old-school tough-guy thing going for him."

"I know all of that, and I am grateful. But I haven't heard from him since he left the week after Easter. I don't even know where he is. Or if he is alive. For all I know he might have gotten knifed in a bar-fight in Nebraska or something."

"You have his cell phone number."

"True, but he hasn't called me, so why would I call him?"

"Maybe he's busy with some important things that are important to him, and he thinks maybe you don't care about him anymore, that he's not important to you, because you haven't called him? Maybe he's thinking the

48

same thing you are, 'he hasn't called me . . . why should I call him?' I mean, you two were meeting every week, and you were helping him unpack his past. He was moving toward faith in Jesus, wasn't he?"

"Yeah, he was. In fact, if you'd pinned me down on it, I'd have said he had crossed that line, whatever that line may look like in a life as complicated as his, toward true and genuine faith in Christ. But that was right when he packed up and left. I don't know why he left, but he did. We had made great progress and then, poof, he was gone."

"Call him, Butch. You're going to need him."

"I've got Terence. He's a pretty smart guy, too. But I promise you, Lucy, if we get in a bind, I will call Wyoming. Okay?"

"I think you should call him tonight, but I'll take that. Tell me, are you ready for dinner?"

"Absolutely."

Lucy and Butch left the dining room and ate their dinner at the small table in the breakfast nook. Lucy had mashed potatoes and tossed a salad to go with the ham. Butch ate like he'd not eaten in a week. Most of all, he enjoyed the safety of home. He never had to be on guard in his home.

Their conversation turned again toward family things. They spoke about Paul's lack of progress in reading and how they might need to schedule an appointment with his teacher. Lucy told Butch that Sarah's boyfriend had broken up with her by text message that morning. They'd only been boyfriend and girlfriend for four days, but still, his daughter was upset. This made Butch upset, and he made a few comments questioning the integrity and genealogy of Sarah's now ex-boyfriend. Butch told Lucy that he'd had a good breakfast with Terence, and made her laugh as he relayed the horrible vomit-filled wedding story. He told her about the lawn mower purchase Robert made, and how graceful Erin was about it. Then he reminded her of the time she chased him with a wooden spoon when he booked their family a luxurious vacation in Chicago in February, the coldest month of the year. She reminded him that she still had some frostbite on her pancreas from that trip.

***

By 5:30 PM he was out the door again, headed back to work. After the excitement of the morning, he'd spent the afternoon working on his sermon for the coming Sunday, and hadn't gotten ready for the Wednesday night prayer meeting. The coming sermon was on Psalm 27, "The Lord is my light and my salvation, whom shall I fear?" Butch wanted to talk about trusting in the Lord when our instincts and experiences tell us we should be afraid. He wanted to link that passage to Romans 12:2 and the idea of transforming our way of thinking. He didn't yet know how he would bridge those two texts just yet, but he knew something would come up.

He went straight to the main building when he arrived at Sydney Community Church. The first thing he did was turn the heat on. He'd forgotten to do that earlier. The building wouldn't be warm by the time everything started, but it would be soon thereafter. Then he unlocked all the doors and turned on the lights. He noticed that one of the lights in the children's classes had been left on, and probably had been left on since Sunday. He made a mental note to send out another email reminding everyone to make sure and turn the lights off when they left.

His phone rang.

"Can someone give me a ride to youth group tonight?"

"Ah, Dylan, let's see. Have you called The Robinsons? They live out by you and might be coming in to church tonight."

"Yeah, and they said they have the crud, so they are not going to church tonight."

"The Hills, they live out by you. Have you called them?"

"No."

"Okay, let me give them a call, and then I'll call you right back, okay?"

"Okay."

Butch ended the call, then found the Hill's home number in his contacts.

"Hey, Florence, are either you or Mike coming in for church tonight . . . You are, good. Hey, do you think you could swing by the Vista apartments and pick up Dylan Martinez on your way . . . I know it is short notice . . . you can, thanks . . . I'll let him know."

Butch ended that call, redialed Dylan, and told him to expect the Hills within the next ten minutes.

He made two pots of coffee. He unclogged the toilet that had still not been fixed from Sunday. The heat had still not come on in the education wing. He knew that meant the pilot light was out again. He said his prayers asking the Lord to keep him from blowing himself up, then he went into the furnace room and wrestled with the ancient fire machine until the pilot light was relit and heat poured out of the vents. When he washed the dust and soot off his hands in the church kitchen, he noticed there were dirty cups and dishes everywhere, so he loaded the dishwasher and ran it. The trash overflowed, and smelled like the missions ministry potluck, so he took it out to the garbage bin and replaced the liner in the can.

When he came out of the kitchen, he saw Tamara Rey and her mother Nikki coming in the front door. When Tamara saw him, she sprinted as fast as she could and gave him a big hug. He hugged her back, asked about her day, and she complained about seventh grade which made Butch smile, and he told her she should probably hurry on to the Junior High group. He gave Nikki the classic sideways pastor hug before she headed off to the children's wing to do the mid-week children's club.

He walked over to his study and picked up his Bible and the prayer list Mildred printed out for him. He had fifteen minutes now until the prayer meeting started. He checked his email. There was one from Miss Betsy's son. The surgery to replace her hip was scheduled for next Monday. He wrote that onto his prayer list. He needed to make certain to mention that one, for even though Miss Betsy was a saint in the first order, those around her could be petty, and the smallest slight could have negative repercussions for Butch. Such was the politics of prayer. Butch replied to the email, making certain to find out which hospital the procedure was in and what time. He highlighted it on his prayer list.

There were several emails from the media. One was from a television station wanting to interview him on the evening newscast. Two others were from local newspapers and some from newspapers he didn't recognize. He suspected the story might have been picked up nationally. He deleted all of them.

Apparently, Detective Wright told the news media who it was that called in the murder and it took no time for them to show the file footage from two years ago. Both KOMO Channel 4 and KING Channel 5 had called his office that afternoon. Mildred successfully deflected them, though, and safeguarded her boss from their inquiries. She didn't do it for Butch as much as for herself. She enjoyed disappointing people. Her job was church secretary, but her hobby was disappointing people. Pastor Butch believed it was her spiritual gift.

Butch took another couple of minutes to sit in silence and gather his thoughts. It wasn't so much prayer as it was preparation. When he glanced at his watch, it was already 6:32 PM. He was late. He grabbed his Bible and prayer list and left for the sanctuary.

There were more people than usual at the Wednesday night prayer meeting at Sydney Community Church. The youth and children's ministries were always well attended, but adults didn't normally attend the prayer meeting. On a good night, Pastor Butch would have twenty or so people. Most of these were senior adults who valued the mid-week prayer meeting. The majority of people who comprise Sydney Community did not value it.

However, tonight was different. Nearly fifty people were in the sanctuary waiting for Pastor Butch when he came in at 6:33 PM. He should have known. People had seen his name on the television reports.

He walked down the middle aisle to the portable music stand in front of the altar table on the floor of the sanctuary. Even though he knew the room was cooler than normal because the heat was turned on late, the room still felt unusually warm to him. He took off his coat and draped it over one of the sanctuary chairs.

"Good evening everyone. Let's start with a little Scripture." He opened the hardback devotional Bible he'd had since college and read from the Gospel of Matthew.

> Come to me, all you that are weary and are carrying heavy burdens, and I will give you rest. Take my yoke upon you, and learn from me; for I am gentle and humble in heart, and you will find rest for your souls. For my yoke is easy, and my burden is light.

Pastor Butch left his Bible opened and then gave the opening prayer.

> Almighty God, we come tonight needing you to take the burdens we carry from us. Some of us are weary of work, of school, of poor health, or poor economics. We need rest, spiritual rest. For me personally this has been a very hard day; now I pray that for the next several minutes this place, here, where we pray and share our burdens, will be a place of holiness, trust, and peace. In Jesus' name. Amen.

"Are there any prayer requests tonight for those who are sick or ill or have surgeries?"

"I have some, Pastor Butch," a man named Lawrence said, "but before we do that, what can you tell us about, you know, the stuff over at TLC and Pastor Michael?"

An affirming "yeah" flew out of several mouths.

"There is not much to tell, really. I was supposed to meet Pastor Michael at 10:00 this morning. When I showed up, he wasn't in his office. The re-

52

ceptionist told me he was probably over in the sanctuary so that is where I went. When I got there he was, well, you've seen the news. He was dead. It was clear that he'd been murdered."

"The television said that Pastor Michael had been beaten up pretty bad. Is that true?" Lawrence asked.

"Not from what I saw. However, I'm probably not supposed to talk about it too much. The police are investigating it, I'm sure. So, let's take this meeting back to where it should be. Let us take any prayer requests. I know that Miss Betsy is having a hip replacement next Monday. Pastor Philip had his wisdom teeth removed yesterday, and he'd like to get off the Vicodin. Anything else?"

For the next several minutes Pastor Butch recorded the usual organ recital—spleens, kidneys, livers, hearts and the occasional brain. Then there was the never ending requests for people who had various types of cancers. After a season of prayer for those needs, Butch then took prayer requests for personal needs—relationships, marital strife, unemployment, and addictions. Pastor Butch always found those the hardest to pray for, but perhaps the most important to pray for. Finally there were the several requests for prayers about church programs and ministries. Most people had the upcoming Thanksgiving banquet on their mind. There was always fear about having enough food.

Pastor Butch wrote all of these down, and then he asked the congregation if there was anything else before they took these issues to prayer. He saw a hand shoot up in the back.

"Yes, Stephanie, I see your hand up." Pastor Butch appreciated Stephanie Colson because she bucked the trend. She was always at the mid-week prayer meeting, whether her husband came or not. She was not just there tonight for the spectacle of information about TLC and Michael Westgrave. She was also one of the few younger people who came on Wednesday night. Stephanie had settled into Sydney when the Navy sent her husband to one of the nuclear submarines. She was from Arkansas and he was from Tennessee. They'd initially had a difficult time adjusting to the Northwest, and Sydney Community. The cultural differences were large, but the religious differences were larger. Stephanie and her husband, David were from fundamentalist church backgrounds, and the fit was awkward. However, they stuck it out because they made friends in a hurry with some of the other younger couples and had since settled in. Stephanie was also his favorite teller at the bank.

"Pastor Butch, would you pray for me? A friend of mine has an important meeting soon with a, with a supervisor, that might not go so well. I just ask the church to pray that she will have wisdom to know what to do and the strength to carry through with what is right, and that I will be able to help, however possible."

"Ooohh," Pastor Butch said, "those kinds of meetings are the hardest ones. I will pray for that, Stephanie. You know, what I've learned is that sometimes the best way to approach those moments is to be like Jesus was in the upper room with the disciples. Everything was happening so fast and the cross was looming on the horizon, and that was when Jesus took the time and washed the disciples' feet as an act of service. It was also a teaching time. He was able to show that being vulnerable in service to others is important, but being willing to let your feet be washed is also important. I encourage you to try to have a servant's heart, even as you have to help your friend work through some difficult news or a hard situation."

"That's a good idea, Pastor Butch. Thank you."

Chapter Eight
Stigmata

Monica parked her white Volvo on the street instead of the driveway. She walked along the picket white fence and then up the sidewalk. Tiny sprinkles fell from the sky into the koi pond in front of the door. After a deep breath and a slow count to ten she rang the doorbell.

Nicole answered the door smiling. The smile evaporated from her face, disappearing into the worried look that replaced it.

"I knew you'd come eventually."

"Of course you did. One of the hallmarks of The Judys is attention to detail. We never overlook or forget anything. You know that. You yourself are a very detailed oriented person, which is what made you such a promising candidate. Now, before we go any further, will you invite me in, or will this become more difficult?"

"Oh Monica, of course you can come in," she swung her left arm around and beckoned the leader of Judith's Servants into her home. "I am here alone, but I just made some fresh coffee if you like."

"No thank you on the coffee. I know you're alone. Your husband left for work before the sun came up this morning and you just took your two sons to school. That is why I am here now."

A lump formed in Nicole's throat. Her worst fears were being confirmed.

"I also know," Monica said, "that you have acted wisely the past two days. You knew I would be coming, yet you made no effort to run away, notify any kind of police authority, or anyone else. In other words, even though you made a mistake, you've been a good girl. That is to your credit. You should be commended for such nobility, such honor, and I certainly have taken it into consideration. Others, in the same situation you are in, have not acted so honorably."

"Thank you, Monica, I think. I feel like there is a 'but' coming."

"Very perceptive. Again, that is a credit to you. However, you did make a mistake the other night that could have jeopardized not only the mission, but the entire mission of Judith's Servants. I have consulted with Stephanie and the Signet Four, and we feel you need to be taken off the Remove Team and put back on the Discovery Team. We know you're committed to the cause, but you're just not up to the emotional situations or the challenges that come up at the moment of action. You lack courage."

A loud sigh of relief came out of Nicole. "Thank the Lord. That is exactly what I was praying for, what I've been praying for over the past two days without ceasing. I do believe in The Judys and their calling to remove false teachers. It's just that when I saw him, I fell apart."

"We know. As I said, you lack courage. I am glad that you see the truth in all of this. It is not a demotion. It is a reallocation of gifts. To some he has given the gift of discovery, to others he has given the gift of investigation, and to still others he has given the gift of removal. There are many different gifts, but one Lord. There are different abilities, however there is only one Servants of Judith, and we all work together for the good of the Kingdom of God, each according to her gifts."

Nicole recognized that Monica was repeating the initiation liturgy. She knew her line was next.

"I willingly give my gifts to the service of the Kingdom of God through the Servants of Judith. I submit to their leadership. I covenant to obey their rules, under penalty of death for the rest of my life." She repeated the last line with a wince. The use of the initiation liturgy was an ominous signal to her that punishment was coming.

She was right.

"Nicole," Monica said, "sit down. You made an oath to the Servants of Judith, but you also made a commitment to the Remove Team when you agreed to the mission. You could have backed out before departing for the mission, but once everything was go, you were locked in, and we were counting on you. Your team counted on you. God was counting on you. Your refusal to help, and your lack of cooperation during the mission, indicates that you violated your promise and went back on your word. Our whole ministry is tied to the bonds of our word. If we don't do what we say we will do, if we lie about our future activities, then we have undermined everything we stand for. Because of that, you must be punished. Our intention is not to hurt you for the sake of revenge or retribution. Instead, as the Scriptures teach us, 'Despise not thou the chastening of the Lord, nor faint when thou art rebuked of him: for whom the Lord loveth he chastened, and scourgeth every son whom he receiveth.'

"Now, receive the chastening discipline of the Lord as a beloved daughter whom he loves. Do not despise it, but receive it. It is for the salvation of your soul and for the purification of your labors, that, as you mature and grow, you might become as refined gold in the cause of Christ."

Nicole hung her head low and stared at the floor. She accepted the truth of what Monica was saying, and remembered her oaths. Guilt, shame, and self-loathing washed over her, drowning her in an ocean of disgrace. She despised herself. Fear of punishment now turned into a desire for pain. Dread of penance became a need for relief. Pain that would be penance to assuage her feelings and restore her. She deserved to suffer. Nicole craved the suffering like a child craves an ice cream cone. She embraced the coming scourge the way she embraced her sons when they cried. The woman yearned for the pain the way she yearned for the touch of her husband in the middle of the night. Her desire for the cleansing pain overpowered her fear.

Nicole ached for the ability to put things right. Suffering seemed the only way toward restoration.

Monica allowed the pregnant moment to build until her student was fully ready to accept her sin and give birth to propitiation.

Nicole turned her gaze from the floor and upward into Monica's dark eyes and said, "What must I do?"

"Your penance is light, because I am gracious." Monica reached into her bag and pulled out a small knife with a ceramic blade, an alcohol swab, gauze, a large towel, an equal sized piece of thick plastic and a yellow legal pad. "I believe that punishment should fit the crime. Take off the shoe on your left foot."

Without question or hesitation Nicole took off the shoe.

"Now take off the sock."

Nicole removed the sock. Monica knelt down with the towel. She rolled it up, then laid it in a circle around Nicole's foot on the laminate floor. She then placed the plastic over the towel and put Nicole's foot on the plastic.

"When Jesus washed the disciples' feet," Monica said, "he taught them about service and about trust. To be at someone's feet is a vulnerable position, but to let someone touch your unclothed foot, so close to so many vulnerable parts of the body, requires trust. It was an intimate act.

"I believe Jesus was also teaching us that when we want to teach someone a lesson, maybe it is best to start with the feet, and then work our way

57

up to the heart." When Monica said the word heart, she looked right at Nicole's chest. Then, with the knife in her right hand, she lifted up Nicole's naked foot and sliced the bottom of it from heel to toe. It was not a deep cut, but it was enough to bring the bright flow of blood.

Nicole squirmed in her seat, but never pulled her foot back from Monica, and never made a sound in protest or in pain.

Monica held the foot at an angle so the blood ran down lengthwise where it dripped off the heel. At first, there were small splatters on the plastic where the first few drops hit, but then it trickled, like water from a leaky showerhead, onto the bloody plastic crater that was forming on Nicole's floor.

"The beautiful thing about a wound on the foot is that no one will ever see it. Even if you are wearing sandals in public, the scar on the bottom of your foot is invisible. However, it is a part of your body that takes, perhaps more than any other part, a physical pounding every day. We feel every step in our feet, and until this heals, you will feel pain with every step. With every flinch of discomfort I want you to remember that you turned your back on your sisters when they were in need. When your foot hurts, remember that with this same foot you walked away from your commitment. You took the Judas route. You betrayed The Judys by leaving them in limbo. You did not fulfill your commitment to the Lord and to his people. When you are an old woman, you will wash your feet and see the scar. Long after I and the other two women you left in the lurch have forgotten it or even died, you will see the scar in the tub and remember this day, this moment, and your sin. When you die, the undertaker will dress you. He will hold this foot in his hand, see the scar, and wonder how you got it. Of course, he will not know what it is or why it is there, but he will be the last person to see it. When you are in heaven, in your transformed body, there will be no scar on your foot. But when you see Jesus, and all of the scars on his body, you will know that it is your sinful scar he is carrying around for all eternity. Jesus died to take away your cowardly sins."

Nicole's only answer was tears of sorrow.

Finally, the bleeding began to stop as the biology of clotting took over, ending Monica's sermon. She then tore open the alcohol swab from its package and disinfected the wound. Nicole took a deep inhale at the sting of the antiseptic. Monica wrapped the foot in gauze with the care of a nurse, then tied it off tight.

58

"Now, we're not done yet. Come down here on the floor with me."

Nicole obeyed.

"You are to never speak of this to anyone. Ever. Not even another Judy. It is between you, me, and the Lord. If someone should see the scar when you are at the beach swimming, or if your husband should inquire, you are to say that it got cut one day around the house when you were barefooted. That is not a lie. Let him fill in the gap of details. Should he ask for a more explicit answer simply say, 'It was nothing.' Do you understand?"

"Yes, Monica. I understand."

"Good. Should the wound become infected, contact me. One of The Judys has access to antibiotics and prescription medicines. There is one more thing, though, before we are finished. Dip your finger into your blood that is pooled in the plastic. With that finger and your own blood write on this pad of paper, 'My word is my bond.'"

Nicole did exactly as she was told.

When she'd finished writing her penance, Monica pulled a small glass jar, like what might be used to hold pimentos, and poured Nicole's leftover blood into it. Then she wrote on the lid with a black marker, "Nicole—11/5/14" and put the jar of blood into her bag.

"The paper is for you to keep. I would store it somewhere private. However, I think it would be wise for you to pull it out once a day and meditate upon it."

Chapter Nine
Illuminatio

Butch's phone lit up. "Meet @ 2. Ok? Ebenezer?" It was Terence. They had texted each other the night before about meeting this morning, but now it looked like Terence needed more time. That was okay, because he could use the time as well. His sermon still needed some work, and it was already Thursday morning, but now he had all morning because there was nothing scheduled until lunch with Lucy at the country club.

He didn't eat at the country club often, mostly because it was expensive. Nevertheless, one of the older men in his church organized a monthly luncheon there for his friends and their wives. Because almost all of them were members of Sydney Community, somewhere along the way Butch and Lucy had become regular attenders. Pastor Butch loved these luncheons, and accepted it as a positive to his ministry. It gave him a regular, non-invasive point of contact with at least six families in his church and it cost him nothing. Literally, it cost him nothing because someone always paid Lucy and his bill, and he always had a good time. He'd come to believe it was just as good for him as it was the others involved. It wasn't exactly the same as Jesus eating with the sinners and tax collectors, but it still felt like the spiritual thing to do. It felt more to him like the disciples having all things in common in the second chapter of Acts.

He looked at his watch. It was a little after nine. The luncheon started at half-past eleven. He would have plenty of time to meet Terence at his place at 2:00 PM. He tapped out a reply to Terence on his phone.

"Great. C U then."

He turned his attention to the sermon and Psalm 27. His eyes scanned the two commentaries he'd looked at yesterday and his background work on some of the grammar, but he still struggled to bring it altogether. Butch knew there was some kind of spiritual connection between not being afraid, the point of Psalm 27:1 and transformed thinking in Romans 12:2. The only way to overcome fear was to control the mind, or better yet, let the mind take control of the body. That is the true measure of courage, to make your body do things you're afraid to do. How to help people make that transition from fear to action was the real question.

> Lord, help me know how to do this. Show me the illustration, the example, the story, the supporting text, the statistic, or the cultural reference that will bring this point of the sermon out. I can't do this without you. I am woefully inadequate for this task, but somehow you have seen it in your divine will to make it my assigned duty. Therefore I plead to you for assistance. Help me. Open my eyes to see how to do it. In Jesus' name. Amen.

He felt better after the prayer. He usually felt better after praying.

He picked up his large leather bound preaching Bible and read the Psalm text again, then he read Romans 12:1-2 again. He closed the Bible, sat back, sipped coffee from his favorite daisy patterned mug and let his mind roam.

The Latin title for Psalm 27 is Dominus Illuminatio. Perhaps a good translation of that would be 'The Lord enlightens." The Lord enlightens. The Lord lights up. The Lord illuminates. The Lord shines.

Dominus illuminatio. Dominus illuminatio. Why did that sound so familiar to him? Dominus illuminatio. He knew it from the prayer book, but it had some other sound to it in his mind. Where? Where had he heard dominus illuminatio before? The thought was almost there, he could feel it. Dominus illuminatio, dominus illuminatio, dominus illuminatio. Where was that from? Aha! From Harry Potter. Well, not exactly, but he thought to himself that dominus illuminatio sounds like one of the spells those kids were always shouting out in the Harry Potter novels and movies. That's why it sounded so familiar.

Wouldn't it be nice? If we could just snap our fingers or wave a wand, utter the magic words and make everything change before our eyes so that we could see what was really going on. Dominus illuminatio we could say and then supernatural light from above would flood over our situation and through our mind and we would be able to see the struggle with our finances is really a gift from God to keep us from the hell we would make for ourselves if we had excesses.

Dominus illuminatio, point the wand. Suddenly, light would radiate our relationships and we would see exactly how destructive that friendship is to us or how those kind, over-flattering words were really meant to poison us.

Dominus illuminatio, presto! Suddenly we can see the way forward, whether we should stay or go, fight or flee, persevere or quit, do or don't.

Wouldn't it be nice indeed?

Magic is easier than faith.

Magic is not the way of Christ. There are no easy prestos, and those who sell Jesus as a cure-all are charlatans of a false gospel which is no gospel at all. There is nothing easy about following the Lord. It requires work. Commitment and perseverance.

Light is all about seeing. In darkness sight is absent, or strained. In light everything is visible. Jesus is light. We are light. Jesus sees different. We see differently.

He picked up his Bible and thumbed to the Sermon on the Mount and found the passage that was on his mind:

> The eye is the lamp of the body, so if your eye is healthy, your whole body will be full of light; but if your eye is unhealthy, your whole body will be full of darkness. If then the light in you is darkness, how great is the darkness.

How great is the darkness? The hardest work of the Christ-follower was to maintain the glow of light, divine light from God, the light of truth from science, ethical truth in our relationships, and the light of love and hope. When these go out, all that remains is darkness, violence, hate, and pain.

The eye was the key to everything. How we see things matters. But how can we see differently?

People learn to see differently by changing their perspective or their point of view. They transform their mind.

Pastor Butch Gregory took another sip of coffee and began pounding out words on his laptop.

***

"I have an idea," Butch said to Lucy. He drove his blue Honda Civic along the winding road that led to the country club. "Michael was a member of the country club, right? He ate there at least twice a week and he golfed there when the weather was good. In the summer he was there almost every day. Right?"

"If you say so. I barely knew him, and you told me yesterday that you barely knew him, too. Remember, your whole 'we turn in different circles' talk?"

Butch ignored her sarcasm. "Well, he did. Also, I was thinking that we almost always have the same server whenever we have these luncheons out there. She knows us, and I think we tip well. I bet if I can get her talking, I might be able to find out something. Maybe she knows some country club gossip. She might even know a fact or two, like when Michael might have been at the club last, or who was with him. Or something."

"Do you really think that will work?"

"No. Chances are really good that I'll discover nothing, but I need to start somewhere. Don't you think?"

"I think you should call Wyoming. You're trying to act like you know what you're doing. You don't, and I'm not going to validate you by telling you it is a good plan. Sorry."

"That's not very nice."

"I didn't intend for it to be nice. I intended for it to be truthful. Don't ruin our lunch trying to be clever. Let's just enjoy our friends and the delicious clam chowder. You should order the fish tacos. As to your plan, if you get a chance to talk to the server in a natural or pastoral way, then go ahead. That makes sense to me. But scheming a way into it seems sordid. It seems beneath you." She fidgeted with the heater vent, then said, "It seems like something a pastor shouldn't do."

Butch didn't say anything.

Chapter Ten
Inner Sanctum

Butch arrived at Ebenezer five minutes late. Terence was waiting for him out in the reception area.

"You're late, old man."

Butch said, "Well, I got caught up in churchy stuff."

"Yeah, that happened to me this morning. Let's go back here to the inner sanctum where we can talk. I have something to show you."

"When that is over, I need to tell you about what happened at lunch."

"Sounds interesting." Terence turned to his right and spoke to his secretary. "Shondra, hold all my calls. I don't want to be disturbed while I'm back here with Butch."

"Yes, Dr. Harrison."

When they were halfway down the hall Butch whispered, "You make them call you Dr. Harrison? Really?"

"No, it is not my idea at all. I'd rather them just call me Terence—no pastor, no reverend, and definitely not Brother Terence. Nothing. Just plain old Terence."

"Then why did she call you Dr. Harrison?"

Terence puckered his lips, kissed the air, and said, "There is a strong tradition in some black churches to highlight the educational experience of their leaders. Think about it, we always refer to MLK as Dr. King. That he achieved that educational status means something to the rest of us, and we want everyone else to remember it too. It is encouraging. Butch, it goes back to that evil man named Jim Crow. Back in those days, and really ever since Africans were trafficked to North America, it was almost impossible for a black person to get any kind of education or credentials. So, whenever someone did, it was a big deal for him, but a bigger deal for the community. What you just saw there was a woman who wasn't just showing deference to me by calling me by my title, she was also taking pride in her community. So, I just let it slide."

"I'd never thought of that before." Terence's lesson gave him something to ponder.

"You've never thought of it because you are white."

Butch nodded that he understood, but he wasn't quite sure he did. He followed Terence down the hall with his head down and his brow furrowed.

It had taken Terence almost the entire two years he'd been at Ebenezer to get his office set up the way he wanted it. Terence was a scholar as much as he was a pastor. He got that tendency from his father, who was a professor of ancient literature at UCLA. His father gave him the first name of Terence after the ancient Roman who wrote comedies during the time of the Roman Republic, before the rise of the Roman Empire and the Caesars. He gave him the middle name of Simon after the man who carried Jesus' cross. These two literary figures, both black men, served as inspirations for Terence's father, and he'd hoped it would do likewise for his son.

It did. After seminary Terence earned a Ph. D. in Old Testament narrative. He enjoyed the academic work of the ministry more than the programmatic leadership at which Butch excelled. Because of this academic penchant, he arranged his personal space at the church building a little different than most other pastors. He designed a front reception room with a sofa and a couple of comfortable chairs; nice pictures hung on the wall. That was where he met people when they came to see him at church. Down the hallway, behind the storage room, and in an old janitor's closet was Terence's inner sanctum. It was a private study area. It was ugly, not very well lit, and not very big. The floor was chipped tile with an area rug thrown over part of it. The desk was small, and filled with books and notepads. Enough space was pushed out on the desk for a laptop. There was almost no room to sit, as it was crammed full of bookshelves and books. Books were piled one on top of another all the way to the ceiling. Wadded up paper littered the floor and desk. There were no windows and only one vent in the ceiling for heat. A two-cup coffee maker plugged into the wall and an old fashioned-clock radio were the only two luxuries in the room. There was no table for the coffee pot, so it sat atop a stack of volumes from the New American Commentary. The radio played jazz. The room smelled like a mix between a library and jail cell. The only person who had a key to this room was Terence. The janitor was not allowed in, neither was the secretary. Most of the people in his church did not even know the room existed. It was Terence's private space where he could be alone with his books, his research, and his thoughts. It was Terence's happy place.

Butch had only been back here once before. It was in the summer. Butch remembered it being hot and a small fan oscillated, blowing papers and pages all over the room effectively creating a theological tornado. Today it was cold. Butch stuck his hands in his coat pockets as he crowded in alongside some books with titles in German.

"What do you want to show me?"

"This," Terence said, pulling a piece of paper from a drawer in his desk. "I got it this morning by email. I took the liberty of printing it out. I did that myself, mind you. No need in getting the Shondra involved."

"I can see why," Butch mumbled as he began to scan the document.

Butch Gregory held in his hands the official Blackjack County report on the crime scene as well as the Blackjack County Coroner's autopsy report.

"How did you get this?" Butch said.

"If I tell you, I'll have to kill you." Terence didn't smile.

"For reals?"

"No, not for reals. Don't be ridiculous. But I had you for a second. Remember I told you that one of the officers was in our church choir. Well, I kind of went all Holy Ghost—pastoral authority—do your duty for God—on him last night over the phone and told him that he needed to help me get as much information on this case as possible. This was in my inbox this morning. So, it looks like we have a friend on the inside. You're welcome."

"Thank you. Have you had a chance to look over it? What do you make of it?"

"Why don't you sit at my desk and look over it yourself. I'm going down to the other end of the building and rid myself of some of the coffee I've been drinking all day. When I get back, we'll compare notes."

"Sounds like a good plan."

Terence disappeared into the hallway and Butch sat down behind the cramped desk. He pushed aside a half-eaten sandwich and a Philadelphia Phillies coffee mug to make room. He thought the mug was empty, but when he pushed it aside it toppled over. Cold, black coffee ran off the edge of the crowded desk and onto the floor. Desperate for something to clean up his mess, Butch looked around the room for a towel or a napkin. Hanging on a hook on the back of the door was a pure white baptismal robe. He lifted it up, not sure if he'd use it or not; it seemed sacrilegious to use a holy garment to clean up spilled coffee. Fortunately, underneath the robe on the same hook was a white towel.

With the towel he mopped up the coffee on the floor, the bits that dripped down the side of the desk and the small amount still on the desk-top. It was a minor miracle that none of it got on the numerous papers. But what to do with the towel? In a capricious act he threw it across the room. It landed on the floor against a bookshelf. With all the mess in the office, Butch assumed it would be weeks or months before Terence found it; he would never know how it got there.

His butterfingers crisis solved, Butch turned his attention back to the document. There were several pages in the crime scene report, but most of it was decidedly 'in-house' issues, things only a trained eye would make sense of. Nevertheless, he persevered.

He discovered no fingerprints were found in the sanctuary or on Michael's body.

A single strand of blond hair was found on Michael's coat. It was being sent for DNA testing.

Butch read the description of the crime scene closely and noticed there was no mention of the bullet he and Terence found in the parking lot, although they did mention the missing socks and the pair of wet socks in Westgrave's office.

He also learned they found the parking lot ticket in Michael's Lexus as well as his busted watch. There were pictures of both in the crime report. The detective who filed this document concluded the alarm system was de-activated using some kind of network hack from the outside. This conclusion was reinforced with a two page readout from the alarm company detailing the exact time the network was compromised as well as the override commands that deactivated the sensors, turned off the cameras, and unlocked the doors. The music team did indeed turn the system back on when they left, but someone deactivated it later.

Butch turned to the last page. His eyes almost fell out of his head when he read the last paragraph.

> Detailed analysis of the photo-electric footprints found numerous footprints, from reporting officers, the individual who found the victim, and those who used the building the previous evening. However, footprints found around the body indicate that there were three assailants. All three of the footprints were small and likely female. Shoe sizes 6, 6, and 7. Shoe type—common athletic shoe.

Women. Michael Westgrave was murdered by three women. Butch didn't see that coming.

Butch moved from the forensics document to the coroner's report. It was a little easier to read than the crime scene report. The cause of death was strangulation, which Butch and Terence already knew. No poisons or any other trauma could have accounted for his death. The wound on his head was superficial and would not have killed him, but was most reasonably assumed to be the method his attackers used to subdue him. His right foot was swollen, likely the result of a sprain or twisting before he died. There was a scrape on his right hand with loose gravel in some of the wound. The coroner speculated that the wounds were consistent with a runner who had fallen and braced himself with his right hand as he fell.

Were you running from those three women, Michael?

Where were you running? He thought about the parking receipt in the car.

You were running in the park, weren't you?

A small amount of alcohol was found in his blood, but his stomach was empty except for the pages of the Bible that were found. Michael hadn't eaten all day.

Pages from the Bible were found in his stomach, lungs, throat, mouth and nose. Several photographs showed the pages, smoothed out and straight on a table. The coroner's report noted some of the pages had specific passages highlighted. These were being sent to the FBI lab for further analysis.

The report ended with the coroner's official conclusions.

> The victim died of strangulation caused by the pages of a book being forced down his mouth and throat, causing him to suffocate. There is no evidence the victim ever struggled with his assailants as no dirt or skin tissue were found under his fingernails. Given the location of the body, the type of death, and the implement used, my judgment is that this was ritual execution by people wanting to send a message.

Execution? Ritual? Michael was executed by three women trying to send a message.

Just as he finished, Terence came back from his bathroom break.

"So, what do you think?"

"I think we have some crazies on the loose in Sydney." Butch circled his index finger around his temple, making the universal sign of insanity.

"Yeah, that's kinda what I thought. Did you catch the part about the footprints?"

"That is the part that frightens me the most. Not only do I wonder why—why would three women want to kill a pastor, but I also wonder how they were able to so easily catch him. You saw that Michael had a pistol on him. Why didn't he use it?"

"Maybe he never got the chance. Whether you're female or male, if you sneak up behind someone with a big enough stick, they have no fighting chance at all." Terence pushed aside some of the books from the corner of his desk and sat down on top of it. "But Butch, the question I'm asking is, and this is the man inside of me, not necessarily the pastor, but as a man, what on earth was Michael doing to make three women want to kill him? Three women who knew the Bible very well, yet felt like murder was something they were allowed to do."

"What makes you say they knew the Bible well? Anybody knows enough about it and church to use it as a weapon against a pastor if you're mad at him or her."

"Yeah, but did you look at those photos? The three in the report had highlighted sections on them. When they were on my computer, before I printed them, I zoomed in and got the Scripture references. Every one of them is some passage about false teachers, lying prophets, or immoral leaders. Most of them are from the Hebrew Bible, primarily Isaiah and Jeremiah, but others are about some of the ungodly kings from the history books."

Butch put his hands on his head, "What you're telling me is that not only do we have three crazy women running around Sydney who murdered a man two nights ago, but you're telling me they are also Bible scholars?"

"Bible scholars on a mission. Zealots. Fanatics."

"But that doesn't fit with them being women?"

"Sure it does, Butch. You know better than to be sexist. Even though most violent crime is committed by men, primarily young men in organized systems of violence, women are just as capable of using violence as a means to an end. Besides, never forget that it was Kipling who said that the female of the species is the most dangerous."

"Great. So where do we go from here? What is our next move?"

"I don't really know. I was hoping you would have an idea or two. After all, you're the one with experience at this sort of thing."

"Don't remind me." Butch stood up. Then he handed the two reports to Terence. "You should put these in a safe place."

"You're right." Terence folded the papers neatly in two. He turned around and moved his index finger along the bookshelf until he found what he was looking for. "Yes, that'll work." He pulled Gesenius' Hebrew lexicon off the shelf, then stuffed the grisly report somewhere in the middle of Lamedh. "It should be safe in there."

"Let's go for a walk," Butch said to Terence. "I need some fresh air."

"But its drizzling rain outside."

"I know. That is perfect walking weather. If you're going to minister here in Sydney you'd better get used to the weather."

"Fine, but now?"

"Walking helps me think. Come on. Grab that heavy coat of yours."

"I'll need my hat. Those are at the front on the coatrack. Let me get them, then we will slide out the backdoor."

"There is a backdoor?" Butch said. He didn't remember a backdoor.

"Yeah, just around this corner is a small wooden door," Terence turned away, then looked back over his shoulder, "it is so seldom used that it sometimes doesn't even get locked."

Terence walked down the hallway toward the front of the administration building and disappeared. Within seconds he was walking back. He had donned his trench coat and hat. Butch made fun of him for his decidedly Northeastern attire, then he popped out the hoody from the nape of the neck on his Gor-Tex coat and pulled it over his head.

Ebenezer Church was located on the hillside overlooking downtown Sydney. It was an older part of town, but not in a gentrified way. This was the part of town middle-class people abandoned a generation ago in favor of the housing developments on the outskirts. Years ago, all of the churches in town were located down on the hillside, but the mainline, mostly white churches left the area when the people left, leaving older, vacant church buildings. In the early 90s, Ebenezer purchased the old Nazarene Church building and remodeled it. The other buildings often saw start up congregations or church plants make a go. However, these ventures, usually begun by disgruntled church people, blew away like chaff in the wind. Ebenezer, however, had thrived in the midst of town. In its previous location, out near the industrial plant, its congregants had been almost entirely black people. Since moving to this location, the diversity of the congregation steadily grew. At first, it added a couple of white families who still lived in the neighborhood, then a slow trickle of people from Asian backgrounds began to attend. In the past five years, a growing Mexican and Latin American demographic had started attending Ebenezer. One of the first things Terence did when he arrived was add a Spanish speaking associate pastor to start a Spanish worship service. Nevertheless, Ebenezer was still a majority black congregation.

The two men walked out the back of the administration building, then up a small hill toward the sidewalk. The rain put a frown on Terence's normally cheery face.

"I had lunch at the country club today. I thought I might be able to find something out because Michael was a member out there and he loved to golf."

"I don't know if Michael loved to golf as much as he loved the prestige that went along with being a part of the country club," Terence said.

"I see your point," Butch patted his friend on the shoulder. "I've been thinking about my relationship with Michael and the way he did things, and it seems like he was always striving for some level of social acceptance, or maybe an idyllic way of life where everything was picture perfect."

"You and I know what that means?" Terence lowered his voice as if betraying a state secret. "It means that he was compensating, overcompensating, for something that probably happened a long time ago. You know, the guy who makes his kids eat dinner at the table every night is probably a guy who grew up without a table to eat at or without a family to eat with."

Butch nodded, then added, "I was thinking along similar lines. The problem is I don't know enough about Michael's past. He grew up around Seattle, and I know he started a church over there before he came to West Sound. That's about it. Did he ever talk about his past with you? Maybe his childhood or high school or anything like that?"

"Never. All Michael ever wanted to talk about was the latest ministry gimmick." Terence held his hand up, "Sorry Butch. I shouldn't have said gimmick. I guess he meant well. It's just that I don't think his particular type of church life matches what I read in Scripture or what I see in the early church. I think the Apostles, if they were here today, would slap most of us around and defrock us as incompetent to lead."

"You mean you feel like most pastors are chasing off after Baal, Molech, and Jupiter?"

"Yeah. That's exactly what I mean," Terence stopped walking and grabbed Butch's shoulder. "And maybe that is part of what was going on

71

with Michael. I mean, that report we saw was pretty descriptive of the methodology of his death. We might be dealing with religious zealots who view themselves as judge and jury for God's righteousness or something, and they are punishing him for his worldly ways. Think about it, if we can see the way Michael lived and ministered, and not like it, then it stands to reason that someone out there might see it and come to some very misguided and dangerous notions about righteous indignation and retribution."

"You mean," Butch said as they started walking again, "like three women who know their Old Testament very well."

"Yeah, three women armed with a stick, duct tape, a Gideon Bible along with a deranged sense of divine calling."

"That is a frightening thought, Terence. You know why?"

"Yeah, I know exactly why. These crazies might decide at any moment that any pastor or ministry leader needs to be punished for his or her sins." Terence stroked his chin whiskers. "You know what else is frightening? Some of these women might be in our churches. Although, I'm pretty sure most of the crazy women are in your church and not mine."

Butch frowned and opened his hands up wide, "Why would you say something like that?"

"Because everyone knows black women don't sneak around and hide when they are mad like these killers. Black women just come at you full tilt, swinging their purse at you as they yell, 'Get thee behind me Satan!'"

"I thought that was a stereotype?"

"Tell that to the woman who swung her oversized purse at me last week because I forgot to mention her grandmother's birthday during the announcements. She was half-playing when she did it, you see, but that is the personality type indicative of strong character. It is a stereotype, Butch, but it is grounded in the very real temperament many black women have, a temperament which has helped our people survive the brutal treatment we've received for the better part of American history."

"Point taken."

The two men walked down the hill and turned the corner toward the Happy Beans Coffee and Espresso shop. Neither one of them indicated that was where they were going, but they both knew that was where they were headed. It was Butch's second favorite hangout, right behind the Sydney Diner.

Next door to Happy Beans was the marijuana store that opened in the summer. Both men scowled as they walked by Pot Paradise. Their pace picked up until they were safely beyond the brownie and bong lined windowpanes. At the counter of the coffee house, Terence ordered a cappuccino and Butch got the drip of the day, a blend called Navy Strong. Butch paid the bill. They walked back outside. Neither one of them wanted to talk in a public space.

They were silent as they walked across the street at the crosswalk. They found their way to the water's edge and looked out across the inlet at the Shipyards.

"You said you were at the country club today. Did you find out anything?" Terence pulled his coat around him. The wind blew over the water's frigid waves.

"Sorta. It's weird though."

"Of course it's weird. That fits the theme of the last 36 hours. If it were anything other than weird I'd think something had gone wrong."

"Sad, but true."

Chapter Eleven
Premonition

Butch took a sip of his coffee. It was smoother than he expected. He sipped again, then began the story about the bizarre lunch at the country club.

"Lucy told me not to go snooping around as we drove out to lunch. I didn't really pay attention to her. I should have listened. Of course, that is the way most of married life goes anyway. When we got there, our server was a woman named Katie. She is always the waitress for our little luncheon group—we meet there every month—and have for at least three years—wait, I think it is more like five. The point is, she knows us and she knows me. Katie goes to the Pentecostal church out on the highway and she knows that I'm good friends with Pastor John because we've been in there together to eat before. A few times she's even asked me to pray for her when things are tough—a surgery or something—when she brings my food out or fills my cup. Anyway, Katie knows me and trusts me. I thought I'd take advantage of that relationship a bit and ask Katie if she'd heard about Michael's death and all.

"The problem is, I didn't have any idea of how to do that, and as I told you earlier, Lucy was no help. When Katie came around to our table, I ordered the salmon on a cedar plank with a rice pilaf and green beans. I substituted the green beans with fresh cut pineapple and cottage cheese. The country club is one of the few places in town where you can get cottage cheese and fresh pineapple. After she took our order, I watched Katie walk over to the kitchen and put the order in. I decided that was when I should make my move so I got up from my chair, excused myself as if I was going to the bathroom, but I walked in the direction of the kitchen. When I crossed her path, I asked her if she'd heard about the horrible situation with Pastor Michael. She told me that she'd not only heard about it but had been praying for his family. I asked her if Michael had been out to the country club lately. She said yeah, he comes all the time. She guessed at least twice a week, usually more. She was kind of sheepish as she spoke, and she got hush-hush when she told me he spent a lot of time at the bar drinking. I can

74

imagine how she felt, and how that really embarrassed her. Pentecostals are pretty much the only teetotalers around anymore. Well, them and Mormons.

"She went on to tell me that Pastor Michael was at the club the day he died. She said he was having lunch down in the clubhouse. She took his salad to him and just as he got it his phone rang. Well, whatever the phone call was must have been very important because he left, without eating his salad.

"She told me, 'I simply figured that it was church related or something. I can only imagine how herky-jerky a pastor's life can be. I assumed that someone was in trouble and needed him. I guess now that maybe it was something else. I don't know.'

"Terence, I thought that was a very interesting development, and it makes me certain we need to get our hands on his phone records. I wish I'd lifted his phone from his pocket the day I was there by myself.

"But anyway, after listening to Katie's story, I gained a little courage and pushed the point. I asked her if there were some kind of way that I could look in Michael's locker. She told me that normally absolutely not, but then because Michael was dead and she knew me, she might be able to make an exception. She asked me if I was working with the police. I told her no, not officially.

Terence interrupted the story. "You're not working with the police at all. Not officially or even unofficially. You need to be straight about that preacher man."

Butch ignored Terence's rebuke. "That was when Katie said she had to get back to work. She told me to come find her after she served dessert. I smiled like a cat that just ate the canary as I went back to my seat beside Lucy. Lucy glared at me, like she knew something, but she didn't say anything. I hate when she does that.

"The salmon was delicious, and I passed on dessert. Lucy ordered a fudge pie of some sort, but as soon as Katie served it, I swiped a bite of Lucy's dessert and then made a beeline for Katie. She said the issue would have to go through her management, particularly through the security manager. I should have known something was wrong then and chickened out. But apparently, I'm not that smart. She walked me across the building, down a hallway, up a flight of stairs and through a cubicle maze to a corner office. I had no idea that it took that many people to properly administrate and run the country club. I guess I always just thought of it as the restaurant and a few caddies out on the golf course, along with maybe a few maintenance and lawn care people. Apparently, it takes a small army. Eventually, we found ourselves in the office on the far side of the cubicle maze.

"The office, more of a control room really, looked like something from the CIA or FBI, or at least movies about the CIA or FBI. There were video and computer screens with live feeds from video cameras all over the club, golf course, and roads leading in and out. About three different computers with keyboards were set up around the room. At a sleek desk in the middle of it all sat a middle-aged woman. Katie introduced her to me as the chief of security. 'Pastor Butch, this is Jeannie. She runs all our computer systems and security. She is a computer genius,' Katie told me and then she added, 'It's her call to make as to whether or not you can get in. Good luck.'

"Well, that's when things got weird. Jeannie stood up and shook my hand. When she did, Terence, I had the strangest sensation. It wasn't a vision, I've had those before. It wasn't the Lord talking to me, either. I know what that sounds like. It was more like a premonition. A lot like a hunch, but much stronger than that. Foreboding maybe a good word too. I know you probably think I'm crazy, if you don't already think I'm crazy, but Terence, as I held her hand in my hand, shaking it, I knew that somehow she was involved in Michael's murder. There was a cold feeling that came up my arm and moved into my shoulder. It felt like it took fifteen minutes, but I know it was only a split second. As the coldness came up my arm, I suddenly knew that this woman whom I shook hands with was evil, and that she was guilty. I also knew she was dangerous and that in this moment, for the first time in two years, my life was in mortal danger. It was like Jesus was giving both good news and bad news, all at the same time.

"I wish there had been more to the feeling. I wish there had been something in the thought about how she was involved or what else was going on, or even how many and who else was involved. However, there was nothing. All I was left with was a certain knowledge that the person I was standing in the room shaking hands with was one of the people who killed Michael Westgrave.

"It scared me to death, and my first instinct was to run, but I knew that would be unwise. Instead, I needed to carry through with what I told Katie. She smiled and asked me how she could help me, and I asked her if there were any way I could get into Michael Westgrave's locker. I told her that I was investigating his death. She asked me if I had a search warrant. I told her that I wasn't with the police. That was when she showed me the door and said that I needed to keep my nose out of other people's business. It was a very terse, quick conversation. When she finished she pointed to the door and said to me, 'Go back to your dining table and enjoy your wife's fudge pie. She left you two bites.'

"The creepiness of her knowing our dessert, along with the feeling that somehow she had a special eye on me, and perhaps my wife, ran through my mind all the way back to the dining room. I tried to smile and act as if nothing special was going on as I sat back down, but Lucy noticed. I'm sure of that. When we got back in the car she told me that I was as white as a sheet. She asked me what happened. I told her I would tell her later. Which I know I will. I always do.

"What I'm worried about, Terence, is that now this woman, this Jeannie, who, if my premonition is accurate, is a part of the murderous clique, now she knows I'm snooping, which makes me a target. Plus, I don't know if she felt maybe the same thing I felt when we shook hands. What if it were reciprocal or something, some kind of supernatural spiritual highway with information traveling both ways? If she does, then she knows that I am onto her.

"So, what started out as a little plan to do a little snooping has turned more than a little serious. And I am a little frightened."

Terence tossed his empty cappuccino cup into a trashcan. Then he told Pastor Butch Gregory, "You'd better be worried. And you'd better pray."

***

It was two minutes after 3:00 when Butch arrived at Blackjack Elementary. He felt tired. There was little emotional energy left in him after the events of the past several days, plus the encounter at the country club and the talk with Terence. He just wanted the day to be over already. But Mildred had called him, telling him Paul's teacher called the church office. The teacher wanted to speak with Butch between 3:00 and 3:25 today.

He walked down the corridor of the elementary school toward his son's classroom. This was the same elementary school both his children attended, and he had a good relationship with the principal and many of the teachers. Some of the greatest people he knew, and kindest folks at Sydney Community, were teachers. Paul's teacher, however, was someone he didn't know and still hadn't figured out. Sarah had a different teacher in sixth grade, Mr. Mosely, who was benevolent and gentle. Butch knew Mr. Mosely's pastor.

Paul's teacher was Mrs. Hastings, someone he didn't know. Lucy had felt cold toward her at their October parent conference, and there was no connection.

However, he was feeling optimistic, which is how he usually felt when he thought about his children. They'd been worried that Paul's reading comprehension was weak, and when he got the message from Mildred that Mrs. Hastings needed to see him today, he assumed it was her picking up on the same thing. It would be nice to talk to her about some strategies to help his son. Sarah was a strong reader, and he wanted Paul to be the same.

He arrived at the room, and the door was closed, but no children were inside. He knocked on the door and opened it all in one motion. Mrs. Hastings was sitting behind her desk. When she saw him she waved him into the room. Her face had the countenance of someone who had just lost their pension in a Ponzi scheme. She did not get up. Butch walked over to her and extended his hand, "Good afternoon, Mrs. Hastings. It is a pleasure to see you again."

"Not really," she said. "Please have a seat," she waved her hand toward the tiny children's chair beside her desk.

"You want me to sit in that chair?" Butch didn't realize he'd said that out loud. It popped out of his mouth before he edited it.

"Yes, that chair. That is where all the parents sit when their children have been naughty."

"Naughty? What are you talking about?" Butch looked at the chair with disdain. There was now no power on earth that would make him sit in that chair. "What has Paul done?"

"This," Mrs. Hastings said, handing him an iPad with a picture on it. "I took the picture this morning when we came in from music class. He denies it, but I am certain Paul is the little boy who wrote this on the dry erase board."

The picture was simple. It showed a three verse poem written in black dry erase marker on the whiteboard. Butch smiled when he finished reading it.

> Roses are red.
> Violets are blue.
> Penis.

His smile turned into an audible laugh. Mrs. Hastings did not look amused. Butch tried to be serious again, tugging at the bottom of his jacket.

"You say Paul denies he wrote this."

"Yes, but I am almost certain he did."

"Do you have proof?"

"It had to be him. None of the other boys would have done this."

"Are you sure it was a boy?"

"Of course it was a boy."

"You mean you don't think a girl would do this?"

"Quite frankly, no. I do not. Girls, although they have their issues, do not generally act out in this way. Boys are far more demonstrative in their ill behavior than girls. Girls tend to keep secrets and hide things, whereas boys want the whole world to see their wickedness."

"Isn't 'wickedness' really strong language there for sixth graders?"

"No. I thought as a pastor you would understand that."

Butch rocked back and forth on his feet. He couldn't believe he was having this conversation. It was surreal.

"Other than your gender bias, what makes you so certain Paul did it?"

"I can see it in his eyes."

"His eyes. Really?" Butch's cheeks turned red. "That is the sole determination of the burden of proof, you can see it in his eyes? I'm sorry Mrs. Hastings, but my son can be lazy, and I've even heard him say a dirty word or two, but he has never, ever lied to me or his mother. If he says he didn't write that, I believe him."

"I assure you, he did write it," Mrs. Hastings said. "Are you going to believe a child over his teacher—"

"Don't go there." Butch had now regained control of his feelings, but he was still angry. "This is not about whose word I take. It's just that you have no proof. You didn't see him do it. You didn't find marker smudges on his hand. He didn't sign it. No other kid said he did it. You just think he did it. Rest assured I will talk to Paul about this incident. I will give him a chance to tell me the truth, to tell me if he really did it or not. However, I think you are blowing this completely out of proportion. It is actually kind of a funny thing to write, and if he did write it, well," Butch shook his head, "I actually don't think he did that bad of thing. I mean, he is an eleven year old boy, and at that age the humor is definitely tilted toward bodily functions and body parts."

Butch finished his impromptu speech by pointing his finger at the whiteboard. Then he turned around and walked out of the classroom. He fumed all the way to his car. He sent a text message to Lucy saying that the meeting was over and he'd tell her all about it later. There was no way he could communicate what had just happened in a text message. He didn't think there was an emoji for stupid teacher.

Before Butch was even to his car, Mrs. Hastings called her friend from church, Shawna, the one who asked her to arrange the meeting with Butch Gregory, and told her that she didn't think much of the man's parenting technique.

Mrs. Hastings had no way of knowing, but she had put a lethal set of events in motion.

Chapter Twelve
The Signet Four

"We have a problem," Jeannie said to Monica.

"What is the problem?"

"I'd rather not talk about it over the phone because I am still at work."

"Do you propose a meeting?"

"Yeah, but only with the SF."

"Tonight, then. I will notify the other two and confirm the time later."

"Be careful Monica. Something here just doesn't feel right."

"I am always careful. You should know that Jeannie, and you should also know your place. Never tell me what to do."

***

There was a break in the clouds of the western horizon just enough to see the last dying rays from the orange sun as it dipped behind the Olympic Mountains. Monica had called the meeting for 5:30 PM, but she left early from work in order to see the last bit of sunset. One of the perks of being the boss, both at work and of The Judys, was that she was able to arrange her schedule according to her wishes and desires. She liked that.

She also enjoyed the sunset. It reminded her of God's orderly working of the world. He made the world according to his purposes, and his purposes are for everything to work perfectly, on time, and with predictable regularity and precision. The sunset could be calculated and anticipated because it always worked the same way, every single day, whether a person could see it or not. She loved numbers, tables, and calculations. Her affinity for mathematics made her a good banker while attention to detail made her an ideal leader for the Servants of Judith. She enjoyed both roles with the unique delight of knowing that her work had meaning and purpose.

She took a deep breath.

To the east, the glow of city lights oozed through the mist and over the water. Seattle was the opposite of God's design. It was unpredictable, chaotic, vulgar, and uneven. Every manner of immorality and deviance was celebrated in the wretched city. A chill ran down her spine. She imagined the fornication, violence, and neglect that went on inside the shimmering towers of steel. Men could forge a façade of painted beauty over death, but the city was nothing but a whitewashed tomb. A tomb that made her sick. She gagged as her mind literally caused her nose to smell the filth.

Monica hated the human world. People had polluted the world with sin, rebellion, and irregularity. People were not as predictable as tables and graphs, except in the area of sin. People could always be counted on to sin. The Scriptures promised that. That is why Jesus died on the cross and rose from the dead, and that he left the church as an immortal testimony to the need for repentance. He gave leaders to the church, pastors and teachers, to guide her in that endeavor.

But some of the pastors and teachers had been corrupted by the worldly ways of greed, sin, lust, and pride. Jesus would not be happy with his church until such evil had been rooted out. The church had become Gomer, the whore whom God made the prophet Hosea marry. Monica knew how Hosea felt, forced to live with the putrid smell of adultery, the faces of bastard children, and the filthy rags of unfaithfulness. But as Hosea had redeemed Gomer, so she would redeem her world by cleaning out the filth, one evil shepherd at a time.

Monica's thoughts were interrupted by the sound of footfalls.

"Is that you, Jeannie?"

"No, it's me, Shawna. Stephanie is right behind me. We ran into each other at the trailhead."

"Good. All we're lacking is Jeannie then. Did you guys have a good day?"

Shawna said, "It was okay. Nothing special. My daughter stayed home today from school with a sore throat. I took her to the doctor. That was where I was when I got the message about the meeting. The doctor said she has strep throat, so she'll be out of school at least until Monday. That means she won't be able to go to church on Sunday, which means I will not be able to be there, which is a real bummer because I wanted to see all the sad faces on the sheeple at TLC. If only they knew what kind of man Michael Westgrave really was, they wouldn't be sad at all. Better a few tears now than gnashing of teeth in hellfire."

"I'll watch your daughter for you," Monica said. "Bring her by Saturday afternoon and she can spend the night. I'll go to church, as usual, on Sunday morning. Abigail can stay home and watch her for us. She owes me one anyway. That way you and Jim can both go to church. I think it is important that you be there."

"That'd be great."

"What'd be great?" Jeannie said, still on the trail. "Did I miss something? You guys already make a decision without me?" Her words came fast, and finished with a grunt. "Because if you did, that would be a flagrant violation of our covenant agreement. It only takes three of the Signet Four to approve removal, but you still have to take a vote on it."

"Calm down, Jeannie." Monica walked over to her friend and gave her a long, intimate hug. "Do you really think we'd do something like that? That I'd do something like that? Shawna and I were talking about me keeping her daughter for her this weekend, that's all. We don't even know what this meeting is all about, remember? You were the one who brought us together. We have no agenda and no plans. We are here for you. Now, please calm down."

"You're right. Sorry," Jeannie said. "I guess I'm just a little tense after what happened today. The whole thing has me worried."

"Yes, we need to get to work," Monica said. "Let us all go inside, out of the rain."

The four of them walked underneath the roof and onto the dry concrete slab. The Signet Four held their meetings at the abandoned artillery bunkers built by the United States Army to protect Puget Sound from Japanese naval vessels during World War II. The meeting was in complete darkness, and no records of the meeting were kept, which was rare because Monica loved reports.

Monica formally began the meeting by quoting the covenant.

> The Signet Four—Leaders of the Judith's Servants—Heroines of the True Faith—We are gathered together in the name of Jesus Christ to discuss the holy work of cleaning impurity from the pure church, the sacred task of rooting out worldliness from the heavenly saints, and the just removal of false teachers and shepherds. What we decide here is binding upon us and all the Judith's Servants. May we each seek wisdom, courage, and strength to fulfill our mission, even if it means our very lives are forfeited in the endeavor. If any of us should fail to guard the integrity and secrecy of the group, may she be torn asunder and her soul burn forever in the fires of hell, separated from God and all that is good for eternity.

As Monica had been giving the invocation, the votaries moved to the four corners of the concrete slab and held those positions. They held their arms straight up, in sincere praise. Then all repeated the pledge which bound all Judys together.

> I am a Servant of Judith, called to execute God's judgment.
> We are Servants of Judith, called to remove impurity.
> Together, we are the Sisterhood of Saints, called to guard the true Church from evil.
> This is our solemn task.

When they finished the ceremonial liturgy, Monica added the Aramaic word, "Amen." Stephanie followed with her "Amen," then Jeannie and finally Shawna. They had each repeated the affirmation in order of rank within the Signet Four.

Monica said, "Jeannie, you were the one who called this meeting. Please go ahead and tell us what happened."

Jeannie started, "Today at work, Pastor Butch Gregory from Sydney Community Church, who I'm sure you've all heard about, came specifically to my office. He was inquiring about the false teacher we recently removed. He wanted to look into his locker. I don't know why he thought I, or any security officer would allow him to do that. I didn't tell him that the police had already been by that morning to do the exact same thing, and they cleared his locker out. In hindsight, the smart thing to do might have been to let him in and see that it was empty. But I didn't, I told him to mind his own business."

"Well now," Monica said, "that is very interesting. I think there is more to this than just Butch Gregory snooping around today. Stephanie, please tell the other two what you learned about the connection between the false teacher and Pastor Butch Gregory?"

"The night we removed Michael Westgrave," Stephanie said, "I checked his phone to see if he'd called anyone to notify them about us after the initial meeting in Sealth Park. The only phone number he had called from the time we contacted him earlier that day and when we removed him was Pastor Butch Gregory, who he called from his office, about twenty minutes after the confrontation in the park."

Stephanie twirled her hair in her left hand. "I don't know what the connection is between them, but for some reason, he was the one on the false teacher's mind. Maybe he was warning him to look out, perhaps because they are both involved in the same immoral activity. I suggested to Monica that we might need to put his name to the Investigation Team."

"Which I did," Monica said. "Shawna, I know your team hasn't had much time to work with, less than a day really, but have you been able to find anything out?"

"Not much. Pastor Butch Gregory has a very impeccable record both in the world and in the church. Most of you know about his endeavors two years ago to rescue that little girl. That must be held as a positive in his ledger. The Investigation Team has only had a day to investigate and I've not gotten anything like a thorough report yet. On the flip side, one of my contacts is the teacher for Butch's son. She informs me that she does not think highly of Pastor Butch's parenting technique, and that he has not managed his household well. Apparently there are issues with his son, Paul. Aside from that, we don't have that much yet. Monica, how are his bank records? You might know more than we do, actually."

"I checked his records. He is clean. He makes a good salary from Sydney Community, but it is not flamboyant. His deposits are regular and nearly always identical. There are never any large deposits or money movements. Of course, older activity might take longer to get at. I drove by his home today and it, too, is modest. Stephanie, you go to his church, what do you know about his character?"

Stephanie grinned, although none of the other women could see it in the dark. "Pastor Butch is a very likeable man, although sometimes he can be stuffy. His wife, Lucy is adorable and everyone loves her. Paul and Sarah, his children, have always seemed well-behaved. I can't speak to what Shawna said about her information regarding Pastor Butch's parenting, but that doesn't seem to match what we see at church. He drives a basic car, not flashy at all. I don't think he drinks alcohol, and there has never been an accusation of philandering. Jeannie, does he ever go to the country club? That seems to be where the other false teacher met his mistress. If Pastor Butch has any, it might be the only place he'd meet them."

"Not often. He and his wife Lucy come once a month and have lunch with a bunch of old married couples. Every now and again he eats with another colleague, always male. I've never seen him there with a woman. Unlike the false teacher, Pastor Butch is not a member of the club."

"Well, the false teacher did indeed call Pastor Butch the night he was removed. That must mean something." Monica could feel the group losing intensity to act against Pastor Butch, so she pushed the issue. "We must remember that the absence of evidence doesn't mean he is innocent, and just because we haven't found anything yet doesn't mean it isn't there. Perhaps Pastor Butch and the false teacher had some kind of financial arrangement or, as outlandish as it sounds, they may have been intimate."

"That doesn't even sound possible," Stephanie said. "I mean. No. If it were anyone else maybe, but not Pastor Butch. If we don't have proof, we can't really act."

Jeannie said, "What more proof do you need? The false teacher called him to warn him about something. Pastor Butch was nosing around the club, probably wanting to get rid of any incriminating evidence that might be found there. Plus, never forget it was Pastor Butch Gregory who found the false teacher the next day. That sounds like plenty of evidence to me. Or, perhaps, maybe I should say, that would be plenty of evidence for anyone not biased."

Stephanie scowled. "How dare you accuse me of bias! It was me, after all, who suggested we look into him. I am the one who noted the phone call in the first place. Besides, do I need to remind you that I outrank you here, dear sister? It seems far more likely to me that you got a little close for comfort today, and it scared you. You usually hide away behind your computers and cameras, but today it got personal, didn't it? Welcome to my world."

"Ladies," Monica knew Stephanie was just getting warmed up. "We know how both of you feel. Now, Shawna, what do you think about Pastor Butch?"

"Thank you, Monica. In a perfect world, I'd like more time to investigate. That probably goes without saying. We usually take months in our investigation of false teachers, and have from the very beginning. The one we're currently investigating has been under our microscope for four months, but it took two months before we really found anything. So, yeah, I'd like a little more time."

"We may not have time." Jeannie just wouldn't let it go.

"Shawna," Monica said with poise and assurance, "So we do have evidence that the other person, the Methodist false teacher we've been investigating, is indeed guilty."

"Yes. The research is done. For the most part he is financially clean, but he smoked marijuana when he was in college. He views pornography on his computer at the church office. He has been carrying on several affairs, usually at the church property. Last month when he went to a denominational

86

meeting in New York he was unfaithful to his wife. I have pictures of him gratifying himself in the church bathroom."

"Yuck," Jeannie said.

"Thanks Shawna," Stephanie said. "I will never get that image out of my mind."

"Then what you are saying, Shawna" Monica laid out the pieces of her logic, "is that every time the Discovery Team has sent a candidate to the Investigation Team, all of them eventually come up guilty. Correct?"

"I suppose that would be correct."

"I think it is safe to assume that everyone we nominate for discovery is eventually found to be impure and needing removal. If we believe, therefore, that there is enough circumstantial evidence to move forward with Pastor Butch Gregory, then we should be able to skip the Investigation Team altogether."

Stephanie understood what was coming. "That would be highly irregular and way off course. I object."

It was too late. The other two were swayed by Monica.

It only took another six minutes for the Signet Four, by a vote of three to one, to decide that it was necessary to speed up the removal of the false teacher under current investigation, and then when that was finished, to proceed without any delay with the removal of Pastor Butch Gregory.

Chapter Thirteen
The Boss

Stephanie was angry. It was a quarter after six when she arrived home, cold and hungry. Her husband, Nathan, picked up a plastic bag filled with cheap fried chicken at the grocery store for dinner. For that, she was thankful. The last thing she wanted to do after a long day at work and then a frustrating meeting was to prepare dinner. After her cozy family of four ate their less than tasty meal in the dining room, she went upstairs to take a hot shower. Nathan asked her why she was so soggy. She told him she had a business errand late in the day that caused her to be outside, and she got caught in a downburst. It wasn't a complete lie. It was business. It just wasn't bank business.

Stephanie had just finished drying her hair when her phone rang. She could see it was Monica. She didn't want to answer it because she knew what it was about, and she knew what was coming. Yet she'd made a promise. An oath. She must fulfill her oath, even if it was inconvenient or she disagreed.

"Hello, Monica."

"Good evening, Stephanie." Monica's voice was calm and collected, and as always, professional. "I know that you are frustrated. I understand your frustrations. However, we still have work to do. Can I count on you to fulfill your oath? Are you ready to go to work?"

"Of course I am. I'm just upset, but I'll get over it. I submit, willingly to the group's decision even if I don't agree with it. I made a covenant to The Judys. Be assured, I will honor it. Now and forever." Even though she was angry, she felt pride at being a woman of her word. She was honored to be a part of such a noble venture.

Monica said, "Outstanding. I have emailed you a copy of the report from the Investigation Team on the next false teacher. Do you think you can get him taken care of before the weekend is over?"

"Maybe. I was expecting to act after Thanksgiving, as we had discussed earlier but it shouldn't be too hard to push the timeline up. From what I've already heard, he is a sluggard of a man and will not be much of a challenge."

"Have you assembled your team?"

"No, but I know I will not need Jeannie on this one because we have something else planned. For this one, I should only need one other Judy. I will probably take along Michelle, but I haven't talked to her about it yet. The two of us can probably handle it."

"I think that is a good choice." Stephanie sensed Monica smiling on the other end of the phone. It unnerved her, but what Monica said next unnerved her more.

"Stephanie, I just want you to know, as a heads up, that when we get ready to move on the next false teacher, Butch Gregory, I will be going along."

"Why?"

"The reason doesn't matter. I am going along. It feels important to me to be involved."

"Well, whatever floats your boat. Monica, I hope you're not worried I won't go through with it, because I assure you that I will do what needs to be done."

"No, it is not that at all. I just want to be there. I think this particular false teacher, because he has been so esteemed in our community, no doubt leading a double life of lies and shame, needs to have a particularly symbolic and ceremonial removal."

"If that is what you want. You're the boss."

"Yes, I am."

Chapter Fourteen
Transported

Pastor Butch stood in front of his seat on the front row. He tried to sing along with everyone else as the worship leader belted out the praise chorus. Butch didn't know the song. This was the first time he had ever heard it.

Pastor Philip stood beside him. Philip seemed to know the song well. He looked behind him and to the left and found Lucy, Paul, and Sarah. All three of them sang along without problem. They obviously knew it. He turned square around and looked at the congregation. There was a decided age demarcation on who was singing and who was not. People his age and older were trying to sing, but clearly had no clue how the tune went or what the words were. They stared at the digital projector screen like people being abducted by aliens. Those younger than him, more Lucy's age and below, not only knew the song, but seemed to enjoy its irregular rhythm.

About the time Pastor Butch finally got the hang of the tune, it would change into something else altogether with a whole new chorus. He finally stopped trying to figure it out and decided to just stand there and look at the platform. He stuck his hands in his pocket, content to wait on the parts of the worship service he comprehended.

Mercifully, the song ended. Pastor Butch sat down with the congregation. Pastor Philip stepped forward, walked up the three stairs to the dais. He closed his eyes. He raised his hands in an open gesture about hip high, then began the prayers.

"We come this morning to worship the Almighty God: Father, Son, and Holy Spirit. It is fitting and right for us to make our prayers known to him. As we take a collective moment of silence, I encourage you to make your needs and petitions known to the Lord, and then sit in the silence and listen for the Lord."

Pastor Butch had trained Philip to lead this sort of prayer. The young minister was finally catching on. Butch often lamented how Protestants rarely utilize the act of silence in worship, but it requires skill to do it well. The first thirty seconds of silence are usually the hardest; coughing, sneezing, moving around and other miscellaneous sounds betray the uncomfortable, awkward feeling people have when holy moments are near. Butch taught Philip to resist the urge to end the silence at the first minute. That was when most people felt the psychological or sociological pressure to 'wrap it up.' Instead, Butch wanted Philip to hold the silence until at least three minutes. Or more.

Philip held it out longer today. It was half-past the third minute when Divine Silence seized Pastor Butch.

He lost himself in the sound of nothing. He felt his hands tremble as he knew he was somehow, in a unique way he'd never experienced before, in the presence of the Lord. His hands went from trembling to quaking. His legs buckled. A thrill, a jolt of electricity shot up and down his spine, tingling neurons and nerves from the top of his crown to the sole of his foot. Tears formed in the corner of his eyes, but he couldn't wipe them. He was immobile, frozen still. Snot ran down his nose. He felt like screaming, but couldn't even move that much. His body was no longer under his control.

In his mind he heard from the depth of silence the sound of God. The sound got closer, and louder. Butch wanted to run, to escape the holy presence. There was nowhere to hide. His heart, mind, body, and soul were all splayed out before the Lord's ever searching eye. Every part of Butch, inside and out, wobbled. The voice of God came over him with images and sound.

He saw a middle-aged woman, whom he recognized, but didn't know.

He saw a gun.

He saw the word "abomination" written on a piece of paper.

He saw a newspaper.

He saw blood.

"Please don't shoot. Please."

His knees shook.

He saw a man in a car.

He saw the car smashed to pieces.

He saw a woman floating lifeless in water.

He saw an old man's body, burnt to death.

He smelled perfume.

He tasted death.

Then it was over, the moment passed. Pastor Butch was moved so much by his encounter he was thankful for the piano solo after the silent prayer. It gave him time to recover.

He wiped his eyes and nose. He checked his clothing and breathed deeply. There would be time later to figure out what it meant. For now, he had work to do. When the solo was finished, he rose from his seat and walked up the platform, his preaching Bible tucked underneath his left arm, and his mind firmly engaged with the outline he'd worked up for the sermon.

"Open your Bibles to Psalm 27. In just a moment, we are going to read from this text, and then we're going to try and put some concrete notions to the idea of light—that God is our light and our salvation, as well as try to figure out how to not be afraid in a world that is constantly trying to scare us to death. Think about that for a moment, if you will. It seems like everything is designed to scare us. The news is always telling us how dangerous the world is, both here at home and around the globe. It is too dangerous to travel and too dangerous to go to the grocery store, it seems. Then there are medical reports that tell us all the foods we eat are killing us. On top of that, religious leaders across the globe often manipulate with fear and terror to get people to do what they want them to do. And then as if that were not enough, when we have a few moments of time to ourselves, so many of us spend it watching scary movies or reading scary books. It feels like the whole world wants to scare us.

"In the midst of these frightening prospects, the Lord gives us, through the pen of King David, these wonderful words: The Lord is my light and my salvation; whom shall I fear? The Lord is the stronghold of my life; of whom shall I be afraid?"

After he read the text, Pastor Butch was off to the races. He moved through his prepared material with professional skill. He first gave explication of King David's life and the possible fears and trauma he might be referring to in the text. Then he moved forward with the metaphors of light and salvation. Sometimes, Butch told his congregation, salvation is only a metaphor for the future, the future when we believe things will get better. King David was confessing the Lord was his future. He was certain no matter how bad things looked now, it would eventually, someday, get better.

After handling the easier concept of salvation, he returned to light. He followed the line of thought that came to him in his study earlier in the week. He mentioned the Latin title of Psalm 27, Dominus Illuminatio, and then said it reminded him of a Harry Potter spell. There was a great amount of laughter when he said that, but he noticed it was right then, at that moment in the sermon the younger group, the same ones who were singing that song he didn't know, became engaged. They leaned in to listen.

Pastor Butch explained that there was no such thing as a magic formula for overcoming our fears or for removing darkness in the world. Instead, we had to do the hard work of cultivating light. Just as salvation, he told them, was a metaphor for the future when things get better, light was a metaphor, a way of saying something in poetic language, about seeking understanding. It is important for God's people to understand what is going on. Once we grasp the meaning of something, we are able to tap into wisdom, and wisdom keeps us from being afraid. Courage, he told them, is a byproduct of knowledge.

Then he moved the sermon through Matthew 6:22-23 and a discussion about the eye, seeing, and perceiving. Butch told them when the ability to see the light in the dark world is gone, then the moral center is gone because perception is altered. He reminded them of the way Jesus put it, "How great is the darkness!" Darkness is fear and sin. Light is courage and faith.

Onward he pushed the concept towards Romans 12:1-2, as he brought application to the concepts of being transformed in the way we perceived what was right, what was wrong, how we should behave, and what we should do.

When the service ended, Butch gave the benediction. He walked to the back of the sanctuary to the traditional post of the preacher after church. It was the place where he shook the hands and hugged the necks of people leaving the worship center. The first wave to come through were the teenagers. Several of them gave him a high five or a fist bump. Butch didn't quite know what a fist bump meant, but he hoped it was a good thing.

A random sampling of the congregation passed by after that initial wave. He took a moment to pray with an older woman who was telling him about her sister in Florida that had just been diagnosed with pancreatic cancer. Then he spoke with Robert and Erin about their new lawnmower. The three of them had a great laugh, but Butch went ahead and prayed for them—putting one hand on top of each of their heads, mimicking the motion he'd made when he married them. He prayed that through the years their relationship would grow stronger and stronger, forming the unbreakable bonds of wedded bliss. A nervous man named Skye Jones was behind them. Butch had only seen him at church twice. Skye asked Butch if he could talk to him sometime this week. Butch pulled out his phone and scheduled the appointment for Tuesday afternoon at 1:30. Butch preferred to schedule appoints for the afternoon.

Stephanie and Nathan Colson came through the line. Butch asked, "How did that meeting go with your co-worker, the one we prayed about on Wednesday night?"

"I haven't heard. I guess I should check on it," she stuck her hand out to shake Butch's hand.

When Butch's hand met hers, he thought he saw a flash of light above his head. He looked up, but there was nothing. "Did you see that?" Butch asked.

"See what?"

"That light—like an old fashioned flash bulb going off."

"I didn't see anything," Nathan said. Stephanie shook her head.

Butch grunted, "I guess it was just my eyes. Oh well, you guys have a great and relaxing afternoon." The Colsons shuffled along with their two boys, and more folks came through the line as Butch talked, prayed, hugged, shook, laughed, scheduled, listened, frowned, smiled, encouraged, rebuked, and blessed until everyone was gone. He turned off the heat, made certain to double check if all of the lights were turned off, armed the alarm in the sanctuary, washed his hands with antibacterial soap, locked the building, and then went home to eat the chicken and dumplings Lucy promised him before he'd left for work that morning.

Chapter Fifteen
A Walk In The Woods

Stephanie and Nathan, together with their sons Matthew and John, left the worship center of Sydney Community Church and headed straight for home. Stephanie had put a pork roast in a crockpot early that morning. It was ready to eat when they got home, and they were ready to eat it. She made a box of macaroni and cheese to go along with it while the boys changed out of their church clothes. There was a leftover garden salad from yesterday in the fridge, so she put that out. They talked about Pastor Butch's sermon as they ate. Nathan liked it. He believed there was so much darkness in the world, and said he saw a lot of it in the Navy.

"Some of those guys," Nathan said, "don't have a clue in the world as to what is right and what is wrong. All they ever think about is themselves and what they are doing right now. They don't even think about the future. It is just all in the moment, right now. They live in darkness, and I feel sorry for them. They don't have wisdom. They don't have knowledge, and because of that, they often live their lives in fear."

The boys said they liked the sermon because Pastor Butch mentioned Harry Potter.

"I've never heard a preacher say something nice about Harry Potter," Matthew said, smiling.

"Me, neither," Stephanie said, frowning.

"Does that bother you, hon?" Nathan asked his wife. "Our last church, back in Tennessee, vehemently protested and objected to all those books as witchcraft and devilry. I remember well the three week sermon series that the pastor did on how Harry Potter would be the end of western civilization and the Christian church."

"I remember that," Matthew said again. "I was only, I think, eight years old then, but I remember that because all my friends at school were reading it and we weren't allowed to."

"And you're still not allowed to read it. You got me on that?" Stephanie said.

"Yes ma'am," both Matthew and John said. "But mom, you know we've seen the movies at friends' houses. You know that, right?"

"Yes, I know. I don't like it, however, I can't put that genie back into the bottle so, it is in the past. But I still feel very strongly about this. I don't want witchcraft in my house. And what's more, I don't like that our pastor mentioned it in church. Surely there are more spiritual ways to talk about Psalm 27 than to breathe its words in the same breath with black magic."

"Come on Stephanie, don't you think you're being just a little harsh? I mean, I don't think Pastor Butch is exactly involved in the day-to-day work of black magic or some secret society dedicated to the propagation of black magic. Come on. It's just entertainment."

"I don't want to talk about it anymore. You boys go to the T.V. room and watch the Seahawks. I think the game starts soon, doesn't it?"

"I think the Hawks are going to stomp all over the Giants, don't you, Daddy?" John was far more engaged in this conversation than he was the one about church.

"Yep. I don't think the Giants will even score ten points. The 12th Man is going to be very loud today. But first, let's help Momma clean up the kitchen. The game doesn't kickoff until 1:15 PM."

The four of them made quick work of putting dishes away. John cleaned the table and swept up the floor. Matthew wiped down the kitchen counters. Nathan rinsed the dishes in the sink as Stephanie stacked them in the dishwasher. Then the boys took their Sunday afternoon positions in the den. Nathan, as the patriarch, took the best spot, the couch. If the Seahawks made it a blowout by halftime, he'd be sound asleep by the third quarter. Matthew, as the older son, took the second best place. He sprawled out in the recliner. John, as the younger son, laid on the floor in a bean bag. He pulled his lucky Seahawks sleeping bag over him. John was the true football fan in the family, memorizing every stat, every player's number and position. Even if the score were ninety to nothing, he'd watch every last snap, and then listen to the local postgame show on the radio.

Stephanie entered the television room just after the game started. She had changed out of her church clothes and into jeans, a dark t-shirt with a rain jacket over it and tennis shoes. "I'm going over to a girlfriend's house, and then we are going for a walk out at Banner Forest. I should be home before dark, but if I'm not, don't worry about me. There should be plenty of leftovers in the fridge. Someone might even have left some ice cream in the freezer."

"I knew there was a reason I love you so much," Nathan lifted up from the couch and kissed his wife on the cheek as she walked towards the door. "Have fun. We'll be right here."

Stephanie drove away from the domestic bliss of her home and went to the Skookum Mart. Michelle was waiting for her, standing behind the building, out of sight. The two women drove away from the convenience store, and headed northeast along shoreline road on their way to Ferry View Methodist Church.

The false teacher, who preferred to be called Reverend Peters, was right where he was supposed to be, right where the file she'd received from Shawna said he would be, in the church building. Alone.

A Judy on the Investigation Team named Melody had been targeting Reverend Peters for several weeks. His custom was to have lunch on Sunday afternoons at La Cabana Mexican Restaurant with his wife and some of the more prominent members of his parish. They had installed hidden remote cameras throughout the building, and Melody's report was brutal with specifics about what Peters did after that.

> Rev. Peters drops his wife off at home, and then he returns to the church by 1:30 PM. At the church he counts the money from the Sunday offering, sometimes palming a ten or twenty dollar bill if it is loose in the collection plate. When that work is finished, he takes a nap in the youth room, where there is a sofa. At approximately 3:00 PM he rouses himself, makes a pot of coffee, and then goes to his own office. That is where he often consumes pornography on his computer. Around 4:30 PM he returns to the sanctuary where he tidies it up and prepares the meeting room for the Altar Guild that he meets with at 5:00 PM. When that meeting is over he goes home to his wife.

Although the report had been sickening in the extreme, it revealed to Stephanie and Michelle the perfect opportunity to remove him. As they prepared to make their entrance, Stephanie half expected that this would be the first one of their victims to fully repent on the spot, and thus spare his own life. She hoped so. Killing was not her purpose, even though she'd become efficient at it.

As the name implied, The Ferry View Methodist Church was located on a scenic bluff that gave a great view of Puget Sound. The sanctuary was built in such a way that one entire wall was windows, and from their pews, worshippers could see the majestic handiwork of the Almighty. The distant

Cascade Mountains were in view, with the cobalt blue of the Sounds' frigid waters spreading out like a marble floor between the place of worship and the snowy heights. It was not unheard of for an otherwise downcast worshipper to suddenly be lifted up in spirit at the sight of an eagle soaring out over the terrain, or for the entire congregation to gather by the window to watch if an aircraft carrier were spotted entering the inlet toward its home port. The view from the sanctuary was an endearing aspect of the church. Ferry View Methodist was one of the oldest constituted churches in Sydney and could trace its spiritual legacy to the original white settlers who formed the several small villages on the peninsula that would eventually become the incorporated city of Sydney.

The view, however, was not on Stephanie's mind as she drove along the water's edge. She and Michelle had already looked at the photographs from the Investigation Team, and she had done a little reconnaissance herself Friday night when she went out for pizza. Although Ferry View Church afforded itself a majestic vista of nearly everything—mountains, ferries, boats, and Seattle—it was, ironically, isolated. It's location on the bluff meant there were no neighbors near the building. A mile after the shoreline road turned back south, there was a turnoff that went uphill to the church. However, there was another, almost never used back road that was built by loggers fifty years ago. The turn off for it was unmarked, beside a cow pasture, two miles further down the main road. That unmarked road, really only a trail, was what Stephanie discovered Friday night on her elongated pizza errand. It circled around behind the bluff and came out conveniently to a dead end in a thick stand of Douglas firs twenty-five yards from the church building.

It wasn't dark in the trees, but Stephanie slowed the car down to a crawl. For obvious reasons she didn't want to turn the headlights on, but she didn't want to get stuck either. The typically heavy November rains had turned the trail to slop. If she were to get stuck or slide off the road into the trees, she had no good explanation for why she was here in the first place. As she came around a sharp curve her rear tires spun out. She felt the car give. It lost traction; Stephanie had no control. It spun forty five degrees in the middle of the trail, then began to slide sideways along the road down the hill. She turned the steering wheel wildly to the left and to the right, hit the brake and even punched the gas. Nothing worked. The car continued to slide sideways down the hill.

"Are we about to crash?" Michelle asked.

"Probably," Stephanie said, as the trees kept getting closer and closer out her driver's side window. The car lurched. Stephanie shouted an obscenity.

The mud had overtaken the road, and it forced the two women to sit in the tin can and passively wait for the slow ride to end, which it did as soon as the left rear wheel slid off the road and onto the grass. That wheel found a rather fortunate bit of hardy grass, grass which somehow managed to hold on throughout the autumnal rains barraging the old logging path, grass with deep roots and strong fiber. When the wheel hit that grass, it finally had something to grab, something to generate enough friction to halt the slow but certain descent of the car into the row of trees below. Stephanie felt the car slow down and then finally stop on the grass. Something from driver's ed, way back from her adolescence in Arkansas came to mind, something about driving on ice. She moved the car's gear from drive down past the number two until it stopped at the last option on the dial, the number one. With the car in low gear, she applied a small amount of pressure to the gas pedal. For the first time in what seemed like forever, the car moved forward, up the road. She continued to apply a gentle pressure to the pedal until the car lurched forward. Finally, with better road under her tires, she felt comfortable to speed up a bit until they finally came to the dead end. They could see the church building through the trees.

The weather outside was nasty, and neither Stephanie nor Michelle were native to the Northwest. Therefore, they sat inside the car and changed their clothing from the happy pink, green and purple colors of their casual jackets and athletic pants to more appropriate attire for people on a holy mission. The duffle bag was between Michelle's feet on the floorboard. She opened it up and put it between the two of them on the middle console.

Neither one spoke as the sound of zippers moving up and down filled the car. Michelle untied her white tennis shoes, then pulled down on her elastic waistband, ripping her pants off. Then she removed her jacket and white t-shirt. Stephanie did likewise, removing her black and green walking shoes, unbuttoning her jeans and pulling them down. She struggled to get the denim down over her knees and off her feet because of the steering wheel. She felt as clumsy as the night she lost her virginity to a football player named Tony. He had taken her clothes off in his pickup truck, and then he took from her what she didn't want to give. She had told him to stop; but he wouldn't stop. The sting of his roughness hurt, but he was finished and the ordeal ended in less than a minute. The shame he gave never ended, and she hated him for it.

She never dated Tony again, and met her husband after high school. Tony was now a pastor of a Baptist church in Mississippi.

For some reason these thoughts crept into Stephanie's mind.

Stephanie took off her jacket and University of Washington sweatshirt. The two women wore identical black panties and black sports bra, although Stephanie filled hers out a bit more than Michelle. Sitting there half-naked in the car, Stephanie saw the effects of Michelle's black belt in karate upon her physique. No wonder Monica had promoted her so quickly onto the Removal Team.

With the car and the heater off, they had both gotten cold. The nearly naked women made short work of getting the black cotton pants on along with the black tank top and gray fleece hoodie that went over it. They laced up their black athletic shoes. Michelle pulled a ski mask out of her duffle and pulled it over her short cropped head and face. Stephanie opted for a dark purple bandana tied above her nose in such a way that it hung low, covering her mouth, chin and cheeks. She pulled her long blond hair back in a hair tie and tucked it down into the tank top and brought the hood of her fleece up over her head.

"You know," Michelle said, "I'm going to have to tell Monica about your profanity. Judy's are not supposed to talk like that."

"I know." Stephanie exhaled. "It was an unguarded moment. I planned on telling Monica myself, but you go ahead and tell her, too. Keep me accountable. Okay, partner?"

"You got it."

Stephanie took hold of Michelle's hands. They both bowed their heads. Stephanie spoke the incantation.

> Judith, Judith our mother, help us to hold tight the sword. Make us strong enough to cut off evil's head.
> Miriam, Miriam, our sister; may your song throw the horse and rider into the sea.
> Deborah, Deborah, our sister; make us brave enough to take leadership from the evil men.
> Jael, Jael, our sister; show us where to put the tent peg.
> Esther, Esther, our sister; grant us a whole day to destroy our enemies with the sword.
> Tamar, Tamar, our daughter; today you be avenged.

They whispered two quiet amens when the litany ended. Then they exchanged a hug, which was not part of the rite, but was nonetheless some-thing Stephanie and Michelle had done since their very first removal togeth-er. It seemed fitting for the bonds of sisterhood.

Stephanie checked her watch. It was 1:20 PM. They walked from the car to the building and started their grisly work.

Chapter Sixteen
Your Sins Will Find You Out

Evelyn Frost loved Sunday evenings more than Sunday mornings, although she would never admit that to anyone. Sunday mornings had their pleasantries—the hymns, seeing people you hadn't seen all week, coffee and doughnuts in Fellowship Hall, dressing up, and of course getting all the latest news on who was in crisis, jail, rehab or divorce court. Yes, Sundays were one of the highlights of her week.

But Sunday nights had a very different thrill. As a member of the altar guild, she was able to exert significant influence on the direction of the church. This power came from two different avenues. The first, and most obvious avenue, was the decision about liturgy, songs, litany, prayers, and themes for the worship services. Over the past two years, she had been able to steer the liturgy in the direction of environmental awareness and feminism. It had not been easy, because that fat-faced pig Doris Templeton kept trying to force the issue with anti-war liturgy and prayer. It wasn't that Evelyn was for war, she simply didn't think the church needed peace-activist prayers every week. Then there was the pressure from Her Royal Majesty Mavis Cobb to remember the missionaries and the blessed past in the congregation's weekly prayers. It was a never-ending struggle, but she believed she was winning.

The second power came from the prestige and unofficial power of the group. Although the altar guild had no official governing authority, they were the true secret society that ran the church. Rev. Peters always ran ideas through them and gave them the place of privilege to veto or alter any of his plans for sermons or programs. Even though there were only five people, all women, on the altar guild, they, along with Rev. Peters, made all the decisions for Ferry View Methodist Church, from budgets to the color of the bulletin paper.

There were other benefits besides the intoxication of power that made Sunday nights the most thrilling part of the week. Since the guild met in the evenings, the group always shared a potluck, and Evelyn loved to eat and share recipes. Tonight she brought a gumbo dish she was experimenting with. She'd made the first batch on Friday, but it was dreadful. The second batch she made Saturday morning. It was better, but still drab so she tossed it out. Last night she made the third batch and it was delicious.

Perhaps the greatest thrill, though, was Rev. Peters. That she loved Rev. Peters was not a secret. Even her oafish husband, whom she'd left behind on the living room couch in a football and beer induced stupor, knew that Evelyn loved Rev. Peters. Evelyn would expound to anyone who would listen that Rev. Peters was the best thing that ever happened to Ferry View, that the bishop had done the smartest thing ever by sending him there five years ago, that Rev. Peter's sermons rivaled the Apostle Paul's letters, that his voice was like butter, and his touch was therapeutic. What most people didn't know, however, was that Evelyn and Rev. Peters were also lovers. Each Sunday night, after all the members of the altar guild left, Evelyn would turn her car around and go back to the church where they would light the altar candles and make love as the moonlight poured in through the sanctuary glass. Their little trysts had begun a year earlier when the two of them went to the general conference meeting in Spokane. The first night they had separate hotel rooms. By the end of the week-long conference, they were having breakfast in bed together.

For all these reasons, Evelyn loved Sunday nights. It was with a great level of anticipation that she left her house and made the fifteen minute drive to the church. She hummed several Wesleyan hymns as she drove including "And Can It Be," which she hummed until it somehow turned into "O For a Thousand Tongues to Sing." She didn't care if the tune wasn't quite right, she was in a happy mood. Even the dreary weather couldn't bring her mood down. The road was dark, but she drove with great care so as not to spill her gumbo. When she arrived, Evelyn realized she was the first one there, which was normal. She checked her cell phone for the time, 4:48 PM. Rev. Peter's car was parked in the spot that had a large sign in front, written in large blue letters, "Reserved for Rev. Peters." She parked right beside it.

The wind was gusty when she got out of her car. It seemed the wind always blew hard in the front of the church building. The wind came down the Strait of Juan De Fuca blowing across the water while the Olympic Mountains and the Cascade Mountains functioned as a geographical wind tunnel. As the wind came off the water from the north, it swept over the bluff where the little church building sat. The wind wasn't nearly as bad in

103

the rear of the building, but no one ever went around back. Why would they? The best view in all of Blackjack County was in the front of the building. All that can been seen in the back were those ugly trees.

Evelyn hoisted her mid-sized pot of gumbo from the backseat and walked up to the front door of the sanctuary. It was odd that there were no lights on in there. Rev. Peters always came over and had the lights on, the heat going, and coffee made. The door was locked.

How odd.

She sat her pot on the ground and rummaged through her purse. She eventually found her church key. She would have to tease Rev. Peters for that, and if possible use that to blackmail him into doing that thing she liked so much. This minor inconvenience could work out to her advantage.

When Evelyn opened the door she was met with a damp chill. The heat was still off. She left her gumbo on the stoop while she turned on a few lights. No tables were set up. She was beginning to worry if maybe Rev. Peters was called away to a hospital visit or something worse, because it was very unlike him to not have everything set up. But he would certainly have called her to let her know they wouldn't be meeting tonight. Wouldn't he?

She retrieved her dish, but her nerves were so rattled that she sloshed okra and sausage juice all over the polished cherry wood entryway table as she sat it down. The juice slid down the tabletop and made its way to the flower print doily that sat underneath the large vase of plastic autumn-colored flowers. The dry fabric sucked it up. Evelyn groaned. Now she would have to take that home and clean the stain out before next Sunday. Great. Just great.

Evelyn turned on one more bank of lights, then she walked down the middle aisle of the sanctuary toward the back. The single building that Ferry View Methodist had was a classic "L" shape common in many church buildings designed in the 50s, 60s, and 70s. The longer leg of the L was the sanctuary, with the right side facing the water, mountains, and other viewpoints. Evelyn went through the sanctuary door behind the piano on the left hand side of the sanctuary and then turned down the dark hallway. First she walked by the two small preschool classes, then the children's Sunday School, the youth room, and finally the two office rooms at the far end of the L. Rev. Peter's door was closed, but Evelyn saw the line of light in the crack between the floor and the door.

She put her hand on the doorknob. Should she open the door? He might be doing something important because his door was closed. Rev. Peters never closed his door. He might be praying, or studying, or talking to someone else. He might be with another woman.

The thought was a blazing fireball of anger exploding inside her. She'd always assumed that she was his only girlfriend, and that they had something of an arrangement. Neither one of them wanted to leave their spouse. She didn't love her husband, but she was comfortable in her life. He didn't want to leave his wife because it would probably ruin his career, although that was not a certainty. Their former minister, a man named Rev. Kennedy had been divorced, and it was rumored that he'd cheated on his wife. It seems the ministry was getting far more tolerant of these issues. But Rev. Peters had told her he didn't want to leave his wife because he still loved her, but he loved Evelyn too. So he said. He was a very complicated man with many passions.

Standing there in the dark, with the faint glow of the sanctuary lights behind her, she contemplated for the first time that the jerk had another girlfriend in the church. Maybe she wasn't the only one? She didn't see any other cars out front, so it wasn't someone from the altar guild. Besides, all of the other women on the guild were over the age of 70. She was the spring chicken at forty-nine, the same age as Rev. Peters. Who could it be? It might be that hussy Marcy. Or could it be Sally?

She put her ear to the door to see if she could hear any erotic sounds. She heard nothing.

Maybe they were finished and were trying to get dressed quickly?

Should she just barge in? Maybe catch them *in flagrante delicto*? She wondered who would be more embarrassed, them or her?

There was no lock on the door, she knew that from personal experience. Rev. Peters had asked for one when he first arrived, but was denied. The property committee didn't want a lock, because they philosophically objected to a minster with a locked door. Rev. Peters asked again last year, but they denied it again. Now Evelyn was beginning to wonder why he would have wanted a locked door anyway.

Of course she knew why.

She turned the doorknob, careful and slow. However, when the latch was clear of the doorjamb, she flung the door open and, anticipating what she would see, she screamed out "You no good son . . ."

She never finished the sentence. What she saw was not what she expected. It was far worse.

Blood. Vulgar images. Putrid odor. Death.

The scream that came out of her mouth was the loudest and most frightened noise Evelyn Frost had ever made. She wanted to run, but couldn't. Her initial shock, along with the accompanying scream, passed. Now she needed to see the rest of the scene. Her mind failed to process all that she was seeing. It was beyond belief, beyond comprehension. She began to breath in short, shallow gasps. Her hands broke out in sweat. Her eyelids twitched.

Her body began to tremble, slow at first, then it quaked with violence. Her tremoring hand came up to her mouth, which was wide open and still searching for a good breath of air. Evelyn turned her head to the left and to the right, looking for something, anything to help her, something to explain what her eyes were revealing to her.

She spun around, facing the wall the door was on, the door that Rev. Peters would have looked at if he were sitting behind his desk, and saw the message. Spelled out in blood was the sentence, "Your sins will find you out."

Evelyn collapsed onto the floor, screaming and yelling. Her mind told her to run, but her body would not obey. She was afraid, sad, and confused all at the same time. On the floor she smeared Rev. Peters' blood all over her shoes and legs. She gathered her knees up under her chin and shook. Her mouth open, but no sound coming out and no air going in.

She sat in that same position, rocking and shaking until Doris and Mavis found her, and Rev. Peters' corpse.

Doris sat down beside Evelyn, putting her arm around her. Mavis called 911.

After she reported the scene to the operator, she ended the call but noticed she had a new email from Rev. Peters, which was odd given his current state. She looked at him on the desk, splayed out like a pig for slaughter, and then down at her email. It had been sent to her at exactly 5:00 PM.

Doris was on the floor beside Evelyn, attempting to console her. Mavis looked at her and said, "You won't believe it. I just got an email from Rev. Peters."

"Really," Doris said. "Let me check mine." Doris forced her nervous hands to pull her smartphone out of her coat pocket. "Me too."

"Should we read it?" Mavis said.

"I just opened it." Doris said, then took a minute to scroll through it. Mavis went ahead and opened her email as well.

"Oh my God," was all Doris said as both women sat in silence until the emergency personnel arrived.

The email had been sent from Rev. Peters to the entire church membership as well as several newspapers and television stations. The email was mostly photographs of him in intimate situations with various women. One of the images was of him and Evelyn on the sanctuary altar. The only text of the email was a line from the last verse of the book of Isaiah.

> They shall go forth, and look upon the carcasses of the men that have transgressed against me: for their worm shall not die, neither shall their fire be quenched; and they shall be an abhorring unto all flesh.

Chapter Seventeen
Lucy's Perspective

"Are you watching the news?" Pastor Butch sat in his bed with the television on and the phone to his ear.

"Yeah. I turned it on to get highlights from the game." Terence was in his recliner. "Turns out the Seahawks won, and oh, what's more, the news tells me that God apparently has me investigating serial killers. But wait, there is more. They are serial killers tracking my own profession. And they like a spectacle."

"It's worse than you think, brother."

"How could it get worse?" Terence chuckled, but not the kind of chuckle that meant laughter. It was the kind of chuckle that meant disbelief.

"Well, I don't want to talk about it over the phone. Can we meet tomorrow?"

"Yeah, but wait, didn't you tell me, the last thing Michael Westgrave told you was 'can we meet tomorrow,' and 'I don't want to talk about it on the phone?'"

"True," Butch did not like where this conversation, or this investigation, was headed. "The difference is that I don't have any girlfriends."

"You better not, fatboy or I'll beat your head in. Got it?"

"I'm not worried about you, Terence. My wife would beat you to it. Lucy would kill me and bury me in the backyard. I wouldn't have to worry about any serial killers. Can you come by the house, say around eight?"

"I'll see you then. Just make sure you have the coffee hot."

"You got it." Butch ended the call. He turned the television off. He knew that now the news would just be repeating the same information over and over on infinite loop. He went back to what he had spent the entire evening studying. His fingers moved quickly on the iPad, checking and cross checking. He saved the files and then powered down his tablet.

"Lucy," Butch said to his wife, who was reading a Patricia Cornwell book. "Why do you think people would want to kill a pastor? I don't mean just be angry with a pastor because the Lord knows I've encountered plenty of angry people. I mean, I guess I mean, they really want to kill a pastor, end his life? Keep in mind these are people who clearly know the Bible and therefore must know what it says about violence and murder, I mean, I assume they know the sixth commandment. What would tip someone into that kind of destruction?"

"I don't know, honey," Lucy closed her book and rolled over onto her side. She'd known that this conversation was coming the moment she'd heard the news about Ferry View Methodist and Rev. Peters. "Maybe it is people who know something."

"What could you possibly know that would make you want to murder a spiritual leader?"

"Maybe they know something he did. His past, or his present. You asked me, remember. It strikes me that you're a little naïve because you think every spiritual leader is like you. I've got a news flash for you, they are not. Many of them, far too many if you ask me, are in it for the power trip or the prestige."

"Like Michael Westgrave?"

"Yeah, just like your friend Michael Westgrave. I am sure he was a nice person and all, but from everything you've told me it sure seems like his eyes were not on Jesus, but instead were on himself."

"Enough that someone would want to kill him?"

"Maybe. Apparently, yeah. He's dead, right? Now you've got Rev. Peters. So, someone out there has apparently had enough with phoney baloney pastors. That's the way I read it, anyway."

"You sound as if you kinda sympathize with the killers?"

"No," Lucy said, rolling back over onto her back. "Not really. I mean, I can understand their frustration. When I was a teenager, before I ever met you, we had a pastor of our little Baptist church who everyone loved. He was outgoing, charismatic, and very handsome. All of us teenage girls had a very big crush on him. We didn't use the term back then, but Sarah would use the phrase 'fangirling' to describe how we were at church. Anyway, my senior year we came to church one Sunday morning, I think it was in January, and discovered that our pastor was gone. We learned from the deacon chair and the treasurer that he had taken twenty thousand dollars out of the church's account, and literally skipped the country with one of the women in the choir."

"I remember you telling me about that. I didn't know it affected you so much."

"It doesn't anymore, but it did then. We were all young, impressionable women who expected and wanted spiritual," Lucy turned to look at Butch, "or at least moral leadership from our pastor. When he failed at that, and we realized how he'd deceived us, I can tell you the idea of killing him wasn't far from how we felt. We felt like he deserved to suffer."

"How long did those emotions last?"

"Oh a week or so, tops. We had a good group of church leaders to help us. Our youth minister spent a lot of time helping us work through it. Eventually, another pastor came and we learned to love him, but trust was hard to give. By the time I went to college, I wasn't mad about it anymore, but the incident wouldn't leave my thoughts. It actually caused me to question some of my beliefs about God and church."

"That was when you met me, and I took you away from all those doubts and fears, right?" Butch poked his wife in the side with his finger.

"In a way, yeah. You helped me heal, because when I met you, and you were already in the ministry, I knew that I couldn't judge the whole Christian church, or all Christians, on the actions of one bad guy. Besides, who could resist your incredible nerd charm?"

"Nerd? Who are you calling a nerd?"

"You have a sweater vest for every primary and secondary color, and that my dear, makes you a nerd. Adorable, yes, but still a nerd."

"Now you're just being mean," Butch reached over and turned off the lamp on the nightstand. "But I was thinking I'd wear the yellow sweater vest tomorrow, with that blue pinstriped oxford."

He leaned over to kiss his wife good night. When he did, she grabbed him by his t-shirt, pulled him close and planted a long kiss on him. "I don't care what you're wearing tomorrow, but I feel like right now you're wearing too many clothes."

She began to kiss him again, repeatedly, and Butch, in between kisses said, "Funny you should say that, because that's exactly what I was thinking about you."

Chapter Eighteen
Second Breakfast

"Come on in," Butch told Terence, waving him in from the front porch. "The coffee is hot and Lucy made us some buttermilk biscuits."

"Thank you, Lucy!" Terence shouted out toward the kitchen.

"She would say thank you if she were here, but she's not. Lucy had to take Sarah in early to school, so she went ahead and took Paul too. She'll be back any moment, but she set the table for us before she left, so come on over here. Just throw your coat and hat on the back of the sofa."

Butch poured coffee for his friend from a French press decanter filled with steamy Italian roast. In front of the two pastors sat a glass platter with a half dozen home baked buttermilk biscuits. Each biscuit was golden brown, and about double the size of a regular biscuit. Small serving dishes of butter, strawberry jam, grape jelly, and fig preserves sat on the table.

Butch held up a dish that had a small decanter of creamer, a tiny sugar bowl, and packets of artificial sweetener. "After all these years, I couldn't remember if you took your coffee with cream or sugar or not."

Terence said, "Nope. I like my coffee like I like my women, strong, hot, and black."

"I would have laughed at that tired, old, clichéd joke a lot more a week ago."

"Oops," Terence said, feeling the gentle rebuke. "I suppose I should be careful with things like that, seeing how we have crazy killer women on the loose. By the way, I've got some details about Ferry View. Wanna hear them now?"

"Sure. I'll share my news next."

Terence started, "After I talked to you last night, I sent an email out to everyone in my church telling them to be in prayer for Ferry View and for our community. You know, it was a generic pastoral concern kind of letter. I'm sure you did the same thing."

"Uh, no. I was, well, I was busy last night. But I will shoot one of those type emails out this morning."

"Anyway," Terence continued, "I got a reply this morning to my personal account from one of our few white members. Her grandmother, whose name is Mavis, was one of the women who found poor Rick Peters last night at the church when they showed up for some kind of committee meeting. She said her grandmother described the scene as something out of a horror movie. Said Peters was all cut up and bleeding all over his desk. Said his body was stripped nude. The next part is very interesting, if what she said is true."

"What's that?" Butch worried about third party information, but the way things had been going, he didn't think this sounded too far from the truth or from what the television reporters were hinting at last night.

"She wrote me in the email that Mavis said his right hand was cut off and his eyes were gouged out. Doesn't that sound a lot like Matthew 5, in the Sermon on the Mount to you?"

"If your eye causes you to sin, pluck it out, and if your hand causes you to sin, cut it off. But Terence, does Jesus say hand or right hand? I can't remember."

"It says right hand."

"Are you sure, because I don't think Jesus was that specific?"

"Look it up, preacher boy."

"I will," Butch stood up and went to his study. He returned with his hardback Bible. He thumbed through the worn, heavily annotated pages until he came to Matthew 5. "I guess you're right. Jesus specifically says right hand."

"Of course I'm right. That means our killers were quoting that verse, in a way, in the way they killed that poor man. They are crafting a living, or rather dying, sermon out of it."

"A very gruesome sermon," Butch added.

"Yeah, but I can't argue that it was boring. But check it out, the killers did even more. Mavis told her family that there was also a message, written in blood on the wall."

"I know about that, Terence. KOMO was reporting that last night."

"Yeah, but what KOMO didn't say was that part of that message was Peter's testicles and penis nailed to the wall."

Butch squirmed in his seat, and instinctively looked down to his own privates. "You mean they used Peters' own peter against him? That's just not right." Butch felt physical pain. "Do you know what the message written on the wall was?"

"No, but I'm not finished yet. These killers did one more thing. Somehow, I guess before they killed him, they managed to get Peters to log into his email account. Then they scheduled an email to go out to all of Ferry View Methodist at exactly 5:00 PM, when the committee meeting was supposed to start, and when they knew the little old ladies would find his body."

"I'm afraid to ask what the email said."

"The email was pictures of Peters in bed with all different women, some of them from Ferry View and some others no one knows who they are." Terence took a sip of his coffee, then smothered a biscuit in fig preserves.

"Oh dear," Butch said. "Terence, this means the killers are not only biblically literate, they are methodical. They must have been investigating Peters for a long time to get photographs of him like that."

"Exactly what I thought," Terence said, but his words were only half-intelligible because of the large bit of biscuit he was chewing.

The temporary silence ended when the door coming in from the garage shut on the other side of the kitchen. Lucy walked in through the kitchen and sat down beside her husband.

"How's breakfast?" she said.

"Delicious," Terence shoved the last of his biscuit into his mouth, then reached for another. "I really love fig preserves. Thanks for putting them out for us."

"Oh, you're so welcome, Terence. I love them, but Butch and the kids don't. I took a gamble and thought you might enjoy them as a change of pace. Now, what'd I miss?"

"I," Terence stuttered a bit, "I was just filling in Butch on some details I learned about what happened last night at Ferry View."

"What details?" Lucy asked as she poured herself a cup of coffee.

Butch said, "I'll fill you in later." Dear Lord God, please let her forget to ask. Please.

"You look a little pale, honey," Lucy said. "Are you alright?"

"I will be. Here, have a biscuit," he handed her one. "Was there anything else, Terence, and please, I hope there isn't, that you learned about last night?"

"No. I think that is all."

"Praise the Lord," Butch said. "Well, then I'll go ahead and tell you what I learned. It is not as graphic as your report, but it might be more consequential."

"How's that?" Terence asked.

"Well, after church yesterday I was bothered about something in my spirit. I don't want to go into any details about it, but suffice it to say I was restless. So, I began doing a little research on the internet and through a couple of Google searches and lucky clicks, I discovered that a pastor was killed three months ago over in Pierce County, just this side of the Narrows Bridge."

"A pastor, killed? How would we not have heard about it?" Lucy shook her head.

"I don't think they knew it was that kind of murder at the time. I think that it looked so normal, so run-of-the-mill that no one noticed it was a well-planned homicide."

"Who was it and how did he die?"

"That's just it. It wasn't a he, but a she."

"Oh, that is interesting," Lucy said. "What happened?"

"Yeah, what happened?" Terence said, then he took another bite of his second biscuit.

"*The Tacoma Tribune* reported that Pastor Joan McMullen died on a Friday night back in July when she and her partner got into a domestic squabble. The report said that she killed her partner and then turned the gun on herself. It also said that a notepad found beside her body contained a one word note from her. It was the word abomination."

Butch pulled out his iPad and showed his wife and friend the news article.

"This looks like a terrible violence, Butch," Terence smacked, "but why do you think that her death is connected? That kind of thing does happen, ya know. It might be that you're grasping at straws, trying to find patterns that don't exist." Terence voiced the doubt and Lucy nodded.

"You seem to be looking for connections where there are none, dear." Lucy snatched the last biscuit, "And you have had enough," she waved her hand at Terence. "Save one for the cook."

"You might think that," Butch said. "However, I had heard this Pastor Joan speak before. She was a very likeable woman and eloquent speaker. Of course, I didn't agree with anything she had to say, but she seemed energetic, persuasive, and like I said, likeable. Pastor Joan was the pastor of a mid-size to small, but influential independent congregation located just north of

114

the bridge. It was influential because its people had a lot of money, as well as the fact that Pastor Joan preached a very progressive form of political engagement through the church. You see, Joan was a lesbian, and her partner was a woman. She was one of the most vocal advocates for gay rights within the Christian community in all of Washington.

"Doesn't that," Butch paused while he buttered his biscuit, then he continued, "sound exactly like the kind of person our local band of wicked women would be after?"

"It most certainly does." Terence was dumbfounded.

"Wait, don't you need more proof?" Lucy still was skeptical. "People actually do get into domestic squabbles and sometimes kill each other. Remember that couple from some months back, they just lived a few blocks from here. Wasn't that a perfectly normal looking family, except that when the dad came home from work one day something inside of him snapped. He took a gun and shot his wife and then he shot himself, right in front of their baby daughter. Right? I mean, it is horrible, and it happens but it doesn't always mean conspiracy or anything. Right?"

Butch said, "That's true. But it is the word 'abomination' that is written right beside her dead body. I doubt she would have written that. The Seattle PI reported that the police believed the note was a last word about her conflicted emotional state as she wrestled with her sexual identity. I don't buy that for a minute. That word was a warning from her murderer to others. If we include this one, then we have three pastors, murdered, with theological messages left at the scene every time. I suspect, but can't prove, that there was probably more evidence at this site, but the police didn't know to look for it."

"Oh God help us," Terence said.

"That's kinda my prayer too. I found this out before we heard about Peters, so I was a little dubious at first myself. But not now. I'm fully convinced that they have killed three, not two."

"At least three," Terence reached across the table for the coffee pot. "Who knows how many they've killed or where they've killed."

Lucy shook her head. "No, guys, I don't think it has been that many. We would know about it. For starters, there aren't that many pastors around Sydney. Look how these two deaths are so widely publicized? If they'd been killing off spiritual leaders for a long time, I'm pretty sure it would be common knowledge. Second, notice how each murder is more brazen than the other. It's like the killers are gaining confidence with each one. The first murder, if I buy into Butch's theory that this Pastor Joan was the first one, is sloppy. They probably didn't mean to kill the other woman, just the pastor. Then there is the written message. The word 'abomination' is much weaker than the other two, where poor Westgrave had a Bible shoved down his throat, and then Rev. Peters was stabbed in his office."

"Not exactly stabbed, honey," Butch cringed. "Mutilated is probably a better word, but I get your point, and you're right. I don't even want to think about how much more elaborate they could get for the next one."

"You think there will be a next one?" Lucy's face turned white as she realized the implications of the question.

"Yeah. They will kill again, now that the machine is revved up, so to speak." Terence looked at Butch, then to Lucy as he explained, "They are just getting started. I don't know exactly what their entire motive is, but once you start down that road of violence it is very hard to stop. They will keep looking for pastors to kill, justifying each action as the right thing to do because the pastor didn't fit their prescription for what a man or woman of God should be. Just let that sink in for a minute. Once a person or a group of people cross the line into believing that certain people have to live up to their ideals and values, it is not too long before no one outside their group lives up to those values. It is only a matter of time before they decide that the nice priest at the Episcopalian church should be killed because he can be seen walking around the city parks with a cigar in his mouth. Then they will decide that the Lutheran pastor needs to be killed because he doesn't preach that Jesus bodily rose from the dead. Then, they will come for me, because maybe I'm guilty of pride or they don't like that sometimes I forget to bring the trash can in from the curb. We are all in danger. Every man and woman who carries the title pastor, priest, reverend, and probably rabbi, too. These women are out for blood.

"Perhaps the worst part is the elimination of grace in the equation. I know of more than one man who made a serious mistake in ministry, got caught with the checkbook or someone else's wife, then was justifiably fired from church leadership, but over a period of time was reconciled, restored and now is effectively leading again. However, that kind of process doesn't matter to these murderers. Grace, healing, and restoration no longer have any meaning for them, in their view of what Christianity is." He kissed the air, "The metaphors of war, the imagery of battle, the language of killing sin, and the concept of dying for Christ has become a way of life for them. They will not stop until they have been stopped. They have more in common with jihadists than Jesus."

Terence paused as the danger in his words and his line of thought weighed on all three of their minds. Then he said, "Have you been able to find anything out about that woman you told me about from the country club, the one who gave you the heebie-jeebies?"

"A little. I'm glad you asked because I'd almost forgotten about that. I checked out the club's website and found the staff listings. I got her name, but that was all that was there. Then I Googled her name, but I cross referenced the search with 'church' to see if there was some kind of connection. I didn't get much, but I learned that she is on the governing board of Christ Emmanuel Lutheran."

"Are you sure it is the same woman?" Lucy asked the question, working hard at getting her mind off of the terrible implications of what Terence had said earlier.

"Yes, because the Lutherans had a picture of her. Very convenient."

"How do you think she is connected to the group? Do you think," Lucy said, "she is the leader?"

"She might be, but for all I know there might not be a leader. It could be a democratic kind of group where everyone speaks and they make decisions by concession."

"Oh, there is a leader." Terence said. "I guarantee it. Listen, we suspect this is a church group of some sort. Have you ever seen a church group that didn't elect a leader? Call him or her what you want, but church folk love a good hierarchy. I guarantee you there is a leader, an organized structure with levels of leadership, and probably even rules for who is in control in certain situations along with a policy manual, complete with job descriptions." Terence nodded to Butch, "You say this woman is a Lutheran. A Lutheran woman who works at a country club? Oh yeah, there is a leader alright, and whoever she is, she is probably one of the sweetest and most dedicated people in her church, and she probably serves on a board or committee or something. She probably volunteers in the nursery."

"What if it is a he? What if the mastermind is a man?" Butch Gregory didn't really mean to say that out loud, but it jumped out of his mouth. However, he continued with the line of thought. "It could be that a man somewhere, maybe even a pastor, a male pastor, has organized these women into a group of mercenaries. Maybe he gives them the targets and they carry it out?"

Terence didn't buy Butch's idea. "No, I don't think so. Mind you, it is not outside the realm of possibility, but my suspicion is that if there are three killers we know of, and all three are women, and then your premonition about that woman over at the country club, well it all adds up to a women's only murder club."

"Club?" Lucy asked. "When I think of a club, I think of little old ladies playing bridge. I think of the book club sitting around a coffee table eating cheesecake while they discuss the newest Oprah book selection. Club is not the first word that comes to mind when I think of murder."

"What word would you use, then?" Terence said, with a smile. "How about a sinister sorority? Maybe we could call them murderous mavens? I'm leaning toward the Pastor Killer Club myself."

"You're making fun of me," Lucy hit Terence on the shoulder with a soft punch. "But seriously, what do you call a group of women who are engaged in evil?"

"A coven." Butch said. "A coven bound by a covenant. That is what we are up against. We are stuck somewhere between evil, between two different kinds of evil. On one hand we have religious leaders, pastors, who are abusing their positions for their own pleasure or gain. On the other hand we have people, who I presume to be women, who are serving as judge, jury, and executioner in some kind of terribly misguided coven."

"A coven on one hand, blasphemers on the other," Terence added with an air of solemnity. "A coven, a secret society hiding in the shadows. It could be five women, it could be five hundred women. They could be in every church in Sydney."

Chapter Nineteen
Bitter Caviar

"Well done, good and faithful Servant of Judith. I am exceedingly pleased with the results from your removal of the false teacher at Ferry View."

"Thank you, Monica." Stephanie sat down opposite her leader. "But I'm sad. Not sad as much as disappointed. I thought this one would repent of his sin and agree to leave without having to be permanently removed. I'd hoped that we wouldn't have to kill him. All of our research indicated he was a coward, but at the same time an emotional man. I thought that might tip his direction toward repentance and voluntary removal."

"I am not surprised," Monica said. "Sin hardens the heart, and the evil one convinces the sinner that they've done nothing wrong, that they're only being human, and that Jesus understands their weaknesses and will forgive. The Devil tells them these things, as well as many other lies. The lies become a part of their way of life. The result is they are incapable of admitting their sins even when confronted with the truth. That is why our Lord made hell. Some sinners will never repent, even if Jesus were standing right there in front of them. So the only righteous thing to do is destroy them."

Monica stared right into Stephanie's eyes and said, "Without repentance there can be no forgiveness of sins."

Stephanie looked down. She knew exactly what it was that Monica was getting at.

"While we're on the subject of repentance, I need to tell you something important about yesterday's mission."

"I'm sure you will include all the relevant details of the operation in your always excellent reports. It can wait till then, I'm sure."

Monica toyed with Stephanie. Why does she do that?

"Actually, Monica, I feel it can't wait. While we were on our way to the location, we had an incident with the car."

"Did the car break down?"

"No, it fixed itself. We were slipping in the mud and the car was tumbling, sliding, but it felt like tumbling, down the side of the hill. Eventually the tires found a patch of hard ground that gave it the traction and everything was fine."

"If everything is fine, then why do you feel the need to tell me this?"

"Because when the car was sliding, I had an unguarded moment. I allowed a dirty word, an expletive, to come out of my mouth. It was not pretty, it was not Christ-like, and it most certainly did not honor the work of The Judys. I am deeply sorry. I voluntarily submit to the punishment I deserve."

"The word," Monica's face turned serious, "what word was it? Was it the Lord's name in vain? Did you blaspheme?"

"No. I would never be able to blaspheme the name of the Lord God no matter what the situation is. What I said was dirty, not blasphemous. It was impure."

"Did you say the F word?"

"No. I did not. What I said was a euphemism for excrement."

"Ahhh. I see." Monica touched her top lip with her tongue. "Michelle already informed me of this development last night in her oral report. I am very pleased that you self-reported your indiscretion, however, I expect nothing less from the number two person in this group. Your punishment, though, will be light."

She paused for effect and raised her eyebrow, obviously waiting for the expected chuckle at her number two pun. Stephanie recognized the pun, but did not react to it. "Thank you," was all that she said.

"Your penance is simple," Monica said. "You have to pay for lunch."

"That sounds more than fair. Thank you, again."

The server finally arrived at the table. "Welcome to Umami Wok. My name is Robert, and I'll be serving you today. Would you ladies like to start off with any drinks or appetizers?"

Tapping the edge of her menu, Stephanie said, "I'll have an iced tea." Then she added, "Don't I know you from somewhere?"

"Yes," Robert said. "We go to the same church."

"That's right. That's right. Erin—that is your wife's name, right?" Stephanie snapped her fingers while she tried to conjure the name.

"Yes, we've only lived here for about a year though, so we don't know that many people just yet."

"It'll come," Stephanie said. "This is my friend from work, Monica."

"Hello, Monica," Robert said.

Monica ignored his greeting. "I'd like a small pot of that ginger tea that is so good here, and please bring out some pot stickers while we decide what else to have."

"You got it, I'll be right back with your drinks and those pot stickers."

After the server turned the corner, Monica spoke. "Stephanie, do you remember when I formed The Judys?"

"Yes, I do remember when we formed our little group." Stephanie couldn't tell if Monica had caught her slight correction of pronoun. It was the Signet Four who had founded the Judys. Monica was the most vocal of them all, and it was her original idea, but it was a group decision to form. Together they wrote the covenant, decided on the rituals, prayers, and scriptures. Shawna and Jeannie did most of the recruitment work. Monica organized the work into the three different functions, just like she would have done with any work at the bank. It was her gift, but she'd never went on a removal before. She'd never done any of the tedious work that the Discovery or Investigation Teams do, though Monica was the only one who knew all twelve of the Judys.

Stephanie pushed aside the resentment. She needed to focus. This was turning into a trap.

"Stephanie, do you remember why we did it?"

"Yes, because it was something we all felt strongly about. It was six, maybe five years ago, right? Yeah, right after that Mega-Church pastor in Seattle was arrested for stealing church money. Then it later came out that he was having a homosexual affair with some druggie who was a male prostitute or something. I forget all the details of that case, but I remember we were very distraught and the four of us were having coffee one day and we decided we needed to pray for all of our churches because it seemed like there were bad pastors all over the place, not just this guy in Seattle."

Monica said, "That is the way I remember it. We got into this because there was a real problem with the churches, and we thought that we had an obligation to do something about it."

"Right." Stephanie didn't know where this history quiz was going, but she played along. "We didn't remove him, because he backed away from his place of position, but about nine months later when another false teacher in Puyallup was exposed, we took action. Jeannie and I sent him an anonymous letter. He refused to confess, so we arranged the little car accident."

"Exactly," Monica said. "We acted because there was a problem. Early on we moved much quicker than we have of late. The problem of false teachers is very real, but we are moving too slow."

"What are you getting at, Monica?" Stephanie looked at her watch.

"What I'm getting at is that the worst kind of hypocrite, of false teacher, is the one who fools everyone into thinking he is so righteous and so much better than everyone else. He hides behind past glory and bravado in order to keep his present evil hidden, and he is right in front of us—God has revealed him to us. Now God wants us to act quickly, just like in the old days, to remove this type, this most vile of all of them. I know that when we met as the Signet Four, we agreed to move forward in the investigation, but I want to go further. I want to act tonight."

"Tonight?" Stephanie's face turned red.

"Yes. Tonight. Don't you think two removals in two days would be quite a powerful statement to the other false teachers in Sydney, not to mention the rest of the nation? I mean, that will get everyone's attention."

"Excuse me ladies while I set this down," Robert said as he pushed the condiments from the middle of the table to the edge. Robert gave Stephanie her iced tea, then he placed the ceramic tea pot in front of Monica. She inhaled, and smiled.

"I love that smell. It is so delicious."

"I agree," said Robert. "The ginger tea is one of my favorites here."

He put the pot stickers down on the table and put two small plates in front of the women. "Have you decided what you'd like?"

Stephanie ordered the number seven, which was a chicken teriyaki. She was okay with Chinese food, but it wasn't her favorite. For years she always ordered the chicken nuggets and fries off the children's menu whenever she was forced to eat Chinese. She'd learned that chicken teriyaki was tolerable. Umami had a good salad, so she substituted that for the much heavier fried rice.

"Please put ranch dressing on the side," Stephanie told Robert.

"You got it. And how about you?" he said as he looked at Monica.

"Well, I'm thinking about the sushi bar today. I heard from a coworker that you just recently started offering a caviar roll? Is that right?"

"That's right. It was rated as a five star dish by the food and wine editor at the *Seattle Times* and also by *Seattle Magazine*."

"Do you think it lives up to all the acclaim?" Monica clasped her hands as she waited for Robert's reply.

"Absolutely. They served it to all the wait staff, so we could talk about it, and I tell you, it is delicious. I've never before put anything as decadent in my mouth as our caviar roll. It pairs nicely with a Washington State Riesling, if you're interested, as well as a side of our world class lobster bisque."

"I'll skip the wine," Monica said. "Alcohol is an intolerable evil. But go ahead and bring me the caviar roll and the lobster bisque."

"You got it," Robert said, then, as if remembering an important detail at the last minute, "Of course, you know that the caviar roll is very spendy. It costs a little over a hundred dollars. That's not as much as a new lawn mower or anything, but it is a lot for lunch."

"I know," Monica said as she glared across the table at Stephanie.

Robert left, and Monica picked up where she'd left off. "The false teacher who leads your church usually has a Monday evening men's Bible study, doesn't he?"

"Yes," Stephanie responded.

"That is what I thought," Monica poured tea into a cup. "Do you think he will have it tonight as usual?"

"Pastor Philip announced it yesterday at church, so I assume it is a go. I don't see any reason why it wouldn't be."

"Good, that is what I wanted to hear. Sydney Community's website says that the study lasts from 6:30 PM to 7:30 PM. I will come by your house around 7:00 PM. We will catch the false teacher as he comes out of the building tonight."

"There might be a problem with your plan, Monica. Pastor Butch is—"

"No! No longer use his proper name or title. He is now a false teacher, an enemy of God."

That was hard for her to hear. As much as she believed in the mission of The Judys, she just couldn't believe this was true of Butch. Yet she had to obey. The Signet Four had elected her as the leader.

"Yes, Monica. I understand. But you have to realize he is known for being a talker. It is not unusual for him to hang around after the class ends and chat with some of the guys, sometimes in his office, in the classroom, or even in the parking lot. It is just one of the things he does. So that might throw our timing off. We might want to rethink any plan with him that involves apprehending him right after something, because he will no doubt be gabbing with someone, and probably surrounded by many other people."

"Hmph. That might be a problem. We'll just have to wait it out then. I really want him tonight. I very much dislike the idea of waiting."

"There is another problem. My clothes are still muddy from yesterday. I haven't had a chance to wash and dry them, because the boys were all home yesterday and this morning I had other chores."

"That is not a problem, Stephanie. I know that you have today off from work, because I am the one who makes your schedule. When lunch is over, go home and launder up."

"Okay, I will, but that doesn't let us know if Michelle is available tonight."

"We don't need Michelle. You and I can handle this one."

"With all due respect, Monica, I don't think that is true. Michelle is the best, physically speaking, of all of us. The Methodist false teacher yesterday actually put up quite a struggle. Michelle, however, was able to subdue him with three quick karate moves. I would not be able to do that, and unless you've developed a skill set I don't know about, neither would you." Stephanie casually snatched a pot sticker with her chop sticks and plopped it into her mouth. She didn't really like the pot stickers, but she needed something to focus her agitation on. Talking through her food, she said, "I think you're wrong. We need her."

"Oh Stephanie, you are so wise in so many ways, but you still lack faith. God is with us. If he is with us, it doesn't matter who we bring."

"Don't you think you're being a little too overconfident? I mean, things can still go wrong. Don't you think God wants us to use all of the assets and gifts he gave us? It is foolish not to take Michelle. We should see if she's available and if she is not, then we should wait for another day."

"I have made up my mind."

Robert arrived again. He laid out Stephanie's chicken teriyaki in front of her, then he, along with two other servers, prepped Monica's side of the table in an elaborate show of fancy tablecloths, plates, spoons, chopsticks, and sauces. The caviar rolls were elegantly placed in five points, as if it were a star. Lines of mixed vegetables, cut fine, were used by the chef to complete the star image. Each slice of the caviar roll served as a point in the star. It was beautiful to behold.

Monica applauded as the wait staff finished their display and then Robert said, "Enjoy your meal."

"I'll be at your house tonight. Be ready, and stop making excuses. I hope you've not gone soft on us, not now that we've gotten so close to ridding

Sydney of evil. Remember the covenant. You got off easy this time for your little dirty word," Monica waved her hand, indicating the expensive lunch. "You will not get off so easy next time."

Monica took a whiff of the dish in front of her, then frowned at Stephanie. "I hate caviar. Besides, it is time for me to get back to work. Enjoy your day off." Then she stood up, grabbed her purse, and walked out of the restaurant leaving Stephanie alone and one hundred and fifty dollars poorer.

Chapter Twenty
Memorial

The memorial service for Pastor Michael Westgrave was scheduled to begin that Monday afternoon at 2:00 PM at TLC. Pastor Butch waffled on attending until the leader of the ministerial alliance sent out a group email over the weekend encouraging the pastors to be present *en masse*. He said it was important to maintain solidarity in these moments of tragedy. He believed the presence of Sydney's pastors would be a comfort to TLC as well as the rest of the community.

The email was sent before the news of Rev. Peters' murder. Butch knew that whatever people might be feeling was now probably multiplied tenfold. He was also afraid that the funeral might turn into even more of a media spectacle, being the very next day after another high-profile murder. It truly was a delicate situation and he didn't know which direction to go. He felt like going was the right thing to do, but at the same time he felt like being there might cause more disruption and call more attention to himself and the other pastors than needed to be done at what should be a moment to focus on Michael's family and church. Terence had decided to go, which put even more pressure on Butch to attend.

Terence's reasoning was a little different, though. On one hand, Terence thought he'd be safe at the funeral. It would be public and there would likely be armed police and guards. If he was the only pastor who didn't go, and if all the police were at the funeral, he thought that might be exactly when whoever was killing the pastors might pick him off like a stray hyena that got too far away from the herd. He didn't want to be brought down and eaten by the lioness.

On the other hand, Terence also thought it was equally possible for the killers to decide to blow up the whole funeral and kill all the pastors gathered at one spot. It would be very convenient for the assassins to have all of their targets lined up like ducks in a row at the shooting gallery. Or fish in a barrel. Or pastors at a potluck.

That neither option was brimming with security had Terence almost convinced that he should drive down to Portland for the day. He didn't know what to do, so he flipped a coin. It was heads. He decided to go to the funeral.

Neither of Terence's lines of thought were much comfort for Butch. Lucy had wanted to go with Butch, but, after hearing Terence's morbid logic he decided it was safer for her to just stay home.

It was 1:15 PM, the moment of decision, and he'd still not decided whether he'd go or not. He asked himself the age old WWJD question, What Would Jesus Do, and with all apologies to Charles Sheldon, that wasn't helping. Jesus famously skipped the death and funeral of Lazarus. However, that was because he later called him forth from the grave. Jesus also said, "Let the dead bury the dead." Butch, however, never fully understood what the Lord meant when he said that, so no help there either. He glanced again at his watch. It was now 1:20 PM. What would he do?

By sitting in his chair in his office, he'd come to the conclusion that he'd decided he wasn't going. Then, out of nowhere, a Bible verse came to his mind. Paul said in Romans 12 that we should, "weep with those who weep."

Crap. Now he knew he was going. In his bottom desk drawer were two neckties. One was blue. The other was red. Butch pulled out the blue one. He buttoned up his neck and pulled the tie around to knot it. Then he pulled on the blue sports coat that he'd grabbed from his closet on the way to work, just after Terence left him and Lucy at breakfast.

Butch ran a comb through his hair, not that his thinning hair needed it. He gargled with mouthwash, which was also in his bottom drawer, because he did need that. He opened his window and spit it on the rhododendron.

"I'm off to the funeral," Butch told Mildred as he walked by her.

"I knew you'd go. It's the right thing to do."

"I wish you'd told me that earlier, because I didn't know I was going until five minutes ago. You could have saved me some time by telling me ahead what I would choose."

"You didn't ask me. But if you want my opinion, you'd save yourself a lot of time and trouble by just asking me what you should do."

"You'd like that a lot, wouldn't you?" Butch put his hand on the doorknob, then turned back toward Mildred, "I don't know if I'll be back this afternoon, but I have the Men's Bible study tonight. Could you possibly make a note to blast out an email to all the guys in that group? Oh, and pretty please turn the heat on in our meeting room before you leave?"

"Consider it done. You men meet in the room that is right off the fellowship hall, right?"

"Right. That room has its own thermostat."

"That's what I thought. Have fun at the funeral," Mildred hesitated as she said it, realizing the oddness of the statement. "I didn't quite mean it that way, although, isn't it queer that the first three letters of the word funeral are f-u-n."

"I'd never thought of that," Butch said, opening the door. "But I think this will technically be a memorial service, as his body has already been cremated. At least, that is what I think. One can never be too certain what a family might do."

The word 'do' was swallowed by the sound of the door closing. Butch hopped in his blue Honda and made his way toward TLC.

He arrived at TLC in five minutes. The parking lot was a disaster. Three different news vans were there, broadcasting live and interviewing people as they went into the sanctuary. The state police were there, overseeing security. It took him twenty minutes to park. Butch walked through a makeshift metal detector in order to enter the building. He was patted down again on his way into the actual sanctuary. Terence wasn't the only person who thought the murderers might take advantage of a group setting.

Once inside he found Terence and the other pastors who were there. Most of them had made the same decision that Butch made. The only colleague missing was his friend Dwayne from First Baptist, but everyone knew he was in Yakima for a denominational conference. Butch often wondered how Baptist pastors ever get any work done because they spend so much of their time going to conventions, conferences, meetings, and trainings. He'd asked Dwayne once how that all worked, and all he'd said was that Baptists valued networking. And big travel budgets. And all you can eat breakfasts.

The memorial service was long, and in Butch's eyes, not very Christian. Many things were said, but not much of it was about the sure and certain hope of the resurrection.

One of the speakers was a member of TLC who was also a Sydney city councilman. He told the congregation about how Pastor Michael had helped him overcome his own doubts and insecurities. He said that it was on the golf course, playing golf one day, during a meaningful conversation with Pastor Michael, when he decided to run for city council. Then he listed all the wonderful things he'd done for the city while serving on the city council, and finished his speech by saying, "None of that would have been possible unless Pastor Michael had given me the confidence to go ahead and run for office. He made me believe in myself."

The mayor gave a speech about the importance of partnerships between the faith community and the city. He said that one of his last conversations with Pastor Michael Westgrave was about that very issue. He hoped, the mayor said, that TLC would continue to honor Michael's work and memory. Then the governor gave, what sounded to Butch, like a campaign speech for reelection. The whole thing tasted sour to Butch.

Someone from the church stood up to read scripture. He read from Ecclesiastes, but he only read two verses. Then a worship team took the platform. They led the congregation in about a half hour of up tempo praise music while pictures of Michael flashed across the two digital screens. It was difficult to tell if the praise music was about the Lord or about Michael.

The most uplifting thing for Pastor Butch was at the end of the two hour, thirty-seven minute service. A soloist came onto the platform and sang a beautifully arranged rendition of the popular song *I Can Only Imagine*. It was the closest thing to gospel that was said that day. As the woman sang, Butch thought about heaven. It was something he'd not thought about in a while. He thought about his brother, Shark, who died while still a young boy playing in the backyard. His mom and dad came to mind as well. It occurred to Butch that he was likely the next person in his family to graduate to eternity.

His mind went toward some of the people he'd buried from church. There were far too many to remember them all; but he anticipated seeing them in heaven—Rebecca Thurston, the first funeral he'd ever done, came to his thoughts. She'd been a dear woman whose funeral he did while he was still in seminary. Louise May, Edward Smith, Jordan Baker, and so many more. Lester Wooley. He missed Lester.

Then he thought about Amber, and her brother Adam. Amber was killed while rescuing little children from evil men, and Adam, like Michael, had been a pastor, killed violently in his sanctuary, although under very different circumstances.

Tears formed in Butch's eyes. Here he was trying to imagine heaven—and all the wonderful people who populated it right now. Yet, all he could think about was the hell on earth—the violence, the abuse, and the pain. No one had spoken of the way Michael had died at the funeral, and that was probably a good thing, nevertheless, it was on his mind. It had to be on everyone's mind. Once again, evil was loose in Sydney, in Butch's life. It swelled up into unbelievable acts of violence and degradation. Why, oh Lord, why was he tasked with shepherding a church through such evil times? Why not someone else? Why must he feel the sting of death?

When the song ended, a video montage of clips from some of Pastor Michael's sermons played. In the last clip Michael said, "Live for now; don't worry about the past. Live for now. Don't worry about the future, live for now. The past is irrelevant and the future will take care of itself. Live for now. God wants you to live in the present and to enjoy the gift of life. Live for now." There was a huge smile on Michael's face as he said it. The video showed how the congregation of TLC applauded him and his statement. Then, as if on cue, the people at the memorial service applauded what Michael had said.

Pastor Butch did not applaud. Neither did Terence. They were both thinking the same thing. Michael had lied to himself when he said those words. Somehow his past was relevant. Somehow it had caught up to him.

But how?

That clip was the last element of the memorial service. The house lights came up, just as if they had been at a movie or play. A disembodied baritone voice came over the sound system and announced, "Thank you for attending the memorial service for Pastor Michael Westgrave. Please note, the family is requesting in lieu of flowers donations in his honor be made to the building campaign for a new sanctuary for TLC, as we seek to continue what Pastor Michael started."

"How could they possibly need a new sanctuary?" Terence said to Butch.

"I was thinking the same thing myself," Butch said as the two men made their way down the row toward the center aisle. They were moving slowly because the congestion was heavy. Butch and Terence waited so long that they decided to just stand there and wait for it to clear out a little more. Canned music was blaring over the speakers, and that made it difficult for the two men to talk, so they stood there looking around and at each other.

They were both still on the aisle when they'd come to a stop. They gazed downward toward the platform. Both men noticed the array of flowers and the pristine look of the platform environment. It was a stark contrast to the last time they'd seen it, with Michael dead and duct taped to a chair. They were both looking that direction when they felt the touch of a hand at their shoulder. They both swiveled around.

"I need to talk to the two of you." It was Detective Wright.

"Right now?" Terence asked.

"Yes. Now would be good. Follow me."

Detective Wright gave them no choice to argue. He turned his back on them and walked the opposite direction toward the side wall. Butch looked at Terence, who looked back at him with an expression that said, "I don't know what is going on." Butch shrugged his shoulders and lifted his hands, then proceeded to follow. Terence was right behind him.

"Do you think he found out we snooped in Michael's office?" Terence asked.

"Shush," Butch put a finger over his mouth.

Detective Wright led them down toward the platform. They walked past two state police officers who were still guarding the now empty platform. They made their way up onto it, and then they exited stage right and into a green room of sorts. Butch had never seen a sanctuary with a green room before.

The room had a sofa, a side table with a pitcher of ice water, a thermos of coffee, a couple of plush leather chairs. Ubiquitous large framed photographs of Pastor Michael engaged in leadership poses hung on the walls. The largest was of Pastor Michael preaching. Another fascinating image was him sitting in the green room with a well-known musician.

"Why don't the two of you have a seat," Detective Wright said.

"Do we have a choice?" Terence wondered, because he didn't feel like he had a choice.

"Certainly you have a choice, Rev. Harrison. You could leave right now, go back to your car, and get along with your work. You are not being detained or questioned as suspects. However, I would like it very much if you and your friend chose to sit down and talk with me. I just want to pick your brains."

"Yeah, well, since you put it that way I suppose it is fine. Police just make me jittery."

"Is that because you're guilty of something, Rev. Harrison?"

"Please just call me Terence. And no, I'm not guilty, I'm black. I've learned to be jittery around police. I guess, Detective Wright, it is a defense mechanism that comes from being pulled over a few times for the heinous crime of driving-while-black."

Detective Wright ignored Terence's answer. He said, "Why don't you and Butch just call me Richard and we'll all dispense with the formalities. I assume both of you are aware that a second pastor was murdered yesterday in his office at Ferry View Methodist Church. Am I correct in that assumption?"

"Yeah, we know about that," Terence said.

"Good," Detective Wright pulled out a notepad and opened it up. "It looks like Rev. Peters had been at Ferry View for a little over seven years, just like Pastor Michael was here. Did either one of you know Rev. Peters very well?"

"No, not really," Butch said. "I hate that I can't be more helpful, but he was not one of the more involved pastors in the community. Rick Peters tended to do his own thing. I think part of it is that his church was located out on the tip of the peninsula and that caused a bit of a sense of isolation. Don't get me wrong, though, there was nothing wrong with him, that I was aware of. It's just that he wasn't very involved, that's all."

"Would you say the same thing, Terence?"

"I've not been in Sydney as long as Butch has been, so I can't really say. I knew who Peters was, but I don't think we actually ever met. It is terribly sad what happened. I can't even imagine."

"Do either of you know who might have wanted to kill him?"

"I assume it was the same people who killed Michael." Butch said, then added, "Don't you?"

"Yes and no." Detective Wright took a deep breath. "See, we have the phenomena nowadays of copycats. The weirder the case, the more publicity it gets, the more prominent the victims, the more likely there are to be copycats. It could also be that someone who has always held a grudge against Rev. Peters used the opportunity to stage his death like Michael's to make us think that it was the same person who killed Rev. Westgrave.

"But at the same time, there are a lot of similarities between Peter's death and Westgrave's death. Both were at their church building. Both were intended to send a message. Both scenes were staged for dramatic effect. So there are a lot of similarities that usually can't be faked."

"Should we tell him about the other one?" Terence looked at Butch.

"What other one?" Detective Wright said.

"I didn't want to, but, well, I guess," Butch glanced at Detective Wright, then Terence again, "I guess we have to now, don't we Terence?" Butch frowned.

"What other one? What are you two talking about?"

"I did a little poking around on the internet and discovered that a pastor was murdered in July. It took place in Pierce County. She was a very well-known liberal pastor, or progressive is probably the right label, who also happened to be lesbian and she championed the gay rights movement within the Christian community."

"You say she was murdered? How? How is it connected to these two murders?"

"Well, that's just it. I am certain that when the police investigated the scene, they had no context like we do now, so they weren't looking for crazy women going around killing pastors. Her name was Joan, and she was shot in her home along with her partner. According to the newspapers the police ruled it a domestic violence case. But what got my attention was that there was a one word note written at the scene. The note said 'abomination' on it. To me that sounds like our killers here."

"When did you discover this?"

"Just yesterday. I came home from church feeling bothered by the whole thing with Michael so I did some internet research. Within fifteen minutes I had found this case with Pastor Joan. I think it is the same people, and Joan might have been the first one. Then, Michael was the second one. Now, Peters is the third one. They are getting better, faster, and more brazen in their procedures. I believe it is only a matter of time before they kill again."

Terence nodded his head, "I'm afraid he's right. In fact, Butch," Terence turned and looked at his friend, "I know we haven't talked about it, but the more I meditate upon the subject, the more convinced I am that there are probably more victims than even these three. They've probably been doing this for a while. It might be smart to cross check all the pastors who've died for the past five years or so. There might be a connection."

Detective Wright raised his hand, "The problem with that, Terence, is these two murders are so different from any other kind of death I've read or heard about anywhere in Western Washington. Nothing comes even close."

"Like anything," Terence paused before he finished his thought, then he puckered his lips and kissed the air, "like anything else in life, it takes time to get confident. They have become confident in their work, and want to send messages to the rest of the world. Now that they are in full swing, they can't help but act again. They want the attention, and they want to scare every spiritual leader in Sydney."

Detective Wright kept scribbling in his notebook, and without looking up he said, "I tell you what, I'm going to try to get the file on that case in Pierce County with that Pastor Joan and see what I can learn about it. I should be able to get more information than what the newspaper had, although I can't promise it. Pierce County doesn't play well with others, if you know what I mean."

When he finished writing, he brought his attention back to Butch and Terence. "But for now, I want to just think about Westgrave and Peters."

Detective Wright walked over to the table where the water jug was. He opened up a drawer and pulled out a manila file folder. He sat back down opposite Butch and Terence, then handed them the file.

"I know you know Westgrave's details because you were both here, but I want you to look at this file from Ferry View, mostly the pictures in it because that is really all we have at this point. Does anything stick out to you that might give us a clue as to motive, or even means? Now, be warned, these are some pretty gruesome pictures."

The two men opened the file. Both of them turned their heads in disgust at what they saw. They knew what the pictures would show because of the email Terence received earlier that morning. However, seeing the images in color was a far different experience from a generalized description. There were pictures of the computer with its pornographic site, the naked body, the cut off hand, gouged eyes, and even the genitals tacked to the wall. Those things they already knew about. What they didn't know was what the message written in blood on the wall was.

They saw in full color what was written—Your sins will find you out.

Terence took off his glasses then wiped his hand over his eyes. "That makes sense," he said, putting his glasses back on.

"What do you guys make of it all?" Detective Wright said.

"You go ahead Terence, you tell him."

"Yeah, well, okay. Detective, whoever did this is doing a little more than sending a message. It is actually a sermon based on Jesus rather cryptic words in the Sermon on the Mount. In it Jesus tells his followers that if their right hand offends them, cut it off. If your eye offends you, pluck it out. Many Bible teachers believe that the Lord's words there are about sexual temptation. Now, notice that Peters' right hand and eyes are gone. The killer believes he has committed a sin, probably a sexual sin given the way they

134

mutilated his manhood and all. They are making him a eunuch for God. Plus, it also fits with the email that was sent out to his church. The killers were not just wanting to kill Peters, they wanted to expose him and his iniquity as a warning to others. Whoever killed Westgrave and Peters is motivated by some kind of religious, biblical sentiment. They think they are punishing evil pastors. It is not personal, it is programmatic. At least, that is the working hypothesis Butch and I have."

Detective Wright said, "It's an interesting hypothesis. You don't think that maybe it is someone, or group of people, who are against God or religion, Satanists maybe, or radical Islam. Could it be people who have been hurt by clergy and they want payback, like victims in the clergy sex-abuse scandal?"

Pastor Butch answered, "I don't deny that there could be some complicated political, psychological, or sociological issues going on with the killers. They might be women who have been hurt in the past by a pastor, that's true. However, given the Bible verses that were found inside Michael's throat and stomach, I think the killers believe they are punishing these pastors for their sin."

Detective Wright was again writing down all of this in his notebook. Then he looked up from his pad and smiled at Butch. "How did you know about the paper we got from inside Westgrave? That was never released to the public, and it happened in the morgue, not here at the crime scene? And, I noticed you slipped earlier and said it was crazy women killing pastors. Why do you think it is women?"

"Good going Butch! That was unbelievably stupid." Terence hit his friend on the arm.

"Ouch," Butch said. "That hurt." He turned his attention to Detective Wright. "Well, we may have gotten a copy of the police report. Maybe. So, that is how we know that it was probably three women who did the murdering of Michael, and we knew about the Bible verses. But back to the Peters incident," Butch wanted to change the subject. "That message on the wall, 'your sin will find you out,' fits with the emails that the murderers sent out with all those pictures of him with the different women, some of whom I bet are in his congregation. Remember, the killers think they are doing a favor for the people in the churches by exposing, confronting, and punishing sinful leaders."

Terence stood up and walked around the sofa, his arms clasped behind his back. "If you want to find out who is doing it, you have to think like militant, super-zealous church people. That is why we can be certain these are not Satanists, atheists, or a competing religion. It is people who think they are doing what God wants them to do for the church. They actually believe they are helping. Most bad guys think they are the good guys. Our killers here are no different."

"How did you know about the email with the pictures? That was not released to the media either."

"Detective Wright," Terence said, "This is a small town, and church folk, even if they go to different churches, are very well connected. We live in the same neighborhoods, we intermarry, we stand at the school bus stop together. Our network is two millennia old, speaks its own language, and has survived every empire that has come and gone. Something like this is not going to stay secret for long. To us this is now no longer a legal issue only. It is something inside our community that has gone very wrong. It affects us more than anyone else, so yeah, we're going to talk about it and collaborate together until it is solved."

"Don't preach to me, Terence." Detective Wright now stood up, taking a slightly confrontational posture. "I don't object to religious people doing their thing, but I've never seen much good come from it. People are filthy and dirty, just like animals. They kill for twenty dollars, lust for anyone that walks by, and lie at every opportunity. I've seen it all, and church people are no different, as our little homicides prove. In fact, they might be worse." He took a deep breath. "But I don't want to get into a debate with the two of you. You seem like decent enough people. Thanks for your help. I may contact you further if I hear of anything, and Terence, if that network of yours turns up any evidence I might not know about, please let me know. If I find out either one of you are snooping around on this, or doing anything that might get in the way of our work, I will not hesitate to arrest you for obstruction of justice."

Detective Wright stood up and gestured for the two men to head toward the door. "Be careful out there. It might be unsafe for your kind right now."

"The thought had occurred to us," Terence said.

The Sanctuary was empty of people. Butch and Terence walked out through the big doors and down the hallway. They parted ways in the parking lot, as they were not parked near one another. Just before Terence turned to his left to move toward his car, Butch grabbed him by the shoulder.

"Hey," Butch said. His face was solemn, almost stern. "Not all bad guys think they are good guys. Some know they are rotten. They just don't care."

***

Back in the green room, Detective Wright called into the office.

"Yeah, it's me," he said. "I want you to dig all you can on Butch Gregory and Terence Harrison. I've got a gut feeling that something isn't right. I can't put my finger on it, but it seems like those two know way too much."

Chapter Twenty-One
In The Dark

"That is an excellent point," Pastor Butch said to Bill. "Why do you think that is?"

"It has to be because of Romans 8:28, right? I mean it does say, doesn't it, that 'all things work together for good, doesn't it?'" Bill's knee bounced up and down with excitement, showing the other men in the room he believed he had won the point. It wasn't an argument as much as an ongoing debate between Bill and Pastor Butch. The debate often punctuated the Monday night men's Bible study at Sydney Community Church.

As a confirmed five point Calvinist, Bill was always looking for an angle to bring everything back to his systematic view of theology and the Scriptures. Pastor Butch never went looking for the quarrel, but he was decidedly Arminian in his leaning. The result was Monday nights sometimes turned into a contest to see who could first claim Romans 8:28, "We know that all things work together for good for those who love God, who are called according to his purpose."

It was ironic to Pastor Butch that a passage which was written to bring comfort and confidence in God's power had become a tool for shaking others confidence, spreading discomfort, all with a tablespoon of uncertainty. It was the understood rule of the two debate partners that whoever could logically bring Romans 8:28 in defense of their argument, whatever that argument, was the winner. Bill, as the Calvinist would often call on the verse to support God's sovereignty and predestination. Pastor Butch, would use the verse to emphasize the choice to love God and the way in which "good" goes along with the purposes of God. Bill used the verse to describe the universe and our role in it as a *fait accompli*. Pastor Butch used the verse to describe the universe and the life of faith as a work in progress.

Neither would ever convince the other of anything.

Bill won tonight. Pastor Butch now needed to decide whether or not to engage the argument. He could easily bring his theological acumen, which was deeper and broader than Bill's, into the discussion. He could win the argument, but would the cost be worth it? Many arguments are won at the expense of relationship. Plus, if he did engage the topic, it would probably add another fifteen minutes to the Bible study. Most of the men didn't seem interested. He checked his watch. It was already 7:35 PM, and all but the two of them had closed his Bible.

Butch played the pastor card. "Well, we are out of time, but how about we pick up that discussion next week? Right? I'll email you guys out a summary of tonight's discussion, an outline to go over before next week's study, and a list of prayer requests tomorrow. Let me pray and then we'll get out of here."

Pastor Butch closed his Bible and folded his hands.

> Dear Lord, we thank you for our study in Mark's gospel tonight. Our prayer is that you would grant each of us the courage to recognize Jesus when he is moving in our midst. Show us Lord about how to be better husbands, fathers, friends, and followers of you. I pray that the rest of our week be one of peace, joy, and fruitful labors in all our endeavors. In Jesus' name. Amen.

"Hey, Tom and Greg, can you guys give me a hand for a moment and help me set these tables back up and clean the kitchen?"

The two men nodded at their pastor, but all the men helped. As they wiped down the kitchen area, folded tables, and stacked chairs they talked about sports, hunting, and cars. These are the topics that men speak of when they are together, the things that seem superficial, but in reality are the stuff that builds the bridges to authentic relationship. It is through the medium of sports, outdoors, and cars that men stumble upon genuine discussion, the stuff of brotherhood and meaning. The artificial construct of such things, although odd and not ontologically necessary, helped otherwise self-absorbed, self-conscious, self-doubting people discover friendship.

Pastor Butch reveled in the moment. It had been a tough week, but he loved hearing men talk, laugh, and slurp coffee. It was moments like this that reminded him of why he loved ministry so much. He could live without budgets, bulletins, and boards. What he could not live without was this—this blessed *koinonia*.

Butch turned off the heat. Then as the men filed out of the front door into the soft rainfall, he talked with Bud about the upcoming community wide turkey basket drive for Thanksgiving. Butch locked the door, and he and Bud walked out into the rain. It was dark, even though there were three large lights on poles in the lot. The gigantic bulbs did little more than glow in the foggy rain, like nightlights in the bathroom that provide direction, but do not help seeing the toy fire engine or spaceship on the floor.

"Crud!" Butch shouted. "I think I left my phone in the classroom." Butch turned and walked back toward the dark building. "I'll see you Sunday, Bud. Tell Mona I said hi!" With that Bud walked out to his car. Butch unlocked the door, which frustrated him because he'd just locked it. He flipped the light switch for the tiny chandelier that hung over the front door. That was all the light he needed to navigate his way back toward the classroom.

When he turned the classroom light on, he saw his cell phone on the floor, where his chair had been, right where he put it when the small group began. Out of habit he checked it to see if anyone had called, messaged, or updated his social media in the past five minutes that he'd been separated from the phone.

Butch turned off the light in the classroom and exited out through the kitchen. The faint glow from the green clock numbers on the two stoves gave him just enough illumination to find his way out toward the main hallway.

He didn't notice that the light near the front door was no longer on until he rounded the corner and encountered darkness. He froze.

He had left that light on when he came back into the building. He was certain. Now it was not.

Someone else was in the church with him. Tingles formed at the base of his back.

"Bud? Is that you?"

There was no answer, but he knew someone had to be in the building. Sweat erupted on his back, shoulders, and brow. His knees shook. Butch swallowed hard and sought his courage.

If someone was in the building, then they were waiting for him in the shadows by the front door. He could turn around and leave the opposite direction and exit around the corner and toward the backdoor. But if there were more than one of them, they would probably be waiting for him there as well. He knew there were at least three of them, with petite female feet.

He fingered his phone. Did he have time to call 911? Probably not. That would give away his position in the church building, likely doing more harm than good.

The front door was still unlocked. Maybe he could run, run fast, right by whoever was waiting for him and dart out into the parking lot and make a run for his car. The problem with that was, maybe someone was waiting for him by his car. There were three of them, so there were zero good options.

His prayer was silent and desperate.

Jesus—this is quite a jam here. Show a way out. Save me. Please. Amen.

Just as the prayer left his mind and slid into the ether of divine presence, a memory of playing hide and seek with the youth group in the church struck him.

Several years ago the youth minister, a young woman named Selena, had insisted that Butch spend time with youth at the annual church lock-in. He ate pizza, sang a few songs, and then Selena forced Butch to play hide-n-seek with the group. They turned off the lights in the church and whoever was 'it' had to find people in the dark. The catch in the rules was that a person couldn't stay in one spot and hide for the whole game. The hiders had to change where they were hiding every two minutes or so.

The students always found Pastor Butch immediately, every time. He finally asked one of the seniors, a boy named Brad, why he was so easy to find. Brad told Butch it was because they could hear his shoes on the squeaky tile or linoleum. So for the last round, Butch took off his shoes and wore just his socks.

They never found him.

This memory flashed through his mind at lightning speed. Butch pushed off his shoes with his feet. Then he tip toed back into the kitchen. The best course of action might be to wait them out. Sooner or later his stalkers will get tired and leave.

Butch crouched down in the corner, making himself as small as possible. He was glad that he'd decided to wear a fleece pullover tonight instead of his usual waterproof winter coat. That coat would have rubbed against itself as he moved, making enough sound for Blind Bartimaeus to find him. The dark blue fleece was silent.

The only sound he was making was his breath. Butch worked hard at keeping his breathing calm and balanced. That wasn't easy, because fear is a heavy panter.

His eyes adjusted to the darkness. The hallway he'd just come from had looked pitch black before, but now as his eyes adjusted he could see the faint glow from the parking lot lights coming through the windows. He kept his eyes locked in on the doorway to the kitchen. He'd been there a couple of minutes when he saw a shadowy figure inch by. Butch's pulse raced.

They're in the hallway.

He heard the sound of someone stumbling, and he knew that the figure that just walked by tripped on his Florsheims.

It occurred to him that now might be a good time to make a run for the backdoor. Whoever just walked by had probably been the rearguard. He thought better of it. Staying put seemed like a better plan right now.

In another minute he was glad he'd not done that, because now two distinct voices could be heard in the hallway. One voice whispered, "Where did he go?" The second answered, "I don't know. But he's still in here."

Oh God, help.

Both of the shadows now moved into the doorway. Butch held his breath.

The first one crept into the room, followed by the second. Once they were both in, Butch couldn't see their outline anymore. He didn't know what he would do if they came upon him, because they would just bump into him in the dark. His mind formulated a hasty plan. He knew there was a knife block on the other side of the refrigerator. If they came from his right, he would try to run that way and grab a knife and slash at them.

If they came from his other side, from the left, then he would try to open the refrigerator door and slam the door into the person's head.

Neither plan had much of a chance for working. He was slow, slightly overweight, and terrified. But a bad plan was better than no plan.

That was when he saw the creeping shadows move between him and the digital clock on the stove. Both of them were on the other side of the kitchen. Butch stayed low, but he rose just enough to duck walk around the table in the middle of the room and make his way toward the kitchen door. When he got to the kitchen door he could see from the faint red glow of the exit sign that the two figures had gone into the classroom where he'd taught the Bible class. Butch again duck walked out the door and then once he got into the hallway he walked upright.

Mindful of where he left his shoes, he tiptoed toward the front door. He was almost there when he heard the door down the hallway to his right open. In an instant he had to decide whether making a run for his car was the best action, or if he should continue to stay in the shadows.

Butch opted for the shadows. He moved to his left, crouched down and squatted on the opposite side of a table that was set up with sign-up sheets for the Thanksgiving banquet. There was a large tablecloth, which gave Butch a good amount of cover as he squatted behind it.

If his predators turned the lights on, he was done for. They probably don't know where the light switches are though, so he should be okay in that department. As that comforting thought moved into his mind, it was immediately displaced with a fresh and disturbing thought. Whoever was chasing him knew that there was another door in the classroom and that it joined a smaller hall that came out into the main hallway. They had to know because they navigated from the dark room and into the hallway where Butch was without lights and with speed.

Whoever was chasing him knew the layout of his church. That can only mean someone from Sydney Community Church was trying to kill him.

Something like disillusionment overtook him. Why? Who? How had he gone so wrong as to nurture this kind of violence? How could someone be a part of his community and end up a murderer?

Butch pushed those questions aside. Survival demanded his focus. He stuck his head out from the side of the table. There was a soda machine on the far end of the hallway that glowed. The soda machine had been a great point of contention with the deacon board. Most of them liked it, because it gave people who didn't like coffee something to drink besides water. But others, led by Pastor Butch, were opposed to it because of the soda company's name in lights in the church building. They had objected to the commercialism of it.

Butch had lost that battle.

Crouching beside the table, hiding to save his life, he was glad he'd lost that battle. The light from the soda machine showed him the silhouette of the two people trying to capture him. He watched as they opened up a door to the large teaching classroom. As soon as the door closed, Butch Gregory knew that if he was going to survive the night he had to take the chance and leave now. He dashed down the hallway. At the door he slowed his actions. With great care he pushed opened the door and then slid out of it. He held the door until it came back to rest in its place. No clicks.

Butch crouched down again. He again did his duck walk along the exterior wall of the church building, certain no one from inside the building could see him. His car was parked about thirty feet from the building. He was almost there, but from behind the shrub against the building it felt like there was a great chasm between him and it.

The moment he unlocked the car, the lights would flash. If his assailants didn't see that, then they would probably see the interior dome light come on when he opened the door. If he did it fast enough that shouldn't be a problem though. He'd be out on the road before they could get to him.

Unless they had a gun and shot at him.

It had been a gunshot that killed Pastor Joan.

He figured the best plan would be to minimize the amount of time between the flash of lights and the starting of the car. He didn't want this to be like one of those movies where the person fiddles with the keys trying to get it into the ignition switch. He reached into his fleece pocket and pulled out the keys.

Lord, let this key find its way, and let the lights not be seen. Amen.

He counted to ten, took a deep breath, and then sprinted across the parking lot. He hadn't anticipated the pain he felt in his feet. The sharp rocks atop the asphalt pushed through his socks. It felt like needles to his tender soles. The pain was so strong that he wanted to yell. He stifled that to a low grunt. When he reached the car he squatted down behind it on the side opposite from the main door to the church building. The driver's side, though was the side closest to the building. He thought about going in through the passenger's side, but the time he would lose moving over the seat would be less than the time of the lights going on and the starting of the car.

He held the keys in his hands. He'd made it this far. He believed the Lord would get him the rest of the way. He rested his left hand on the back of the car, looking at the church building for any sign of his pursuers. The parking lot lights that had aided him when he was hunched down in the kitchen now worked against him. The illumination coming from above made it nearly impossible for him to see any details inside the building.

He rested his left hand against the side of the car, but it slipped on the rain. It was no big deal. Butch steadied himself, but when he did, the thumb of his right hand pushed ever so slightly on the panic button of his Honda's key fob. The blue sedan exploded with light and sound.

The bit was up.

The church building went supernova as every hallway and exterior light came on. They knew where he was.

Butch pushed the panic button to silence the alarm, then the unlock button as he ran around the car to the driver's side. Now he was doing exactly what he'd worked so hard to avoid, fumbling with the keys at the steering column of his car. He flipped through the house key, his office key, the key to the church post office box, then finally he located the right one and jammed it into the switch.

The car started. Butch stamped down on the gas as hard as he could.

When he did, the car stalled.

Jesus, don't let this happen. Please deliver!

He started it again and slammed it into drive. The Civic lurched, then died. Butch turned the key again and it started. Just as he did his door opened, someone wearing a ski mask reached and grabbed his arm off the steering wheel.

How had he forgotten to lock the door!

His windshield shattered in front of him as a tire iron, wielded by another set of hands, came down hard against his car. Butch let out a shriek. He swung with his left hand at the person trying to pull him out of his car. It felt like his fist found a target. That moment was all he needed. He pushed the gear lever to drive, pushed the gas, but not too hard. The car moved forward.

He reached out with his hand to close the door. Right as it clicked, he heard, felt, the crash of the tire iron come down on the door. The window frame took the force of the blow. Whoever they were, they missed the glass, which was good for Butch. One more blow and the glass could be gone and he'd be vulnerable.

But now he was moving forward. He entertained the thought of circling around and trying to run over his assailants with the car—to end this right now. In the car he had the advantage. Then he remembered that they might have guns. Living another day was a better plan, so he drove on out into the street in his battered sedan and sped away.

Chapter Twenty-Two
Shoes

"Be careful, Terence, and I'll call you later if I learn anything. I called the police, and I am waiting for them to come." Terence said a prayer, and then Butch ended the call.

Butch sat in his living room recliner, stunned. His eyes were red and his face ragged. All his mind could think about was that someone who called him Pastor Butch, some woman, or several women, who listened to him preach about love, compassion, and kindness every week, souls that at least publicly confessed to follow Jesus, had tried to murder him tonight.

Lucy brought him a cup of tea. The two sat in silence.

There was a knock at the door. Butch looked out the front window. It was Detective Wright. He didn't expect him to arrive that quickly..

"You're pretty fast there, Detective. I just called you four minutes ago."

"We're pretty good at speed when murderers are roaming about." Detective Wright didn't wait to be asked into Butch's home. He just walked in. "Where is the car? I'd like to look at the physical evidence as soon as possible. I've already sent a team to the church. This will only take a second, Butch, and then if you don't mind I'd like to take you up to the church with me, and you can let me in so I can look around. Are you up for that, or do you need medical attention?"

"I'm fine. My nerves are rattled, but other than that I'm fine." Butch realized he seemed distant. He could feel himself preoccupied. "I'm sorry detective. I guess I'm a little foggy right now. People have tried to kill me before, but never at my own church."

"That is understandable. Just take me to the car."

"Of course, I'm sorry. Follow me." Pastor Butch led the detective through the kitchen side door and into the garage. Lucy followed behind them. Detective Wright took several pictures of the damage with his cell phone.

"It looks like they were really trying to hurt you," he said. "I mean, sometimes this is simple vandalism or some kind of generalized rage coming out. But these were all aimed at your head. Seriously, they intended to harm you."

"I know."

"Could you open the car door for me so I can see inside?"

The bent frame of the door creaked against the Honda's shell when he opened it.

Detective Wright took a couple of pictures on the inside.

"I know you're probably anxious to get this car repaired, and need to call your insurance company, but before you do it would really help me out if you'd let me get a forensics team to check for fingerprints or any other physical evidence. Is that okay?"

"Yeah sure, like I said, whatever you need."

Lucy spoke up. "Do you think we're safe from these crackpots?"

"No," Detective Wright said. "Your husband is clearly a target. If what we suspect is true, then they have killed family members before. I cannot guarantee anyone's safety. The truth is these people may come after you or your children."

"I was thinking, honey," Butch stuttered a little because he knew what he was about to say was something Lucy wouldn't like one bit. "Why don't you pack a little, and you and the kids go off to your folk's house over at Ocean Shores. They have already left for their winter trip to Arizona, so you'd have privacy. It'd be like a fall vacation for the kids, on the beach and all. I'm sure their teachers can send school work down, plus doing things over the internet. It just seems like the safe thing to do right now." He gave her a hug then added, "I want you and the children out of here."

He expected a fight from her. But she didn't. Instead, she nodded up and down and then said, "That is a good idea. You can tell the church you'll be gone a few weeks, and Philip can take over for a while."

Butch tilted his head. "No. I have to stay here."

Lucy jerked back from her husbands arms.

Detective Wright took note of the coming squabble. He stepped away to the other side of the garage. He called the forensics team.

"Butch," Detective Wright said, "can you open up the garage door? It'll make it easier for the forensics team."

"Sure," Butch said. He pushed the button on the wall. The garage door motor hummed to life.

Lucy's face was flush. "You don't have to stay here," Lucy raised her voice more with each word. "You don't have to stay anywhere. You can come with me and the kids. You don't owe anyone anything."

"You know better than that. Do you really want me to turn my tail and run? I don't think you do."

"Yes, I do. I want you to be safe. I want you to get out of this alive."

"I believe that," Butch said, "but I also believe you also want me to be in the will of God. I told you, something about this involves me at a deeper level. I'm supposed to find out who is doing this. I feel like I'm close. You know I'm right."

Large tears formed in the corner of her eyes. Lucy Gregory believed her husband was right, but she didn't like it. Conflicting emotions all swirled up inside of her. Part of her was very angry at her husband for putting the needs of others ahead of her needs, ahead of the needs of their children. It was the same old story of the pastor and his family, everyone else's crisis is what matters while their crisis is pushed to the side of the road.

The anger spilled over as anger at God. It wasn't a disobedient or disbelieving anger, but it was palpable frustration that the Lord seemed to delight in torturing her husband. Why couldn't someone else do it this time? Hadn't Butch already done enough of the dangerous stuff?

Along with those emotions came the maternal instinct to protect her children. Her husband, as much as she loved him, was an adult capable of making his own decisions. Sarah and Paul were not. She knew that Butch felt the same way she did, that they both would do anything to keep their children safe and to protect them. Taking them away from Sydney for a while was the safe thing to do. She knew that it was true.

At the same time that these complicated emotions were waging war inside her, she also felt pride in her husband. It was one of his endearing qualities that he always strove to do the right thing. Not the thing everyone expected of him, and not what someone else thought was right for him. Butch wanted to do the right thing in the right way. Whether he was correct or not was irrelevant. Butch Gregory believed that it was right for him to stay in Sydney. He was willing to face the danger if it was the right thing to do. She loved him for it, and she was proud of him for being that kind of man.

Butch could see his wife working through these feelings. He reached out to her and drew her close again. In the embrace she said, "I know you're right. I'll call my folks, pack some things up. You do what you have to do. But you promise me one thing preacher boy."

"What's that?"

"Don't get yourself killed. You hear me. I don't plan on being a widow. I'm too young for that. Besides," she wiped tears from her eyes, "you haven't earned enough retirement yet to die. I'd have to get a job or something." She held him at arm's length, and added, "Make certain you don't get Terence hurt either. I mean it."

"Yes dear."

Detective Wright made a fake cough. "I hate to break this up, but I need to get over to the church and check things out there. Mrs. Gregory, there will be a forensic team here in about fifteen minutes. If you can just leave the garage door open that would help them come and go. They will knock on your front door when they arrive to let you know they are working. Other than that, you shouldn't even know they are here. There are two officers in the front yard, and I'll have one of them come around here to the side. I will leave them here overnight."

"Thank you. I'll leave the garage opened."

"Butch, are you ready to go?"

"No, not really. But I know we need to. Let me put my shoes on and grab my coat."

Ten minutes later Detective Wright pulled into the parking lot of Sydney Community Church. Butch road shotgun.

"Where were you when they hit the car?"

Butch pointed out the parking slot where he'd been. Detective Wright pulled up beside it. They both got out of the car. There was, surprisingly, nothing there to see. For some reason Butch had expected to see glass on the ground. Standing there, though, he remembered that the glass on his car shattered, but didn't fall out.

"I guess there is nothing here to see," Butch said. "No evidence at all."

"Not exactly," Detective Wright said, waving a flashlight around the pavement.

He bent over on the far side of the parking spot, closest to the church and stared at the ground. Then he pulled a plastic bag from his coat pocket. "One of the nice things about the slow, drizzly rain we have here in Sydney is that it acts like a sealant sometimes. It just seals everything down and keeps it in place. A heavy rain would wash everything away, but slow rain makes it soggy and heavier. High winds, too, would blow everything away, but our typical fall and winter rain is just a slow, steady drizzle."

From nowhere, it seemed, Detective Wright produced a pair of tweezers.

With those tweezers he grasped a sliver of blue off the pavement. "This is the blue paint from your car."

"What, is that a big deal?"

"Well, it is a big deal for two reasons. One, it corroborates your story. But two, and more important, if we can find the tool they used to do this, it should have tiny little particles that match this paint, and ties the owner of the tool to the scene of the crime."

"Oh." Butch was impressed, but he didn't see how that could be of much use in finding the killers. He didn't worry about proving anything. He wanted to find them first.

Detective Wright looked around.

"Which door did you use to come in and out, because I see two doors from here?"

"There is also a backdoor that one of them came through."

"There should probably be signs of forced entry there. Let's walk through the front door and then we'll work our way back."

"Okay," Butch said. "But I bet there are no signs of forced entry."

"Do you usually leave the backdoor unlocked?"

"No."

"What are you trying to tell me, Butch?"

"I think that the person who came in from that backdoor probably knew what she was doing."

"Are you telling me that the person had a key? Is that what you mean?"

"Yes."

"What makes you say that?"

"Well, for starters, I don't remember any noise, or delay for that matter, in the person coming in from around the back. It was as if they had already prepped the scene while I was in the Bible study. The only way to have done that was probably to have had a key. But also," Butch scratched his head, "when they were looking for me in the building, like I told you about over the phone, I could tell by their movements that whoever it was knew the layout of the building. It was someone who knew every door, every hallway, every light switch. The only reason I survived is I know this building better than anyone else in the world."

Detective Wright walked toward the building and reached inside his coat. He stopped halfway to the building, pulled out his notebook, and wrote. Butch opened the unlocked front door. The lights were turned off.

Detective Wright told Butch, "Go ahead and turn all the lights on."

Butch's shoes were in the middle of the floor where he'd left them. A circle drawn with ruby red lipstick outlined the shoes. Around the perimeter were words. It took Detective Wright a moment to orient himself. It was another message, written in same red lipstick.

"The false teacher who walked in these shoes will soon die."

Chapter Twenty-Three
Insight and Brilliance

Monica locked the door to the employee's bathroom.

There were more people at SeaTown bank than was usual for a Tuesday. The latest news from New York was that the prime lending rate was about to go up. Whenever that happened, people came rushing into the bank branch to try and lock-in the lower rate before it spiked. This morning she had already approved two car loans, one refinance on a mortgage, and two new home loans. All the while, she'd kept an eye on Stephanie. As soon as Stephanie went to the restroom, she dashed the same direction and locked the door behind her.

On a normal day Monica would have called her over to her cubicle to talk, in coded and guarded language, about what to do next. That typical stratagem was foolish today because of so many extra ears around.

They had not spoken about the failed effort to remove the false teacher the previous night. After he drove away they turned the lights off and left their private message for him. Stephanie had not wanted to leave a message, since they had failed, but Monica insisted it was spiritually necessary. She had argued that claiming victory by stating your intentions was important. Other than that, they said nothing to each other.

Monica checked under the three stalls. Only Stephanie's blue pumps. The other two were empty.

"I've been thinking about last night."

"I figured you would," Stephanie said. Then she flushed. "But I didn't think you would be so desperate to fix your foul-up that you would actually follow me to the bathroom. You must be afraid."

"Me? Me? You think I'm the one who fouled up? It was you who let him get away. Somehow you let him slip right through your fingers."

"You're unbelievable. I told you that Monday night at the church was a bad idea, didn't I? I told you there were too many variables, we hadn't re-searched it enough, and that we needed Michelle with us. If we'd had Michelle he wouldn't have gotten away."

"Are you saying that I made a mistake?"

"I guess that's exactly what I'm saying. In your mad dash to do something grand and spectacular you neglected one of the pillars we are built on—thoroughness. We never miss details. Remember? Men miss details, but women don't have that luxury. Churches miss details, The Judys don't. The world misses details, but God doesn't. Didn't we learn our lesson with the removal of that gay false teacher this summer? We thought we had it all figured out, but we didn't count on her partner being there, did we? Then we were in the middle of a mess with no backup plan, so we had to kill them both. Remember? Because I sure do."

"You killed them both. That is the way I remember it."

"Nice." Stephanie's eyes narrowed and her mouth curled. "Very convenient. Very convenient indeed. Real nice. Of course I was the one who did it. I was there. You were at home knitting or something. We had to make a decision on the ground and we made it. I think you've been so distant from the actual process that you don't really know how dangerous and messy it is. People don't just lay down and let you kill them. There is always a struggle. That is why Michelle is so important. Sunday she took the false teacher out in his office with one kick to the head."

"The Judys are bigger than any one woman. I think you depend too much upon Michelle. It is a weakness."

Monica stepped backward. She was beginning to consider the possibility that Stephanie might take a swing at her. She knew that Stephanie could physically take her. Monica put her hand in the outer coat pocket of her blazer and fingered her pistol. Just in case.

"That is where you are wrong again. Any other woman last night would have sufficed. Once Pastor Bu-," Stephanie caught her slip and then corrected, "once the false teacher knew we were in the building we were spread too thin. One more person would have been enough to catch him. But no. You insisted that the two of us do it together, and you insisted on coming along. You, who have no experience at all with this. I'm not dependent upon Michelle, I am dependent upon the team. It was your arrogance last night that split the team up."

There was a moment of silence as the two of them stared at each other. It was the first argument the two of them had ever had out loud. Stephanie had fantasized many such arguments in her mind. In her imagination every argument ended with her slapping Monica across the face.

Someone shook the door handle. "Is anyone in there?" a voice called.

153

"Yes," both Monica and Stephanie called out.

"It'll be clear in a minute," Stephanie again shouted.

Monica scowled and said, "Great, now the office will think that we are having a fling in the bathroom. Just great."

Stephanie laughed, releasing some of the tension between the two women. "I wouldn't worry about that. Everyone knows that Beth and Robin have been carrying on in here for weeks now."

"I didn't know that!"

"That's because you're the boss. No one tells the boss these things. That is one of the advantages to not being management. I know more than you do."

"You should have told me that sooner. I guess I'll have to fire them now."

"That's why no one tells the boss anything."

Monica checked her lipstick in the mirror. Then she waved her hand through her hair as she said, "We need to put our differences behind us, Stephanie." She pivoted, then faced Stephanie straight on. "Tonight, the Signet Four need to meet, and we must disclose what happened. Then we can all decide what to do next."

"Agreed. I assume you are making the arrangements?"

"Of course. Don't I always?"

Stephanie opened the door and the two women walked out together. Whoever it was that was waiting for the room to become empty must have decided to try again in a few minutes.

Stephanie walked back to the counter. While she was gone the line grew, overwhelming the one teller on duty who was working both the drive through and the front. She logged into her computer, put her anger aside, looked up with a smile, and said, "May I help the next customer?"

Monica had an application for a pre-approval of a mortgage waiting for her. That was followed by a default. She took a ten minute break after that and enjoyed a handful of cashews with a glass of water. During her break she sent text messages to Jeannie and Shawna. She knew the women would not like it, but tough. Before she could chew through another handful of nuts, replies came from both of them affirming that they would be there.

Then she decided that Stephanie had become a problem. She was no longer an asset but a liability. She was too close to the false teacher. His distorted teaching and malignant ministry had infected her with his poison. His

154

worldly ways worked on her. She was compromised. It would not be enough to ask her to leave the group. She would never go quietly. Discrediting her would not work either. Too many on the team were loyal to her.

Monica needed to kill her. It was clear. She knew that was why God had made her the leader of the Judys. She made decisions fast because she saw what needed to be done. Monica did not need analysis, waiting, or investigation. She had allowed all of the research apparatus to be put into the original work of the Servants of Judith as an accommodation to Jeannie and Stephanie. Neither one of them were willing to take action and actually remove a false teacher without proof of some sort. So, she gave in.

She, though, didn't need that kind of evidence. She knew. She knew that Butch Gregory was evil and needed to die, just like she knew that Stephanie had been appointed by God for death because of her lack of faith.

The trick would be how to do it and make it look accidental. If the other women ever suspected that she killed Stephanie all would be lost. She could do it tonight at the Signet Four meeting. If she could arrange for Stephanie to die in front of the other two, and it looked like an accident, then she would be innocent in their eyes. The problem was if she died in those circumstances, the police might become a problem. It could be too much attention.

No, some other way needed to be found to kill Stephanie. She couldn't wait too long. The more she thought about it, she decided to wait until after the meeting. If she could turn the other two against her, create doubt and distrust toward her, then it might be possible to kill Stephanie and make it look like a suicide. Then the other two, and eventually all ten of the other women would believe that she killed herself in a kind of honorable way because she knew she was standing in the way of the group.

Yes, that is exactly what she would do, and she knew how to do it. She'd done it before, more than once. She pushed a rival from a high rise in college. In high school she typed an eloquent suicide note that she left at the feet of her ex-boyfriend as he swung from a noose she made. This time, neither one of those methods would work. She would need something better, something cleaner. Police were so much smarter now with all their forensics and science.

The hardest part would be to get her away from her family long enough to do it. Her two boys and husband were always there. Maybe they could meet somewhere, like out in the woods on a hike, and she could kill her there? Slit her wrists to make it look intentional? She could always take a pistol and leave it in Stephanie's hands. That might work?

Monica sat at her cubicle pondering the different ways she could kill Stephanie until a better idea formed in her disturbed brain. The better idea had the benefit of being much easier to accomplish.

She crossed herself.

Monica was so pleased with her insight that she rewarded herself with a candy bar from the top drawer of her desk. She deserved it. She was blessed by God with insight and brilliance.

Chapter Twenty-Four
Benevolence

His appointment was early. Mildred was not happy that Skye Jones arrived at the church office at 1:15 instead of 1:25 or 1:30. She thought it was rude to be that early, and it was certainly inconsiderate. When she buzzed Butch, he told her to bring him on down to his office. He was thankful for the distraction. It had been very difficult for him to focus. He kept thinking about his wife and kids, his church, and how close he came to dying the night before.

"Come on in, Skye," Butch said as Mildred opened the door. "Do you want some coffee, a soda, or water or something?"

"No, thank you. I'm good."

"Okay, have a seat."

Skye sat down in one of the two modest chairs opposite Butch's desk. Butch came around and sat beside him. Butch had no idea what this meeting was about. After church Sunday, Skye had only said that he wanted to talk to Butch, but he didn't say why. Butch guessed it was one of three things: Marriage or girlfriend problems, he wanted to be baptized and/or join the church, or it was financial.

"Let's start off with prayer," Butch said.

> Father, I thank you for our time today. Help me to hear what is on Skye's heart, and allow him to feel comfortable speaking with me. I pray that you grant me wisdom and insight in what a good course of action might be. I pray you bless him by revealing yourself to him. In Jesus' name. Amen.

When the prayer was over, Butch decided to slowly ease into the conversation, since he had no background with Skye at all.

"It has been nice having you in worship the last three weeks or so. Have you had a chance to visit one of the small groups?"

"No," Skye said, looking down. "Our lives are a little crazy right now, and just getting to church has been a struggle."

"Our lives," Butch said. "Who is the our?"

"My wife and daughter. We just moved here from California, and we've yet to settle into any kind of rhythm."

"Navy?" Butch asked with a raised eyebrow.

"Yeah, I'm on a submarine."

"I know a lot of great people who are on those subs. I'm sure once you guys get adjusted to Sydney and Western Washington, you'll love it." He paused, still unsure of what Skye needed. "So, what is your spiritual background? Have you always gone to church?"

"Not really, no. In fact, we just started going to a small church about six months ago before we left. That was right after my daughter Zoe was born."

"Zoe is a beautiful name. What is your wife's name?"

"She is Marta."

Skye then became silent, not filling in any of the details. Butch decided to go for it, "So, what is on your mind today?"

"Well, it is about Zoe. She hasn't been right, physically, since we got here. We keep taking her to the doctors, but they haven't helped much. They are still trying to figure out what is going on. Her being sick is why Marta hasn't been to church. She is always at home taking care of Zoe.

"To make things worse, we kinda got extended on money when we moved up here, and then the medical bills—even with the military coverage, we were surprised at how expensive the deductibles were. We've only been in our apartment for three months, and we are already a month behind on the mortgage."

Again Skye paused. Butch could tell that it pained him to be in this situation.

"We were wondering, Pastor, is there any kind of financial assistance from the church? We would pay it back when we got on our feet. It's just, we don't have any family, we don't know anyone here, and we feel so helpless."

Skye's eyes moistened, and he sniffled.

"Pastor Butch, I just don't know what to do."

Butch said, "Yes, of course we can help. Relax. You have friends here. Give me just a couple of minutes, okay."

Skye nodded, then looked down.

Butch walked out of his office and down to Mildred's desk. "Call John Hall, please Mildred, and ask him to come down here with the Deacon checkbook. If he is unavailable, call Sandy Fields. If that doesn't work, keep calling down the list until you get a deacon with a checkbook to get down here ASAP." Butch pulled a benevolence request form from the file cabinet. He hated those forms, but they were a necessary evil to help guard against those who abuse the system. About once a year he sat down with the other five churches that regularly do benevolences in town and compared notes to weed out those who were playing the church con game. It was obvious to him that Skye was not one of those kinds of people, but it was a required part of the benevolence process at Sydney Community Church.

He took the form back to his office and handed it to Skye. "Take a moment, if you will, to fill this out. It will help our folks figure out some of the best ways to help you."

"No problem," Skye said, taking the form. Butch handed him a pen.

"While you fill it out, I'm going over to the food pantry we have here to put together some groceries for you to take home to your family. I'll be back in about ten minutes or so. If you need anything, my ministry assistant is down the hall."

Butch grabbed the key to the church's food pantry and made the long walk back to the main building. He'd almost forgotten the ugly incident from the night before, but then he saw the message from his attacker still scrawled into the floor. The police had already done their work with it, but no one had cleaned it. The scene was as fresh as the wound was in his psyche.

The Bunn coffee pot rumbled as he walked past the kitchen; he jumped.

This is pathetic, I'm afraid in my own church.

He pushed those fears aside and went down to the pantry, which was located near the children's wing. Once there he filled three boxes with cereal, noodles, macaroni and cheese, canned vegetables, beans, crackers, canned meat like tuna and Spam, Hamburger Helper meals, and diapers. He put in a can of baby formula as well. He'd forgotten to ask if Zoe was on formula or not, but he figured it was better safe than sorry. If she was sick, she might have dietary restrictions, but he'd hate for the baby to need it and not have it. The price of baby formula was highway robbery, anyway.

When he finished he carried the boxes one at a time to the front door of the church building, the one he'd escaped out of last night. When he walked back to his office, John Hall was already there waiting for him. Butch smiled for the first time all day when he saw the large man in the red flannel shirt with the burly salt and pepper beard.

"Hey John," Pastor Butch said, "Thanks for coming down so quickly. We've got a young sailor with a sick daughter and medical bills who is a month behind on his rent. I just put together some boxes of food for him. Do you think the deacons can pay his rent this month?"

"Yes, if the rent is modest. The benevolence fund is flush right now. The church has been gracious and generous in its giving. How much is his rent?"

"I don't know. Let me go check. Stay here."

Butch walked down to his office. Skye had already completed the benevolence form. "Just a couple of more minutes, Skye. Let me take that form from you."

He brought the document back to John. Skye's rent was only five hundred and fifty dollars. John said that wasn't a problem, and that he would swing by the apartment manager's office and pay it.

Butch brought John back to his office and introduced him to Skye.

"I recognize you," John said. "You sat in front of me Sunday at church."

"Yes, I think I did," Skye said, "over on the right side near the back."

Pastor Butch said, "Skye, can you bring your car by the front door, over at the front of the church? John and I will load the food up, and then John is going to swing by your apartment complex later this afternoon and catch you up on your rent."

Outside of the church's front door, John and Pastor Butch put the boxes of food in the trunk of Skye's Toyota Tercel. When they had finished, John asked Skye, "Do you know where the Albertsons is on this side of town?"

"Yes, it is not far from the Skookum Mart, right?"

"Exactly," John said. "Follow me over there, and we'll get you some milk, fresh food, bread, and some things we just can't keep here in the pantry."

Skye looked completely dumbfounded when John said this. "That would be more than I could ever hope for. Thank you guys so much."

"Don't thank us," John said. "Everyone, and I mean everyone, has times when things are tough. There is not a person I know who hasn't needed a hand-up at one time or another. Jesus understands that, which is why he told us to take care of each other."

"I'll pay you back when we get on our feet. I promise."

"No, you won't," Butch said. "That is not the way this works. We don't keep ledgers like that. Neither does God. All we ask of you, is that when you are in a position to help someone else out, do so. That is what Jesus has taught us to do."

Then he bowed his head, and the other two men followed suit.

Lord, I pray you heal Zoe of her infirmities, and help the doctors figure out exactly what is going on with her. Soon let there be a plan for getting her well. I pray that you comfort Skye and Marta during these tense, anxious days, and allow their family stability and peace as they transition to their new lives in Sydney. In Jesus' name. Amen.

Chapter Twenty-Five
Failure and Opportunity

"Looks like we're all here," Monica said to the other three women. Then she went through the invocation that solemnized the meeting of the Signet Four.

> The Signet Four—Leaders of the Servants of Judith—Heroines of the True Faith—We are gathered together in the name of Jesus Christ to discuss the holy work of removing impurity from the pure church, the sacred task of rooting out worldliness from the heavenly saints, and the just removal of false teachers and shepherds. What we decide here is binding upon the four of us, and all the Servants of Judith. May we each seek wisdom, courage, and strength to fulfill our mission, even if it means our very lives are forfeited in the endeavor. If any of us should fail to guard the integrity and secrecy of the group, may she be torn asunder and her soul burn forever separated from the love of God.

They each added their own amen to the creed.

"I gather this is about the debacle last night." Shawna did not hide her displeasure.

"What debacle?" Jeannie said.

Monica said, "Let me bring everyone up to speed and on the same page. I'm sure Shawna has heard some of the information from a different perspective. When I'm finished she can flesh out new data, and of course, I know Stephanie will have her own perspectives."

"So everyone knows what is going on except me?" The darkness hid Jeannie's scowl.

"Not by design. It's just the way it happened. Now, let me begin." Monica could not afford to lose Jeannie, or she would lose the group. "Last night Stephanie and I attempted to remove the false teacher we had targeted at our last meeting. I know that it was a quick turnaround, and that I didn't clear that with the other two of you, but as the leader I felt like it was the wise thing to do. We needed to act fast against this one because he was onto us. I also wanted to go along, to lend moral support to Stephanie because it was obvious, and understandable, that she was having a hard time with it because of the personal nature. I take full responsibility for rushing the project. It was my idea to just take two of us, but we should have taken a full compliment. If we'd had Michelle with us I'm certain that the whole thing would have succeeded."

"You didn't take Michelle?"

"No, Shawna, it was just Stephanie and I. Everything was going according to plan, but somehow the false teacher became aware of our presence in the building."

"He became aware because you turned off the light he'd turned on. That's what clued him in." Stephanie said.

Keep defending yourself, Stephanie. Please keep defending yourself, because that is exactly what I need you to do.

Monica said, "That may or may not have been exactly what happened. The light needed to go off for us to catch him by surprise. Somehow, though, he eluded us."

"How? How could he elude you? Stephanie, that is your church. You should have known that place inside and out, and certainly better than any of the other places we'd conducted removals before. I mean, what did he do, fly away?"

"Very funny, Jeannie," Stephanie said. "Of course I know that church very well. I even had my keys to get into the backdoor. The problem wasn't the layout; the problem was that once he was alerted to our presence, he was able to hide and then slip away."

"Whatever he was able to do," Monica said, steering the conversation, "he got out of the building and into his car. Our last ditch effort to get him resulted in me smashing a tire iron over his car windshield and against his door. Stephanie had him by the hand for a split second, but somehow he got away.

"We left him a nice message, though."

Shawna said, "The police department is really scrambling this morning. The lead detective has already interviewed the false teacher and done an analysis of the church building as well as the car. He didn't really find anything substantial, except for some paint chips on the ground. I advise you to get rid of that tire iron, Monica. Throw it in a lake or something.

"The false teacher was petrified this morning. Detective Wright's report used the words 'distracted' and 'distressed' more than once. It looks like the false teacher is sending his wife and kids away to keep them safe."

"He's not leaving?" Stephanie said.

"No. He is staying behind. He might be a false teacher, but he is no coward."

"I don't think he is a false teacher." Stephanie took the opening made by Shawna to press her point. "I told you that before. If he were, he'd be running away frightened right now. His bravery proves he is not evil. I think we've made a mistake. We need to back off of him and get back on track."

Monica said, "I sympathize with your feelings Stephanie, but we're not here to rehash old arguments."

"The blazes we're not!" Stephanie said. "That is exactly what we need to do. Don't you think it odd that the first time we don't succeed is the one time we weren't in unity about who to go after? I think that might very well be the hand of God telling us to back down."

"Or," Jeannie said, "It could be that you have pooped in the pool."

"What does that even mean?" Stephanie said.

"It means," Jeannie said, "that you didn't really believe in the mission, so you were the one who sabotaged it. This should have been a no brainer. You know the false teacher and his habits, you know the building, you are experienced. You should've been able to remove him all by yourself for crying out loud."

The meeting of the Signet Four could not have been going any better for Monica if she'd scripted it. All the pieces were falling into place. She'd had hoped Jeannie might be the one to push the point, but not as forcefully as this.

"You think I intentionally let Pastor Butch get away?"

"No. We don't think that at all." Now Shawna was getting in on the idea. "I suspect that you subconsciously just couldn't bring yourself to remove him. You thought you would be able to but in the heat of the moment, the darkness of the night, your heart betrayed your mind and like Lot's wife, you looked backward instead of forward. In that hesitation the false teacher got away."

"I can't believe you're saying this," Stephanie said. "I warned Monica this was a mistake to act so fast. How is it you are blaming me for this—this—this disaster." Stephanie raised her voice even louder and said, "It is her fault," pointing right at Monica.

"I freely admit," Monica said in a soft, contrite tone, "that I did push the issue too quickly. That was my mistake. I will submit to whatever punishment the other Signet Four require. None of us are above the rules."

"Monica, you didn't do anything wrong," Shawna said. "I think we all have a pretty clear idea of what happened. But we need to get back on task. There is more that the police department worked on today. Apparently the false teacher has formed a partnership with another pastor named Terence Harrison. He is at Ebenezer Church."

"I know that church," said Jeannie. "They partnered with our church last year for an MLK celebration thing in the park."

"Do you think that this Pastor Terence is a false teacher, too?" Monica said. Monica had already come to that conclusion when Shawna told her about Terence earlier in the afternoon.

"I don't know. But I do know this, Pastor Terence was with the false teacher the day they found Westgrave. In fact, the police records indicate that the first person the false teacher called was Terence Harrison."

"What?" Jeannie gasped. "Oh my. Logically that means, if the false teacher from Sydney Community, from Stephanie's church, was in league with the false teacher from TLC, and this Terence was with him when he found the other one, then he's a false teacher, too."

"No, it doesn't!" Stephanie was livid. "It absolutely does not mean that. It simply may mean that the two of them were genuinely concerned. Look at it from their perspective. They found someone murdered in a sanctuary. I know from our view we were simply removing him, but, you have to admit, it is pretty shocking."

"Oh Stephanie," Jeannie said. "Why do you persist in not seeing the evidence right before your face? It is becoming painfully clear that all three of these men, Westgrave, Gregory, and Harrison are all false teachers and were connected. You need to accept the truth."

Stephanie didn't respond.

Shawna was all in. "It looks like we need to act fast on both of them, especially after our botched attempt last night. What do you recommend, Monica?"

"As you ladies know, I have a certain penchant for irony and symbolism. Wouldn't it be great if we could somehow use this to our advantage? Every crisis is really just an opportunity. Let's make the most of this opportunity."

Chapter Twenty-Six
Wyoming's Sunrise

Wyoming Wallace drank coffee by his campfire. To Wyoming, the best coffee in the world was not found in a fancy coffee house, with frap that and mocha this. Coffee should be brewed over an open fire, with water drawn from the river, boiled, and then filtered through a slow drip coffee pot. His blue kettle with white speckles was the identical technology the cowboys on the open range used to make their coffee. And that is the way Wyoming Wallace liked it.

He had rolled out of his tent just before dawn and poked at the coals in the fire pit. A light snow had fallen Tuesday night, but he'd still managed to coax enough glowing ember from last night's roaring campfire to get the breakfast fire going again. Wyoming pulled on his Wolverine boots and coat. He also stuck his .45 revolver into his pants. Human beings were not the only predator out here. Then he walked down to the banks of the Wenatchee River. He splashed some of the cold water on his face. Although cold, it was refreshing. The water that gathered on his beard began to freeze almost immediately. That didn't bother Wyoming.

He scooped up water into his coffee kettle, then walked back to camp where he boiled it.

It takes longer to make this kind of coffee, but to Wyoming Wallace it was worth the trouble. The main reason it was worth the trouble was the atmosphere. Wyoming needed the pristine, clean, rugged outdoors to help him clear his thoughts. He couldn't change his past, no matter how hard he tried. Learning to live in the present was a mere cliché to him. How could he separate the past from the present? Everything he'd ever done was always in his mind. The past six months were supposed to be a respite, a time for him to heal and learn what he was becoming. That is what he'd told himself, anyway.

But it hadn't worked out that way.

It was enough for him now, to sit by the campfire in the early morning hours and enjoy his million dollar view. The river's undying, calming and soothing sound filled his ears. In the background was nature's symphony.

The vocals for the eternal aria were provided by various nearby birds singing, or the occasional call of an owl. Sporadically a wolf or coyote pitched in a chorus or two. The whole orchestra was given direction by the giant sun rising in the east, painting the sky and the snowy mountains with masterful strokes of the cosmic pigments orange, pink, blue, and amber.

The view made the coffee taste even better.

Wyoming sat in his folding chair, thinking that he soon would have to break camp. He didn't really know who owned this track of land anyway. Eventually, someone would show up and make him move. Besides that, winter was coming. This was the third morning in a row he'd woken up to snow. He knew enough of the weather in the Cascade Mountains to know that a major snowstorm could come through at any moment and dump several feet right on top of him.

Wyoming didn't fear the snow; it would simply be uncomfortable.

More than that, though, he could feel that it was almost time to go home. He'd left in a hurry; he told no one where he was going or what he was up to. Wyoming regretted that, but it had to be that way. No one could know what he'd been asked to do. No one. Not even his friend Pastor Butch.

What Wyoming was still trying to figure out was whether he wanted to go straight home, or maybe he'd spend some more time on the road. He had plenty of money. He didn't need much to get by. The thought occurred to him to travel to the high desert in Oregon. That might be a nice place to spend the winter. The thought occurred to him that he could go to Arizona. He had an army friend there. If he left today, Wyoming figured he could pull into Phoenix sometime early tomorrow morning.

Chorizo and eggs sounded good.

Wyoming had just about made up his mind. He would be a snowbird this year, spend the winter in Arizona, and then return to Sydney in the spring. He calculated in his head how many times he'd have to stop for gas. He would have supper in Salt Lake City. It would likely be a late supper, but who cares. IHOP is open twenty-four-seven, three-sixty-five.

That was when the wind began to blow.

From the east, from the direction of the rising sun, the wind rushed through a stand of evergreens. It came so hard that it cleaned the branches of their snow. The gusts flew over the river and pushed the water into whitecaps, as if it were a tempest on the sea. Wyoming saw the approaching gale and shook his head.

Here it goes again.

"I give up—I surrender even before you say anything."

He expected an answer, but the wind kept coming. It stirred up the bank, picking up snow, autumnal leaves and small pebbles as it came. The wind came right at him. Wyoming dropped his tin coffee cup and clutched the arm of his chair. He closed his eyes as he braced for the impact.

The blow never came.

The wind turned left and then spun around his campsite—encircling his black Jeep, the fire, his tent, the makeshift table he'd built out of two old stumps and a piece of aluminum siding he found by the highway. When Wyoming opened his eyes there was a wall of snow all around him, spinning. He was at the center of the wintry cyclone.

The campsite was undisturbed, the calm at the eye of the storm.

"What?" Wyoming stood up and yelled above the wind's noise, hands lifted heavenward.

There was nothing.

"What, come on, I'm listening. I know better than to fight you. This is the third time now, I've learned my lesson."

Still nothing. Only the swirling wall of snow and the furious sound of calamity.

He was about to sit back down in his chair. That was when the wind stopped, the snow wall fell to the ground, like the electrical plug making the whole thing run had been pulled out of the wall socket. Wyoming raised his arms in disbelief.

"Where is the message? Are you just trying to scare me these days, is that it?"

"Take," a voice said. The voice was not internal—it was not a thought he heard, it was an audible voice, as someone speaking directly to him. The voice was not a shout, nor was it a whisper. It didn't have a creepy, other worldly sound to it. It was simply a voice. "Take," the voice said again. "Take and read."

Read what?

Even before that thought fully formed in his mind, he saw it. There where the part of the snow tornado that had been between him and the river, a piece of paper flapped on the ground. It was half buried in snow. Wyoming could feel no breeze, yet the paper flapped as if it were on the beach and partially covered in hot sand.

He pulled the paper out of the snow.

He took it and he read it.

It was the Seattle Times, the front page of the B section. Wyoming mouthed the headline, "Local pastor murdered in sanctuary." Beneath the byline was a photograph of Michael Westgrave shaking hands with the governor from an archived file. Then there was a photograph of his body being carried out toward an ambulance. Beneath the fold Wyoming saw what he was supposed to see. It was a photograph of Butch Gregory. Underneath the picture of Butch was written, "Westgrave's body was found Wednesday morning by Pastor Butch Gregory of Sydney Community Church."

Wyoming began to read the article, but was unable to finish because the rest of it was on B-5, but only that one page of the section had flown in with the wind from the nostrils of God. All Wyoming could really learn from what he had was that Butch had found the body of another pastor, one he'd never heard of, and that it was a big deal.

"What have you gotten yourself into now, Reverend?"

"Go!" the voice said.

"Yes, sir." It was the only reply Wyoming could think of that made sense.

Twenty minutes later his campsite was completely packed. It would take him at least an hour to get out of the gorge he was in, even in his reliable Jeep. He expected he would be in Sydney by lunchtime.

Wyoming reached into his glove box and pulled out a photograph of Amber Smith. It had been a while since he'd looked at it. He kept the old five by seven picture with him always. Her parents had given it to him at Amber's funeral. Of all he owned, that photograph was one of his greatest treasures.

He stuck it on his steering wheel. Then he pulled a small case that looked like a fisherman's tackle box from behind his seat. He unfastened the box, and took a long, dark, fat cigar out of it.

"I wish you were here to go with me. You understood the Reverend better than me."

He grabbed the guillotine cutter from the middle console. He snipped off the end of the stogie.

"What do you think Butch has done? Do you think someone is trying to kill him? Did he kill someone? That seems unlikely," Wyoming's voice slowed down to a near crawl as he talked to the photograph. "The Reverend couldn't hurt anyone. No, I think he's in trouble."

He dug his trusty silver Zippo from his jeans' pocket and lit the cigar. He took a big draw.

He held the picture up to his face. "How about this time we make sure no one gets killed?

Wyoming waited to see if there was response.

There was none.

He didn't like that kind of silence.

Chapter Twenty-Seven
Like Before, Except Different

Pastor Butch Gregory sat behind his desk and tried to concentrate. His favorite mug filled with coffee, Bible opened, computer running, door closed. He was ready to study and write. Everything was there except his mind.

His mind was an untamed beast roaming the countryside of his memories and imagination. He thought about Lucy, Sarah, and Paul and the phone call he had with them last night. They arrived safely on the Washington coast, where Lucy's parents kept their summer home. His mind drifted to the previous July when they'd visited his in-laws. They flew kites all day, and when they grew tired of flying them he tied all four of their kites to the car bumper. They swam in the shallow surf, walked into town, and ate so much ice cream that Paul got sick. It was a great summer vacation. Horseback riding. Mopeds. Bicycles. Seafood. Sandcastles. Saltwater taffy. Yahtzee. Cards. Dominos. Movies. Sunburns and aloe.

He longed to be with them now, there at the beach, worrying about how to stay warm in the cold wind. But he wasn't. He was in Sydney, where someone from his own church was trying to kill him.

Someone he trusted.

Someone he thought trusted him.

Someone he had prayed with and worshiped with.

Why? What had he done? In no way did he defend the murder of the other three pastors, but their death at least made sense in the twisted, sick logic these women were using. How did he fit in? Killing him was illogical, unless it was because they knew he and Terence were onto them? But even that doesn't fit the super spiritual motive. Or that they pretend to have. Perhaps the group is really just a bunch of killers hiding behind spiritual pretext.

Or maybe the leader is.

Butch was dragged out of those thoughts when he heard the door to his office open.

Butch couldn't believe his eyes. Standing before him was Wyoming Wallace. Although Butch was happy to see him, and, a great sense of relief swept over him, the first words out of his mouth must have sounded accusatory. "Did Lucy call you?"

"Why would Lucy call me?"

"Well, because—because she thought I should, and I told her that I wanted to leave you alone and respect your privacy."

"Are you sure," Wyoming's words slowed to the pace of a banana slug after a large meal, "that she didn't want you to call me because she knew you were in trouble?"

"You didn't answer my question. Did she call you?"

"No, Reverend, she didn't call me. I promise on a stack of Bibles. I guess you could say that I got a different kind of call."

"What kind of call?"

"Like before, except different. You know what I mean."

Butch knew exactly what he meant. After Amber died rescuing Tamara, Wyoming finally told Butch all his secrets. He told him about the awful shooting in Iraq, and how he'd carried that guilt with him every day since. He told him about why he had shut God out of his life, and he told him why he'd refused to help when he and Amber had asked for it.

The last secret Wyoming told Butch was about the unusual event that led him to change his mind. He said that God visited him in some kind of tornado, but the tornado was in his trailer house. In the midst of the whirlwind the Lord had told him to help, and the only other choice was certain death.

Butch assumed the Lord had spoken to Wyoming in the same kind of way as before.

Except different.

Whatever that meant.

"So, Reverend," Wyoming said, "What kind of trouble have you gotten yourself into? It looks pretty serious."

"How much do you know?"

"Only what is on this uninformative scrap of a newspaper article." He pulled the newspaper section out of his coat pocket and handed it to Butch. Butch recognized it and laid it on top of his desk.

"Well, then you don't know that much. Let me start at the top. Before I do, would you like some coffee or something?"

"I'm good."

"By the way, how did you get past Mildred? She's usually quite the bulldog about keeping people from coming down the hallway uninvited."

"You mean the old woman at the desk?" Wyoming grinned his patented devilish grin, lifted his Seattle Mariners ball cap off his head, ran a hand through his curly hair and said, "Well, she never saw me."

Butch took off his reading glasses and laid them on his Bible. "How? No wait, I don't want to know." Then he told Wyoming everything that had happened. He began with the odd conversation he had with Michael Westgrave the night he was killed. Then he told every detail, including the pilfered police report Terence got, the gruesome murder of Rick Peters out at Ferry View Methodist, and finally the attempt on his life two nights earlier.

"Sounds like quite a racket you've uncovered. Was life too boring for you? Did you miss the action of crime syndicates and pistol-toting bad guys? I mean, good grief, you don't do anything halfway do you? Your life is either as boring as watching paint dry or its dig your own grave life and death situations. No in between, huh?"

"I wonder Wyoming, I wonder. Trust me when I say I didn't want any of this."

"Oh I believe you, but," he smiled at him again, "down deep inside there is obviously some part of you that does want this or you wouldn't go sticking your nose where it doesn't belong."

"But God is the one who—"

"No, this ain't just God, Reverend. Have you ever considered that maybe God talks to all kinds of people in different ways? They just don't listen because they don't want to? You, however, kind of want to, so you listen and answer."

"Wyoming, did you spend the last six months reading psychology or something?"

"Not exactly. But I think I'm right about some of it."

"Where were you, anyway?"

"I had some things that needed doing in Texas. I don't really want to talk about it right now. Maybe later."

"Later, then." Butch knew from experience with Wyoming that it was not a good idea to press him when he didn't want to talk. He would open up when he was ready. "I won't ask again, but I will say that you look wretched and smell worse. Have you been living in that old ratty Jeep of yours? I see that you've let your Vandyke grow into a full beard. You need a haircut. Maybe you should go home and get cleaned up. Lucy and the kids are out of town; I sent them away where it was safe. You can come by tonight. I'll introduce you to Terence, and maybe order a pizza. Then we can talk about what we need to do next."

"That sounds like a good idea. A hot bath, clean clothes, and a shave would feel good."

Wyoming stood up to leave. Before he could get far the intercom on Butch's book-covered desk blinked and buzzed.

"Yes, Mildred?"

"Someone is here to see you, Pastor Butch."

"Who is it?"

"It is Stephanie Colson. She says it's urgent that she speak to you right now."

Butch's gut told him, in the same way it always did, that this was something important. The Lord spoke to him through his bowels, and right now it was unmistakable that he needed to talk to Stephanie, regardless of what he and Wyoming had planned.

"Send her back."

"Do you want me to go?" Wyoming asked.

"No. I feel like whatever she has to say is intended for you to hear, too. The timing that you both show up today is not a coincidence. I feel we are about to learn something that may change this whole situation."

"Looks like I showed up at just the right time, then."

"Looks that way."

"As usual, I might add."

Mildred opened up the door and showed Stephanie in. Mildred did a double-take when she saw Wyoming in Butch's study.

"How did you get in here, you ragamuffin?" Mildred raised her hand as if to take a swipe at an a pesky insect.

"Mildred, be nice. Wyoming just dropped by. He came straight in. Apparently you didn't see him."

Mildred grunted, then shut the door.

"Stephanie, what a pleasant surprise. Please have a seat."

"Thank you, Pastor Butch," Stephanie said, but her eyes were on Wyoming Wallace. Butch noticed it. "This is my friend, my very dear friend. His name is Wyoming. He just arrived about a half hour ago. Like you dropping by, his arrival was rather unexpected. We were catching up as you arrived,"

Butch swallowed hard but tried to look pastoral, "when Mildred told me you were here," Butch brought is hands and placed them palm down on the top of his desk, "for some reason I felt like the Lord wanted Wyoming to hear whatever it was you have to say. I trust him like a brother."

There was a moment's pause. Stephanie sat on the edge of her chair; she looked she might flee the room at any second.

Butch turned on his pastor voice—the one Lucy hated, but he'd worked on for years, to the point where he had mastered it with complete perfection. "Now Stephanie, you came here for a reason," he brought his hands together, still on top of the desk, "go ahead and tell me what is on your mind."

Stephanie still had not said anything. She stared at him, and then she glanced at Wyoming. Doubt about the betrayal she was about to commit swirled through her. It clouded her judgment. She was confused about what was right and wrong. She didn't know what to do, but running felt like the right thing so she stood up and walked to the door.

"Stephanie, please sit back down." Butch remained calm. He knew she wasn't going to leave, and he was already beginning to feel like he knew what she wanted to say. He took a gamble and said, "I know why you are here."

"Do you really?" she said. "Do you really know why I came? Because if you did, you'd probably have run away with your wife."

The mention of his wife made him flinch.

"I think, I hope, my wife is safe. I think I am doing what I must. The question for you, Stephanie, is are you going to tell me what you need to tell me. You know that this can't keep going on. Sooner or later everything done in darkness comes out into the light. You know that, I know you do."

Butch's choice of metaphor punctured her imagination and took her back to the dark meeting from the night before.

"Okay," she said as she sat back down. "But, Pastor Butch, this is extremely difficult." Tears filled her large, blue eyes. "I don't know what to do. Any step I take, in any direction, feels like an unfaithfulness, like I've done something wrong. I, I . . ." She couldn't finish the sentence without breaking down completely.

"It's okay, Stephanie. Look at me. Look at my face. I am not going to hurt you. I want good things in your life, not bad. Do you believe that? Do you believe that I want what is best for you? Have I ever lied to you?"

"No, you haven't." Stephanie gathered strength from that statement. The confession of simple truths, that Pastor Butch Gregory had never lied to her and that he wanted good things for her in her life, helped her see at least the way forward.

She said, "The people who tried to kill you are not going to stop. They believe you are a false teacher, like the others, and that you must die. I tried to tell them, but they wouldn't listen to me."

"How do you know this?"

Stephanie said, "Never mind that. What matters now is that you know they are after you and your friend."

"How do they know about me?" Wyoming said, raising his arms in protest. "What did I do?"

"Not you. They are after Pastor Butch's other friend, Pastor Terence Harrison. In fact, right now they are probably getting him. It is their impatience that will do them in. I tried to stop them, but they refuse to listen to me."

"What do you mean they are after Terence? Right now, in broad open daylight?"

"Probably. She has the day off, and I think she will act."

"Who has the day off? What are their plans?" Wyoming had heard enough circular talk. He was ready to do something.

"I don't know specifics," Stephanie said. "They kept me out of the loop. But I know that they are aware of your partnership with him. I also know that they are arrogant and brazen, which leads to carelessness." Her eyes swelled with giant tears again. "I'm actually thankful that we were careless," her chest began to heave; her face shook. "If we'd been more careful, I probably would have killed you Monday night. I'm so sorry, Pastor Butch. I didn't want to. I'm so sorry." The crying turned to wailing.

"So it was you. I knew it was someone who was familiar with the church building. I never dreamed it was one of the leaders of our preschool ministry."

"Where is your friend Terence right now?" Wyoming stood up.

"He is probably studying or working on a sermon at his office, the same thing that I was doing when the two of you arrived. At least, that is my guess, anyway."

"How far away is that?"

"Three minutes." Butch looked at his watch. It was almost noon. "Maybe four."

"Let's go."

"Should we call him?"

"Yes," Wyoming said, then he thought better of it. "No. Don't. If he is not in trouble, then calling is no use. If he is in trouble, then calling could only alert the bad guys to our presence. In a rescue situation, stealth is vital."

Just hearing Wyoming say things like that, like he knew what he was talking about, which he clearly did, made Butch feel so much better. He realized he'd made a mistake by not calling his friend earlier. Maybe if he'd done so, Rick Peters would still be alive. Maybe his wife and children wouldn't have had to leave. Why had he been so stubborn? Why had he been so arrogant? Only a fool doesn't recognize when he or she needs help.

He made a mental note to confess his sin in this regard later.

"Should we call the police?" Butch said to Wyoming.

"Do I ever recommend calling the police?"

"That would be no. By the way, I'm glad you're here. I missed you."

Five minutes later Butch, Wyoming, and Stephanie were standing in front of Ebenezer Church.

"Terence is here." Butch pointed. "His car is here."

"Well, that's good news, I guess." Wyoming said. He had complained the whole way over that it was probably a trap, and that Stephanie was leading them into it. But Wyoming was always suspicious.

"I swear to you it is not a trap," she'd told him. "If it were a trap, do you think I would have said anything in front of Wyoming? Everyone at Sydney Community knows who you are and what you've done. If this were a trap, I would never have spilled my guts in front of you."

That line of logic seemed to win the moment in the Ford Fusion that was serving as Butch's rental car.

Wyoming planned their course of action the whole way toward Ebenezer.

Now that they were there, Wyoming took the lead. He grabbed the other two by the arm. "Look, it still smells like a trap to me. So, why don't the two of you go on in there, go on into the building and act natural." His words slowed to a painstaking crawl. "Act like everything is fine," he squinted as the sun popped out from behind a cloud. "Everything is fine and you just want to see your friend. When you get a chance to see him," he paused, "well, then the three of you just come back here to the car and we'll catch him up and figure out what to do next." He looked around the property. "I'm going to sneak down the backside of the building and try to listen," he sniffed the air, "or look for clues."

Butch nodded. "Sounds like a good plan to me."

"It is not a trap," Stephanie said. "I promise you."

"If it is not a trap, then that is fine and we're just being cautious, because you never know when things might get," Wyoming smiled big, "a little dangerous."

"It's not a trap." Stephanie repeated, smiling back.

"Stephanie is married, Wyoming, so knock it off."

"What?" Wyoming said.

He'd been around Wyoming enough to know when he was flirting, and he was definitely flirting with Stephanie, which would have been weird for anyone else. Wyoming Wallace was one of those men who, the odder and more dangerous it was, the more excited he was. Stephanie was certainly proving to be odd and dangerous.

Butch and Stephanie walked down the sidewalk toward the front door. Butch had already been working on saying what Wyoming told him to when they got inside. He worked at remembering the secretary's name. Shannon? No, that's not it. Sheerah? No, definitely not it. Samantha? No.

It finally hit him just as he opened up the door. Shondra. Her name was Shondra.

Shondra was not there.

"Good. She must be at lunch or in the bathroom or something." Butch thought this was a good development. "Follow me. Terence's office is this way."

Stephanie walked behind Butch as the two crept down the hallway. Butch whispered, "Let's not be too sneaky. I don't want to scare him."

Butch knocked on the door of Terence's inner sanctum. There was no reply. Butch put his ear up to the door. He could hear the radio playing jazz. He turned the knob then he and Stephanie walked in.

Chapter Twenty-Eight
We Know Everything

Sitting behind Terence's desk was Shondra.

"Oh, Shondra. I didn't expect to see you there." He turned to Stephanie and said, "This is Shondra, she is the church secretary here at Ebenezer." He turned his attention back to Shondra, "Where is Terence?"

Shondra grinned. "I didn't really believe her when she said you'd come, but here you are. I guess that will teach me to doubt Monica again. She is always right."

"Monica? Who is Monica?" Butch was confused.

Shondra ignored Butch's questions. "She also said that you would be with him. She said that you were a snitch, a traitor. A Jezebel. Looks like she was right."

Stephanie exhaled. "I didn't see this coming."

"Surprise." Shondra gloated.

Stephanie turned to Butch, "Shondra must be a Judy. Probably on the Discovery Team, but I'm not sure. I don't know all of them—Monica said it was better that way."

"So," Butch gulped. "It is indeed a trap."

"Yep," was all Stephanie could say.

"Trap is a good word. Like a pig led to slaughter, trapped by its own greed at the feed trough." Shondra said these words and at the same time pointed a pistol at the two of them. Butch didn't know much about firearms, but he could see that the barrel on the pistol was longer than usual. He guessed that it was some kind of noise suppression device.

"Come on Shondra, this is ridiculous. Where is Terence?" Butch was having a hard time processing what was happening.

"Terence is in a very safe place. You'll be with him soon."

"Have you killed him?"

"Not yet. Monica has something special planned for the two of you."

"Oh joy," Butch said. "But you," Shondra said pointing the gun at Stephanie, "I'm supposed to give you a personalized message. I'm supposed to tell you that you have violated your covenant, and now you must pay the price for disobedience." Shondra squeezed the trigger. The bullet ripped through Stephanie. She fell backwards, clutching herself. Butch caught her before she hit the floor.

There wasn't enough space in the room to lay her down flat, so he sat her down and propped her up against a bookcase.

"Leave her to die. She deserves a slow, reflective death. It gives her time to repent before she meets the Lord."

"You are a sick woman," Butch said as he ignored her directions. He moved his head to look around the room for something to use to stop the bleeding.

On the ground beside Stephanie was a white towel. It was the coffee stained white towel Butch threw across the room the previous week when Terence showed him the autopsy report. The wound was above her right breast, closer to the shoulder. Butch knew the bullet had gone through her body, because blood came out of her back onto his hands as he lowered her down.

Oh Lord, I pray the bullet missed her lung. Amen.

"I'm sorry," he told Stephanie, then he pulled the purple and gold UW hoodie she wore over her head. She wore a black tank top underneath it, and Butch pushed the dirty white towel against the bullet's entry wound under the strap. His hands moved faster than they ever had. He snapped the hoodie wide open, tied it across her shoulder and back, wadding the fat part of it over the exit wound. He had finished tying the arms together when Shondra put the gun at the back of his head.

"I'm not supposed to kill you," she said. "But I will if I have to. Stop what you're doing and stand up."

He stood up, lifting his hands up as he did. "I'm sorry," he said to Stephanie.

"No, I'm the one who is sorry. I can't believe what I've done." Butch thought he saw more tears in her eyes; but it wasn't from the pain of the gunshot wound. It was from regret.

"That's enough," a new voice said from the doorway.

"Monica," Shondra said. "I've done as you ordered."

"You did well, good and faithful servant. You've made The Judys proud. Now, I want you to stay here with the traitor. Stay with her till she dies, which should be soon. Take those makeshift bandages off; she'll bleed out in about twenty minutes. It might be quicker than that if you got lucky and hit something important in there. If you shut the door and keep quiet, you should be fine. However, if anyone comes in here, even by mistake, kill them. We can't take any chances."

"Yes Monica. What should I do if the police show up?"

"That probably will not be a problem, but in the outside chance it does, you should quickly put a bullet in Stephanie's head to finish her off, then shoot yourself in the arm or leg. Then you tell the police that they shot you when you came in on them, but you didn't get a good look because they were wearing ski masks. Got it? Just make sure you toss the gun aside so they will not know it is yours."

"Now you," Monica said to Butch, "come with me." She pulled out her own single round Lady Derringer, complete with a pink grip and a pink tipped barrel. "I have plans for you and your friend."

"What have you done to Terence?"

"Don't worry about your little false teacher friend. He is waiting for you at your house."

"My house?"

"Yeah, with your wife and kids gone, no one was using it anyway. Your wife really does have good taste. I adore her decorative motif; she has a real gift for it. My favorite is the way she blended the colors of the area rugs with the paint on the walls. Very nice. Very chic.

"Now come on, enough small talk." Monica waved the pistol at him like a bad actor in a gangster movie. "I'm getting claustrophobic in this miserable, cramped room." Monica shoved the gun right in Butch's gut. "Walk slowly toward me as I walk backwards out of the door. Any quick or sudden move and you will find yourself in the same predicament as our pretty little traitor over there."

Butch did as he was told. Monica backed into the hallway.

"Shondra, lock the door behind us." Monica never took her eyes off Butch. With her left hand she crossed herself.

In the hallway, she spun Butch around. "Shut the door." He did, then she pushed him toward the back of the building. "Now, walk slowly to the back door. Do not go out of the door until I tell you."

"I'm surprised you know about Terence's back door."

"We know everything."

Not everything. Not even close.

181

Chapter Twenty-Nine
What They Didn't Know

Wyoming Wallace saw Butch leave the building. He also saw the woman in the fancy business suit right behind him.

He almost missed them because he had taken cover behind a giant shrub in need of pruning beside the exterior wall of the main sanctuary. It gave him a clear view of the whole administrative building side, particularly the front door. His eyes had been so focused on the front that he almost missed the two walk out the back.

It didn't look good. Wyoming couldn't see a weapon, but the woman was so close to Butch that Wyoming assumed there was a pistol or knife shoved into his back. Heck, as exotic as these people were in their execution practices it could have been a syringe filled with bubonic plague.

Wyoming pulled his pistol out from the shoulder holster underneath his coat. He aimed it at the woman's head. They were not walking fast, so targeting wasn't a problem. Distance, however, was. Wyoming was at least forty yards away, and they were moving diagonally away from his position. His pistol, though powerful at close range, could not be trusted at such a distance.

He put his gun away.

Where was Stephanie?

Her absence led him to believe that either she was in trouble inside the building, or he'd been right after all. She'd led them into a trap.

Forget her. He was told by God to take care of the Reverend, and that was what he intended to do. Stephanie wasn't his problem, even if she was cute. Wyoming used the concealment provided by the overgrown bushes along the church wall to scoot toward the sidewalk that came out of the backdoor. He wanted to get as close as possible to the woman holding the gun, or knife, or whatever at Butch's back so he could tackle her from behind. It was risky, but he believed the woman would never get a shot off before he could sweep her arm toward the ground.

He made it to the sidewalk by the backdoor where Butch and the smarty pantsuit woman had come out. When he did, he heard something. Wyoming didn't hear it with his ears; he heard it with his spirit. It was a beckoning to go inside the building. He'd already decided to save Butch. Now, in a moment that required action, he was immobilized by his inner dialogue.

He couldn't just stand there; he had to do something.

Angry with his decision, he turned his back on Butch and moved toward the door and opened it. He reached into his jacket and again pulled out his .45 revolver. The hallway in front of him was short, and then it turned to the left. Wyoming crouched down low as he neared the turn. He was about to perform a duck and roll into the hallway and come up ready to shoot. Then he remembered that in his coat pocket he still had a tiny mirror from his camping trip. He'd used it to groom a bit down by the river, before the weather got too frigid to do even that.

He used the mirror to peek around the turn. No one was there.

Wyoming made the turn. He was thankful that his boots were soft leather soled instead of hard, because the tile on the floor would have given him away otherwise. He could see down to the end of the hall where it came out in what looked like a reception area. He came to the first door in the hallway, and it was closed. It looked like a janitor's closet, so Wyoming almost skipped over it. However, he noticed the doorknob had something on it.

It was red.

Wyoming's eyes got wide when he realized it was blood. He took a deep breath, pulled the hammer back on his pistol, and he burst into the room.

He expected mops and brooms, but his eyes were filled with books and papers. It was quite the shock. He didn't have time to figure out what was going on, because someone shot at him. He turned to see a woman point a pistol at him again, ready to pull the trigger. Wyoming ducked, but there was no space at all in the room to maneuver. He was down beside a metal desk while his enemy was on the other side of the desk. He glanced to his right. That was when he realized Stephanie was beside him, bleeding.

Another shot rang out in his direction, but it hit the desk between them and ricocheted off, hitting the spine of Strong's Exhaustive Concordance.

"Did I kill you, yet?" a female voice said.

"Not yet. And not today." He expected her to stand up and shoot him. When she did, he would shoot her first. But so far she hadn't stood. She was still behind the desk. She must have seen his gun when burst through the door.

Wyoming was mad. He had started the day looking at the most beautiful scenery in the world in the great expanse of the wilderness. Now, he was being shot at by a crazy woman in a tiny room filled with books while another woman bled to death right beside him. He had to do something or this lunatic would kill them both.

An idea came to him.

He looked underneath the desk. He saw white shoes at the bottom of bare ebony legs. For a millisecond he thought about shooting one of her feet. But that was not his plan. Wyoming put his pistol down on the floor and grasped the bottom of the desk with both hands. Then, with all the strength he had, he lifted the desk up. In one motion he overturned the desk on top of the woman. Books, paper, pencils and pens flew everywhere. Wyoming stepped beside the desk to see his attacker. She was a well-dressed woman in her 30s. She squirmed to get out from underneath the weight of the metal desk. The pistol had been knocked from her hand. Her eyes were wide with panic.

He retrieved his pistol and pointed it at her head. He wanted to kill her, but he knew it was wrong. He spotted the oversized Philadelphia Eagles coffee mug lying on the floor. He smashed the cup over the woman's head and rendered her unconscious. Then, with swift, brutal efficiency he broke her leg.

Wyoming turned his attention to Stephanie. "What happened?"

Through the immense pain, she laughed a little. "It was a trap."

"I told you."

She smiled. "They took Pastor Butch," she coughed right after she said it.

"Do you know where they took him?"

"They took him to his house. I think Butch's friend is there too. Monica has something special planned." Stephanie screamed in agony as she tried to sit up.

"Who is Monica?"

"Monica is the woman who runs everything. They all answer to her." Stephanie passed out.

Dangit. He knew he needed to call an ambulance, but he also needed to get to Butch's house. He couldn't be more than five minutes behind them, but that might be all the time it takes. That woman over there with a desk on her chest was going to wake up, and if she woke up before the ambulance got here, she might finish off Stephanie.

What to do?

Wyoming decided to move forward with it. He threw Stephanie over his shoulder and carried her out to the rental car. The Reverend had left the keys in it, just in case something went wrong. He laid her down in the backseat, trying to be as gentle as possible. She woke up a bit as he jostled her. "What's happening?"

"We're trying to get you help."

Wyoming called nine-one-one on his cell phone.

"What's your emergency?" the woman in the phone asked.

"I have two emergencies," he said as he drove away from Ebenezer Church. Send an ambulance and the police to 87 Trinity Drive."

"Okay sir, what are the emergencies? I can't send the units until you tell me why?"

"I have a gunshot victim in transit to that location. Also, be advised that I'm pretty sure someone else is about to get killed unless you get the police there in a hurry."

"Did you say gunshot?"

"Yes, gunshot. Make sure the police know that. It is a dangerous scene."

"Do you have the contact name the police should look for?"

"Butch Gregory. Pastor Butch Gregory. Now I haven't got any more time for this. Send them out to 87 Trinity Drive."

Wyoming ended the call. He was driving fast, blowing through stop signs and swerving around corners. Ebenezer Church was not very far away from Butch's home; so by the time he ended the call with nine-one-one, he was already there.

He left the car door open so that the paramedics would be drawn to it. He wanted them to find Stephanie in the backseat.

Wyoming knew the layout of Butch's house. He decided that the back-door was the best option. If there were well-armed femme fatales inside of the house, they would blast him to pieces before he got through the front door.

His gun at the ready, he walked around the back of the home, and took notice that there were no cars parked in the driveway or on the street. He slipped through the gate to the backyard, then walked up on the deck. He hoped the backdoor was unlocked.

He turned the knob. The door cracked open.

As soon as he opened the door he heard voices. Male voices.

Chapter Thirty
Lessons From The Internet

Terence's eyes were shut. Not squeezed shut as in fear, but closed as in repose.

Butch prayed.

> Dear Lord, it looks like this is the end. I have tried to live my life to serve you, be a good husband and father, and serve the church the way you asked me to. I haven't always been perfect, but I tried. I commend myself to you; I trust you for eternity. Receive me now as your child.

Butch paused in his prayer and Terence took over.

> Yes, Lord. Everything my friend said I agree with. I do ask that you somehow let my wife know that I love her very much and that I regret not being there for her in the years to come. I pray that you would let my work be blessed by your Spirit long after I'm gone. Let it endure. Oh, and Lord, please don't let them split up my library— give them the good sense to give the whole thing away to one person and so keep it intact. In Jesus Name. Amen.

"Really." Butch turned his head as best he could toward his friend. "We are about to die, and what happens to your books is on your mind. Really? That's just twisted."

"Hey—I've spent my entire life collecting all those books—theology, history, philosophy, literature, ethics—I don't want them to just be put on the internet and sold piecemeal. I wish I'd told someone how I felt about that, but I never got around to it so now it came into my mind. It makes sense to me."

"You're the only one it makes sense to. I can think about a thousand other things that matter more to me than books." Butch laughed at his ridiculous friend, even though the two of them were in the direst of straits. "Before that thing goes off, I'd like to say, although we've only reconnected the last couple of years, it has been a real privilege and joy to be your friend. It is an honor to leave this world with you. Aside from Lucy, I can't think of anyone else I'd rather die with."

"That's the sickest thing anyone has ever told me. You're glad that if you have to die that I do, too?" Now Terence was laughing.

"That's not how I meant it, but I guess you could take it that way."

"I just wish we'd had a chance to catch that woman and put her out of commission. I am sure she will go after someone else before—"

"Shhhh" Pastor Butch said.

"Don't shush me. If we're about to die I think I have a right to say whatever I wa—"

"Shhhh," Pastor Butch said again. "Do you hear that?"

They both extended their neck, as if to hear better. Butch took a gamble and shouted out, "Help! Anyone who might be there, help!"

"Is that you, Reverend," came Wyoming Wallace's distinct voice.

"Yeah, we're in the living room. Hurry."

"You sure no one else is with you?"

"We are alone. But if you don't hurry, we will be in pieces and parts."

Wyoming sprinted through the back area of the house and into the living room. He saw the two pastors sitting in two of Butch's dining room chairs, back to back. Their hands and feet were tied with rope, but they were also duct taped into the chairs and to each other. It was a very snug captivity.

"I can't believe you boys are still alive," Wyoming said. "In fact, given what these women have done, I thought for sure your pieces and parts would be all over the house forming some kind of weird pentagram, maybe writing out six-six-six in Latin or something." He holstered his gun.

"Yeah, well, before you get too comfortable you might want to look at that," Terence said, pointing his head underneath his chair.

"What is it?"

"Death." Butch said. "I'm not quite sure how it works, but she said it was a bomb she built herself. That evil woman took such delight telling us all the gears and gizmos she put in it. She said there was broken glass, nails, tacks, and even a few old kitchen knives she bought at Goodwill."

Wyoming knelt down to get a good look. "Yep," he said. "It is some kind of pressure cooker bomb. It works much like the I. E. D.'s we used to run up against in Iraq. They're quite simple to make."

"That's what she said," Terence said. "She said that it was amazing what you can learn on the internet."

Butch snorted a laugh, "That was when you told her she needed to get off the internet and read a book or something. Then she hit you with her pink pistol."

"I have a way with people."

"Hey Wyoming, how long do you think we have? She seemed to indicate we didn't have long at all. In fact, I'm surprised it hasn't gone off yet."

"Well, it looks like she has it set with a digital watch, but I can't see the watch. She has it attached to the device, backwards, I suppose so you can't see the countdown. Theoretically, we could just turn the watch off and that would stop it." Wyoming lifted his ball cap off his head, then he stroked his beard. "The problem," the words crawled out of his mouth, "is she might have rigged it to blow if anyone messed with it."

That was when they heard the sirens. Seconds later they saw the flashing lights.

"I don't think we can take a chance on diffusing this thing," Wyoming said.

He opened the front door. "Stay clear—there is a bomb in here," he yelled to the emergency team that arrived. He then pulled out his pocket knife and began cutting the tape off the two men. Then he worked through the ropes. While Wyoming cut, Butch and Terence pulled at the tape and the rope to free themselves. They were moving fast, too fast for Wyoming. He raised his voice and said, "Listen, hurry, but be careful. She put that thing right under you for a reason. If you kick it, it might go off. So please be careful. If not for your sake, then mine."

They did. The thought crossed Butch's mind of how horrible it would be to have the bomb blow up just as it looked like they might survive.

The last bit of tape was off, and all three ran for the front door; but Butch fell and knocked over Wyoming. Terence stopped, and bent over to pick them up. As he did, they all three heard a click inside the bomb.

With renewed fervor they made for the door. As they cleared it, Wyoming slammed it closed. The bomb exploded as they stepped off the front porch. The blast hurled them off the steps and threw them into the front yard. Wyoming landed out near the sidewalk. Butch slammed hard against the old apple tree in the front yard. Terence flew through the rose bushes, rolling out into the street beside a police squad car.

The blast of the pressure cooker bomb was tremendous. Investigators would later determine that shutting the front door probably saved their lives, and possibly the life of two police officers standing in the front yard. All the windows in the home blew out. The walls buckled where they met the roof, and part of the roof was ripped open. All of the furniture in the living room and dining room was destroyed. The kitchen, likewise, was a total loss.

The bomb cratered the floor and blew out into the basement. The explosion ripped open the wall to the garage and tore into the upstairs bedrooms.

Pastor Butch Gregory laid on the ground with his hands over his ears. They rang with intense pain from the sound of the explosion. It hurt so much that he couldn't believe he wasn't dead; he didn't believe he'd ever hear again. His vision was blurry, but he could see, and his eyes told him his home was destroyed.

He tried to stand up, but wobbled when he did. His arm hurt, as did his chest. He looked down at himself, pulled open his coat and lifted his shirt. His chest was scraped and bloody. He felt something running down his head. It was blood. He was dizzy, like he might be sick. He bent over and vomited on his front lawn beside what was left of his favorite rocking chair that had blown out of the window.

After retching, he scanned the area. His vision was still blurry, but he saw police, firefighters, and paramedics; Wyoming Wallace stood beside a policeman. When Wyoming saw Butch he and the policeman both walked over to him.

"Where is Terence?" Butch called out, raising his hand in their direction. Then he collapsed back to the ground, unconscious.

Chapter Thirty-One
Interrogation

Butch, Terence, Wyoming, and Stephanie were taken to the regional hospital. Wyoming was the first one they discharged, although he didn't leave. Pastor Butch was treated for minor cuts, and they told him he had a concussion. He would have fared better had he not hit that apple tree. Physically, Stephanie was fine. The bullet wound was clean. It had missed her lung, but not by much. The problem for her was that she was also under arrest and under the supervision of two of Blackjack County's finest.

Terence was in the worst condition. He woke up in the ambulance ride to the hospital, but they sedated him afterward and he went back to sleep. Terence had a broken arm, two broken ribs, a deep gouging laceration on his back, as well as head trauma much worse than Butch's. It was uncertain whether or not he would live, and if he did, permanent brain damage. When Butch was cleared, sometime that early afternoon, the first thing he did was go to Terence's room in the ICU.

Wyoming followed.

Muriel sat in a chair beside her husband, stroking his arm. When Butch entered the room she said, "This is all your fault! If he dies, I will never forgive you. Do you hear me, never!" She kissed Terence on the forehead, then walked right by Butch out the door. Butch didn't try to say anything to her, because she was right. It was his fault.

Pastor Butch had been in the ICU of this hospital many times, more than he could even remember. He had seen people die in these rooms; he had seen people miraculously recover from terminal illnesses in these rooms. He had seen shattered and fractured families become whole again in these rooms; he had seen the things people say tear families apart in these rooms. He had witnessed sinners repent of past evils and seek forgiveness in these rooms; he had seen people curse God and choose bitterness in these rooms.

He thought he'd seen it all, but Pastor Butch had never seen his best friend cling to life here. He stood at the foot of Terence's bed. It felt like he was in a dream where he watched himself as a passive actor at the whirlwind happening around him. He closed his eyes hard.

Dear Lord, help me wake up from this nightmare.

He opened his eyes. He was still there in the room and Terence was still lying on a hospital bed; wires and tubes everywhere. Terence's head was swollen. A cervical collar held it in place. It looked like the whole right side of his body was in a cast. Monitors beeped and chirped.

A crushing weight of grief pressed against Butch's chest, tighter and more painful than the bruises and scrapes from the explosion. He was losing his ability to compartmentalize the areas of his life—it all crashed on top of him. Every pain and every grief he'd ever felt seemed like a new emotion. He would rather die himself than have one more person taken from him. How much would he have to give?

Grief metamorphed into anger. As the tears filled his eyes he raised his fist upward and said, "No more. Please God, I can't take any more. It's not fair."

Wyoming Wallace stood behind Butch, watched him, but he didn't interfere.

"How much must I sacrifice? Huh? I thought you died on the cross to save the world; why do I have to keep crawling on a cross again and again? Now, here is my friend fighting for his life and you feel so terribly distant. It feels like you said to us, 'do the best you can' and then you walked away. Why? We need you. Where are you? Why do you let these people do such evil things? Please don't let my friend die. Please."

"Watch out," Butch heard a weak voice say. "You're barking up the wrong tree." It was Terence. His words were just above the sound of raspy whisper.

Butch dried his eyes and came around to the side of the bed. "It seems like the only tree to bark up is God's, so how can I be wrong?"

"Blaming God is stupid," Terence said, still whispering his words, struggling to form them. "I know that you're not as smart as I am, but you're not stupid either."

Butch showed a faint smile through his tears. Terence couldn't move, but there was a hint of his wry smile.

"Butch, don't give into bitterness. Jesus knows what he is doing, and he doesn't owe you any explanation at all. We would both be dead right now if it wasn't for that redneck friend of yours."

"I know, Terence. I just don't want to lose you."

"I don't belong to you. Whether I live or die, I belong to the Lord."

"Don't go quoting scripture to me, preacher man," Butch said as he put his hand on Terence's hand just below the cast. "But if you insist on quoting scripture, then I insist upon praying."

Butch waved Wyoming over to the bed. "Wyoming, come pray with us."

Wyoming walked toward Terence from the other side. "I knew at some point you'd want to pray." He took off his ball cap. "You'd better make it a good one. We still have a crazy dame out there on the loose."

> Dear Lord, please heal your servant Terence. He has served you faithfully with his heart, mind, soul, and body. Remember him now in his time of need. I pray that you help us put an end to this violence. I don't know what to do next; I feel so helpless, hurt, and frustrated. I just know that I depend on you to show me the way. If it weren't for your grace we'd all be dead right now. In Jesus' name.

Butch squeezed Terence's hand. He held it until his friend's eyes closed again, and he drifted off to sleep.

"Dream good dreams, Terence."

When the moment ended, Wyoming said, "We need to go see that woman from your church who tried to kill you. We gotta figure out what is going on."

"Let's go."

Muriel was standing outside the automated doors of the ICU along with several other women, whom Butch assumed were from Ebenezer Church. He stopped and looked her in the eyes.

"I know you're angry at me, and I understand why. I just want you to know that I'm sorry he was in the middle of this, I'm sorry for what happened. God knows I wish it were me instead of him." Butch realized how weak his words were. He looked down at the ground. "I guess that's all I wanted to say. I'm sorry."

He looked back up at her, but before he could fully find her eyes he found himself on the receiving end of a bear hug. She squeezed him hard, like a drowning person holding on to a raft.

"Butch, I could never be mad at you, at least not for long. We love you too much for that." She squeezed him again with fresh vigor, then let him go and pulled back. "Terence loves you like a brother, and it wasn't you, it was him. He and I talked about it a lot the last few days. He knew what he was getting into, and that was okay with him because he was in it with you. I was just mad, and when I'm mad I don't always make sense. It doesn't make it right, and I shouldn't give in to it. I guess I had to be mad at somebody; it was either you or God."

"Thank you," Butch said, pulling back from Muriel. Snot ran down his nose as he cried. "I'm pretty angry too. I think we should be angry with those people who've done this. We will find out who they are and where they are, I promise."

"Well, when you do, I want the first swing at that low-down-dirty-rotten Shondra. I can't believe she did that to my husband." The women behind Muriel did not release their scowl, indicating they had not so easily forgiven Butch.

Muriel put her arms around Butch again and said, "Okay, now you be careful. You're no use to him," she pointed toward the ICU, "if you're dead."

"I'll make sure the Reverend is okay," Wyoming said. "But we need to go talk to that cute little crazy chick."

"You go, Butch," Muriel said, "do what God wants you to do."

The two hugged one more time. He and Wyoming walked away.

After they'd turned the corner Butch said, "Wyoming Wallace, did I hear you use the word 'dame' back there when we were talking to Terence? I don't think I've ever heard that word used anywhere except in old black and white movies."

"Reverend, I was editing my words as I spoke. The word I was thinking of was stronger than dame, but it didn't seem proper to use in front of two holy men. Had it just been you I probably would have let fly, but I don't know the other guy as well. I guess dame was just the first word that came to my mind. It does sound kind of funny, doesn't it?"

"Especially coming out of your mouth." Butch could feel the despair he'd felt earlier lifting off his soul. Terence was still alive, Muriel forgave him, his wife was safe, Wyoming was helping him now, and it was clear that Jesus was looking out for them because they were all indeed still alive.

"Hey," Wyoming said, "While we're on it, did you notice he called me a redneck?"

"He was drugged up. He didn't know what he was saying."

"I think he knew exactly what he was saying. What have you told him about me?"

"Nothing that isn't true."

"Truth is in the eye of the beholder."

"Beauty. Beauty is in the eye of the beholder."

"Well, beauty and truth are two sides of the same coin. Speaking of beauty, do you know what room that murderous Stephanie gal is in?"

"She is in the other tower."

It took fifteen minutes to navigate the labyrinthine hospital corridors. Pastor Butch knew it's layout like the back of his hand, but it still took them a long time to move through the numerous elevators, escalators, and stairwells needed to get from the basement ICU where Terence was to the second tower on the opposite end of the complex. When they finally arrived, Butch was winded.

"Let me take a moment to catch my breath."

"Sure," said Wyoming. "Take your time. I guess it stinks getting old, huh?"

Butch shot Wyoming an evil look. "I think it has more to do with the bruises on my chest, oh, and the concussion."

"You keep telling yourself that if you want to."

"Besides, we'd had more time to clear out of that doomed room if you'd gotten to my house faster."

"So now it is my fault? I might be wrong, but I think I saved your life about four hours ago, or was that someone else who put his red neck on the line?"

Butch grinned, "Oh, and about that. Thank you. I owe you one."

"I'm gonna hold you to that."

"Okay. I think I'm fine now, let's go on in."

Two sheriff's deputies stood outside the room. Butch saw Stephanie inside. He waved at her. She waved back with her one good arm. Wyoming said, "Can we go in and visit her?"

"Yes, but I'll have to pat you down first."

"Fine. Let's get it over with. They took my pistol and knives when they brought me into the hospital."

One officer frisked Wyoming while the other watched. He then frisked Butch. "You can go on in, but you only have ten minutes, and I'm watching you."

"Thanks," Butch said.

Stephanie's face beamed joy.

"You look like you just came from a day trip to the spa," Butch said. "For some reason I expected you to be, well, somewhat more broken up, or at least sad that an innocent man is fighting for his life down in the ICU."

"I am, sorta. It hurts a lot where I was shot, and moving is not fun at all. The doctor said sometime in the next couple of days they will have to operate to permanently stitch up the insides."

"I meant emotionally; spiritually." Butch's voice was flat.

"Well, I was for a while. Slowly, though, I began to feel better than I have in ages."

"Adrenaline junkie, huh?" Wyoming said.

"No," Stephanie said. "That's not it at all. The secret is out. I didn't realize how much it was eating away at my soul. The violence, the plotting, the deceit. Now that it is all out in the open, the burden is gone. I just feel better now. I mean, I know I've done horrible things. I will have to pay for those, but that can't be as bad as the prison I put myself in."

Butch coughed, then said "I guess that is one way of looking at it. But Stephanie, that woman is still on the loose."

"Her name is Monica. She was my boss at the bank. That is where we met. We started having a little Bible study on Tuesday mornings at work before we opened. The next thing I knew, I was at a Saturday morning Bible study at someone's house that she knew from her church. There were several of us studying and praying together. Then, when the big scandal happened with the mega-church pastor in Seattle, well, we all began to focus in on the problem of corruption within the church. We decided that we would never have revival or spiritual health as long as evil shepherds and false teachers were leading churches."

"So you decided that killing them was a good idea?" Wyoming said. "It's a mighty big leap from praying to shooting."

"We weren't thinking about violence, not at first, no. We didn't want to kill anyone. But it seemed like we just organically moved that direction." Stephanie pursed her lips and squinted her eyes. "Actually, now that I think about it, Monica drove the process the whole time. I think she made us think it was our idea. She manipulated us into believing we were in charge, that it was a democracy of some kind, and that decisions were made together. In reality, though, she was the one steering the whole thing." She paused, then added, "It's funny how I can see it so clearly now. I was blind."

"Not funny at all, I think." Butch pointed his finger at Stephanie. "And not so fast with the wave of relief and forgiveness, either. You made a decision, all by yourself. It wasn't Monica or anyone else. It was you—a mother, wife, Christ-follower, preschool volunteer, an otherwise perfectly normal person—you chose to become a murderer. How could you do such horrible things? We saw the pictures of Rick Peters. I found Michael! Both of those are images that will stain my memory like a psychological tattoo for as long as I live."

Butch trembled. "I can only imagine how horrible their death was. It doesn't make any sense to me how anyone could do that to someone else. How you could do that to someone. You tortured people, Stephanie. You tortured them to death."

Stephanie wiped her eyes with the bed sheet, but she didn't say anything.

Wyoming saw his friend's distress, and took over. "Do you think that you maybe can see clearly as to where this Monica woman is right now? I hate to be rude and pushy, but the cop outside told us we only had ten minutes in here with you. We've used up seven. You and The Reverend can get together later and hash out how you went all psycho all over everyone." Wyoming's speech slowed. "But what we need to know is, where do you think this Monica woman might have gone? Do you think she'll run away and let it all drop now that her secret is revealed and she's out in the open, or do you think she'll instead double-down and come out with all pistols blazing?"

Stephanie's face hardened. "She will never, never let up. Monica lives by a philosophy of balance sheets. She feels incomplete until everything is balanced out, until it is all put in the right column."

"Oh, she's a legalist." Butch said. "Terence was right in his assessment. She is a Bible scholar, but she misses the whole point."

"Pastor Butch," Stephanie said. "You are not safe. She will keep on and on until she has killed you. She thinks you are a heretic. Nothing I could say would change her mind; she believes she is doing God's work."

Wyoming shook his head. "I thought I left behind all the religious zealots in Iraq. Now they are here in my backyard. Great. Just great." He stroked his beard, "So, do you know where the Ayatollah-ette of Sydney might be hiding out?"

"I know that she is resourceful. She usually plans well in advance. That was, until you. For some reason she came after you with a blindness to details and planning. It was very uncharacteristic of her."

"I wonder why?" Butch said.

"It might have something to do with your reputation." Wyoming thought out loud.

196

"What do you mean, my reputation?"

Wyoming Wallace said, "Well, for starters you're probably the most-squeaky clean person in the world. I am sure a little research taught Monica that, if she didn't already know it. Everyone in town knows you and loves you. You're the poster-boy for good living and righteousness. She might have assumed you were evil to the core, that no one could be that innocent. From there she deduced that your image was hypocrisy. Then she felt even more compelled to bring you down. If someone assumed you were a bad apple passing yourself as a shiny red one, then they would want to get rid of you that much more."

Stephanie nodded, "Exactly. That is the kind of intensity she brought to it. Nothing would deter her once she decided that Pastor Butch was a false teacher."

"Do you think she will go after my family?"

"She never has gone after anyone's family before," Stephanie said.

"What about that one pastor, Joan, and her partner. They both ended up dead." Butch realized as he said it that it sounded judgmental. He didn't want it to be, but he also didn't care too much about Stephanie's feelings. His wife and kids were on his mind.

"That was a mistake."

"Too bad for her, huh?" Wyoming said. "So you messed up on her because she was the first one?"

"Oh no, she was like the fourth. The first one was in Puyallup about five years ago."

"Terence was right about that, too," Butch whispered.

Wyoming checked the clock. "Keep it moving, people. We're running out of time. Stephanie, do you know where she might be?"

"We might make better time, Mr. Wyoming Wallace, if you didn't talk so slow." Stephanie tilted her head sideways a bit.

Butch couldn't believe it. In the distress of the moment, Stephanie was flirting with Wyoming. What was it about that guy?

Stephanie said, "She has only been in Sydney for about ten years. Before that she was in California somewhere. She never really talked about her past. The more I think about it, she might have a past in things like this. She seemed very eager for it."

"The same might be said of you, Stephanie." Butch twisted the words like a dagger. It felt good.

"True. And I'm sorry. I don't really know what to say."

"What I want to know," Wyoming Wallace's words came out of his mouth at a painfully slow pace, as he worked on every word, "is how come you didn't know the secretary at Ebenezer was one of your co-workers? Seems to me you'd all know each other."

"Even though I helped form The Judys, each team leader made recommendations, and Monica made the final selections. She told us it would be better if we didn't know everyone, in case one of us was ever caught."

One of the deputies walked in. "It is time for the two of you to go. I even gave you an extra two minutes out of the goodness of my heart."

"Thanks," said Wyoming. "Don't break your arm patting yourself on the back."

"Watch it, tough guy, or you'll find yourself being carted off to the jail."

"For what?"

"Calm down, Wyoming. Let's not provoke the nice policeman. Remember, they've had a bad day too. Besides, the last thing we need is to make this more complicated." Butch gave a frown to Wyoming.

"Too late." Detective Wright was standing outside of the hospital room when they left. "It is already complicated."

"I suppose you've been listening to our entire conversation?" Pastor Butch said, pointing a finger at the detective.

"Not all of it. Just the important parts."

"Is there such a thing as privacy anymore?" Wyoming said. He threw his hands up in mock disgust.

"No," said Detective Wright. "But you already knew that, Mr. Wallace. Besides, that woman is a suspect in a rash of serial killings. Do you really think we'd let her have the luxury of guests without our being aware of her every word?"

Wyoming said, "I can't say that I'd argue with your rationale."

They walked into the lobby for that floor, then sat down on three different, but equally uncomfortable, chairs.

Detective Wright pulled out his notebook. "While all of you were getting stitched up I had a chance to do a little research on you, Mr. Wyoming Wallace. I have to say, I'm impressed. You seem to have an uncanny knack for finding trouble on almost any continent in the world. Tell me, does Butch know about London, Rio de Janeiro, or Iraq?"

"I know about Iraq," said Butch, raising his hand as if he were at school.

"The other two, no." He looked at Wyoming. Wyoming grinned, the way the proverbial cat does regarding the unfortunate canary.

"Reverend, the detective here is just trumping up small things. London was just a street scuffle with a couple of guys who thought I should give them my wallet when I didn't want to. Rio, well, that was a simple misunderstanding between me and her father."

"Whose father?"

"I can't remember her name, but her father's name was Manuel. He was some kind of boss or something."

Detective Wright flipped back several pages then read from his notepad, "She was the daughter of a drug lord in one of the Brazilian drug cartels. Her name was Bianca."

"Yes!" Wyoming grew animated. "Her name was Bianca. Boy, could she dance. She was a redhead, but I don't think it was natural. God really knew what he was doing when he made Brazilian women. You know what I mean, Reverend?"

"No, I don't know what you mean. When exactly did all this happen? Is this what you've been up to these last six months?" Butch's face turned red.

"Nah, Reverend. That all happened before I met you," his voice trailed off, "before, you know."

Detective Wright didn't look up from his notes. "Quite right. Does Butch know, Mr. Wallace, about your most recent escapade down in Texas?"

"Please call me Wyoming. And no. I just got into town this morning, and things have been happening so fast I've not had time to tell Butch much of anything."

"What happened in Texas?"

"Like I said, I'll tell you later, Reverend." Wyoming looked at Detective Wright with exasperation. "How do you know so much about me? You only just learned of my existence a few hours ago."

Detective Wright said, "Let's just say that you are a heavily flagged person of interest on the various websites and databases used by law enforcement. Everyone has a file on you—the FBI, CIA, Homeland Security, and even INTERPOL. If I had more time, I suspect I might find some information from the Mossad."

"Very funny," Wyoming didn't laugh. "But, I have a feeling you do not want to talk about me. What you really want is to talk about that crazy woman who is trying to kill Butch and Terence, and apparently anyone else who gets in her way."

"That would be yes," Detective Wright paused for effect, "Wyoming." Wyoming nodded at the use of his first name, then the detective continued. "But first let me say that I do hope your friend Terence pulls through. I believe he will. The doctor tells me that his injuries, though severe, are probably not fatal. If he makes it through the next twenty four hours he will probably have a full recovery by Christmas."

"I've seen injuries like that several times," Butch said. "Usually from car crashes. Once the swelling goes down, and if there is no hemorrhaging, then the body tends to heal up nicely all by itself. Of course, that assumes there is no internal bleeding."

Detective Wright nodded then said, "Now, I need you to tell me everything that happened today. I've already gotten a pretty good picture from Stephanie Colson. She was the first one ready to talk. I didn't even have to threaten her or offer a plea bargain or anything. She just confessed it all, almost faster than I could write. The only thing I didn't get from her were the other names of all her co-conspirators. I'll get those later. For now, though, I'd like to hear from the two of you. I'll talk to Terence later, once he's recovered."

Butch said, "I hope you've found that woman and this is all over long before Terence recovers."

For the next fifteen minutes the two men relayed to Detective Wright everything that happened. They even rehashed their argument about whether or not Stephanie should have gone to Terence's office in the first place. Wyoming insisted that none of it would have ever happened had he been with Butch, because Shondra the receptionist at Ebenezer would have never had time.

Wyoming told his story, about waiting beside the building, watching Butch be led away, checking on Stephanie, fighting Shondra, calling the ambulance, sneaking into the house, and untying the two of them before it was too late.

Butch told his story. He told how Shondra was sitting behind Terence's desk, how she shot Stephanie, how he tried to clot the blood and how Monica showed up. He then said that another woman was in the car waiting for them. He said that the other woman drove while Monica kept the gun pointed at his ribs. Butch explained how two other women were at his house, waiting for him, and that they had Terence already tied up in the chair.

"After they tied me up beside Terence," Butch said, "Monica brought out the bomb. She secured it underneath us. I assume that is when she set the timer. I can't be for certain."

"Did she say anything?" Detective Wright asked.

"She wouldn't shut up. She kept talking about how I was a false teacher and Terence was my ally. She mentioned how we were in league with Michael Westgrave. She went on and on about how she knew it because we had talked on the phone the night he was killed. She said she couldn't prove how we were connected, but God had told her to kill me."

"That's not a very nice thing for God to do," said Detective Wright.

"I agree with you, Richard." Wyoming threw the detective's first name like a dart.

"Of course, God had nothing to do with that." Butch felt compelled to state the obvious. "Anyway, she kept talking about how it was appropriate for Terence and I to be joined together in death, and that the death should be explosive. She seemed to pin a lot of symbolic meaning on that explosive idea. She kept talking about how the revelation about the false teachers would explode in the hearts and minds of Christians, sparking some kind of revival or renewal."

"Sounds frightening." Detective Wright kept writing.

"She was absolutely diabolical."

"Now, Wyoming, I don't know where you came into all of this." The detective kept writing. "You say you just got into town today. That is quite a coincidence, don't you think? Just showing up, happy-go-lucky on the day your good friend almost gets blown up?"

"Well, when you put it that way, I guess it might seem so. But," Wyoming looked across at Butch, "ever since I met the Reverend, it has become clearer and clearer to me that chance, or," he paused and slowed his speech, "as you call it coincidence, doesn't really exist too much. I can't explain it as well as he can," Wyoming pointed at Butch. "But I believe it. I was brought home today, like a soldier brought from one place to another to do a specific thing. Today I was brought in to untie those two men and save their lives."

"Fine, Wyoming. But why wouldn't God have brought you, or someone else even, in earlier to save the other pastors who were killed by these women?"

"I don't rightly know, except to say that maybe in some way they were actually guilty. Not that I mean they were deserving death, but they weren't completely innocent, either. It is hard for me to put into words. I've dealt with people, actually Butch and I have dealt with people, who did deserve to be killed on the spot, and that is different. What I mean is that because there was a level of guilt in them, when they needed help it wasn't available. But Butch and Terence, as innocent people, or as innocent as a human can be in this fouled-up world, had a reprieve from the Lord. At least, that is the way I figure it."

"That's an interesting hypothesis. According to your logic everyone who is murdered or killed is guilty of something, and that only the morally pure are rescued?" Detective Wright stopped writing. He looked at Wyoming with suspicion.

Wyoming said, "That is not what I am saying. I've seen innocent people die too, and it stings every single time I think about it. I'm just saying that here, for some reason, God was working to protect Butch and Terence."

Detective Wright said, "I don't believe in coincidence too much. You can leave superstition out of it. I believe in motive. I don't really know what is going on right now, but I will find out. This case is very complicated, with many moving parts, but I will solve it."

"We hope so." Butch tried to emphasize the word hope.

"So," Wyoming said. "Do you know who this Monica woman is? Do you have any kind of idea where she is?"

"Not too much. We know where she worked. Her daughter is under state protection and care. Her husband is a sailor and we're trying to contact him through the Navy. That isn't always easy. Right now we're searching through her home. For now, that is all we have to go on."

"I'd feel a lot better if she were in jail." Butch shivered.

"Likewise," said Detective Wright.

The needy sound of a cell phone vibrating crinkled the air. Detective Wright pulled out his phone. "This is Detective Wright." He then held up a finger and whispered the words, "Don't go away," to Butch and Wyoming as he walked out of earshot.

After several minutes Detective Wright returned. "Well, gentlemen, that was the FBI. Just as I expected, they will be here tomorrow morning, along with Homeland Security. This is now officially an incident of domestic terrorism."

Wyoming looked at Butch and said, "Do you think we'll see our old friend Agent Lapp-Bench again?"

"That was Agent Lapp-Bench on the phone," Detective Wright raised his hands in surrender, "how do you know her?"

"Next time you talk to her, tell her I said hi." Butch wanted to smile, but he couldn't. He was running on adrenaline, and his body was almost depleted. He was nearly emotionless.

Detective Wright stuck his phone back in his pocket. "If I have any further questions I'll contact you." He gave them both a card with his contact information.

"I already have three of these," Butch said.

"I know. It is a habit, but Butch, you know you can't have too many of them? Now, please don't leave the area while this investigation is still open, or if you do, let me know where and why. Got it?"

"Sure, we got it."

Just as they were finishing their conversation, Pastor Philip from Sydney Community walked through the doors of the lobby. Butch was relieved to see Philip, and behind him was Gerald Land, one of their Bible teachers. Detective Wright took a couple of steps backward and allowed the four men to form a conversation circle while he eavesdropped.

"You look awful," Gerald said. He wrapped his arms around Butch and gave him a long hug.

"You should see my house," was all Butch could say in response.

"I have. The whole town has. It is crawling with all kinds of police. Every car in Sydney has driven by in the last two hours. It is the most interesting thing to look at in town since the ferry ran aground last summer. Remember that?"

"I remember," Butch said.

"It's good to see you alive," Philip said to Butch. "Then he turned to Wyoming and said, "It is good to see you, too, Wyoming. Although, I should have expected that when you showed up stuff would start exploding."

"It wasn't my fault."

"How is Terence?" All Philip knew was that Terence had been involved.

"He's in ICU. I have a feeling he will pull through. He is strong." Butch said that trying to reassure Philip, but he was really just trying to reassure himself.

Philip looked at Butch and said, "The Blackjack Presbyterian Church is hosting a prayer service tonight. All this, with Westgrave, Peters, and now you and Terence has everyone very concerned. All the churches are coming together to lead in some of the prayers, Father Juan from the Catholic Church organized it."

"That's great, Philip," said Butch. "I look forward to seeing everyone."

"Well, you're not going." Gerald said. "The last thing you need is to be in a crowd of people pawing over you. So you're not going. Doctor's orders."

"You're a dentist, Gerald. I don't think you can give orders like that." Butch finally worked up a smile.

"No matter," Gerald said. "This town loves you a lot, and though well-meaning, they will smother you tonight if you show up. You let us pray for you, while you take care of yourself. Right now you need a place to stay because obviously you can't go to your house. I've got a cabin out on this side of the Hood Canal. We mostly use it in the summer. Here are the keys to it. You're welcome to stay as long as you need, and I mean that. Even if it takes a couple of years to get all this sorted out, that would be fine with us. My wife is stocking the kitchen right now for you with food and putting fresh linens out." Gerald turned to look at Wyoming. "And you, Mr. Wallace, are welcome to stay as well."

"That is very kind, but I have my own place, and it still should be in one piece, although I haven't been there since I got back into town." Wyoming pointed at Butch, "But the Reverend being on Hood Canal is perfect, because that will make him actually closer to me in case something should come up."

"Very well," said Gerald. "Now, how about we get you boys out of this hospital. Where are your cars?"

Wyoming said, "Butch's rental car is at what's left of his house. My Jeep is at the church."

"Gerald," Philip said, "Can you take Butch to his house to get his car, I'll take Wyoming back to Sydney Community Church. I need to stop by the church anyway."

"You got it."

Butch scanned the room and found Detective Wright, "Bye, Richard. I guess we'll be seeing you later. For now, I think we're going to grab something to eat and try to get some rest. You will be in my prayers."

"You will be in my logs and reports," Detective Wright said. "Before you go, can you give me the address to this cabin you'll be? I'd like to have that information, just in case."

"That's no problem," said Gerald. He told the address to Detective Wright, who wrote it in his notes. Then the four men walked down the hallway to the elevator.

Detective Wright watched Butch and Wyoming walk away with Philip and Gerald. When he was certain they were gone, he made a phone call. "I want you to put a tracking device on Butch Gregory's rental car and Wyoming Wallace's Jeep. Have it done right now. You got that? Don't waste time because they are on their way to their cars. Butch's car is at his house and Mr. Wallace's jeep is at Sydney Community Church."

"Yes, Detective Wright," said the female voice on the other end of the line.

"If you can spare another detective from the explosion site at Butch's house, I'd like you to try to tail them. I suspect they will be together for the most part."

"Should we treat them as suspects?" she asked.

"Absolutely. I wasn't sure until today, just now actually. That Wyoming guy's showing up wasn't a coincidence. When I asked him about it he started spouting off a lot of god-talk. In my experience when people start talking about god that usually means they are guilty. Only the guilty appeal to a god."

"You got it, sir. Is there anything else you want me to get started on?"

"Not now. I'll do some footwork later, that's enough for now. Thanks Shawna."

Shawna made the phone calls to put into place the action Detective Wright asked for, except for the tail. It'd be better to not have officers in the way. Then she sent a text message using her pre-paid phone to Monica.

Chapter Thirty-Two
A Debate about God's Will

Butch didn't realize how much he hurt until he was alone. When the roar of doctors poking, policemen probing, women plotting, pistols pointing, Wyoming protecting, and Terence praying was quieted he finally heard his muscles and bones pleading for relief. Being slammed into that tree trunk hurt him more than he cared to admit, even to himself. He knew that tomorrow he'd be really sore. He hoped his head would clear up. He could tell his concussion wasn't too severe, but he was groggy nonetheless.

The doctor at the hospital had offered him a pain prescription. He regretted not taking it. He found a bottle of naproxen under the bathroom sink. He took three of them. Then he talked to Lucy on the phone. He had already called her earlier in the day from the hospital to let her know the basics. Now he filled her in with all the details.

"How much longer do you think this will go on?" she said.

"I don't know, but I feel like it is coming to a head soon. I think it will all be over by the end of the week."

"Do you want me to come home?"

"What home? We don't have a home. We have a crater. I want you to stay there. I know it is tough, but it shouldn't be too much longer."

He could tell she didn't like that answer.

"I don't like it, either. But it seems like it is the way it has to be. I will see you soon. I promise."

They talked for a long time afterward, then Butch asked her to pray for them. When life was normal, Butch always thought his wife prayed better. Now, he knew she would pray better than him.

After the call ended, he made himself dinner. He fried up two eggs, four pieces of bacon, and placed it all on top of two pieces of toast, open faced. He washed it all down with a tall glass of orange juice. When he finished his meal, he took a shower. After the shower, he decided to spoil himself. Gerald's wonderful wife had not only stocked the kitchen, she also filled up their hot tub with fresh water.

Before he had driven out to the cabin he'd been able to salvage most of his clothes. It surprised him that the explosion didn't do more damage. Wyoming tried to explain it to him, something about shrapnel rather than force being the key to a homemade pressure bomb. It mostly exploded upward through the ceiling, as well as into the living room and kitchen area. His bedroom, though, was mostly intact. While he was there, it never crossed his mind to get his swimming trunks, or even a pair of shorts. Therefore he enjoyed his time in the hot tub *au naturel.*

He was glad that the tub was on their deck facing the Hood Canal. Even though houses were all around, the way the canal jagged and the house was built, the backyard was completely secluded. A soft rain fell just beyond the edge of the deck's roof. It was a soothing sound that refreshed Butch's soul. He was made for the northwest; it was his home. Other people who moved in and out with the Navy or other government jobs often complained about the weather. Butch never understood why they bellyached so much. The rain was a gift of God to bless the land. It washed everything clean. The cool air was invigorating and the occasional snow was exciting.

Thank you, Lord, for the land and weather. The earth is yours, and the fullness thereof.

The rain was a healing balm in the midst of the murderous crisis. He'd almost died today. He was separated from his wife and kids. His friend was very sick. Others had been snuffed out. In the midst of all this turmoil, he found a moment of grace as the hot water massaged his flesh and the rain soothed his nerves. There was still a ringing in his ears, though. He hoped it wasn't a permanent souvenir.

He scooted to the edge of the tub and relaxed in one of the seat molds. He'd turned the lights off on the deck, so he sat in the dark. There was little light from the sky as the clouds covered the stars and most of the moonshine. Enough light escaped the heavens to glow upon the Olympic Mountains on the other side of the canal. It formed a ghostly image, towering above the water's edge, like giant ramparts and fortified walls encircling the kingdom below to keep it safe from outside evil.

Butch felt safe. It was an inexplicable feeling, but he knew God was watching. He'd sent the mountains, the rain, and the smell of the salt water to reassure him. He'd given him Wyoming to see him through. He'd provided a place for his family to take refuge. He'd spared his life twice now. Whether he spared it again or not was irrelevant. Terence's quotation of the Apostle Paul came to his mind. Whether he lived or died, he was the Lord's possession.

It was true for Terence. It was true for him.

A somber thought came over him. Those words were from the liturgy he used at funerals.

His mind jumped from there to the contentious use of Romans 8:28 at the Bible study on Monday night. All things work together for good for people who love the Lord and are called according to his purposes. He believed those words were true with everything in him. He also knew that the way God defines good is not the way most people do. Good often comes from sacrifice, death, and pain. After all, the day Jesus was tortured to death was called Good Friday.

All of these thoughts formed something like a prayer of gratitude. If he did die in this ordeal it comforted him that the mountains were still there. The rain would still fall. The ocean would still swell, because the Lord was still in control of everything. People would still laugh and love, the church would move forward, and eternity would be none the less certain.

He stayed in the tub too long. The cold tingled against him as he emerged from the blanching pool. His skin shriveled up like a raisin. Butch wrapped an oversized towel around himself and scurried back into the cabin. Even though it seemed redundant, he climbed back in the shower to rinse the chlorine off.

He sent Lucy a goodnight text before he drifted off to sleep on the pillow top mattress.

Pastor Butch Gregory's body rested in the bed, but his mind was active. When his eyes began to move rapidly under their eyelids, he was transported into the mystery of dreams.

He sits in the Sydney Diner with Terence and Michael Westgrave. They laugh together and look at Michael's watch. Butch wants one, but Terence tells him no, it is not for him to know the time or hour. Then the server comes to their table, and the server is Stephanie. Stephanie sticks a fork into Michael's throat and he disappears, as in a vapor.

Now he and Terence run away from Stephanie. They are no longer in the diner, but are in the woods. It is a park. Butch knows where he is, but he does not recognize exactly where it is. He just knows he has been there before. He can hear Stephanie chasing them.

They run by a building with no walls. It looks like a church, but it is not a church. Women stand underneath it, all different kind of women. They wear crimson robes and pray. As they run by the women, one by one they leave their prayers and give chase.

Terence grabs Butch's arm and says, "I have an idea. Follow me."

Butch follows. The two pastors are now in a library. Stephanie is there, and Butch is afraid. Stephanie shouts, "Run!" She points toward a staircase that leads to a second floor and they go up. Stephanie stays behind. Butch doesn't look back but he hears her scream as the other women catch up.

When they come to the second floor of the staircase, Terence pushes Butch into a study room. Wyoming is in the room with them, but he ignores them. Then Terence explodes into a million tiny pieces. Now he and Wyoming are running down the highway. It is the highway across the peninsula to the Pacific coast where Lucy is. He wants to get to Lucy. He needs to get to her, but the women are chasing him.

When they reach Lucy, she is inside a giant pressure cooker. Monica is there, forcing Lucy to stay in the cooker. Then he and Monica are underwater, gasping for air.

Butch woke up, startled. It was the kind of dream that felt real. His pulse raced. Sweat was on his brow. The bedroom was filled with sunlight, so he squinted his eyes as he rubbed them. His chest was sore. He reached over to the nightstand to find his watch. Judging from the amount of sun, he guessed it to be around seven.

"Good morning. I hope you enjoyed your sleep and the sunset. It will be the last your eyes ever see." It was a female voice he'd never heard before. He jerked around to see a woman sitting in a chair in the corner. It was the chair he'd laid his pants on the night before.

"Who are you?" he asked. He realized it was a stupid question. Even if he didn't know her name, he knew exactly why she was here.

"What an interesting question. You're the first one to ever ask me that. Usually the false teachers just start begging for their life. My name is Michelle. I used to work with Stephanie, before she betrayed us."

"Look, Michelle, I'm not a false teacher. I don't know what you women think I've done, but I'm not a heretic." He sat up in bed, but tried to keep himself covered as much as possible, as if the blanket would protect him from the vulnerable position he was in.

"As far as I am concerned you're all guilty, but it's not my job to decide guilt or innocence. You've already been found guilty by Monica, and that is good enough for me. Unlike Stephanie, I take orders and do my job."

"What exactly is your job?"

"Another curious question. My job is to remove the people who have been deemed false teachers. Normally, I give them a chance to repent of their sin. If they agree to resign their church immediately and walk away, then we let them live. No one ever does that, so they all had to be killed in order to remove them. You, however, are different. It is too late for you to repent and quietly leave. You have made a mess that will take us some doing to clean up. But rest assured, we will clean it up. It is what The Judys do. We make pure what was previously impure. Your little rebellion is not permanent."

"Who is the we? What are The Judys? I mean, I know you want me dead, but before I go I'd like to know what kind of group are you?" Butch was stalling for time. He didn't know what he might do, but he figured the longer he could drag this out the better it would be. It already occurred to him that this Michelle woman had something special planned, or she would have killed him while he slept. However, he was curious as to the nature of the group. In the rush of yesterday he'd not had a chance to get full answers from Stephanie.

"The Judys are the ones who do God's will. We do the dirty work. The dirty work other people are too weak to do. The dirty work that must be done for purity. It needs to be done, everyone wants it done. The church has become polluted by evil people, evil men like you. You abuse children, womanize, engage in wordliness, abuse power, steal money, and practice cowardice. You worship the Baals and Molechs of this world. You compromise holiness and smear the cross of Christ with the filthiness of your sin. We are the ones who protect the true church. We remove the filth. Filth like you."

"Sounds like you've made yourself the mouthpiece for God. You know, that is evidence of being delusional."

"Someone has to do it."

"So you call yourself The Judys, like Judy Garland? That's kinda tame, isn't it? I would have thought you'd chose a more representative name like, Crazy Killers for Christ. Doesn't that fit better than The Judys?"

"We are," Michelle stood up, "technically called The Servants of Judith. Over twenty-five hundred years ago our mother Judith cut off the head of Holofernes when he threatened the purity of Israel. She was helped by her loyal servant. Monica has showed us how we aid her in the work of remov-

210

ing the threats that would come against the true people of God."

When Michelle stood up Butch saw the pistol that had been aimed at him the whole time.

"It is time for us to get moving," she said, walking to the doorway. "Monica has plans for you."

"Ah, Monica. Why didn't she come along this time? Too busy blowing up other innocent people? Or has Detective Wright already got her in custody?"

"You're the one who is delusional now. Detective Wright is under our thumb, just like everything and everyone else. He doesn't blow his nose that we don't know exactly where he did it and how long he blew. But if you must know, Monica has—"

Michelle went silent before she could tell Butch what Monica was up to. She fell face first onto the floor.

Chapter Thirty-Three
The Smell of Tobacco

Butch looked up to the ceiling, as if God had struck her dead. He heard something, though, and noticed a shadow in the doorway. The bright gray sunlight blocked him from seeing beyond the bedroom into the living area, but it was definitely a person. Was it Detective Wright? Had Gerald come out to check on him?

Then he saw a tiny flame followed by the distinctive smell of tobacco.

"I don't think Gerald would appreciate you smoking your disgusting cigars in his cabin. Isn't it a little early in the morning for that, anyway?"

"Ah, he won't care," Wyoming Wallace said. "After all, I just saved his preacher's life, again. I figure I deserve it. And no, it is never too early to enjoy the finer things in life. This is what you might call a breakfast stogie." He took a big long draw and let it out in a slow blow. "Breakfast of champions."

"I don't think they're ready to put you on a cereal box just yet." Butch shook his head. "Why did you have to knock her out before she told me what Monica was up to? She was just about to spill the beans."

"Because I already know where Monica is. But the real reason is I was getting tired of her speech. What is it about maniacal murderers that they always want to give speeches?"

"It is a part of the pathology," Butch said as he got out of bed. "They have a self-inflated view of their own importance and abilities." He pulled the pink and yellow bathrobe he'd found the night before around his body. "The speeches are how they communicate their superiority and sooth their defective ego. They are just a small group of people in a tucked away corner of the world, but by doing these kinds of things and using this kind of language, they actually believe they are changing the universe.

"Along with that ego comes the human drive to show everyone how smart they are. That is what fuels the speeches. It's also what fuels their actions. Most people think it is a cliché found only in Hollywood movies for plot development, but it's actually a real thing." Butch picked up the pistol Michelle had pointed at him. He handed it to Wyoming. "Michelle here wanted me to know that her merry band of psychopaths had won. She enjoyed gloating over me, helpless in the bed in my underwear. I suspect for her it was a kind of role reversal. She was in the power position over someone she perceives to normally be in power."

Butch sat down in the chair and took a deep breath. He exhaled. "Actually, the more I think about it, if I were a betting man I'd wager that each of these women at some point in their lives had been hurt, and I mean badly hurt, by a pastor." A split second of empathy came upon Butch Gregory. He felt sorry for the crumpled body lying on the floor at his feet. She had been hurt, and now she wanted to hurt the one who hurt her, if even symbolically. Then he said, "The chickens always come home to roost."

"Wow," Wyoming said. "It was just a rhetorical question. If you keep making speeches like that I'm going to bonk you in the head with this fireplace poker."

"Sorry," Butch said. "You gotta remember, part of my job is trying to figure out why otherwise rational people do sinful, destructive, and stupid things." He waved his hand in front of his face as the cigar smoke floated right into his eyes. "Let's tie her up and then we can make some coffee. And crack a window."

"Sounds good to me, but don't get too comfortable in that pretty little bathrobe of yours. We'd need to make that coffee to go."

"Why?" Butch said. "What do you know that I don't know?"

"Well, one, I know that she will wake up in a few minutes. She will probably be a little dizzy with a headache, but we can ask her then what Monica is up to. Anyway, even if she doesn't, I think I already know where Monica is, and, better yet, I know exactly what we need to do about it."

"Oh, well then, let's get started."

Wyoming patted Michelle down to look for other weapons. Along with a pre-paid flip phone, he found a small .22 pistol in a holster on her belt at the small of her back. A six inch Japanese tanto knife was sheathed and tied to her left thigh. Wyoming admired her preparedness, and her physique. "She is firm all over," he said standing up after the pat down.

"Now is not the time for that."

"Not like that, Reverend. I mean she is a lean fighting machine. She was toting two pistols and a dagger. I bet she is the muscle of the group. You should see her abs."

"I'd prefer not, thank you very much."

Wyoming unloaded the two guns and put the knife in his inside coat pocket. Butch rummaged around the various cabinets and drawers looking for rope or string. He finally found bright red duct tape.

"Look," Wyoming told him, "you'd better get cleaned up and dressed. I have a feeling as soon as we finish interrogating her we will be on the road."

"What makes you say that?"

"The same thing that told me to come over here first thing this morning."

"You mean," Butch's voice lowered an octave, "The Lord spoke to you again." Butch's dream, about the women chasing him and Terence came rushing back to him.

"Let's just say I had a tough night."

Butch didn't argue. He obeyed Wyoming's directive to go get dressed. While he did that, Wyoming tied Michelle up. He taped her hands behind her back. He wound the tape around her ankles. Then he put her into one of the wooden kitchen table chairs and taped her to that. For good measure he took the sheet off the bed, wound it as tight as he could, and then wrapped it around her torso and tied it off. Then he taped the chair to the wall.

"Isn't that a little excessive?" Butch asked. "She's not Captain America."

"No, she's no superhero. I do have a feeling she is resourceful. I considered breaking her leg, like I did the secretary yesterday, but we only need to hold her for a while until the police show up." Wyoming pointed at her. "Look, she is coming around."

By this time both Wyoming and Butch had a cup of coffee in their hands.

"Who are you?" Michelle asked Wyoming.

"That is an interesting question," Butch said, mocking her earlier reply to his identical question. "He is my friend. That is all you need to know."

Michelle squeezed her eyes together and wrinkled her face, then shook it. "Never mind. I know who you are. You're Wyoming. She told me you were dangerous. I didn't believe her."

"Did you hear that, Reverend?" Wyoming said, the stogie still between his lips. "She said they think I'm dangerous. I really like the sound of that. I'm dangerous," He pulled the cigar out of his mouth. "But in a good way." Then he turned his attention back to Michelle. "Tell me, who is this 'she' you're talking about. Who is she? How did she know I was dangerous?"

"Do you really think I'm going to tell you anything?" Michelle turned her head sideways and stared out of the window. "I may have made one mistake by letting myself be taken by you. I will not make a second by spouting out names you don't know." She turned her head back to Wyoming. "Nice try, though."

"Let's get to the point," Butch said. "Where is Monica? What is she doing today?"

"Oh foolish false teacher. It is too late. You're too late. I'm certain by now she is already there."

"Where?" Butch demanded.

"The coast," Wyoming said. "She is going after Lucy. This woman was probably supposed to take you down there to her."

"You're smarter than you look," Michelle said to Wyoming, then she turned to Butch. "Your harlot wife and mongrel children will meet the same fate as you. You can't stop it, false teacher. God has appointed it. It is his will."

Butch turned his back to Michelle. He stared out of the window at the Olympic Mountains. His mind raced. Lucy, Sarah and Paul were in danger, and it was his fault. Desperation and despair hovered just outside of his heart.

"We must go get them, Wyoming. Now."

"You're right. But what do we do with her?" Wyoming pointed at Michelle. "I say we kill her."

"No. We can't become like them. If we start working the same way they do, then we are no better. We can't call the police, though." Butch turned around and faced Wyoming again. "She said earlier, before you whacked her, that Detective Wright was under their thumb. If we call the police, then their mole, whoever that is, will let them know that we escaped here. That will make matters worse." Butch chewed his thumb, then put his hands on his hips. "It would be infinitely better if Monica thought her plan had succeeded. If she thought we, or more specifically me, was tied up in the trunk on my way to the beach house then we might have the drop on her."

"That's a good plan Butch. I'm actually quite impressed. But it still doesn't answer what we do with her? Are you sure I can't kill her? I haven't killed anyone, yet. I seem to have a dangerous reputation to maintain." Wyoming pulled the baseball cap off of his head and ran a hand through his curly hair.

"Let's keep it that way. You racked up far too many fatalities last time."

"This is not like last time."

"I hope not, we paid too much then."

Wyoming pulled out of his pocket the cell phone he'd taken from Michelle. He looked for text messages or phone calls. There were no calls in the history, and only one text message. There was no name, only a contact number. Wyoming showed it to Butch.

"That is probably a pre-paid phone too."

"Probably. What does the message say?"

Wyoming scrolled through and clicked it. It was the address for the cabin, followed by the words, "bring him here."

Butch said, "It is safe to assume that Monica sent this."

"You heathen, she did not!" Michelle shouted.

Butch smiled at Michelle. "Yep. She certainly did. That trick usually only works on my kids and deacons, but you fell right into it. You're clearly not as smart as you think you are. Wyoming, send a text to that number. Have it say, "on my way.""

"Do you think we'll get a reply?" Wyoming said.

"No. Actually, if we get a reply that is bad, because that means this is not Monica. But I'd be willing to wager my life that it is Monica, and she will not reply."

"I just want you to know, you're not wagering your life, you're wagering your family's life."

"Don't you think I'm well aware of the stakes," Butch sighed. "Please, don't remind me."

"Okay, but you still haven't told me what we should do with her." Wyoming pointed at Michelle. "We can't call the police because they have an insider. You won't let me kill her. So what do we do?"

"We could take her with us. Throw her in the trunk like she probably planned to do with me."

"Not a good idea. It presents too many variables. If we get pulled over, then that is bad. If she somehow gets out or gets free, or says something in the moment, no, that is not good. But I do have an idea along those same lines."

"What?"

Wyoming looked at Michelle, then at Butch. He grabbed the duct tape and put it over her mouth. "I'll be back in a second," he said as he walked out of the front door.

Butch watched out of the front window as Wyoming walked up the long driveway toward the main road, a cloud of smoke following him. He lost sight of him after he reached the high hedge row that blocked the house from public view. Butch checked his watch. He didn't know what Wyoming was doing, but he'd learned to trust him. This was just one of the things he did.

Five minutes later, a white Kia Sorrento pulled into the driveway and parked between Wyoming's Jeep and Butch's rented Ford Fusion. Wyoming got out of the Kia. When he got back into the house he said, "I solved our problem. Give me your car keys."

"Why?"

"Just give them to me."

Butch handed his keys to Wyoming. Wyoming pushed the button on the fob that opened the trunk to his rented sedan. He hoisted Michelle, chair and all, over his shoulder, and carried her outside and put her in the trunk of Butch's car. Her eyes shot terror at him. "I have a feeling this is medicine you've dished out to others. What goes around comes around, sister."

"I prefer the biblical way of saying that idea, Wyoming. Whatever a man, or woman in this case, sows, so shall she reap."

"Nicely put, Reverend. Now don't worry, crazy lady. After we've saved Butch's family, we will then call the police to tell them where you are. That will probably be in about six or seven hours, nine at the most I think. It all depends on what goes down. You will not dehydrate or starve in that time period. You will, though, probably need a diaper change when they get you." Then he slammed the trunk door shut.

"That was genius, Wyoming. Absolutely brilliant." Pastor Butch Gregory had a new admiration for Wyoming's cognitive ability.

"Thanks, but I'd rather have just killed her. Now she is a dangling loose end."

"Maybe, but I'm not a murderer. I guess we take your Jeep to Lucy."

"Nope. We take her nice new Sorrento. That is the car this Monica the Maniac is expecting to show up."

Chapter Thirty-Four
The Syringe

Paula Dietz looked in the mirror. She mumbled the words, "I can do this. I made a vow that cannot be broken. I can do this." Then she added, "I can do all things through Christ who strengthens me."

Paula checked inside the pocket of her nurse's smock, the pocket that hung over her thigh. She fingered the two syringes. She knew they were there, but in her nervousness she kept checking. She'd never done anything like this before. It was a big honor to be asked. She didn't want to mess it up.

The watch showed 7:55AM. It was time.

She left the bathroom and walked down the hallway. She waved at the two guards standing outside Stephanie's door.

"Good morning, Stephanie," Paula said.

She checked the syringes again, then said, "It is time for your morning pain meds. Doctor says you need these and some anti-inflammatory for the swelling that will keep developing on that wound."

"I only see two pills in the cup," Stephanie said.

"That's because the anti-inflammatory is a shot."

"You'll excuse me if I don't get too excited about being shot again." Stephanie laughed at her own joke. Paula did not laugh.

She checked the syringes in her pocket again.

"Roll over now dear, I need to do this in your bottom."

"You can't do it in my arm?"

"Nope. Don't make this harder than it has to be." Paula seemed to be talking to herself as much as to Stephanie.

She checked the syringes again.

Stephanie said, "I'll be glad when I get out of this hospital. You guys poke and prod me so much I'm beginning to think I might be in more danger from you guys than from the people who shot me."

Paula hesitated, then realized it was a joke. "Roll over, dear."

Stephanie rolled over onto her left side and pulled down the pajama bottom. "Make it quick nurse, my husband is coming to see me in about an

218

hour. He brought me these pajamas last night, but we didn't have time to talk. Then I have to talk to my boys. I've got a lot to explain, and I don't want my rear end hanging out while I do it."

Paula took the tab off the end of the needle. "This will not take but a minute." Then she shoved the needle into her buttock and pressed the contents of the syringe into Stephanie.

"There, that wasn't so bad, was it?"

"No, you were gentle. I barely felt anything."

"Good. Now take your pain medication."

Stephanie popped the paper cup's contents into her mouth and then drank from the glass on her bedside table.

"I—, I—" Stephanie stammered as she wiped her hand over her brow. "It suddenly got hot in here. What kind of medicine was—"

Paula leaned over and whispered in Stephanie's ear. "It was the kind of medicine that bad girls get when they break their vows to The Judys. May the Lord have mercy on your soul."

There was just enough life in Stephanie for her eyes to open wide, she fought just a bit. Paula put her arms on Stephanie's shoulders to hold her down. Stephanie Colson's eyes shut for the last time.

Paula switched the monitor off beside the bed.

"She will sleep for about an hour or two now," Paula told the guard as she pulled the door shut behind her.

She walked back to the same small nurses' bathroom she'd been in before. She locked the door and checked to make certain no one else was in there. Her nerves were shot. She felt queasy, like she might get sick. But she couldn't. She still had more work to do.

Paula splashed water on her chubby face. She dried it with the industrial brown paper towel from the crank dispenser. She took several deep breaths, repeating over and over the covenant oath she'd sworn to uphold.

> I am a Servant of Judith, called to execute God's judgment.
> We are Servants of Judith, called to remove impurity.
> Together, we are the Sisterhood of Saints, called to guard the true Church from evil.
> This is our solemn task.

This is a solemn task.

She was a Judy, the noble army of women who would alone rid the church of its pollution.

Feeling herself strengthened, Paula felt for the second syringe still in her pocket. One down, one to go.

She left the bathroom and found her way to the elevator. Her actual shift in the oncology ward wasn't scheduled to begin until 8:30AM, so she had plenty of time. The worst thing for her to do was to get in a hurry. She needed to look calm and relaxed, just like any other day at work. This was her hospital. She belonged here. She wasn't trying to hide anything. She was just doing her job.

Just doing her job.

On the second floor a doctor, a nurse, and a policeman all got on the elevator with her. Against her wishes, a cold sweat broke out on her forehead. She felt exposed. Her plan would unravel if she couldn't hold it together. Alarmed, she closed her eyes to focus.

"Long shift?" the doctor said to her. "You work in oncology, right? Or is it pediatrics?"

Claustrophobia. Terror. She needed to get away before they found out.

Her hand reached down into her pocket to feel the syringe. It was still there.

"Oncology," was all she said to the doctor. She figured the fewer words she squeaked, the better. She regretted not taking the stairs.

Her fright was short lived because all three of them were going to breakfast in the cafeteria, so they got off on the ground floor. Her destination was one floor down. Finally the doors opened on the basement floor where the intensive care unit was. Her mind was so relieved to be rid of the elevator and her riding companions, she rushed out of the doors as soon as they slid open, slamming straightway into a phlebotomist and his cart. Vials of blood, paper, needles, syringes, and rubber bands flew all over the hallway.

"Watch where you're going," he said, staring at the mess on the floor and on his cart.

"I'm so sorry," Paula said. "Let me help you."

She stooped to pick up the various items and placed them back on the cart.

"It is a miracle that none of the vials broke," she said.

"It is not a miracle. It is thick glass. They build them that way because of klutzy people like you."

"I said I was sorry, what more can I do?"

"You can stay out of people's way, that is what you can do."

His cart was far from put back together, but everything was off the floor so he pushed it into the elevator. The door closed with him scowling at Paula.

Just like in the care tower, no one in the ICU questioned her presence. She was a nurse. She belonged. Even if she was not an ICU nurse, the hospital was such a sprawling institution that people came and went from the various wings and units without question. She walked right by the nurses' station and to room seven. Lying on the bed, asleep, was the false teacher she was looking for.

Her left hand dropped into her pocket to check for the syringe. Her eyes popped open wide. It was gone. It was not there. She checked the other pocket on her right side.

No syringe.

"Jesus, help me," she whispered.

It must have fallen out when she bumped into the blood cart. Her first fear was that somehow it had ended up on his cart. If that happened, she was doomed to failure. Desperate, she retraced her steps to the elevator. She got down on her hands and knees by the elevator door to look.

About the same time a nurse walked by. He laughed at her and said, "What are you looking for?"

Paula didn't think to guard her words. "A syringe."

"Oh dear. Losing one of those could be very bad."

"It is bad," she said.

He squatted down to look. "Sometimes the only way to find something is to get a fresh perspective," he said as he moved a trash can that sat against the wall. "When we keep looking at problems from the same angle all the time we can't see all the different possibilities. Anyway, is this your syringe," he picked up the object, then added, "or is this where all lost syringes go to hide?"

"Oh, thank you," she said. She hugged him.

He held it in his hands. "Is that blue? I don't think I've ever seen a syringe filled with something with that dark of a blue before? What kind of shot is this?"

"I don't know, really. The doctor ordered it for a patient. I am just the nurse, you know. They don't tell me anything."

"I know what you mean," he said. "Anyway, be careful with that."

"Thank you."

Moments later she was again standing just inside room seven of the ICU.

Her finger was on the syringe, gently tapping it over and over with nervous energy.

Paula approached the bed.

She leaned over toward his ear. "I don't know if you can hear me or not, but I have a message for you from Monica. I'm supposed to tell you that heretics and false teachers always get what they deserve. It is now time for you to face judgment. But before you do, she wants me to tell you that your friend, the other false teacher, his wife and kids, they are all dead now. All of you will rot in hell together, forever. Your days of misleading the sheep are over."

Paula lifted up the covers and pulled back the immodest hospital gown. She half expected him to respond, even though she knew he was in a drug induced coma designed to help his body heal. She brought the syringe out of her pocket and popped off the top. With her left hand she pushed Terence's bottom up as high as she could. She finally got the kind of leverage she needed to make the injection. She plunged the needle into him.

Terence twitched.

Her thumb was on the tab.

"Stop!" A voice shouted from the door. It was the nurse who'd found the syringe for her by the trash can. "Back away."

Paula stared at him, then she brought her eyes back down toward Terence.

The male nurse in the doorway realized what was happening. He bull-rushed her, which caused her to take an instinctive backward step. When she did, Terence's body resettled down onto the bed. His body pushed the syringe against the bed, breaking the needle off in his buttock. The syringe fell to the floor. The nurse pushed Paula against the IV rack holding fluids and medicines, and they all crashed against the wall inside the small room.

"Die heretic, die!" Paula shouted as she lunged, summoning her adrenalin and passion, she flung herself on top of Terence. She tried to choke him, but the cervical collar around his neck kept her fat fingers from getting around his throat. The entire ICU staff ran in and pulled her off.

About an hour later, Detective Wright stood in the room beside Terence's bed and spoke with Muriel. He told her how close her husband had come to dying. He told her about the nurse who killed Stephanie, and dropped her syringe of poison, and about the other nurse who found it for her. Detective Wright told her how that nurse had then overheard a conversation between two others in the elevator about how they'd found Stephanie's body, and how inexplicably she was dead. Detective Wright told her that second nurse pieced it together and decided to double back and check on things. Then Detective Wright told Muriel how he stopped the murderer, just as she was about to push the poison into Terence.

By the time he finished speaking, Muriel was weeping uncontrollably.

"Thank God Almighty for that nurse. Praise Jesus!"

***

Detective Wright found an empty lobby with a comfortable chair. His assistant Christine brought him a cup of coffee, then he shooed her away. This case was getting out of control, fast. He pulled out his notebook. He wondered when the FBI would finally show up, because he wasn't making much progress at all.

His earlier hypothesis about Butch Gregory and Wyoming Wallace appeared to be wrong. There was someone else pulling the strings on this puppet show. It appeared to be this woman named Monica. How, though, had she managed to know so much so fast about where Stephanie and Terence were?

For that matter, how did she seem to elude the search for her?

He wrote one word on his notepad. Mole.

Someone in the police department, or the hospital, was feeding her information. That was the only logical conclusion. It was also logical to assume that every woman in his department was to be suspected as the mole.

It was that line of thought that led him to the conclusion that he needed to get out to that cabin where Butch Gregory was, and fast. If this Monica woman knew where the hospital patients were, and could get to them, it was a sure bet that she knew where the pastor and his rogue friend were.

He pulled out his phone and called his chief assistant, Shawna. "Shawna, check your GPS device on Wyoming Wallace's Jeep and Butch Gregory's rental. I'd like to know exactly where they are."

"Sure thing, boss. Give me just a moment." About a half minute later she came back on the line. "Okay, it shows here that Butch Gregory's car is at the address you gave me for that cabin out on the canal. Wallace's car is at the address we have on file for his residence. Do you want me to send squad cars out to check on them, or bring them in for questioning?"

"Negative. I want them to stay right where they are. Let them think that their little plot succeeded. I am going to go back to Gregory's house here in town and look for more clues." Detective Wright added more webbing for his plot. "I want you to check their location every fifteen minutes and tell me the first sign of movement. Okay?"

"You got it."

Now, let's see how this plays out.

Detective Wright left instructions to the uniformed deputies to post two guards at Terence's room and that only doctors and nurses on the list that the attending physician drew up would be allowed in, along with Terence's family. Then he left the hospital and did the exact opposite of what he told Shawna. He went to the cabin out on the hood canal.

Chapter Thirty-Five
Across the Olympic Peninsula

Wyoming merged the pearl colored Kia off of Highway 101 onto the two-lane highway that led to the Washington coast. He and Butch had not said much since they'd left the cabin.

"Did you find the tracking device on your car?" Wyoming said.

"Huh?" Butch was looking out of the passenger side window.

"The tracking device on your car. Did you find it? Mine was underneath the rear bumper. I guess they must have thought I was a greenhorn to not know to look there."

"I didn't even think about it," Butch turned his head toward Wyoming. "I guess I should have expected that."

"Don't worry about it. I didn't check your car because I wanted them to know where you were. But I wanted them to think I was at home. Didn't want them knowing I went after you. I don't think that detective is bad or anything. I just don't think he trusts us, either. You know he was feeding us a line of bull at the hospital. I think he suspects us."

"Us?"

"Yep."

"What makes you say that?"

"Just a hunch."

Butch took a sip from his coffee. "Did you destroy the tracker?"

"Oh, no. Then they might suspect something was wrong. No, I tied it to Olalla."

"You tied it to your dog?" Butch shivered. He didn't have a very good relationship with Wyoming's fanged pet.

"Yeah. I put it on his collar. I figure the police will think I've decided to drive around in the woods all day. At any rate, they think I'm at home and that you're at your cabin. So everything is great."

Butch tilted his head sideways, in marvel at Wyoming's ways. Then a thought popped into his mind. "Who kept Olalla while you were away on your six month odyssey?"

"My folks. Remember, they live right up the road from me."

"That's right, you live in mommy and daddy's backyard."

"That's not exactly how I see it." Wyoming shot Butch a glare that communicated more than five minutes of words.

After a quarter of an hour of silence, Wyoming picked up his thought from earlier. "The second rule," his eyes twinkled, "of subterfuge is misdirection and misinformation."

"Interesting," Butch said. "What is the first rule?"

"Stay alive."

"We've still got about two hours of driving left," Butch said, pointing at the digital clock on the dashboard. "Are you sure I shouldn't call Lucy? I mean, what if this Monica hasn't gotten there? I can warn Lucy to grab the kids and get out of there. That just makes sense."

"I promise you, Reverend," Wyoming spoke at the speed of water freezing, "that she is already there. That is why we haven't heard back from her on the text message. Everything is in place, from her perspective. If I thought calling your wonderful wife would be helpful, you have to believe I would say do it. However, calling her now would only alert Monica to the reality that you're not tied up in the trunk. That would make the situation even more dangerous. If Monica thought you'd escaped her spitfire enforcer, then she'd probably just kill Lucy, and your two kids, on the spot. We don't want that happening."

"No," Butch shook his head.

"And," Wyoming started again, "there is another side to this. Let's pretend just for a moment that somehow Monica isn't there yet, and you did let Lucy know she was in danger and she did escape, it would only be a temporary escape. Eventually Monica would be back. She would be back at a time of her choosing. She would be back at a time when you weren't as ready as right now. She would be back at a time when you didn't have the drop on her. So it is better, infinitely better, for us to go ahead and move quick and decisive right now against her or we'll just have to do it again, under worse circumstances at less favorable odds some other day."

"Wait a minute," Butch raised his voice, "so you're using my family as bait?"

"I wouldn't put it quite like that, but yeah, I sorta guess that is exactly what the plan is."

"I don't like it."

"Me, neither. I don't like any of this. But let's face it, she is already in

226

danger. We are not adding to it one bit. Quite the opposite. We are using Monica's god-complex to our advantage."

"I hope you're right," Butch said. Then he changed the subject because his mind couldn't hold-up the thought of his family in danger any longer. "Why did you want to drive that woman's car instead of one of ours?"

"Well, it was a spur of the moment idea. Mostly I did it in case that might play into our advantage once we are at this beach house. I don't quite know how it could, yet. But it is better to have an ace in the hole. The presence of Michelle's car could, even for a split-second, confuse Monica—make her think all was fine. That is a split-second we could use to our advantage."

"That makes sense."

"Of course it does," Wyoming said. "It was my idea."

"Oh, please."

"There is another reason, though, that I have thought of since then. If the police should come out to the cabin to get you or check on you; finding both of our cars there would add to their confusion. If we took your car, they'd simply track it. If we took my Jeep, there would be an all-points bulletin out all over the state for it. But this way, they don't have a clue where we are or what we're driving. We are practically invisible to them. For all they know we took a walk on the shore to look for whales or something."

Butch was satisfied with that logic, so he moved onto another question that had been on his mind for seventy miles. "Have you thought about what we're going to do when we get there? I assume our plan is not to just go knock on the door."

"I was thinking about that. And, actually," Wyoming chuckled, "driving right up to the front door is just exactly what I had in mind."

Chapter Thirty-Six
She Bites

Detective Wright pulled his Lincoln across the driveway behind Butch's rented Ford and Wyoming's Jeep. He parked in such a way as to block the exit. He didn't quite know what to expect; so he decided caution was in order. He knew that the tracker said Wyoming was at his house, but he wasn't surprised to see the black Jeep. If there was a next time he'd just put an officer on Butch and Wyoming.

If there was a next time.

He pulled the pistol out of his hip holster. He carried an extra-long barreled .38 special. Detective Wright never worried about concealment. He preferred that everyone knew he had a gun, and if he ever had to use it he preferred even more that little extra accuracy that came from the longer barrel. Besides, he had a .380 tucked away underneath his coat.

The detective walked down the driveway with his head on a swivel, but didn't see anything suspicious. He listened from the front porch for voices inside. He heard nothing. After several minutes he went ahead and knocked on the door. No one answered.

Technically, he had no authority to enter the house, but he wasn't the kind of man who let technicalities get in the way of his job. He brought his pistol up to his shoulder with his right hand, pointing it forward. He turned the knob, then with great patience he pushed open the door with his left hand. There was no resistance and no sound as he entered the cabin. It only took him a couple of minutes to check the bedrooms, closets and bathrooms for foul play. There was no evidence of anything. It was empty.

Looking through the cabin a little closer, he saw the note on the bar that separated the kitchen from the living room. Car keys sat on top of the sheet of paper.

> Be careful when you open the trunk. She is a friend of Monica's that came looking for me this morning. Her name is Michelle. We didn't know what else to do with her. I prayed for you. Watch out, she bites!—Butch

A sinking feeling overtook the detective. He had been played, and he knew it. For the past twenty four hours he'd believed that he was in control of this situation, that he was beginning to get a handle on what was happening, of who was right and who was wrong. He held the keys with the car

228

rental company's keychain in his hands and cursed.

Once outside, he pulled his pistol again and pointed it at the trunk. He counted to three, and then popped the lid. Angry eyes stared back at him. He ripped off the duct tape from her mouth. He expected her to shout in pain, but she did not.

"I am Detective Wright from the Blackjack County Sheriff's department. Who are you?" he said.

"Interesting question," Michelle said.

"They are in your car, aren't they?"

"Who?" Michelle said.

"The reverend and his reckless friend?"

"Why should I tell you anything?"

"Because if you don't, I'll just shut this trunk and conveniently forget about you for another day or so."

"You wouldn't dare. It's against the law."

Detective Wright slammed the trunk door shut.

Thirty seconds later he heard her say, "It is a white Kia Sorrento. If you let me out, I'll give you the license plate number."

Detective Wright popped the trunk again. "Where are they going?"

"I don't know."

"Okay then," he put his hand back on the trunk, "have a nice nap."

"Wait, wait, wait," Michelle said. "I thought you said you'd let me out if I told you about the car?"

"I never said that exactly. What I said was that I was willing to shut this trunk if you didn't cooperate. Telling me about the car was a start. I need more information. Now, are you going to help or not, because I have a feeling I don't have time to mess around."

"I think they said something about going to the hospital to see their friend."

Detective Wright knew she was lying, but he decided to play along anyway. He holstered his pistol again and pulled out his pocket knife. He cut the chair she was taped to off.

"Wow, they did a number on you. You must have spooked them real good for them to tie you up like this."

Michelle didn't say anything.

Detective Wright decided it was a tactical advantage to not take the tape from her hands and feet. He pulled her feet out of the trunk and draped them over the edge of the car's bumper. He stood back.

"I bet the fresh air feels good, huh?"

She didn't talk to him, but her dark brown eyes pierced holes in his head.

"I tell you what, why don't you tell me why you were out here, huh?"

"I was delivering a pizza."

"For breakfast?"

"It was a breakfast pizza."

"Somehow, I just don't believe you. Why don't you try again?"

Michelle took a deep breath, "I'd prefer to speak to my lawyer before I answer any more of your questions."

"Okay, suit yourself. But it might be a while before I can do that, because, you see, I think I'm in a situation where I can't call back at the station. You already know that, though. You know that if I radio this in, somehow or another your coven of lethal ladies will find out. I can't let that happen, can I?"

There was no response from Michelle.

"I also suspect that if I were Butch Gregory I'd probably be heading toward my wife and kids right now. I can't very well take you with me. I can't take you to the jail. I can't kill you."

Michelle said, "I'm not going back in the trunk."

He walked over toward Michelle, "I don't like it, but I guess I'm just going to have to stuff you back into this trunk."

"My whole day is one giant déjà vu," Michelle said.

Detective Wright leaned over to grab Michelle's feet. When he did, he felt the force of her knees come hard against his forehead. It was followed by a roundhouse from her left hand, which had found its way to freedom from the duct tape. Detective Wright fell over backwards onto the gravel of the driveway.

"I told you, I'm not going back into that trunk." Michelle said, pronouncing the word trunk as if it were a curse. She ripped the tape off her feet. "Thanks for cutting away the chair," she continued, "I was afraid for a moment that you saw my hand come free when you did that." She kicked him in the stomach. "It was so hard to pretend to still be taped up. But you were so caught up in finding your precious little heretic that you didn't worry about me." She kicked him in the stomach again.

He coughed.

Michelle brought her right leg up and kicked him in the kidneys, pushing

230

him to the ground. She reached down and pulled out his revolver out of its holster. "This might come in handy." She cocked the hammer back and pointed it at his head. "Which pocket is your cell phone in? If you lie to me, I will shoot your head off."

"Don't shoot," he said. "It is in my back pocket. The left one."

She pulled the smart phone from his pocket. "What's the passcode?"

"One, two, three, four," he said.

"Really? That's the password the cops have?"

"I like to keep things simple," He said.

She kicked him in the stomach. "Shut up."

Michelle thought about her next course of action. Monica only had the prepaid phone, and she didn't know the number to it. Shawna, however, would. She took a risk and called Shawna's regular phone number.

"Shawna, it's me, Michelle," she said.

"No, everything is not alright. I've been locked in a trunk for the past several hours. The heretic and his friend are on their way to the beach where Monica is. They might already be there." Michelle began to pace around the front yard. For good measure she gave a quick kick to Detective Wright's stomach. He writhed in pain and then curled into a ball.

"Yes, do that. Call her on the dedicated line and let her know to expect some funny business." Michelle nodded her head as she listened to Shawna.

"I agree. He knows too much. I'll make it look like the heretic did it. This will work out perfect for us yet. God is with us."

Michelle ended the call, turned to face Detective Wright, and then noticed the pinprick of red laser light on her chest.

"Don't move a muscle. Not a single well-toned muscle. I'm a little out of breath from all the kicking you've given me, so my trigger finger might be jumpy."

While she had been preoccupied with her phone call to Shawna, Detective Wright used the writhing in pain to mask his movement toward his backup pistol in the shoulder harness under his coat.

He pointed it at her, then said, "Keep in mind I could have shot you already, but I don't want to. So if you do as I tell you, you will live. Put my revolver gently, onto the ground. Don't throw it. I don't want any scratches on it because it is my favorite pistol."

Michelle paused. She didn't move, but she didn't drop the pistol either. Detective Wright assumed she was calculating, so he added another warning. "I assure you, that I always keep a round chambered in this little beauty. You have no options. It is either put down the pistol or die. Don't be stup—"

Michelle stepped to her left, then waved the revolver in the direction of Detective Wright, who was still lying on the ground. She moved her finger to the trigger and squeezed.

A vase to the left of Detective Wright exploded.

Detective Wright fired his pistol. It penetrated her chest and came out of the back of her neck. The second shot went into her cheekbone and came out of the top of her skull.

Detective Wright got up off the ground. He stood over Michelle's body. "I've never killed anyone before," he told the corpse. "But you needed it."

He picked up his revolver and put it into his holster, then he retrieved his cell phone, which was still in her hand.

Now he knew who the mole was. Shawna. No wonder he couldn't ever make any progress in the investigation.

Chapter Thirty-Seven
The False Teacher

Even in the summer the Washington coast can be gray, dreary, and cold. In November, it was almost a guarantee. Wyoming counted on this for their plan to work. He was not disappointed.

Though it was only a little after lunchtime, the sky was dark. Butch had the headlights of the Kia Sorrento on high beam. He drove the car down the beach drive, through the dunes, and right up to the front door of the beach house. He killed the car, but left the headlights on. Then he sent a text message to Monica—"Help me get him out. He is fat and heavy."

Then Butch got out of the car and walked around to the back.

The timing was perfect. Monica opened the front door. "We've been waiting on you," she said walking down the deck stairs and out onto the sandy yard. "I can't wait to get this over with," she said, rounding the corner of the vehicle.

"Me, neither," Butch said as he brought the aluminum bat he'd bought at Target fifteen minutes earlier across her midsection. Then he pulled the cheap costume wig off of his head. "I'm ready for you to go away for a very long time, you murderer and coward."

Monica was on her hands and knees in the sand. "You!" she said, growling from the depths of her stomach. "You are so going to pay for this." She screamed at him.

Butch told her, "I don't think so. It is you who will pay." He cocked the bat, ready for another swing, then eased in closer to her with tiny, uncertain, steps.

Monica threw a handful of sand into his face. Butch swung his bat wildly, hitting only the air. Monica ran back into the beach house. She went straight to the main bedroom, where she'd left Lucy, Sarah, and Paul tied to the bedposts. She burst through the bedroom door, then screamed in emotional anguish.

All three of them were gone. At the same time Butch drove up to the house wearing his wig, Wyoming Wallace walked down the beach to the house. He saw when Monica ran out the front door. Once he was inside the house, the first thing he noticed was Monica's cell phone blinking from an incoming call from Shawna. Wyoming stuck the phone in his pocket. He found Butch's family on the bed, and used his pocket knife to cut loose the ropes. Then he led them back out onto the beachfront. From there he guided them away to safety.

Butch and Wyoming had argued ferociously about who would do what. Wyoming wanted to be the one to drive up and deal with Monica, but Butch wanted Wyoming to take care of his family. The pastor knew that they would, in all actuality, be safer with Wyoming than with him.

Wyoming had objected, noting that Monica might kill Butch in a one-on-one situation. Butch wouldn't hear it. He responded by telling Wyoming they didn't know what Monica might have planned—that his family might be attached to a bomb or there could be other booby traps. If that was the case, Wyoming would be better equipped to rescue them.

Neither man would budge, so they decided to flip a coin.

Butch said a short prayer in the Target parking lot asking God for it to be heads.

Heads it was.

Wyoming Wallace rescued Butch's family.

Butch, meanwhile, was determined to put an end to Monica's schemes. When she ran into the house he chased after her. He slowed down when he entered the front, expecting either to be shanghaied as he came through the door, or walk into some kind of lethal trap. Neither happened. Then he heard Monica's yell.

Six steps later he was in the bedroom, eyeball to eyeball with his nemesis. He could feel the hate flowing out of her heart, through her skin, piercing out of her eyes, and oozing from her mouth. It was a tangible heat.

"It's over Monica. It's better if you—"

Monica ran headlong into him so fast he didn't have time to swing his bat. She came at his midsection like a linebacker, crushing him against a glass framed map of Cape Disappointment. One of the shards of glass pushed through his coat and into his shoulder blade. He cried out.

Monica dropped him, then began to swing wildly, first at his face, then she kicked him in the groin.

Butch doubled over.

When he righted himself back up, he was looking straight into Monica's single shot Lady Derringer.

"You are a heretic," she said, "and you will die." She panted from lack of breath. "I have seen your kind my whole life. You are no different from the rest. You hide behind a loving family, a good church, the reputation of the job, and the goodwill of others. But I know you. I know who you are. In the secret you hurt people. You do things to people that are wrong. You hurt women and little girls. You must die! All of you must die! There are no good pastors in the world anymore. All of you are evil. It is time for a reformation, a bloody revolution to cleanse the land. Not until we have purged the church of the evil will the Lord bless us."

"Look," Butch said, swallowing hard. "I am not what you think I am. Am I a sinner, yes, of course. We all are. But I try to do right, I really do."

He took a deep breath as if to continue. Monica cut him off. "Stop it. Stop your lies. I don't want to hear any more."

That was when Butch remembered that he had a baseball bat in his hands. In one motion he moved to his left while bringing the bat up with his right hand, swatting the pistol to his left. At the same time, Monica pulled the trigger, and the bullet shot through the bedroom wall and into the microwave oven in the kitchen.

Now Butch had the advantage, and he brought the bat up again to her side, knocking her into the nightstand beside the bed. She threw the empty pistol at him, but missed. Then Monica grabbed the lamp and hurled it across the room at Butch, hitting him on the jaw. Several bright red spots appeared across his face and chin. He brought the baseball bat above his shoulders, like a battle axe, but when he did it shattered the overhead light. More glass rained down on the two combatants.

Monica spotted the power cord to the lamp she'd hurled at him. It had landed upon the bed. She snatched it just as the glass from the overhead light fell everywhere. Butch took another swing at the woman, and missed. Monica made her way around Butch and brought the power cord up around his neck. He dropped his bat as both hands clawed at the cord.

"I will choke the life right out of you, and once you have breathed your last, the church will once more be able to breathe better. Help me Lord Jesus to kill this man. Help me Judith, to take off his head!"

Butch waved his hands, trying to get a hold of the cord, or to grasp Monica. Even as he did so, he thought those were the strangest prayers he'd ever heard. His mind went back to seminary, and the story of Judith. Did she just cast him as Holofernes? And she as Judith? Terence would love to debate the symbolism of these ideas, as well as the neglect of apocryphal writings amongst Protestant congregations.

He didn't have time for symbolism, or for a discussion of deuteron-canonical literature of questionable origin and historicity because he was nearing asphyxiation. He had to do something.

He fell to his knees, and Monica pulled the cord tight, riding his back. A jolt of inspiration crossed his mind. When he was a young boy, he and his kid brother, Shark, used to wrestle. Shark was younger than he was, and shorter, so one of Shark's favorite moves was to jump onto Butch's back and put him in a headlock. Shark would intentionally rub Butch's ears raw and knee him in the kidneys while he had Butch at the disadvantage. But when Butch had enough, he would simply use his greater size and strength to flip Shark over his head.

Monica pulled on the cord. Butch straightened his torso as best he could, then thrust his waist backwards. He bowed his head, like a Buddhist monk in prayer, then lifted up on his toes, making an upside down V-shape. The motion was sudden, and as Monica came over his back he grabbed her hair with his arm and tugged. It worked. She flipped over onto the ground, releasing her throttle on his windpipe.

Butch took a deep breath, then coughed. He didn't know how much longer he could have endured the strangling. It wouldn't have been too much longer. His head pounded from the oxygen deprivation, his lungs tried to recover, and his heart thumped. In his disorientation he failed to notice Monica pick up one of the long shards of glass from the picture frame. She plunged it into his arm, but his coat was too thick for it to penetrate. Her hand slid down the shard and sliced open.

She screamed.

He was still on his knees, but Monica was already back on her feet. She also had picked up his bat. She swung it at his head. A quick head duck helped him avoid a blow that surely would have knocked him out. Butch jumped to his feet and ran out of the bedroom door.

He formulated a plan. In the confines of the house things were equal. There were knives, cords, lamps and many weapons of opportunity. If he could get her outside, then his size would give him the advantage. Assuming, of course, she didn't have another pistol. He darted through his in-laws house, out onto the deck facing the Pacific Ocean, and then ran down the stairs.

Monica followed. "Coward!" she shouted. "Come back here and take your medicine."

Butch ran across two small dunes until he was halfway across the beach. He stopped to look back. Monica was not far behind. She let out something halfway between a yell and a scream. Her speed quickened. Rage had filled her heart and what was left of her mind.

Butch took off for the water's edge. The tide was in, so the waves were near. He did not hesitate when he got to the water, but plunged right into the cold November surf. He waded out, to his knees, then looked backward. Monica was on his heels, running into the water.

Butch continued to wade out until the water was a little over his waist. The waves were smashing against him. He had just enough time to turn around and face Monica's approach. He dug his feet into the sand beneath him. Monica brought the baseball bat up and swung at him. When she did he ducked into the water. The bat came down with a splash just over his head. It did collide with his scalp, but the force of the bat was negated by the water, which is exactly what Butch wanted. He kicked off with his feet toward Monica. The two went under three feet of water. Butch, on top, put his knees into her stomach and pinned her down. He forced her head under the water with his hands.

He could feel her squirm beneath him. Soon she would instinctively gasp, suck in a lung full of water, and then drown. He would be safe. His family would be safe. It was the right thing to do. It is what Wyoming would do.

She kicked and clawed, and he pushed her head further into the bottom of the beach beneath the water.

It felt good. She deserved what she got. God had allowed him victory over his enemies, like David or Moses of old. Was this woman, in essence, any better than Pharaoh's charioteers or the Philistine giant? No. She was evil, twisted, and dangerous. This was right. His hands found her neck and squeezed. He shook her.

"Those who live by the sword die by the sword." It was the words Jesus spoke to his followers the night they came to arrest him.

"Vengeance is mine. I will repay, says the Lord."

His mind struggled with his heart.

Finally, he relented. Butch stood up, then dragged her body to the shore. She was still breathing, but the fight in her was gone. He stood over her.

"You are the false teacher," Butch screamed in her face. "You have twisted everything that is good into something that is evil. God is love, peace, and unity. You turned him into hate, violence, and division. You are nothing more than a common murderer, a serial killer."

Butch caught his breath, and that was when he smelled the distinctive odor of a cigar that followed his friend around. "Where is my family?"

"They are safe. I used this woman's cell phone to call that detective friend of ours. The beach patrol is on its way. That little filly of yours wanted me to stay with the kids while she came back to help you. I talked her into staying there while I came to check, but it looks like you've got everything under control."

"No. Nothing is under control." Butch's body shook.

Chapter Thirty-Eight
Third Breakfast

It wasn't quite the Sydney Diner, but to Butch and Terence both it seemed like the best breakfast they'd ever shared. Butch ate two soggy breakfast tacos he picked up at a fast food drive-thru three blocks from the hospital. Terence had runny, tasteless scrambled eggs, a cup of fruit, and instant coffee. The doctor still didn't want him eating anything that tasted good. However, that didn't stop Butch from smuggling in a cinnamon roll.

When Terence saw Butch pull the contraband from his bag of breakfast he said, "Manna! You are an angel sent by God. They're trying to starve me to death in here."

It had been eleven days since Terence had been one push of a needle away from death. During that time he'd made an almost complete recovery. The neck brace was gone, as were most of the bandages. His swelling had decreased, but he still wasn't back to normal. They had moved him from intensive care over the weekend to a room in the non-critical wing. He shared it with a salty mouthed man who had fallen from a scaffold at work in the shipyards.

A guard, though, was posted outside the door.

"Have you talked to our detective friend?" Butch asked just after he said the prayer over their meal.

"No, I haven't seen Richard at all. They tell me he was around quite a bit after that crazy nurse tried to kill me. I don't remember any of it."

"What do you remember?"

"I remember you and me tied to that bomb, that's for sure." Terence did not intend to be funny when he said that, but both of them laughed at it. "The next thing I remember after that was about four days ago when I woke up in the ICU. Muriel was there. She was sitting in a little chair beside my bed reading a book. I called out her name, and she answered me. That is the next thing I remember."

"So you don't remember talking with me down in the ICU?"

"We talked?"

"Yeah. You even rebuked me."

"I'm sure you needed it, but I don't remember that. I don't remember the fight in my room or the broken needle in my butt. Nothing."

"Terence," Butch took a sip of coffee. "I think I could have killed that woman, there on the beach."

"Does that bother you?"

"It bothers me a lot. It felt so good to have control over her. Since this whole thing began I've felt helpless, like someone else was pulling the strings. It felt great to have her in my grasp. I really wanted to kill her."

"Did you want to kill her," Terence said, tilting his head sideways, "or were you just defending your family by removing a threat? I think there is a difference."

"Agreed. There is a difference, and I know the difference. What I felt wasn't just the desire to remove a threat or to protect my family. It wasn't even revenge. It felt a lot more like hate. Terence, my hands were around her neck. And I squeezed. Hard. I didn't just want her to die, I wanted to kill her, to be the one who killed her."

"That is understandable. I would probably feel the same way in your situation. Most anyone would."

"Unacceptable," Butch said, raising his voice and slicing the air with his hand. "I don't want you to tell me it is understandable. I want you to tell me, I need you to tell me that what I felt was wrong. I need you to tell me that I sinned, because that is exactly what it was. It felt like the darkest depth of hell, and I relished it. I wanted it. I know my heart, Terence. I know in that moment my heart was in a bad place, a place that I had only entertained in my imagination. Violent impulses seized me, with my hands around her neck.. It nourished me, fed me, controlled me. And I didn't want it to end. I just wanted to kill her. I wanted to watch her body go rigid in the struggle, then limp in the release of her soul. I wanted to watch her die." As Butch talked, his arms were stretched out, and his hands strangled a memory.

"I thought I knew how dark my heart was before all of this, but in that moment I found a far darker place. It frightens me. I don't ever want to be there again, because it was evil, it was awful. I need you to tell me how wrong it was. Don't sympathize with me, correct me. Rebuke me. Tell me I am a worm."

"Is that what you do to people who come to you with their problems, beat them up spiritually with their issues?"

"No, but that is not a fair question. This is not about someone else; this is about me. I should know better."

"You should know better, and, let's not lose sight Butch, you did do better. You didn't kill Monica, and that is the real issue here. Why didn't you?"

"That's a good question, brother. It is one that has kept me awake at night the past couple of evenings. The best answer I can come up with is that something inside wouldn't allow it. As she wrestled with me under the waves, a couple of Bible verses came to me, as a form of correction. Those verses let me know that I shouldn't kill her, that it would be wrong."

"Was it Jesus talking to you, directly maybe?"

"No, I don't think so. I think it was, I know this sounds crazy," he rubbed his hand over his mouth, from top to bottom, finishing with a stroke of his chin. "I think it was me talking to myself. I think the verses, I think the voice, came from within me. They came from that part of me that knew what I was doing was wrong."

"I think I see," said Terence. Then he said nothing else, taking a big bite of his cinnamon roll. There was silence for about a minute.

"See what?" Butch said. "You can't just say something like that and leave me hanging while you munch on food. What do you see?"

"What you experienced was metanoia. Metanoia is often translated as repentance, but literally it means a change of mind, a change in thinking. Your mind, which you have transformed all these years by daily prayer and study would not let you carry through with such a horrible action. It was your heart that wanted to kill that woman. Your mind wouldn't allow it. It has been molded ever so slowly, but surely, into the likeness of Christ. That is what happened."

"Metanoia—transformed mind? You think it was spiritual? You think the Holy Spirit guided me in that moment?" Butch's eyes narrowed.

"That is exactly what I hear you describing to me. It happens to people every day, all over the world, in a billion different circumstances. You know this, Butch. The only difference is that the issue at hand was life and death." Terence chewed on another bite of the cinnamon bun, then he changed the subject. "Have you talked to the detective?"

"Richard called me yesterday afternoon, but most of the information I got came from Agent Lapp-Bench. She and I talked yesterday for a good long while."

"Well, what did she tell you?"

"She said they had arrested nine women, plus Monica. If you add in the two fatalities, Stephanie and Michelle, then you have twelve women in all involved."

"Then it's over." Terence sighed in relief. "We know that there were only twelve of them."

"Not exactly."

"What do you mean, Butch?"

"Well," he hesitated. "She said that they had evidence there were thirteen women involved. Somewhere out there is one they haven't found yet, and none of them are talking. They have closed ranks, and so far, maintained silence and solidarity."

"They all want to be martyrs."

"That is probably some of it. That is what Detective Wright thinks. Agent Lapp-Bench believes something else is in play. She thinks Monica might have made some kind of threat against their families if they ever talked. They are afraid."

"Afraid of what? She will spend the rest of her life in jail." Terence did not like where this was headed.

"Afraid that someone on the outside might do something, that's what. She thinks this thirteenth woman was someone who never worked with any of the others. She was set aside for this very purpose. Only Monica knows who she is, but this woman knows all about the others. Whether this mysterious thirteenth person exists or not is irrelevant, really. All that matters is that they believe she is real. They believe that if they cooperate with the police their families will be in jeopardy."

"Then it is not over?"

"Well, maybe. Agent Lapp-Bench tends to think this woman will not come after us because she is something more of an internal policing agent."

"How do you know all about this? Did they leave behind records or something?"

"Actually, no. I was told that most of this came from the deposition they got from Stephanie. The night she was brought into the hospital, the detective questioned her long and hard. She cooperated fully. She told him she was one of the leaders, second only to Monica. They had a falling out when the group decided to target me."

"So we really don't know anything, we just hope it is over."

"There is a bit more than hope."

"Uh oh. When you say things like that, it means you're holding out on me."

"No, Terence, I'm not holding out on you. I'm about to tell, or, I guess, show you."

Butch unfolded a piece of paper he pulled from his coat pocket. He handed it to Terence.

Pastor Butch Gregory,

I address you as Pastor, not as heretic, because I have done my own research into the recent events and decided that the Judys were wrong. I also believe that is why they failed in their effort to remove you. I will, however, uphold our covenants, as I swore on oath. As long as you do not follow after the false teachers, nor lust for the evil of this world, I will leave you, your family, and your friends in peace. Be advised, though, I am watching.

The 13th Servant of Judith

After he finished reading it, Terence exclaimed, "Where do all these crazy people come from? Is there some kind of mill, or factory out in Spokane that cranks them out? We can't trust this woman. Whoever wrote this is certifiable."

"You'll get no argument out of me. The good news is that it looks like we're safe, for now."

"Yeah, until we do something they don't like. Maybe she decides that me playing blackjack on my iPad is evil, or she thinks you bought the wrong kind of car. I mean, this is lunacy."

The two men sat and thought, the way friends can do, in a non-anxious way.

"Did she mail that note to you?" Terence asked after he finished off his cinnamon roll.

"No, that is the funny part. It was taped to the door at church."

"That's pretty brazen," Terence said. "They obviously weren't afraid of being spotted, to walk right up "to the door at church and tape it outside like that."

"Terence, it wasn't taped to the outside church door or to the door of the admin building. It was taped to my office door, inside the admin building. I found it four days ago."

"That means whoever this woman is— "

"She has access to my building. Exactly."

"This just gets worse and worse."

"There is one more thing that has me bothered, Terence."

"Yeah, what's that?"

"It's that these women are right. Don't get me wrong. They are crazy, evil, delusional, whatever word you want to use; and it would be a true description. However, their underlying presupposition is accurate, and that bothers me. Monica is a villain, but she is one that says true things. Her analysis of the situation is accurate. It is just that her conclusions are flawed and her solutions are psychotic.

"Look, Michael Westgrave was a lousy shepherd. I mean, what kind of pastor puts hero pictures of himself throughout his church? Then think about the way he led his congregation in the vanilla-mush teaching he gave. He really was only in it for the show—the prestige—the power trips—the affluence. I don't think he really knew the Lord, even. Then we get Peters. I mean, those photographs of him with all those women are disgusting. Can you imagine what the Old Testament prophets would have thought of him? Ezekiel might have gone after him with a sword, or at the very least thrown a bucket full of poop on him. I mean, that guy was bad to the bone."

Terence looked confused. "What are you getting at, Butch? Do you think those women did the right thing? Tell me you're not saying that."

"Of course not. I'm getting at the fact that we do have a problem with pastors who are improperly motivated at best, and evil at worst. Most of them get away with it. They spend entire careers leading congregations, shaping them into their own image, crafting the dialogue a certain way, fleecing the sheep, and the result is exactly what we have right now—a nation filled with churches that have no spiritual pulse because they are guided by false shepherds. These crazy women diagnosed the situation properly."

"Butch," Terence said. "It has always been that way. The church, both before and after the Protestant split, has always had a problem with bad clergy. Adulterers, power-abusers, greedy, thieves and all kinds of other immoral people have led churches. This is nothing new."

"So we should just let it go? Act like it is not a problem?" Butch looked down at the ground.

"I didn't say that, but violence is not a solution. You know that."

"Yes, of course I do, Terence. I am not advocating for hurting anyone. What these, these Judys did is disgusting. It violates everything that I believe in. But surely there must be some middle ground—something that is more than acceptance and less than violent retribution. I guess that is where I'm bothered the most. What can we do?"

"Well, that is a good question. However, don't forget that for every bad pastor out there, there are a thousand good ones, and hundreds of great ones. These people live their lives for the Lord, usually in anonymity, doing the right things. There are nearly fifty churches in the Sydney area, and those women really only found a couple or so. What about the rest? The rest were people like you and me, doing the best we can in this world to love the Lord with all our heart, mind, soul, and strength and to love our neighbor as ourselves."

Butch knew Terence was right, but he still didn't feel any resolve in his spirit. "What about the wicked, false shepherds and teachers? What do we do about them? We can't just ignore the problem and let them get away with it, can we?"

Terence puckered the air. "No one is getting away with anything. I know that you're shaken right now, but keep your eye on eternity. Jesus is working. For every Michael Westgrave and Rick Peters, there are thousands of pastors and church leaders who have committed grave sins, but have been restored through confession and repentance in the community of faith and the prompting of the Holy Spirit. These *femme fatales* were not solving problems, they were usurping the power of God."

Terence at a piece of cantaloupe on his hospital breakfast tray. "Listen to me carefully, Butch. With all the other things, the greed, the power trippers, the adulterers, and such, you've got to believe that Jesus is Lord, and that you are not. He will deal with those people in due time. Do you not believe the Scriptures which teach us that those who build a house on the sand will watch it wash away? These people are building homes on the sand. It is their choice to be fools. Your job, my job, is to make certain we have built our homes—our real homes with our families but also our ecclesiastical homes—on the solid foundation of truth, of the ministry of Jesus, and the work which we know matters. It really does boil down to a trust issue. You either trust Jesus or you don't. He is the Lord of light, and he will shine the light on the darkness. Everything done in secret will eventually be proclaimed from the rooftops."

"If you say so," Butch said. "After all, you're the scholar."

A Word From the Publisher

ATHANATOS
PUBLISHING GROUP

Did you enjoy Jamie Greening's *How Great is The Darkness?*

Be sure to check out his other works, listed at the beginning of the book. Please consider leaving a review on sites such as Amazon.com. There is nothing more powerful than your recommendation to friends and family.

Thanks for reading!

www.ingramcontent.com/pod-product-compliance
Lightning Source LLC
Chambersburg PA
CBHW050500260626
47157CB00004B/1133